BY AND ABOUT WOMEN

BY AND ABOUT WOMEN
An Anthology of Short Fiction

Edited by
BETH KLINE SCHNEIDERMAN
Los Angeles Pierce College

Harcourt Brace Jovanovich, Inc.
New York   Chicago   San Francisco   Atlanta

ISBN: 0–15–505665–4
Library of Congress Catalog Card Number: 72–96987

Printed in the United States of America

To the memory of
MARION MOONEY DAVIS

Preface

*U*nlike many of the "women's books" currently in print, this anthology is not meant to be a feminist tract. Its purpose is neither to convince nor to convert, for being a woman is neither a trend nor a movement. Women are, to be sure, different from men. In a male-dominated world, they are treated differently and have greater difficulty finding fulfillment in life. Understanding the nature of their difficulties is a step toward easing them, toward fulfillment for women. The purpose of this book, then, is to show the reader what it means to be a woman.

It is my belief that fiction can best accomplish this end. It can do what no other kind of prose can—present the reader with a direct, immediate experience of life. The works assembled in this collection are stories of literary merit. They offer the reader what all good art offers: a view of life sharpened by insight, sensitivity, intelligence, and understanding.

At the same time, the stories represent a variety of experiences encountered by modern women. If there is one common element among them, it is their emphasis on the necessity of coping with life. For some women, coping can result in successful solutions; for others, coping means learning to live with defeat. If the latter experience seems to be the more prevalent one in this collection, it is because I have tried to avoid the sentimental drivel that popular magazines sell as the image of a woman's life—the superficial ideal of satisfied mediocrity or inferiority. Instead, these stories stress the great potential women have to attain fulfillment, and the great waste that results when that potential is not realized.

The title of Part 1, "Promise and Disappointment," reflects what happens to a girl during adolescence. It is a time when all the infinite possibilities dreamed of get narrowed down and become restricting certainties. It is the time when the woman emerges from the images of her childhood. That experience does not have to be tragic, but more often than not it does entail compromise. The stories in this section also demonstrate how pervasive and persistent is the myth that a girl's happiness comes with finding the man of her dreams.

Part 2, "Expectation and Defeat," illustrates the cruelty of perpetuating the falsehood that in marriage alone can a woman find satisfaction and happiness. None of the selections in this section presents an account of real marital contentment; indeed, outside the pages of popular magazines, the concept of marriage as a woman's fulfillment does not seem to exist. It is impressive to note, however, how great a difference exists between what marriage is supposed to offer and what in fact it does. At best, a woman is left to cope with the problems of her married state; at worst, she is left with shattered ideals and an empty life.

Part 3, "Success and Failure," deals with the alternatives to marriage as a source of fulfillment for a woman. For the most part these alternatives are not careers; it would seem that this possibility is still sufficiently rare that there is as yet no real body of literature about it. My concept of fulfillment is a sense of personal liberation, that feeling in a woman that she is a person in her own right. A woman can, with strength and maturity, succeed in affirming her own identity.

Part 4, "Triumph and Death," presents a look at the woman who has coped with the problems of life and who seeks the rewards of rest and tranquillity. Too often what she finds instead are loneliness and neglect. It is the rare woman who achieves contentment in old age, especially in a society that values youth more than wisdom. The elderly woman confronts uncertainty as much as the young, but what she must also face is the prospect of infirmity and death.

Each selection is accompanied by a brief, informal headnote meant to stimulate thought and to focus class discussion. The headnotes contain both analytical comments and questions, but they are neither final nor exhaustive. Students are encouraged to use these notes not as conclusive explanations but rather as an impetus for their own interpretation of the literature.

At the end of the book are notes on the authors that provide brief biographical data as well as a list of the major works by each writer represented in the anthology. Students will discover writers whose works they want to explore in depth, and these notes can serve as a starting point for their investigation.

A bibliography of works that relate to each part of the book is included after the notes on the authors. These works are for the most part available in paperback editions and represent some of the more important nonfiction writing on the subject of women. They offer the reader additional perspectives, primarily sociological and psychological, that can be brought to bear on the short stories themselves and that can aid the student in understanding all aspects of the feminine experience.

I believe, however, that literature is the main source for gaining that understanding. I do not know if the following selections constitute a view of the way life will continue to be for a woman, or if feminine self-awareness in the future will be different. It is possible that the feminist movement will change the ways in which women interpret their experiences as well as the experiences themselves. The fiction of the future may not have to dwell on the waste of unrealized potential; it may shift its emphasis to the special achievements of women and, I hope, to their fulfillment as human beings. The task of the woman writer will be then as it always has been, to create good art.

I wish to express my thanks to Matthew Milan of Harcourt Brace Jovanovich for his confidence in this book and to Louise Marinis for her perceptive editorial assistance. I am also grateful to my husband, David, for his understanding. Most of all, I wish to remember Marion Mooney Davis, a wise and compassionate woman, to whom this book is dedicated and whom I miss.

Beth Kline Schneiderman

Contents

1

Promise
and
Disappointment

The Waltz

DOROTHY PARKER

"The Waltz," by Dorothy Parker, is primarily a very funny story. Part of the humor comes from the blatant contrast between what the girl so sweetly says out loud and what she so maliciously thinks to herself. Most of the humor, however, is contained in the monologue. The girl's repeated use of exaggeration is one of the more obvious comic devices, but the story can also be read as satire. What is the author satirizing? Is the girl more the object or the subject of the satire? Why does the story end with almost the same words as the opening sentence?

Why, thank you so much. I'd adore to.

I don't want to dance with him. I don't want to dance with anybody. And even if I did, it wouldn't be him. He'd be well down among the last ten. I've seen the way he dances; it looks like something you do on Saint Walpurgis Night. Just think, not a quarter of an hour ago, here I was sitting, feeling so sorry for the poor girl he was dancing with. And now *I'm* going to be the poor girl. Well, well. Isn't it a small world?

And a peach of a world, too. A true little corker. Its events are so fascinatingly unpredictable, are not they? Here I was, minding my own business, not doing a stitch of harm to any living soul. And then he comes into my life, all smiles and city manners, to sue me for the favor of one memorable mazurka. Why, he scarcely knows my name, let alone what it stands for. It stands for Despair, Bewilderment, Futility, Degradation, and Premeditated Murder, but little does he wot. I don't wot his name, either; I haven't any idea what it is. Jukes would be my guess from the look in his eyes. How do you do, Mr. Jukes? And how is that dear little brother of yours, with the two heads?

Ah, now why did he have to come around me, with his low re-quests? Why can't he let me lead my own life? I ask so little—just to be left alone in my quiet corner of the table, to do my evening brooding over all my sorrows. And he must come, with his bows and his scrapes and his may-I-have-this-ones. And I had to go and tell him that I'd adore to dance with him. I cannot understand why I wasn't struck right down dead. Yes, and being struck dead would look like a day in the country, compared to struggling out a dance with this boy. But what could I do? Everyone else at the table had got up to dance, except him and me. There was I, trapped. Trapped like a trap in a trap.

What can you say, when a man asks you to dance with him? I most certainly will *not* dance with you; I'll see you in hell first. Why, thank you, I'd like to awfully, but I'm having labor pains. Oh, yes, *do* let's dance together—it's so nice to meet a man who isn't a scaredy-cat about catching my beri-beri. No. There was nothing for me to do, but say I'd adore to. Well, we might as well get it over with. All right, Cannonball, let's run out on the field. You won the toss; you can lead.

Why, I think it's more of a waltz, really. Isn't it? We might just listen to the music a second. Shall we? Oh, yes, it's a waltz. Mind? Why, I'm simply thrilled. I'd love to waltz with you.

I'd love to waltz with you. I'd love to waltz with you. I'd love to have my tonsils out, I'd love to be in a midnight fire at sea. Well, it's too late now. We're getting under way. *Oh.* Oh, dear. Oh, dear, dear, dear. Oh, this is even worse than I thought it would be. I suppose that's the one dependable law of life—everything is always worse than you thought it was going to be. Oh, if I had any real grasp of what this dance would be like, I'd have held out for sitting it out. Well, it will probably amount to the same thing in the end. We'll be sitting it out on the floor in a minute, if he keeps this up.

I'm so glad I brought it to his attention that this is a waltz they're playing. Heaven knows what might have happened, if he had thought it was something fast; we'd have blown the sides right out of the building. Why does he always want to be somewhere that he isn't? Why can't we stay in one place just long enough to get acclimated? It's this constant rush, rush, rush, that's the curse of American life. That's the reason that we're all of us so—

Ow! For God's sake, don't *kick*, you idiot; this is only second down. Oh, my shin. My poor, poor shin, that I've had ever since I was a little girl!

Oh, no, no, no. Goodness, no. It didn't hurt the least little bit. And anyway it was my fault. Really it was. Truly. Well, you're just being sweet, to say that. It really was all my fault.

I wonder what I'd better do—kill him this instant, with my naked hands, or wait and let him drop in his traces. Maybe it's best not to make a scene. I guess I'll just lie low, and watch the pace get him. He can't keep this up indefinitely—he's only flesh and blood. Die he must, and die he shall, for what he did to me. I don't want to be of the over-sensitive type, but you can't tell me that kick was unpremeditated. Freud says there are no accidents. I've led no cloistered life, I've known dancing partners who have spoiled my slippers and torn my dress; but when it comes to kicking, I am Outraged Womanhood. When you kick me in the shin, *smile*.

Maybe he didn't do it maliciously. Maybe it's just his way of showing his high spirits. I suppose I ought to be glad that one of us is having such a good time. I suppose I ought to think myself lucky if he brings me back alive. Maybe it's captious to demand of a practically strange man that he leave your shins as he found them. After all, the poor boy's doing the best he can. Probably he grew up in the hill country, and never had no larnin'. I bet they had to throw him on his back to get shoes on him.

Yes, it's lovely, isn't it? It's simply lovely. It's the loveliest waltz. Isn't it? Oh, I think it's lovely, too.

Why, I'm getting positively drawn to the Triple Threat here. He's my hero. He has the heart of a lion, and the sinews of a buffalo. Look at him—never a thought of the consequences, never afraid of his face, hurling himself into every scrimmage, eyes shining, cheeks ablaze. And shall it be said that I hung back? No, a thousand times no. What's it to me if I have to spend the next couple of years in a plaster cast? Come on, Butch, right through them! Who wants to live forever?

Oh. Oh, dear. Oh, he's all right, thank goodness. For a while I thought they'd have to carry him off the field. Ah, I couldn't bear to have anything happen to him. I love him. I love him better than anybody in the world. Look at the spirit he gets into a dreary, commonplace waltz; how effete the other dancers seem, beside him. He is youth and vigor and courage, he is strength and gaiety and—*Ow!* Get off my instep, you hulking peasant! What do you think I am, anyway—a gangplank? *Ow!*

No, of course it didn't hurt. Why, it didn't a bit. Honestly. And it was all my fault. You see, that little step of yours—well, it's perfectly lovely, but it's just a tiny bit tricky to follow at first. Oh, did you work it up yourself? You really did? Well, aren't you amazing! Oh, now I think I've got it. Oh, I think it's lovely. I was watching you do it when you were dancing before. It's awfully effective when you look at it.

It's awfully effective when you look at it. I bet I'm awfully effective when you look at me. My hair is hanging along my cheeks, my skirt is swaddling about me, I can feel the cold damp of my brow. I must look like something out of the "Fall of the House of Usher." This sort of thing takes a fearful toll of a woman my age. And he worked up his little step himself, he with his degenerate cunning. And it was just a tiny bit tricky at first, but now I think I've got it. Two stumbles, slip, and a twenty-yard dash; yes. I've got it. I've got several other things, too, including a split shin and a bitter heart. I hate this creature I'm chained to. I hated him the moment I saw his leering, bestial face. And here I've been locked in his noxious embrace for the thirty-five years this waltz has lasted. Is that orchestra never going to stop playing? Or must this obscene travesty of a dance go on until hell burns out?

Oh, they're going to play another encore. Oh, goody. Oh, that's lovely. Tired? I should say I'm not tired. I'd like to go on like this forever.

I should say I'm not tired. I'm dead, that's all I am. Dead, and in what a cause! And the music is never going to stop playing, and we're going on like this, Double-Time Charlie and I, throughout eternity. I suppose I won't care any more, after the first hundred thousand years. I suppose nothing will matter then, not heat nor pain nor broken heart nor cruel, aching weariness. Well. It can't come too soon for me.

I wonder why I didn't tell him I was tired. I wonder why I didn't suggest going back to the table. I could have said let's just listen to the music. Yes, and if he would, that would be the first bit of attention he has given it all evening. George Jean Nathan said that the lovely rhythms of the waltz should be listened to in stillness and not be accompanied by strange gyrations of the human body. I think that's what he said. I think it was George Jean Nathan. Anyhow, whatever he said and whoever he was and whatever he's doing now, he's better off than I am. That's safe. Any-body who isn't waltzing with this Mrs. O'Leary's cow I've got here is having a good time.

Still if we were back at the table, I'd probably have to talk to him. Look at him—what could you say to a thing like that! Did you go to the circus this year, what's your favorite kind of ice cream, how do you spell cat? I guess I'm as well off here. As well off as if I were in a cement mixer in full action.

I'm past all feeling now. The only way I can tell when he steps on me is that I can hear the splintering of bones. And all the events of my life are passing before my eyes. There was the time I was in a hurricane in the West Indies, there was the day I got my head cut open in the taxi smash, there was the night the drunken lady threw a bronze ash-tray at her own true love and got me instead, there was that summer that the sailboat kept capsizing. Ah, what an easy, peaceful time was mine, until I fell in with Swifty, here. I didn't know what trouble was, before I got drawn into this *danse macabre*. I think my mind is beginning to wander. It almost seems to me as if the orchestra were stopping. It couldn't be, of course; it could never, never be. And yet in my ears there is a silence like the sound of angel voices . . .

Oh, they've stopped, the mean things. They're not going to play any more. Oh, darn. Oh, do you think they would? Do you really think so, if you gave them twenty dollars? Oh, that would be lovely. And look, do tell them to play this same thing. I'd simply adore to go on waltzing.

Helen

GWENDOLYN BROOKS

This chapter from the novel Maud Martha *describes the emotions
of a girl who isn't as pretty as her sister. Whatever else she is—
intelligent, loyal, sensitive, loving—she isn't beautiful, and the
world values beauty in a woman. Nothing will eradicate the hurt
and the sense of injustice that Maud Martha feels because she is
deficient in this one characteristic over which she has no
control. Is it true, however, that she bears no resentment
toward Helen and blames no one for preferring her sister over
her? Despite Maud Martha's claim of resigned selflessness,
what evidence is there of continued competition between the two
girls? There are three people whose attention and approval
Maud Martha especially seeks: Emmanuel, Harry, and her father.
What is the significance of these characters and how do they
relate to the last line of the story?*

What she remembered was Emmanuel; laughing, glinting in the
sun; kneeing his wagon toward them, as they walked tardily home
from school. Six years ago.

"How about a ride?" Emmanuel had hailed.

She had, daringly—it was not her way, not her native way—
made a quip. A "sophisticated" quip. "Hi, handsome!" Instantly he
had scowled, his dark face darkening.

"I don't mean you, you old black gal," little Emmanuel had
exclaimed. "I mean Helen."

He had meant Helen, and Helen on the reissue of the in-
vitation had climbed, without a word, into the wagon and was off
and away.

HELEN   "Helen" in *The World of Gwendolyn Brooks* (1971). Copyright, 1953
by Gwendolyn Brooks Blakely. Reprinted by permission of Harper & Row,
Publishers, Inc.

Even now, at seventeen—high school graduate, mistress of her fate, and a ten-dollar-a-week file clerk in the very Forty-seventh Street lawyer's office where Helen was a fifteen-dollar-a-week typist—as she sat on Helen's bed and watched Helen primp for a party, the memory hurt. There was no consolation in the thought that not now and not then would she have *had* Emmanuel "off a Christmas tree." For the basic situation had never changed. Helen was still the one they wanted in the wagon, still "the pretty one," "the dainty one." The lovely one.

She did not know what it was. She had tried to find the something that must be there to imitate, that she might imitate it. But she did not know what it was. I wash as much as Helen does, she thought. My hair is longer and thicker, she thought. I'm much smarter. I read books and newspapers and old folks like to talk with me, she thought.

But the kernel of the matter was that, in spite of these things, she was poor, and Helen was still the ranking queen, not only with the Emmanuels of the world, but even with their father—their mother—their brother. She did not blame the family. It was not their fault. She understood. They could not help it. They were enslaved, were fascinated, and they were not at all to blame.

Her noble understanding of their blamelessness did not make any easier to bear such a circumstance as Harry's springing to open a door so that Helen's soft little hands might not have to cope with the sullyings of a doorknob, or running her errands, to save the sweet and fine little feet, or shouldering Helen's part against Maud Martha. Especially could these items burn when Maud Martha recalled her comradely rompings with Harry, watched by the gentle Helen from the clean and gentle harbor of the porch: take the day, for example, when Harry had been chased by those five big boys from Forty-first and Wabash, cursing, smelling, beast-like boys! with bats and rocks, and little stones that were more worrying than rocks; on that occasion out Maud Martha had dashed, when she saw from the front-room window Harry, panting and torn, racing for home; out she had dashed and down into the street with one of the smaller porch chairs held high over her head, and while Harry gained first the porch and next the safety side of the front door she had swung left, swung right, clouting a head here, a head there, and screaming at the top of her lungs, "Y' leave my brother alone! Y' leave my brother alone!" And who had washed those bloody wounds, and afterward vaselined them down? Really—in spite of everything she could not understand why Harry had to hold open doors for Helen, and calmly let them slam in her, Maud Martha's, his friend's, face.

It did not please her either, at the breakfast table, to watch her father drink his coffee and contentedly think (oh, she knew it!), as Helen started on her grapefruit, how daintily she ate, how gracefully she sat in her chair, how pure was her robe and unwrinkled, how neatly she had arranged her hair. Their father preferred Helen's hair to Maud Martha's (Maud Martha knew), which impressed him, not with its length and body, but simply with its apparent untamableness; for he would never get over that zeal of his for order in all things, in character, in housekeeping, in his own labor, in grooming, in human relationships. Always he had worried about Helen's homework, Helen's health. And now that boys were taking her out, he believed not one of them worthy of her, not one of them good enough to receive a note of her sweet voice: he insisted that she be returned before midnight. Yet who was it who sympathized with him in his decision to remain, for the rest of his days, the simple janitor! when everyone else was urging him to get out, get prestige, make more money? Who was it who sympathized with him in his almost desperate love for his old house? Who followed him about, emotionally speaking, loving this, doting on that? The kitchen, for instance, that was not beautiful in any way! The walls and ceilings, that were cracked. The chairs, which cried when people sat in them. The tables, that grieved audibly if anyone rested more than two fingers upon them. The huge cabinets, old and tired (when you shut their doors or drawers there was a sick, bickering little sound). The radiators, high and hideous. And underneath the low sink coiled unlovely pipes, that Helen said made her think of a careless woman's underwear, peeping out. In fact, often had Helen given her opinion, unasked, of the whole house, of the whole "hulk of rotten wood." Often had her cool and gentle eyes sneered, gently and coolly, at her father's determination to hold his poor estate. But take that kitchen, for instance! Maud Martha, taking it, saw herself there, up and down her seventeen years, eating apples after school; making sweet potato tarts; drawing, on the pathetic table, the horse that won her the sixth grade prize; getting her hair curled for her first party, at that stove; washing dishes by summer twilight, with the back door wide open; making cheese and peanut butter sandwiches for a picnic. And even crying, crying in that pantry, when no one knew.

The old sorrows brought there!—now dried, flattened out, breaking into interesting dust at the merest look . . .

"You'll never get a boy friend," said Helen, fluffing on her Golden Peacock powder, "if you don't stop reading those books."

Girl Reading

ELIZABETH TAYLOR

*On one level "Girl Reading" is a story about a young
girl who begins to outgrow her romantic notions and gain a sense
of her own worth. As her awareness of reality develops, she learns
to say "I am I." On another level the story raises serious
questions about personal values. In what ways are the two mothers
dissimilar? How are these differences reflected in the
personalities of the girls? Why does Etta spend so much time
reading, and why is she fascinated by the engaged couple?
What is the relationship between these two preoccupations? What
does the author mean by the contrasting phrases "the things
of the mind" and "the things of the heart"? The story ends with
Etta's "pondering her mounting sense of power." How
significant is it that Roger's letter precipitates this feeling? What
constitutes Etta's sense of power, and how valuable will it
be to her as an adult?*

*E*tta's desire was to belong. Sometimes she felt on the fringe of
the family, at other times drawn headily into its very centre. At
mealtimes—those occasions of argument and hilarity, of thrust and
counterstroke, bewildering to her at first—she was especially on her
mettle, turning her head alertly from one to another as if watching
a fast tennis match. She hoped soon to learn the art of riposte and
already used, sometimes unthinkingly, family words and phrases;
and had one or two privately treasured memories of even having
made them laugh. They delighted in laughing and often did so
scoffingly—"at the expense of those less fortunate" as Etta's mother
would sententiously have put it.

GIRL READING   From *A Dedicated Man and Other Stories* by Elizabeth Taylor.
Copyright © 1961 by Elizabeth Taylor. First appeared in *The New Yorker*.
Reprinted by permission of The Viking Press, Inc., and Chatto & Windus.

Etta and Sarah were school friends. It was not the first time that Etta had stayed with the Lippmanns in the holidays. Everyone understood that the hospitality would not be returned, for Etta's mother, who was widowed, went out to work each day. Sarah had seen only the outside of the drab terrace house where her friend lived. She had persuaded her elder brother, David, to take her spying there one evening. They drove fifteen miles to Market Swanford and Sarah, with great curiosity, studied the street names until at last she discovered the house itself. No one was about. The street was quite deserted and the two rows of houses facing one another were blank and silent as if waiting for a hearse to appear. "Do hurry!" Sarah urged her brother. It had been a most dangerous outing and she was thoroughly depressed by it. Curiosity now seemed a trivial sensation compared with the pity she was feeling for her friend's drab life and her shame at having confirmed her own suspicions of it. She was threatened by tears. "Aren't you going in?" her brother asked in great surprise. "Hurry, hurry," she begged him. There had never been any question of her calling at that house.

"She must be very lonely there all through the holidays, poor Etta," she thought, and could imagine hour after hour in the dark house. Bickerings with the daily help she had already heard of and—Etta trying to put on a brave face and make much of nothing —trips to the public library the highlight of the day, it seemed. No wonder that her holiday reading was always so carefully done, thought Sarah, whereas she herself could never snatch a moment for it except at night in bed.

Sarah had a lively conscience about the seriousness of her friend's private world. Having led her more than once into trouble, at school, she had always afterwards felt a disturbing sense of shame; for Etta's work was more important than her own could ever be, too important to be interrupted by escapades. Sacrifices had been made and scholarships must be won. Once—it was a year ago when they were fifteen and had less sense—Sarah had thought up some rough tomfoolery and Etta's blazer had been torn. She was still haunted by her friend's look of consternation. She had remembered too late, as always—the sacrifices that had been made, the widowed mother sitting year after year at her office desk, the holidays that were never taken and the contriving that had to be done.

Her own mother was so warm and worldly. If she had anxieties she kept them to herself, setting the pace of gaiety, up to date and party-loving. She was popular with her friends' husbands who, in their English way, thought of her comfortably as nearly as good company as a man and full of bright ways as well. Etta felt safer with her than with Mr. Lippmann, whose enquiries were often too probing; he touched nerves, his jocularity could be an embarrassment. The boys—Sarah's elder brothers—had their own means of communication which their mother unflaggingly strove to interpret and, on Etta's first visit, she had tried to do so for her, too.

She *was* motherly, although she looked otherwise, the girl decided. Lying in bed at night, in the room she shared with Sarah, Etta would listen to guests driving noisily away or to the Lippmanns returning, full of laughter, from some neighbour's house. Late night door-slamming in the country disturbed only the house's occupants, who all contributed to it. Etta imagined them pottering about downstairs—husband and wife—would hear bottles clinking, laughter, voices raised from room to room, goodnight endearments to cats and dogs and at last Mrs. Lippmann's running footsteps on the stairs and the sound of her jingling bracelets coming nearer. Outside their door she would pause, listening, wondering if they were asleep already. They never were. "Come in!" Sarah would shout, hoisting herself up out of the bed clothes on one elbow, her face turned expectantly towards the door, ready for laughter—for something amusing would surely have happened. Mrs. Lippmann, sitting on one of the beds, never failed them. When they were children, Sarah said, she brought back *petits fours* from parties; now she brought back *faux pas*. She specialised in little stories against herself—Mummy's Humiliations, Sarah named them—tactless things she had said, never-to-be-remedied remarks which sprang fatally from her lips. Mistakes in identity was her particular line, for she never remembered a face, she declared. Having kissed Sarah, she would bend over Etta to do the same. She smelt of scent and gin and cigarette smoke. After this they would go to sleep. The house would be completely quiet for several hours.

Etta's mother had always had doubts about the suitability of this *ménage*. She knew it only at second hand from her daughter, and Etta said very little about her visits and that little was only in reply to obviously resented questions. But she had a way of looking about her with boredom when she returned, as if she had made the transition unwillingly and incompletely. She hurt her mother—who wished only to do everything in the world for her, having no one else to please or protect.

"I should feel differently if we were able to return the hospitality," she told Etta. The Lippmanns' generosity depressed her. She knew that it was despicable to feel jealous, left out, kept in the dark, but she tried to rationalise her feelings before Etta. "I could take a few days off and invite Sarah here," she suggested.

Etta was unable to hide her consternation and her expression deeply wounded her mother. "I shouldn't know what to do with her," she said.

"Couldn't you go for walks? There are the Public Gardens. And take her to the cinema one evening. What do you do at *her* home?"

"Oh, just fool about. Nothing much." Some afternoons they just lay on their beds and ate sweets, keeping all the windows shut and the wireless on loud, and no one ever disturbed them or told them they ought to be out in the fresh air. Then they had to plan parties and make walnut fudge and de-flea the dogs. Making fudge was the only one of these things she could imagine them doing in her own home and they could not do it all the time. As for the dreary Public Gardens, she could not herself endure the asphalt paths and the bandstand and the beds of salvias. She could imagine vividly how dejected Sarah would feel.

Early in these summer holidays, the usual letter had come from Mrs. Lippmann. Etta, returning from the library, found that the charwoman had gone early and locked her out. She rang the bell, but the sound died away and left an ever more forbidding silence. All the street, where elderly people dozed in stuffy rooms, was quiet. She lifted the flap of the letter-box and called through it. No one stirred or came. She could just glimpse an envelope, lying face up on the doormat, addressed in Mrs. Lippmann's large, loopy, confident handwriting. The house-stuffiness wafted through the letter-box. She imagined the kitchen floor slowly drying, for there was a smell of soapy water. A tap was steadily dripping.

She leaned against the door, waiting for her mother's return, in a sickness of impatience at the thought of the letter lying there inside. Once or twice, she lifted the flap and had another look at it.

Her mother came home at last, very tired. With an anxious air, she set about cooking supper, which Etta had promised to have ready. The letter was left among her parcels on the kitchen table, and not until they had finished their stewed rhubarb did she send Etta to fetch it. She opened it carefully with the bread knife and deepened the frown on her forehead in preparation for reading it. When she had, she gave Etta a summary of its contents and put forward her objections, her unnerving proposal.

"She wouldn't come," Etta said. "She wouldn't leave her dog."

"But, my dear, she has to leave him when she goes back to school."

"I know. That's the trouble. In the holidays she likes to be with him as much as possible, to make up for it."

Mrs. Salkeld, who had similar wishes about her daughter, looked sad. "It is too one-sided," she gently explained. "You must try to understand how I feel about it."

"They're only too glad to have me. I keep Sarah company when they go out."

They obviously went out a great deal and Mrs. Salkeld suspected that they were frivolous. She did not condemn them for that—they must lead their own lives, but those were in a world which Etta would never be able to afford the time or money to inhabit. "Very well, Musetta," she said, removing the girl further from her by using her full name—used only on formal and usually menacing occasions.

That night she wept a little from tiredness and depression—from disappointment, too, at the thought of returning in the evenings to the dark and empty house, just as she usually did, but when she had hoped for company. They were not healing tears she shed and they did nothing but add self-contempt to her other distresses.

A week later, Etta went the short distance by train to stay with the Lippmanns. Her happiness soon lost its edge of guilt, and once the train had rattled over the iron bridge that spanned the broad river, she felt safe in a different country. There seemed to be even a different weather, coming from a wider sky, and a riverside glare—for the curves of the railway line brought it close to the even more winding course of the river, whose silver loops could be glimpsed through the trees. There were islands and backwaters and a pale heron standing on a patch of mud.

Sarah was waiting at the little station and Etta stepped down onto the platform as if taking a footing into promised land. Over the station and the gravelly lane outside hung a noonday quiet. On one side were grazing meadows, on the other side the drive

gateways of expensive houses. The Gables was indeed gabled and
so was its boathouse. It was also turreted and balconied. There was
a great deal of woodwork painted glossy white, and a huge-leaved
Virginia creeper covered much of the red brick walls—in the front
beds were the salvias and lobelias Etta had thought she hated.
Towels and swim-suits hung over balcony rails and a pair of tennis
shoes had been put out on a window-sill to dry. Even though Mr.
Lippmann and his son, David, went to London every day, the
house always had—for Etta—a holiday atmosphere.

The hall door stood open and on the big round table were the
stacks of new magazines which seemed to her the symbol of extravagance and luxury. At the back of the house, on the terrace overlooking the river, Mrs. Lippmann, wearing tight, lavender pants
and a purple shirt, was drinking vodka with a neighbour who had
called for a subscription to some charity. Etta was briefly enfolded
in scented silk and tinkling bracelets and then released and introduced. Sarah gave her a red, syrupy drink and they sat down on
the warm steps among the faded clumps of aubretia and rocked the
ice cubes to and fro in their glasses, keeping their eyes narrowed
to the sun.

Mrs. Lippmann gossiped, leaning back under a fringed chair-
umbrella. She enjoyed exposing the frailties of her friends and
family, although she would have been the first to hurry to their
aid in trouble. Roger, who was seventeen, had been worse for
drink the previous evening, she was saying. Faced with breakfast,
his face had been a study of disgust which she now tried to mimic.
And David could not eat, either; but from being in love. She raised
her eyes to heaven most dramatically, to convey that great patience
was demanded of her.

"He eats like a horse," said Sarah. "Etta, let's go upstairs."
She took Etta's empty glass and led her back across the lawn, seeming not to care that her mother would without doubt begin to talk
about her the moment she had gone.

Rich and vinegary smells of food came from the kitchen as
they crossed the hall. (There was a Hungarian cook to whom Mrs.
Lippmann spoke in German and a Portuguese "temporary" to whom
she spoke in Spanish.) The food was an important part of the holiday to Etta, who had nowhere else eaten *Sauerkraut* or *Apfelstru-
del* or cold fried fish, and she went into the dining-room each day
with a sense of adventure and anticipation.

On this visit she was also looking forward to the opportunity of making a study of people in love—an opportunity she had not had before. While she unpacked, she questioned Sarah about David's Nora, as she thought of her; but Sarah would only say that she was quite a good sort with dark eyes and an enormous bust, and that as she was coming to dinner that evening, as she nearly always did, Etta would be able to judge for herself.

While they were out on the river all the afternoon—Sarah rowing her in a dinghy along the reedy backwater—Etta's head was full of love in books, even in those holiday set books Sarah never had time for—*Sense and Sensibility* this summer. She felt that she knew what to expect, and her perceptions were sharpened by the change of air and scene, and the disturbing smell of the river, which she snuffed up deeply as if she might be able to store it up in her lungs. "Mother thinks it is polluted," Sarah said when Etta lifted a streaming hand from trailing in the water and brought up some slippery weeds and held them to her nose. They laughed at the idea.

Etta, for dinner, put on the liberty silk they wore on Sunday evenings at school and Sarah at once brought out her own hated garment from the back of the cupboard where she had pushed it out of sight on the first day of the holidays. When they appeared downstairs, they looked unbelievably dowdy, Mrs. Lippmann thought, turning away for a moment because her eyes had suddenly pricked with tears at the sight of her kind daughter.

Mr. Lippmann and David returned from Lloyd's at half-past six and with them brought Nora—a large, calm girl with an air of brittle indifference towards her fiancé which disappointed but did not deceive Etta, who knew enough to remain undeceived by banter. To interpret from it the private tendernesses it hid was part of the mental exercise she was to be engaged in. After all, David would know better than to have his heart on his sleeve, especially in this *dégagé* family where nothing seemed half so funny as falling in love.

After dinner, Etta telephoned her mother, who had perhaps been waiting for the call, as the receiver was lifted immediately. Etta imagined her standing in the dark and narrow hall with its smell of umbrellas and furniture polish.

"I thought you would like to know I arrived safely."

"What have you been doing?"

"Sarah and I went to the river. We have just finished dinner." Spicy smells still hung about the house. Etta guessed that her mother would have had half a tin of sardines and put the other half by for her breakfast. She felt sad for her and guilty herself. Most of her thoughts about her mother were deformed by guilt.

"What have you been doing?" she asked.

"Oh, the usual," her mother said brightly. "I am just turning the collars and cuffs of your winter blouses. By the way, don't forget to pay Mrs. Lippmann for the telephone call."

"No. I shall have to go now. I just thought . . ."

"Yes, of course, dear. Well, have a lovely time."

"We are going for a swim when our dinner has gone down."

"Be careful of cramp, won't you? But I mustn't fuss from this distance. I know you are in good hands. Give my kind regards to Mrs. Lippmann and Sarah, will you, please. I must get back to your blouses."

"I wish you wouldn't bother. You must be tired."

"I am perfectly happy doing it," Mrs. Salkeld said. But if that were so, it was unnecessary, Etta thought, for her to add, as she did: "And someone has to do it."

She went dully back to the others. Roger was strumming on a guitar, but he blushed and put it away when Etta came into the room.

As the days went quickly by, Etta thought that she was belonging more this time than ever before. Mr. Lippmann, a genial patriarch, often patted her head when passing, in confirmation of her existence, and Mrs. Lippmann let her run errands. Roger almost wistfully sought her company, while Sarah disdainfully discouraged him; for they had their own employments, she implied; her friend—"my best friend," as she introduced Etta to lesser ones or adults—could hardly be expected to want the society of schoolboys. Although he was a year older than themselves, being a boy he was less sophisticated, she explained. She and Etta considered themselves to be rather wordly-wise—Etta having learnt from literature and Sarah from putting two and two together, her favourite pastime. Her parents seemed to her to behave with the innocence of children, unconscious of their motives, so continually betraying themselves to her experienced eye, when knowing more would have made them guarded. She had similarly put two and two together about Roger's behaviour to Etta, but she kept these conclusions to herself—partly from not wanting to make her friend feel self-conscious and partly—for she scorned self-deception—from what she recognised to be jealousy. She and Etta were very well as they were, she thought.

Etta herself was too much absorbed by the idea of love to ever think of being loved. In this house, she had her first chance of seeing it at first hand and she studied David and Nora with such passionate speculation that their loving seemed less their own than hers. At first, she admitted to herself that she was disappointed. Their behaviour fell short of what she required of them; they lacked a romantic attitude to one another and Nora was neither touching nor glorious—neither Viola nor Rosalind. In Etta's mind to be either was satisfactory; to be boisterous and complacent was not. Nora was simply a plump and genial girl with a large bust and a faint moustache. She could not be expected to inspire David with much gallantry and, in spite of all the red roses he brought her from London, he was not above telling her that she was getting fat. Gaily retaliatory, she would threaten him with the bouquet, waving it about his head, her huge engagement ring catching the light, flashing with different colours, her eyes flashing too.

Sometimes, there was what Etta's mother would have called "horseplay," and Etta herself deplored the noise, the dishevelled romping. "We know quite well what it's instead of," said Sarah. "But I sometimes wonder if *they* do. They would surely cut it out if they did."

As intent as a bird-watcher, Etta observed them, but was puzzled that they behaved like birds, making such a display of their courtship, an absurd-looking frolic out of a serious matter. She waited in vain for a sigh or secret glance. At night, in the room she shared with Sarah, she wanted to talk about them more than Sarah, who felt that her own family was the last possible source of glamour or enlightenment. Discussing her bridesmaid's dress was the most she would be drawn into and that subject Etta felt was devoid of romance. She was not much interested in mere weddings and thought them rather banal and public celebrations. "With an over-skirt of embroidered net," said Sarah in her decisive voice. "How nice if you could be a bridesmaid, too; but she has all those awful Greenbaum cousins. As ugly as sin, but not to be left out." Etta was inattentive to her. With all her studious nature she had set herself to study love and study it she would. She made the most of what the holiday offered and when the exponents were absent she fell back on the textbooks—*Tess of the D'Urbervilles* and *Wuthering Heights* at that time.

To Roger she seemed to fall constantly into the same pose, as she sat on the river bank, bare feet tucked sideways, one arm cradling a book, the other outstretched to pluck—as if to aid her concentration—at blades of grass. Her face remained pale, for it was always in shadow, bent over her book. Beside her, glistening with oil, Sarah spread out her body to the sun. She was content to lie for hour after hour with no object but to change the colour of her skin and with thoughts crossing her mind as seldom as clouds passed overhead—and in as desultory a way when they did so. Sometimes, she took a book out with her, but nothing happened to it except that it became smothered with oil. Etta, who found sunbathing boring and enervating, read steadily on—her straight, pale hair hanging forward as if to seclude her, to screen her from the curious eyes of passers-by—shaken by passions of the imagination as she was. Voices from boats came clearly across the water, but she did not heed them. People going languidly by in punts shaded their eyes and admired the scarlet geraniums and the greenness of the grass. When motor-cruisers passed, their wash jogged against the mooring stage and swayed into the boathouse, whose lacy fretwork trimmings had just been repainted glossy white.

Sitting there, alone by the boathouse at the end of the grass bank, Roger read, too; but less diligently than Etta. Each time a boat went by, he looked up and watched it out of sight. A swan borne towards him on a wake, sitting neatly on top of its reflection, held his attention. Then his place on the page was lost. Anyhow, the sun fell too blindingly upon it. He would glance again at Etta and briefly, with distaste, at his indolent, spread-eagled sister, who had rolled over on to her stomach to give her shiny back, crisscrossed from the grass, its share of sunlight. So the afternoons passed, and they would never have such long ones in their lives again.

Evenings were more social. The terrace with its fringed umbrellas—symbols of gaiety to Etta—became the gathering place. Etta, listening intently, continued her study of love and as intently Roger studied her and the very emotion which in those others so engrossed her.

"You look still too pale," Mr. Lippmann told her one evening. He put his hands to her face and tilted it to the sun.

"You shan't leave us until there are roses in those cheeks." He implied that only in his garden did sun and air give their full benefit. The thought was there and Etta shared it. "Too much of a bookworm, I'm afraid," he added and took one of her textbooks which she carried everywhere for safety, lest she should be left on her own for a few moments. "*Tess of the D'Urbervilles,*" read out Mr. Lippmann. "Isn't it deep? Isn't it on the morbid side?" Roger was kicking rhythmically at a table leg in glum embarrassment. "This won't do you any good at all, my dear little girl. This won't put the roses in your cheeks."

"You are doing that," his daughter told him—for Etta was blushing as she always did when Mr. Lippmann spoke to her.

"What's a nice book, Babs?" he asked his wife, as she came out on to the terrace. "Can't you find a nice story for this child?" The house must be full, he was sure, of wonderfully therapeutic novels if only he knew where to lay hands on them. "Roger, you're our bookworm. Look out a nice storybook for your guest. This one won't do her eyes any good." Buying books with small print was a false economy, he thought, and bound to land one in large bills from an eye specialist before long. "A very short-sighted policy," he explained genially when he had given them a little lecture to which no one listened.

His wife was trying to separate some slippery cubes of ice and Sarah sprawled in a cane chair with her eyes shut. She was making the most of the setting sun, as Etta was making the most of romance.

"We like the same books," Roger said to his father. "So she can choose as well as I could."

Etta was just beginning to feel a sense of surprised gratitude, had half turned to look in his direction when the betrothed came through the french windows and claimed her attention.

"In time for a lovely drink," Mrs. Lippmann said to Nora.

"She is too fat already," said David.

Nora swung round and caught his wrists and held them threateningly. "If you say that once more, I'll . . . I'll just . . ." He freed himself and pulled her close. She gasped and panted, but leant heavily against him. "Promise!" she said again.

"Promise what?"

"You won't ever say it again?"

He laughed at her mockingly.

They were less the centre of attention than they thought—Mr. Lippmann was smiling, but rather at the lovely evening and that the day in London was over; Mrs. Lippmann, impeded by the cardigan hanging over her shoulders, was mixing something in a glass jug and Sarah had her eyes closed against the evening sun. Only Etta, in some bewilderment, heeded them. Roger, who had his own ideas about love, turned his head scornfully.

Sarah opened her eyes for a moment and stared at Nora, in her mind measuring against her the wedding dress she had been designing. She is too fat for satin, she decided, shutting her eyes again and disregarding the bridal gown for the time being. She returned to thoughts of her own dress, adding a little of what she called "back interest" (though lesser bridesmaids would no doubt obscure it from the congregation—or audience) in the form of long velvet ribbons in turquoise. . . or rose? She drew her brows together and with her eyes still shut said, "All the colours of the rainbow aren't very many, are they?"

"Now, Etta dear, what will you have to drink?" asked Mrs. Lippmann.

Just as she was beginning to ask for some tomato juice, Mr. Lippmann interrupted. He interrupted a great deal, for there were a great many things to be put right, it seemed to him. "Now, Mommy, you should give her a glass of sherry with an egg beaten up in it. Roger, run and fetch a nice egg and a whisk, too . . . all right Babsie dear, I shall do it myself . . . don't worry child," he said, turning to Etta and seeing her look of alarm. "It is no trouble to me. I shall do this for you every evening that you are here. We shall watch the roses growing in your cheeks, shan't we, Mommy?"

He prepared the drink with a great deal of clumsy fuss and sat back to watch her drinking it, smiling to himself, as if the roses were already blossoming. "Good, good!" he murmured, nodding at her as she drained the glass. Every evening, she thought, hoping that he would forget; but horrible though the drink had been, it was also reassuring; their concern for her was reassuring. She preferred it to the cold anxiety of her mother hovering with pills and thermometer.

"Yes," said Mr. Lippmann, "we shall see. We shall see. I think your parents won't know you." He puffed out his cheeks and sketched with a curving gesture the bosom she would soon have. He always forgot that her father was dead. It was quite fixed in his mind that he was simply a fellow who had obviously not made the grade; not everybody could. Roger bit his tongue hard, as if by doing so he could curb his father's. I must remind him again, Sarah and her mother were both thinking.

The last day of the visit had an unexpected hazard as well as its own sadness, for Mrs. Salkeld had written to say that her employer would lend her his car for the afternoon. When she had made a business call for him in the neighbourhood she would arrive to fetch Etta at about four o'clock.

"She is really to leave us, Mommy?" asked Mr. Lippmann at breakfast, folding his newspaper and turning his attention on his family before hurrying to the station. He examined Etta's face and nodded. "Next time you stay longer and we make rosy apples of these." He patted her cheeks and ruffled her hair. "You tell your Mommy and Dadda next time you stay a whole week."

"She *has* stayed a whole week," said Sarah.

"Then a fortnight, a month."

He kissed his wife, made a gesture as if blessing them all, with his newspaper raised above his head, and went from the room at a trot. "Thank goodness," thought Sarah, "that he won't be here this afternoon to make kind enquiries about *her* husband."

When she was alone with Etta, she said, "I'm sorry about that mistake he keeps making."

"I don't mind," Etta said truthfully, "I am only embarrassed because I know that you are." That's *nothing*, she thought; but the day ahead was a different matter.

As time passed, Mrs. Lippmann also appeared to be suffering from tension. She went upstairs and changed her matador pants for a linen skirt. She tidied up the terrace and told Roger to take his bathing things off his window-sill. As soon as she had stubbed out a cigarette, she emptied and dusted the ashtray. She was conscious that Sarah was trying to see her with another's eyes.

"Oh, do stop taking photographs," Sarah said tetchily to Roger, who had been clicking away with his camera all morning. He obeyed her only because he feared to drawn attention to his activities. He had just taken what he hoped would be a very beautiful study of Etta in a typical pose—sitting on the river bank with a book in her lap. She had lifted her eyes and was gazing across the water as if she were pondering whatever she had been reading. In fact, she had been arrested by thoughts of David and Nora and, although her eyes followed the print, the scene she saw did not correspond with the lines she read. She turned her head and looked at the willow trees on the far bank, the clumps of borage from which moorhens launched themselves. "Perhaps next time that I see them, they'll be married and it will all be over," she thought.

The evening before, there had been a great deal of high-spirited sparring about between them. Offence meant and offence taken they assured one another. "If you do that once more . . . I am absolutely serious," cried Nora. "You are trying not to laugh," David said. "I'm not. I am absolutely serious." "It will end in tears," Roger had muttered contemptuously. Even good-tempered Mrs. Lippmann had looked down her long nose disapprovingly. And that was the last, Etta supposed, that she would see of love for a long time. She was left once again with books. She returned to the one she was reading.

Roger had flung himself on to the grass near by, appearing to trip over a tussock of grass and collapse. He tried to think of some opening remark which might lead to a discussion of the book. In the end, he asked abruptly, "Do you like that?" She sat brooding over it, chewing the side of her finger. She nodded without looking up and, with a similar automatic gesture, she waved away a persistent wasp. He leaned forward and clapped his hands together smartly and was relieved to see the wasp drop dead into the grass, although he would rather it had stung him first. Etta, however, had not noticed this brave deed.

The day passed wretchedly for him; each hour was more filled with the doom of her departure than the last. He worked hard to conceal his feelings, in which no one took an interest. He knew that it was all he could do, although no good could come from his succeeding. He took a few more secret photographs from his bedroom window, and then he sat down and wrote a short letter to her, explaining his love.

At four o'clock, her mother came. He saw at once that Etta was nervous and he guessed that she tried to conceal her nervousness behind a much jauntier manner to her mother than was customary. It would be a bad hour, Roger decided.

His own mother, in spite of her linen skirt, was gaudy and exotic beside Mrs. Salkeld, who wore a navy-blue suit which looked as if it had been sponged and pressed a hundred times—a depressing process unknown to Mrs. Lippmann. The pink-rimmed spectacles that Mrs. Salkeld wore seemed to reflect a little colour on to her cheekbones, with the result that she looked slightly indignant about something or other. However, she smiled a great deal, and only Etta guessed what an effort it was to her to do so. Mrs. Lippmann gave her a chair where she might have a view of the river and she sat down, making a point of not looking round the room, and smoothed her gloves. Her jewellery was real but very small.

"If we have tea in the garden, the wasps get into Anna's rose-petal jam," said Mrs. Lippmann. Etta was not at her best, she felt—not helping at all. She was aligning herself too staunchly with the Lippmanns, so that her mother seemed a stranger to her, as well. "You see, I am at home here," she implied, as she jumped up to fetch things or hand things round. She was a little daring in her familiarity.

Mrs. Salkeld had contrived the visit because she wanted to understand and hoped to approve of her daughter's friends. Seeing the lawns, the light reflected from the water, later this large, bright room, and the beautiful poppy-seed cake the Hungarian cook had made for tea, she understood completely and felt pained. She could see then, with Etta's eyes, their own dark, narrow house, and she thought of the lonely hours she spent there reading on days of imprisoning rain. The Lippmanns would even have better weather, she thought bitterly. The bitterness affected her enjoyment of the poppy-seed cake. She had, as puritanical people often have, a sweet tooth. She ate the cake with a casual air, determined not to praise.

"You are so kind to spare Etta to us," said Mrs. Lippmann.

"*You* are kind to invite her," Mrs. Salkeld replied, and then for Etta's sake, added: "She loves to come to you."

Etta looked self-consciously down at her feet.

"No, I don't smoke," her mother said primly. "Thank you."

Mrs. Lippmann seemed to decide not to, either, but very soon her hand stole out and took a cigarette—while she was not looking, thought Roger, who was having some amusement from watching his mother on her best behaviour. Wherever she was, the shagreen cigarette case and the gold lighter were near by. Ashtrays never were. He got up and fetched one before Etta could do so.

The girls' school was being discussed—one of the few topics the two mothers had in common. Mrs. Lippmann had never taken it seriously. She laughed at the uniform and despised the staff—an attitude she might at least have hidden from her daughter, Mrs. Salkeld felt. The tea-trolley was being wheeled away and her eyes followed the remains of the poppy-seed cake. She had planned a special supper for Etta to return to, but she felt now that it was no use. The things of the mind had left room for an echo. It sounded

with every footstep or spoken word in that house where not enough
was going on. She began to wonder if there were things of the
heart and not the mind that Etta fastened upon so desperately
when she was reading. Or was her desire to be in a different place?
Lowood was a worse one—she could raise her eyes and look round
her own room in relief; Pemberley was better and she would benefit from the change. But how can I help her? she asked herself in
anguish. What possible change—and radical it must be—can I ever
find the strength to effect? People had thought her wonderful to
have made her own life and brought up her child alone. She had
kept their heads above water and it had taken all her resources to
do so.

Her lips began to refuse the sherry Mrs. Lippmann suggested
and then, to her surprise and Etta's astonishment, she said "yes"
instead.

It was very early to have suggested it, Mrs. Lippmann thought,
but it would seem to put an end to the afternoon. Conversation
had been as hard work as she had anticipated and she longed
for a dry martini to stop her from yawning, as she was sure it
would; but something about Mrs. Salkeld seemed to discourage gin
drinking.

"Mother, it isn't half-past five yet," said Sarah.

"Darling, don't be rude to your Mummy. I know perfectly well
what the time is." (Who better? she wondered.) "And this isn't a
public house, you know."

She had flushed a little and was lighting another cigarette. Her
bracelets jangled against the decanter as she handled Mrs. Salkeld
her glass of sherry, saying, "Young people are so stuffy," with an
air of complicity.

Etta, who had never seen her mother drinking sherry before,
watched nervously, as if she might not know how to do it. Mrs.
Salkeld—remembering the flavour from Christmas mornings many
years ago and—more faintly—from her mother's party trifle—sipped
cautiously. In an obscure way she was doing this for Etta's sake.
"It may speed her on her way," thought Mrs. Lippmann, playing
idly with her charm bracelet, having run out of conversation.

When Mrs. Salkeld rose to go, she looked round the room
once more as if to fix it in her memory—the setting where she would
imagine her daughter on future occasions.

"And come again soon, there's a darling girl," said Mrs. Lippmann, putting her arm round Etta's shoulder as they walked to-

wards the car. Etta, unused to but not ungrateful for embraces, leaned awkwardly against her. Roger, staring at the gravel, came behind carrying the suitcase.

"I have wasted my return ticket," Etta said.

"Well, that's not the end of the world," her mother said briskly. She thought, but did not say, that perhaps they could claim the amount if they wrote to British Railways and explained.

Mrs. Lippmann's easy affection meant so much less than her own stiff endearments, but she resented it all the same and when she was begged, with enormous warmth, to visit them all again soon her smile was a prim twisting of her lips.

The air was bright with summer sounds, voices across the water and rooks up in the elm trees. Roger stood back listening in a dream to the good-byes and thank-yous. Nor was *this* the end of the world, he told himself. Etta would come again and, better than that, they would also grow older and so be less at the mercy of circumstances. He would be in a position to command his life and turn occasions to his own advantage. Meanwhile, he had done what he could. None the less, he felt such dejection, such an overwhelming conviction that it *was* the end of the world after all, that he could not watch the car go down the drive, and he turned and walked quickly—rudely, off-handedly, his mother thought—back to the house.

Mrs. Salkeld, driving homewards in the lowering sun, knew that Etta had tears in her eyes. "I'm glad you enjoyed yourself," she said. Without waiting for an answer, she added: "They are very charming people." She had always suspected charm and rarely spoke of it, but in this case the adjective seemed called for.

Mr. Lippmann would be coming back from London about now, Etta was thinking. And David will bring Nora. They will all be on the terrace having drinks—dry martinis, not sherry.

She was grateful to her mother about the sherry and understood that it had been an effort towards meeting Mrs. Lippmann's world half-way, and on the way back, she had not murmured one word of criticism—for their worldliness or extravagance or the vulgar opulence of their furnishings. She had even made a kind remark about them.

I might buy her a new dress, Mrs. Salkeld thought—something like the one Sarah was wearing. Though it does seem a criminal waste when she has all her good school clothes to wear out.

They had come onto the main road, and evening traffic

streamed by. In the distance the gas holder looked pearl grey and the smoke from factories was pink in the sunset. They were nearly home. Etta, who had blinked her tears back from her eyes, took a sharp breath, almost a sigh.

Their own street with its tall houses was in shadow. "I wish we had a cat," said Etta, as she got out of the car and saw the next door tabby looking through the garden railings. She imagined burying her face in its warm fur, it loving only her. To her surprise, her mother said: "Why not?" Briskly, she went up the steps and turned the key with its familiar grating sound in the lock. The house with its smell—familiar, too—of floor polish and stuffiness, looked secretive. Mrs. Salkeld, hardly noticing this, hurried to the kitchen to put the casserole of chicken in the oven.

Etta carried her suitcase upstairs. On the dressing-table was a jar of marigolds. She was touched by this—just when she did not want to be touched. She turned her back on them and opened her case. On the top was the book she had left on the terrace. Roger had brought it to her at the last moment. Taking it now, she found a letter inside. Simply "Etta" was written on the envelope.

Roger had felt that he had done all he was capable of and that was to write in the letter those things he could not have brought himself to say, even if he had had an opportunity. No love letter could have been less anticipated and Etta read it twice before she could realise that it was neither a joke nor a mistake. It was the most extraordinary happening of her life, the most incredible.

Her breathing grew slower and deeper as she sat staring before her, pondering her mounting sense of power. It was as if the whole Lippmann family—Nora as well—had proposed to her. To marry Roger—a long, long time ahead though she must wait to do so— would be the best possible way of belonging.

She got up stiffly—for her limbs now seemed too clumsy a part of her body with its fly-away heart and giddy head—she went over to the dressing-table and stared at herself in the glass. "I am I," she thought, but she could not believe it. She stared and stared, but could not take in the tantalising idea.

After a while, she began to unpack. The room was a place of transit, her temporary residence. When she had made it tidy, she went downstairs to thank her mother for the marigolds.

Wunderkind

CARSON McCULLERS

"Wunderkind" is the story of a young girl who wants to be a prodigy. Encouraged by her piano teacher, Frances makes this goal her very identity; she works at her music to the exclusion of everything else. When she fails and her rival, a boy violinist, receives the acclaim that she had dreamed of, she is filled with doubts. Her music becomes a terror for her, and her sense of self is destroyed. What kind of man is Mr. Bilderbach? What does his name mean, and what are his motives in fostering Frances' talent? What are his attitudes toward Mr. Lafkowitz and his pupil Heime, and how do these attitudes affect his treatment of Frances? How much of Frances' failure is her own fault and how much is caused by her teacher?

She came into the living room, her music satchel plopping against her winter-stockinged legs and her other arm weighted down with schoolbooks, and stood for a moment listening to the sounds from the studio. A soft procession of piano chords and the tuning of a violin. Then Mister Bilderbach called out to her in his chunky, guttural tones:

"That you, Bienchen?"

As she jerked off her mittens she saw that her fingers were twitching to the motions of the fugue she had practiced that morning. "Yes," she answered. "It's me."

"I," the voice corrected. "Just a moment."

She could hear Mister Lafkowitz talking—his words spun out

in a silky, unintelligible hum. A voice almost like a woman's, she thought, compared to Mister Bilderbach's. Restlessness scattered her attention. She fumbled with her geometry book and *Le Voyage de Monsieur Perrichon* before putting them on the table. She sat down on the sofa and began to take her music from the satchel. Again she saw her hands—the quivering tendons that stretched down from her knuckles, the sore finger tip capped with curled, dingy tape. The sight sharpened the fear that had begun to torment her for the past few months.

Noiselessly she mumbled a few phrases of encouragement to herself. A good lesson—a good lesson—like it used to be—Her lips closed as she heard the stolid sound of Mister Bilderbach's footsteps across the floor of the studio and the creaking of the door as it slid open.

For a moment she had the peculiar feeling that during most of the fifteen years of her life she had been looking at the face and shoulders that jutted from behind the door, in a silence disturbed only by the muted, blank plucking of a violin string. Mister Bilderbach. Her teacher, Mister Bilderbach. The quick eyes behind the horn-rimmed glasses; the light, thin hair and the narrow face beneath; the lips full and loose shut and the lower one pink and shining from the bites of his teeth; the forked veins in his temples throbbing plainly enough to be observed across the room.

"Aren't you a little early?" he asked, glancing at the clock on the mantelpiece that had pointed to five minutes of twelve for a month. "Josef's in here. We're running over a little sonatina by someone he knows."

"Good," she said, trying to smile. "I'll listen." She could see her fingers sinking powerless into a blur of piano keys. She felt tired— felt that if he looked at her much longer her hands might tremble.

He stood uncertain, halfway in the room. Sharply his teeth pushed down on his bright, swollen lip. "Hungry, Bienchen?" he asked. "There's some apple cake Anna made, and milk."

"I'll wait till afterward," she said. "Thanks."

"After you finish with a very fine lesson—eh?" His smile seemed to crumble at the corners.

There was a sound from behind him in the studio and Mister Lafkowitz pushed at the other panel of the door and stood beside him.

"Frances?" he said, smiling. "And how is the work coming now?"

Without meaning to, Mister Lafkowitz always made her feel clumsy and overgrown. He was such a small man himself, with a weary look when he was not holding his violin. His eyebrows curved high above his sallow, Jewish face as though asking a question, but the lids of his eyes drowsed languorous and indifferent. Today he seemed distracted. She watched him come into the room for no apparent purpose, holding his pearl-tipped bow in his still fingers, slowly gliding the white horsehair through a chalky piece of rosin. His eyes were sharp bright slits today and the linen handkerchief that flowed down from his collar darkened the shadows beneath them.

"I gather you're doing a lot now," smiled Mister Lafkowitz, although she had not yet answered the question.

She looked at Mister Bilderbach. He turned away. His heavy shoulders pushed the door open wide so that the late afternoon sun came through the window of the studio and shafted yellow over the dusty living room. Behind her teacher she could see the squat long piano, the window, and the bust of Brahms.

"No," she said to Mister Lafkowitz, "I'm doing terribly." Her thin fingers flipped at the pages of her music. "I don't know what's the matter," she said, looking at Mister Bilderbach's stooped muscular back that stood tense and listening.

Mister Lafkowitz smiled. "There are times, I suppose, when one—"

A harsh chord sounded from the piano. "Don't you think we'd better get on with this?" asked Mister Bilderbach.

"Immediately," said Mister Lafkowitz, giving the bow one more scrape before starting toward the door. She could see him pick up his violin from the top of the piano. He caught her eye and lowered the instrument. "You've seen the picture of Heime?"

Her fingers curled tight over the sharp corner of the satchel. "What picture?"

"One of Heime in the *Musical Courier* there on the table. Inside the top cover."

The sonatina began. Discordant yet somehow simple. Empty but with a sharp-cut style of its own. She reached for the magazine and opened it.

There Heime was—in the left-hand corner. Holding his violin with his fingers hooked down over the strings for a pizzicato. With his dark serge knickers strapped neatly beneath his knees, a sweater and rolled collar. It was a bad picture. Although it was snapped in profile his eyes were cut around toward the photographer and his finger looked as though it would pluck the wrong string. He seemed suffering to turn around toward the picture-taking apparatus. He was thinner—his stomach did not poke out now—but he hadn't changed much in six months.

Heime Israelsky, talented young violinist, snapped while at work in his teacher's studio on Riverside Drive. Young Master Israelsky, who will soon celebrate his fifteenth birthday, has been invited to play the Beethoven concerta with—

That morning, after she had practiced from six until eight, her dad had made her sit down at the table with the family for breakfast. She hated breakfast; it gave her a sick feeling afterward. She would rather wait and get four chocolate bars with her twenty cents lunch money and munch them during school—bringing up little morsels from her pocket under cover of her handkerchief, stopping dead when the silver paper rattled. But this morning her dad had put a fried egg on her plate and she had known that if it burst—so that the slimy yellow oozed over the white—she would cry. And that had happened. The same feeling was upon her now. Gingerly she laid the magazine back on the table and closed her eyes.

The music in the studio seemed to be urging violently and clumsily for something that was not to be had. After a moment her thoughts drew back from Heime and the concerta and the picture —and hovered around the lesson once more. She slid over on the sofa until she could see plainly into the studio—the two of them playing, peering at the notations on the piano, lustfully drawing out all that was there.

She could not forget the memory of Mister Bilderbach's face as he had stared at her a moment ago. Her hands, still twitching unconsciously to the motions of the fugue, closed over her bony knees. Tired, she was. And with a circling, sinking-away feeling like the one that often came to her just before she dropped off to sleep on the nights when she had over-practiced. Like those weary half-dreams that buzzed and carried her out into their own whirling space.

A *Wunderkind*—a *Wunderkind*—a *Wunderkind*. The syllables would come out rolling in the deep German way, roar against her ears and then fall to a murmur. Along with the faces circling, swelling out in distortion, diminishing to pale blobs—Mister Bilderbach, Mrs. Bilderbach, Heime, Mister Lafkowitz. Around and around in a circle revolving to the guttural *Wunderkind*. Mister Bilderbach looming large in the middle of the circle, his face urging—with the others around him.

Phrases of music seesawing crazily. Notes she had been practicing falling over each other like a handful of marbles dropped downstairs. Bach, Debussy, Prokofieff, Brahms—timed grotesquely to the far-off throb of her tired body and the buzzing circle.

Sometimes—when she had not worked more than three hours or had stayed out from high school—the dreams were not so confused. The music soared clearly in her mind and quick, precise little memories would come back—clear as the sissy "Age of Innocence" picture Heime had given her after their joint concert was over.

A *Wunderkind*—a *Wunderkind*. That was what Mister Bilderbach had called her when, at twelve, she first came to him. Older pupils had repeated the word.

Not that he had ever said the word to her. "Bienchen—" (She had a plain American name but he never used it except when her mistakes were enormous.) "Bienchen," he would say, "I know it must be terrible. Carrying around all the time a head that thick. Poor Bienchen—"

Mister Bilderbach's father had been a Dutch violinist. His mother was from Prague. He had been born in this country and had spent his youth in Germany. So many times she wished she had not been born and brought up in just Cincinnati. How do you say *cheese* in German? Mister Bilderbach, what is Dutch for *I don't understand you?*

The first day she came to the studio. After she played the whole Second Hungarian Rhapsody from memory. The room graying with twilight. His face as he leaned over the piano.

"Now we begin all over," he said that first day. "It—playing music—is more than cleverness. If a twelve-year-old girl's fingers cover so many keys to a second—that means nothing."

He tapped his broad chest and his forehead with his stubby hand. "Here and here. You are old enough to understand that." He lighted a cigarette and gently blew the first exhalation above her head. "And work—work—work— We will start now with these Bach inventions and these little Schumann pieces." His hands moved again—this time to jerk the cord of the lamp behind her and point to the music. "I will show you how I wish this practiced. Listen carefully now."

She had been at the piano for almost three hours and was very tired. His deep voice sounded as though it had been straying inside her for a long time. She wanted to reach out and touch his muscle-flexed finger that pointed out the phrases, wanted to feel the gleaming gold band ring and the strong hairy back of his hand.

She had lessons Tuesday after school and on Saturday afternoons. Often she stayed, when the Saturday lesson was finished, for dinner, and then spent the night and took the streetcar home the next morning. Mrs. Bilderbach liked her in her calm, almost dumb way. She was much different from her husband. She was quiet and fat and slow. When she wasn't in the kitchen, cooking the rich dishes that both of them loved, she seemed to spend all her time in their bed upstairs, reading magazines or just looking with a half-smile at nothing. When they had married in Germany she had been a *lieder* singer. She didn't sing anymore (she said it was her throat). When he would call her in from the kitchen to listen to a pupil she would always smile and say that it was *gut*, very *gut*.

When Frances was thirteen it came to her one day that the Bilderbachs had no children. It seemed strange. Once she had been back in the kitchen with Mrs. Bilderbach when he had come striding in from the studio, tense with anger at some pupil who had annoyed him. His wife stood stirring the thick soup until his hand groped out and rested on her shoulder. Then she turned—stood placid—while he folded his arms about her and buried his sharp face in the white, nerveless flesh of her neck. They stood that way without moving. And then his face jerked back suddenly, the anger diminished to a quiet inexpressiveness, and he had returned to the studio.

After she had started with Mister Bilderbach and didn't have time to see anything of the people at high school, Heime had been the only friend of her own age. He was Mister Lafkowitz's pupil and would come with him to Mister Bilderbach's on evenings when she would be there. They would listen to their teachers' playing. And often they themselves went over chamber music together—Mozart sonatas or Bloch.

A *Wunderkind*—a *Wunderkind*.

Heime was a *Wunderkind*. He and she, then.

Heime had been playing the violin since he was four. He didn't have to go to school; Mister Lafkowitz's brother, who was crippled, used to teach him geometry and European history and French verbs in the afternoon. When he was thirteen he had as fine a technique as any violinist in Cincinnati—everyone said so. But playing the violin must be easier than the piano. She knew it must be.

Heime always seemed to smell of corduroy pants and the food he had eaten and rosin. Half the time, too, his hands were dirty around the knuckles and the cuffs of his shirts peeped out dingily from the sleeves of his sweater. She always watched his hands when he played—thin only at the joints with the hard little blobs of flesh bulging over the short-cut nails and the babyish-looking crease that showed so plainly in his bowing wrist.

In the dreams, as when she was awake, she could remember the concert only in a blur. She had not known it was unsuccessful for her until months after. True, the papers had praised Heime more than her. But he was much shorter than she. When they stood together on the stage he came only to her shoulders. And that made a difference with people, she knew. Also, there was the matter of the sonata they played together. The Bloch.

"No, no—I don't think that would be appropriate," Mister Bilderbach had said when the Bloch was suggested to end the programme. "Now that John Powell thing—the Sonate Virginianesque."

She hadn't understood then; she wanted it to be the Bloch as much as Mister Lafkowitz and Heime.

Mister Bilderbach had given in. Later, after the reviews had said she lacked the temperament for that type of music, after they called her playing thin and lacking in feeling, she felt cheated.

"That oie oie stuff," said Mister Bilderbach, crackling the newspapers at her. "Not for you, Bienchen. Leave all that to the Heimes and vitses and skys."

A *Wunderkind*. No matter what the papers said, that was what he had called her.

Why was it Heime had done so much better at the concert than she? At school sometimes, when she was supposed to be watching someone do a geometry problem on the blackboard, the question would twist knife-like inside her. She would worry about it in bed, and even sometimes when she was supposed to be concentrating at the piano. It wasn't just the Bloch and her not being Jewish—not entirely. It wasn't that Heime didn't have to go to school and had begun his training so early, either. It was—?

Once she thought she knew.

"Play the Fantasia and Fugue," Mister Bilderbach had demanded one evening a year ago—after he and Mister Lafkowitz had finished reading some music together.

The Bach, as she played, seemed to her well done. From the tail of her eye she could see the calm, pleased expression on Mister Bilderbach's face, see his hands rise climactically from the chair arms and then sink down loose and satisfied when the high points of the phrases had been passed successfully. She stood up from the piano when it was over, swallowing to loosen the bands that the music seemed to have drawn around her throat and chest. But—

"Frances—" Mister Lafkowitz had said then, suddenly, looking at her with his thin mouth curved and his eyes almost covered by their delicate lids. "Do you know how many children Bach had?"

She turned to him, puzzled. "A good many. Twenty some odd."

"Well then—" The corners of his smile etched themselves gently in his pale face. "He could not have been so cold—then."

Mister Bilderbach was not pleased; his guttural effulgence of German words had *Kind* in it somewhere. Mister Lafkowitz raised his eyebrows. She had caught the point easily enough, but she felt no deception in keeping her face blank and immature because that was the way Mister Bilderbach wanted her to look.

Yet such things had nothing to do with it. Nothing very much, at least, for she would grow older. Mister Bilderbach understood that, and even Mister Lafkowitz had not meant just what he said.

In the dreams Mister Bilderbach's face loomed out and contracted in the center of the whirling circle. The lips surging softly, the veins in his temples insisting.

But sometimes, before she slept, there were such clear memories; as when she pulled a hole in the heel of her stocking down, so that her shoe would hide it. "Bienchen, Bienchen!" And bringing Mrs. Bilderbach's work basket in and showing her how it should be darned and not gathered together in a lumpy heap.

And the time she graduated from Junior High.

"What you wear?" asked Mrs. Bilderbach the Sunday morning at breakfast when she told them about how they had practiced to march into the auditorium.

"An evening dress my cousin had last year."

"Ah—Bienchen!" he said, circling his warm coffee cup with his heavy hands, looking up at her with wrinkles around his laughing eyes. "I bet I know what Bienchen wants—"

He insisted. He would not believe her when she explained that she honestly didn't care at all.

"Like this, Anna," he said, pushing his napkin across the table and mincing to the other side of the room, swishing his hips, rolling up his eyes behind his horn-rimmed glasses.

The next Saturday afternoon, after her lessons, he took her to the department stores downtown. His thick fingers smoothed over the filmy nets and crackling taffetas that the saleswomen unwound from their bolts. He held colors to her face, cocking his head to one side, and selected pink. Shoes, he remembered too. He liked best some white kid pumps. They seemed a little like old ladies' shoes to her and the Red Cross label in the instep had a charity look. But it really didn't matter at all. When Mrs. Bilderbach began to cut out the dress and fit it to her with pins, he interrupted his lessons to stand by and suggest ruffles around the hips and neck and a fancy rosette on the shoulder. The music was coming along nicely then. Dresses and commencement and such made no difference.

Nothing mattered much except playing the music as it must be played, bringing out the thing that must be in her, practicing, practicing, playing so that Mister Bilderbach's face lost some of its urging look. Putting the thing into her music that Myra Hess had, and Yehudi Menuhin—even Heime!

What had begun to happen to her four months ago? The notes began springing out with a glib, dead intonation. Adolescence, she thought. Some kids played with promise—and worked and worked until, like her, the least little thing would start them crying, and worn out with trying to get the thing across—the longing thing they felt—something queer began to happen— But not she! She was like Heime. She had to be. She—

Once it was there for sure. And you didn't lose things like that. A *Wunderkind.* . . . A *Wunderkind.* . . . Of her he said it, rolling the words in the sure, deep German way. And in the dreams even deeper, more certain than ever. With his face looming out at her, and the longing phrases of music mixed in with the zooming, circling round, round, round— A *Wunderkind.* A *Wunderkind.* . . .

This afternoon Mister Bilderbach did not show Mister Lafkowitz to the front door, as he usually did. He stayed at the piano, softly pressing a solitary note. Listening, Frances watched the violinist wind his scarf about his pale throat.

"A good picture of Heime," she said, picking up her music. "I

got a letter from him a couple of months ago—telling about hearing
Schnabel and Huberman and about Carnegie Hall and things to eat
at the Russian Tea Room."

To put off going into the studio a moment longer she waited
until Mister Lafkowitz was ready to leave and then stood behind
him as he opened the door. The frosty cold outside cut into the
room. It was growing late and the air was seeped with the pale
yellow of winter twilight. When the door swung to on its hinges,
the house seemed darker and more silent than ever before she had
known it to be.

As she went into the studio Mister Bilderbach got up from
the piano and silently watched her settle herself at the keyboard.

"Well, Bienchen," he said, "this afternoon we are going to begin all over. Start from scratch. Forget the last few months."

He looked as though he were trying to act a part in a movie.
His solid body swayed from toe to heel, he rubbed his hands together, and even smiled in a satisfied, movie way. Then suddenly
he thrust this manner brusquely aside. His heavy shoulders slouched
and he began to run through the stack of music she had brought
in. "The Bach—no, not yet," he murmured. "The Beethoven? Yes.
The Variation Sonata. Opus 26."

The keys of the piano hemmed her in—stiff and white and
dead-seeming.

"Wait a minute," he said. He stood in the curve of the piano,
elbows propped, and looked at her. "Today I expect something
from you. Now this sonata—it's the first Beethoven sonata you
ever worked on. Every note is under control—technically—you have
nothing to cope with but the music. Only music now. That's all
you think about."

He rustled through the pages of her volume until he found
the place. Then he pulled his teaching chair halfway across the
room, turned it around and seated himself, straddling the back
with his legs.

For some reason, she knew, this position of his usually had a
good effect on her performance. But today she felt that she would
notice him from the corner of her eye and be disturbed. His back
was stiffly tilted, his legs looked tense. The heavy volume before
him seemed to balance dangerously on the chair back. "Now we
begin," he said with a peremptory dart of his eyes in her direction.

Her hands rounded over the keys and then sank down. The
first notes were too loud, the other phrases followed dryly.

Arrestingly his hand rose up from the score. "Wait! Think a minute what you're playing. How is this beginning marked?"

"*An-andante.*"

"All right. Don't drag it into an *adagio* then. And play deeply into the keys. Don't snatch it off shallowly that way. A graceful, deep-toned *andante*—"

She tried again. Her hands seemed separate from the music that was in her.

"Listen," he interrupted. "Which of these variations dominates the whole?"

"The dirge," she answered.

"Then prepare for that. This is an *andante*—but it's not salon stuff as you just played it. Start out softly, *piano*, and make it swell out just before the arpeggio. Make it warm and dramatic. And down here—where it's marked *dolce* make the counter melody sing out. You know all that. We've gone over all that side of it before. Now play it. Feel it as Beethoven wrote it down. Feel that tragedy and restraint."

She could not stop looking at his hands. They seemed to rest tentatively on the music, ready to fly up as a stop signal as soon as she would begin, the gleaming flash of his ring calling her to halt. "Mister Bilderbach—maybe if I—if you let me play on through the first variation without stopping I could do better."

"I won't interrupt," he said.

Her pale face leaned over too close to the keys. She played through the first part, and, obeying a nod from him, began the second. There were no flaws that jarred on her, but the phrases shaped from her fingers before she had put into them the meaning that she felt.

When she had finished he looked up from the music and began to speak with dull bluntness: "I hardly heard those harmonic fillings in the right hand. And incidentally, this part was supposed to take on intensity, develop the foreshadowings that were supposed to be inherent in the first part. Go on with the next one, though."

She wanted to start it with subdued viciousness and progress to a feeling of deep, swollen sorrow. Her mind told her that. But her hands seemed to gum in the keys like limp macaroni and she could not imagine the music as it should be.

When the last note had stopped vibrating, he closed the book and deliberately got up from the chair. He was moving his lower jaw from side to side—and between his open lips she could glimpse the pink healthy lane to his throat and his strong, smoke-yellowed teeth. He laid the Beethoven gingerly on top of the rest of her music and propped his elbows on the smooth, black piano top once more. "No," he said simply, looking at her.

Her mouth began to quiver. "I can't help it. I—"

Suddenly he strained his lips into a smile. "Listen, Bienchen," he began in a new, forced voice. "You still play the Harmonious Blacksmith, don't you? I told you not to drop it from your repertoire."

"Yes," she said. "I practice it now and then."

His voice was the one he used for children. "It was among the first things we worked on together—remember. So strongly you used to play it—like a real blacksmith's daughter. You see, Bienchen, I know you so well—as if you were my own girl. I know what you have—I've heard you play so many things beautifully. You used to—"

He stopped in confusion and inhaled from his pulpy stub of cigarette. The smoke drowsed out from his pink lips and clung in a gray mist around her lank hair and childish forehead.

"Make it happy and simple," he said, switching on the lamp behind her and stepping back from the piano.

For a moment he stood just inside the bright circle the light made. Then impulsively he squatted down to the floor. "Vigorous," he said.

She could not stop looking at him, sitting on one heel with the other foot resting squarely before him for balance, the muscles of his strong thighs straining under the cloth of his trousers, his back straight, his elbows staunchly propped on his knees. "Simply now," he repeated with a gesture of his fleshy hands. "Think of the blacksmith—working out in the sunshine all day. Working easily and undisturbed."

She could not look down at the piano. The light brightened the hairs on the backs of his outspread hands, made the lenses of his glasses glitter.

"All of it," he urged. "Now!"

She felt that the marrows of her bones were hollow and there was no blood left in her. Her heart that had been springing against her chest all afternoon felt suddenly dead. She saw it gray and limp and shriveled at the edges like an oyster.

His face seemed to throb out in space before her, come closer with the lurching motion in the veins of his temples. In retreat, she looked down at the piano. Her lips shook like jelly and a surge of noiseless tears made the white keys blur in a watery line. "I can't," she whispered. "I don't know why, but I just can't—can't any more."

His tense body slackened and, holding his hand to his side, he pulled himself up. She clutched her music and hurried past him.

Her coat. The mittens and galoshes. The schoolbooks and the satchel he had given her on her birthday. All from the silent room that was hers. Quickly—before he would have to speak.

As she passed through the vestibule she could not help but see his hands—held out from his body that leaned against the studio door, relaxed and purposeless. The door shut to firmly. Dragging her books and satchel she stumbled down the stone steps, turned in the wrong direction, and hurried down the street that had become confused with noise and bicycles and the games of other children.

The Child's Day

JESSAMYN WEST

*In this story Jessamyn West describes one special day in the
life of a special young girl. Minta possesses a rare combination of
innocence and insight. The former gives her hope, imagination,
and dreams; the latter brings her strength, intelligence, and
maturity. But she is trapped in a world that will soon destroy
her innocence and slowly dull her insights. What are the indications
that Minta herself is aware of her bleak future? Although she
delights in beautiful words, she scorns using them in her own
poetry, preferring instead a stark and brutal quality. What does
this choice reveal about her sense of herself? How is her poem a
foreshadowing of her life? When Minta dances to celebrate the
beauty of her body, she claims that ugliness cannot touch her.
What details does the author include to contradict her? Minta's last
defiant vow is "I will know everything." Why is it ironic, and
how does the author undercut its impact?*

"I Minta," the child said, "in the October day, in the dying October day." She walked over to the fireplace and stood so that the slanting sunlight fell onto her bare shoulder with a red wine stain. The ashes, so light and dry, smelled raw, rain-wet. Or perhaps it's the water on the chrysanthemums, she thought, or perhaps the bitter, autumn-flavored chrysanthemums themselves.

She listened for her second heartbeat, the three-day tap of the loosened shingle. But it was dead, it beat no more. For three days the Santa Ana had buffeted the house, but now at evening it had died down, had blown itself out. It was blown out, but it left its signs: the piled sand by the east door sills, the tumble weeds

THE CHILD'S DAY From the *New Mexico Quarterly*, November 1940. Reprinted by permission of the author and Russell & Volkening, Inc.

caught in the angle of the corral, the sign board by the electric tracks, face down; the eucalyptus upright, but with torn limb dangling.

"The Sabbath evening," said the girl, "the autumn Sabbath evening." And bright and warm against the day's sober death, the year's sad end, burned her own bright living.

She walked to her own room, across her fallen nightgown, past her unmade bed, and opened the casement window and leaned out toward the west. There the sun was near to setting, red in the dust, and the lights in the distant well riggings already blazed. She watched the sun drop until the black tracery of a derrick crossed its face.

"The day dies," murmured the girl; "its burnished wrack burns in yon western sky."

Then she was quiet so that no single word should fall to ripple the clear surface of her joy. The pepper tree rustled; there was a little stir in the leaves of the bougainvillaea. From the ocean, twenty miles away, the sea air was beginning to move back across the land. "It is as good against the dry face as water." She pushed her crackling hair away from her cheeks. "I won't have a wind break as thin even as one hair against my face."

She arched her bony chest under the tightly wrapped lace scarf, so that she could project as much of herself as possible into the evening's beauty. "Now the sun is down and the day's long dream ended. Now I must make the air whistle about my ears."

She came out of the long black lace scarf like an ivory crucifix —with a body no wider than her arms. Bloomers, slip, green rep dress on, and there she was—thirteen again, and the supper to get, and the house to clean. She had the supper in mind: a fitting meal for Sunday evening. Oyster soup. Oysters that actresses ate, floating in a golden sea of milk, and marble cup-cakes veined like old temples.

She had supper ready when the Duro turned into the driveway bringing her family home from their drive—the cakes out of the oven, the milk just on for the soup.

"Well," said her father when he entered the room, "this is pretty nice." He walked over and held his hands to the fire. "Wood box full, too."

Her mother ran her finger over the top of the bookcase while she unwound her veil. "Minta, you'll burn us out dusting with kerosene."

Clenmie said, sniffing the air, "Did you bake me a little cake, Mintie?"

Minta watched the scarlet accordion pleating in the opening of her mother's slit skirt fan out as she held her foot toward the fire.

Father took off Clenmie's coat. "You should have gone with us, Minta. The wind's done a lot of damage over in Riverside County. Lost count of the roofs off and trees down."

"Is supper ready?" Mother asked.

"Soon as the milk heats, and I put the oysters in."

"Oyster soup!" exclaimed Father. "The perfect dish for a Sunday October evening. Did you get your studying done?" he asked curiously.

Minta nodded. Studying. Well, it was studying. There were her books and papers.

Father had said that morning before they left, "You're a bright girl, Minta. No need your spending a whole day studying. Do you more good to go for a ride with us."

"No, Father, I'm way behind." She could hardly wait until they left.

Finally at ten they got into the car, Mother on the front seat close to Father, Clenmie behind. Father backed out of the driveway and a dusty swirl of wind caught Mother's scarlet veil. They waved her a sad good-by.

She had watched the red Duro out of sight, then turned and claimed the empty house for herself. She was as happy as a snail that expels the last grain of sand which has separated its sensitive fluid from its shell. Now she flowed back against the walls of her house in pure contentment. She stood stock still and shut her eyes and listened to the house sounds: first the dry, gusty breathing of the wind and the shingle's tap, then the lessening hiss of the tea kettle as the breakfast fire died, and the soft, animal pad of the rug as a slackening air current let it fall.

She opened her eyes. In the dining room the curtains lifted and fell with a summer movement in the autumn wind. She felt this to be perfect happiness: to stand in one room and watch in another the rise and fall of curtains. The egg-rimmed dishes still stood on the uncleared breakfast table. She regarded the disorder happily. "Oh," she whispered, "it's like being the only survivor on an abandoned ship."

Stealthily she ran to lower all the blinds so that the room was left in yellow, dusty twilight. Then she made herself a fire of the petroleum-soaked refuse from the oil fields that they used for wood. When the oil began to bubble and seethe, and the flames darted up, black and red, she started her work.

She cleared the fumed-oak library table and ranged her books and papers precisely before her. Now her day began. Now she inhabited two worlds at once, and slid amphibian-like from one to the other, and had in each the best. She moved in Shelley's world of luminous mist, and emerged to hold her hand to the fire and to listen to the bone-dry sound of the wind in the palm trees.

She laid her hand across her open book feeling that the words there were so strong and beautiful that they would enter her veins through her palms and so flow to her heart. She listened to the wind and saw all the objects that bent before it: she saw the stately movement of dark tree tops, the long ripple of bleached, hair-like grass, the sprayed sea water, the blown manes of horses in open pasture, the lonely sway of electric signs along dusty main streets. "Far across the steppes," she said, "and the prairie lands, the high mesas and the grass-covered pampas." She watched the oil bubble stickily out of the wood and wondered how it seemed to feel again after these thousands of years the touch of the wind.

But this was dreaming, not doing her work. She opened her notebook to a half-filled page headed, "Beautiful, Lilting Phrases from Shelley." The list slid across her tongue like honey: "Rainbow locks, bright shadows, riven waves, spangled sky, aery rocks, sanguine sunrise, upward sky, viewless gale." She felt the texture of the words on her fingers as she copied them. The shingle tapped, the wind blew grittily across the pane, the fire seethed.

She finished Shelley and started on her own word list. She was through with the *o*'s, ready to begin on the *p*'s. She opened her old red dictionary. What words would she find here? Beautiful, strange ones? She looked ahead: pamero: a cold wind that sweeps over the pampas; parsalene: a mock moon; panada: bread crumbs boiled in milk; picaroon: a rogue; pilgarlic: a baldheaded man; plangent: resounding like a wave. Her eyes narrowed and her cheek bones ached regarding this rich store.

She rolled her black, ribbed, gartered stocking back and forth across her knee and copied words and definitions. When she finished the *q*'s she put her word notebook away and took out one called "The Poems of Aminta Eilertsen, Volume III." Each Sunday she copied one poem from her week's output into her poem book. Her poems were nothing like Shelley's. Shelley was beautiful, but he was not a modern. Minta was a modern, and when she wrote poetry she scorned the pretty and euphonious. This week's poem was called "You Do Not Have to Wipe the Noses of Your Dreams," and Minta thought it as stark and brutal as anything she had ever done. Slowly she copied it:

> I was lithe and had dreams;
> Now I am fat and have children.
> Dreams are efflorescent,
> Dreams fade.
> Children do not.
> But then you do not have to
> Wipe the noses of your dreams.

"*Yes,*" *she said to her father, having remembered the poems, hers and Shelley's, the long list of words,* "*I finished my studying all right.*"

"*Did anyone come while we were gone?*" *Mother asked.*

"*Mrs. Beal knocked, but she left before I got to the door.*"

She had scarcely moved from her table all morning. Now her back was stiff; she was cold and hungry. She put another petroleum-soaked timber on the fire and sat on the hassock warming her knees and eating her lunch: a mixture of cocoa, sugar, and condensed milk as thick and brown as mud. She spooned it from gravy bowl to mouth and watched the murky flames and listened to the block of wood which was burning as noisily as a martyr. The oil seethed and bubbled like blood. She crouched on the hearth and heard behind the drawn curtains the hiss of sand against the windows. A current of air like a cold finger touched her cheek.

"What do I here," she wondered, "alone, abandoned, hiding?"

She pressed herself closely against the bricks and listened intently. She took a bite and let the sweet, brown paste slide down her throat so that no sound of swallowing should mask the approaching footfall, the heavy, guarded breathing. The room was filled with a noiseless activity. Well, she had known this would be her end. Soon or late they would come, search her out. In some such sordid, dirty, ill-lit hole as this she had been destined to make her end.

"In solitude and from this broken crockery, then, this last meal," she mused, and looked scornfully at the cracked bowl. "And those for whom the deed was done eat from crystal, on linen napery, and talk with light voices."

The wind had died down. But the curtains moved stealthily and the door into the hallway trembled a little in its frame. From somewhere in the house came the light click, click of metal on metal. Light, but continuous. She had not heard it before. She shifted her weight cautiously on the hassock so that she faced the room.

The wind came up again with a long, low, sick whistle; the shingle beat feverishly. She put down her bowl and started the search she knew must be made. She stepped out of her shoes and noiselessly opened the door into the hall. Cold, dark, and window-less it stretched the length of the house. Three bedroom doors opened off it, two to the west, one to the east. She searched the bedrooms carefully, though her heartbeat jarred her cheeks. She lunged against the long, hanging garments that might have con-cealed a hidden figure. She threw back the covers of the unmade beds. She watched the mirrors to see if from their silver depths a burning, red-rimmed eye might look into hers.

In Clenmie's room she finished her search. The loose shingle tapped like the heart of a ghost. Then she heard it: the sound she had been born to hear, the footstep her ears had been made to echo. Furtive footsteps: now fast, now slow, now pausing alto-gether. She leaned against the side of Clenmie's crib and waited for the steps to turn toward the house.

"But how could they know this was the house. What sign did I leave? What clew not destroy?"

The footsteps came on inexorably, turned out of the road onto the graveled walk, then proceeded quickly and resolutely to the front door. First there was a light, insistent knock, then the latched screen door was heavily shaken.

"He must have a force with him," Minta thought, "he is so bold," and waited for the crash of splintering boards, and braced her body for the thrust of cold steel that would follow. She thought fleetingly of Clenmie, and of her father and mother, and wondered if any sudden coldness about their hearts warned them of her plight.

The screen door shook again, and a woman's voice, old and

quiet, called out, "Is there anyone there? I say, is there anyone home?" and ceased.

Slowly, cautiously Minta crept to the living room, lifted the side of the green blind. Old Mrs. Beal, her Sunday black billowing in the wind, was homeward bound from dinner with her daughter.

"I saw it was old Mrs. Beal on her way home from her daughter's," she told her father, giving him as much truth as she thought he could handle.

"Minta, you can get to the door fast enough when some of your friends are calling."

"I was busy," replied Minta with dignity. Her father looked at her doubtfully, but said no more.

Her mother combed out Clenmie's soft, white hair with her rhinestone back comb. "Did you forget to feed Brownie?" she asked.

"Of course I fed Brownie. I'll never forget her. She's my dearest friend."

Against the warm reality of Mrs. Beal's broad, homeward-bound back, the world that had been cold and full of danger dissolved. The dear room; her books, her papers; Clenmie's toys; Mother's tissue cream on top of the piano; the fire sending its lazy red tongue up the chimney's black throat.

She stood warming herself, happy and bemused, like a prisoner unexpectedly pardoned. Then she heard again the click, click she had not recognized. Brownie at the back door!

"O poor Brownie, I forgot you. Poor kitty, are you hungry?" There was Brownie sitting on the back step, with fur blown and dusty, patiently waiting to be let in and fed. She was a young cat, who had never had a kit of her own, but she looked like a grandmother. She looked as if she should have a gingham apron tied around her waist, and spectacles on her nose, and now out of her grandmother's eyes she gave Minta a look of tolerance. Minta snatched the cat up and held her close to her face, and rubbed her nose in the soft, cool fur. When she got out the can of condensed milk she put Brownie by the fire and poured the milk into the bowl from which she had eaten her own lunch. Brownie lapped the yellow arc as it fell from can to bowl.

Minta crouched on the hearth with her eyes almost on a level with Brownie's. It was blissful, almost mesmeric to watch the quick, deft dart of the red tongue into the yellow milk. Her own body seemed to participate in that darting, rhythmic movement and was lulled and happy. "It is almost as if she rocked me, back and forth, back and forth, with her tongue," mused Minta.

When Brownie finished eating, Minta took her in her arms, felt the soft little body beneath the shaggy envelope of cinnamon fur. She lay on the floor close to the fire and cradled Brownie drowsily. Suddenly she kissed her. "My darling, my darling," she said, and caressed the cat the length of its long, soft body. Her hand tingled a little as it passed over the little pin-point nipples.

Some day her mother would tell her the secret phrase, the magic sentence—something the other girls already knew. Then the boys would notice her. Then he would come. Ellen and Margaret and Phyllis already had notes from boys, and candy hearts on Valentine's day, and a piece of mistletoe at Christmas time. The boys rode them on their handle bars and showed them wrestling holds, and treated them to sodas. "But no one," she mourned, "ever looks at me." She pressed her apricot-colored hair close to the cat's cinnamon fur. "It's because mother hasn't told me yet. Something the other girls know. Sometime she'll tell me—some beautiful word I've been waiting a long time to hear. Then I'll be like a lamp lighted, a flower bloomed. Maybe she'll tell me tomorrow—and when I walk into school everyone will see the change, know I know. How will they know? My lips, my eyes, a walk, a gesture, the movement of my arms. But there's not a boy here I'd have, but someone far away, no boy. He will come and we will walk out along the streets hand in hand and everyone will see us and say, 'They were made for each other.' His hair will be like fur, soft and sooty black, and on his thin brown cheek will be a long, cruel scar. He will say, 'Kiss it, Minta, and I will bless the man who did it.' Ah, we shall walk together like sword and flower. All eyes will follow us and the people will say, 'This is Minta. Why did we never see her before?' "

Fire and wind were dying. Brownie slept on her arm. "He will come, he will come." Minta lifted Brownie high overhead, then brought her down sharply and closely to her breast.

"He will come, he will come." She kissed Brownie fiercely and put her on the floor, and ran to her mother's room, undressing as she went. She stepped out of her serge skirt and threw her Norfolk jacket across the room and sent her bloomers in a flying arc. She knew what she wanted. She had used it before—mother's long, black lace fascinator. She wound it tightly about herself from arm-pits to thighs. She unbraided her hair and let it hang across her shoulders. Then she turned to the mirror. "I have a beautiful body," she breathed, "a beautiful, beautiful body."

And because she regarded herself, thinking of him, him who was yet to come, it was as if he too saw her. She loaned him her eyes so that he might see her, and to her flesh she gave this gift of his seeing. She raised her arms and slowly turned and her flesh was warm with his seeing. Somberly and quietly she turned and swayed and gravely touched now thigh, now breast, now cheek, and looked and looked with the eyes she had given him.

She moved through the gray dust-filled room weaving an ivory pattern. Not any of the dust or disorder of her mother's room fazed her, not its ugliness or funny smell. Hair bubbled out of the hair receiver, the stopper was out of the Hoyt's cologne bottle, the mir-ror was spattered with liquid powder. She made, in her mind, a heap of all that was ugly and disordered. She made a dunghill of them and from its top she crowed.

"The curtains, green as vomit, and hanging crooked, the gray neckband on the white flannel nightgown, the dust on the patent leather shoes, I hate them and dance them down. Nothing can touch me. I am Minta. Or I can dance with them," and she clasped the sour-smelling nightgown to her and leaped and bent. "This is evil, to be naked, to like the feel of gritty dust under my feet, the bad smell, the dim light."

She regarded her face more closely in the spattered mirror. "There is something wanton and evil there," she thought, "some-thing not good. Perhaps I shall be faithless," and she trembled with pity for that dark one who loved her so dearly. She shook back her hair and pressed her cool hands to her burning cheeks and danced so that the dust motes in the slanting shaft of light shot meteor-like, up and down.

"I can dance the word," she whispered, "but I cannot say it." So she danced it, wrapped in the black fascinator, with the dust motes dancing about her. She danced it until she trembled and leaning on bent elbows looked deep into the mirror and said, "There is nothing I will not touch. I am Minta. I will know every-thing."

All at once she was tired. She turned and walked slowly to the living room. Brownie lay by the dead fire. "I, Minta," she had said, "in the October day, in the dying October day," and turned to do the evening work.

"*If the milk boils your soup will be spoiled,*" *Mother said.* "*We've been here long enough for it to heat.*"

"*Yes, Sister, let's eat,*" *said Father,* "*it's been a long day.*"

"*Yes, let's eat,*" *cried Minta.* "*It's been a long, beautiful day,*" *and she ran to the kitchen to put the oysters in the milk.*

2

Expectation
and
Defeat

[handwritten annotations across the top of the page:] Similes stated comparison — Extended Metaphor — implied comparison of unlike things — informs

Lappin and Lapinova

VIRGINIA WOOLF

This story by Virginia Woolf begins with a wedding and concludes with the statement "So that was the end of that marriage." It is a kind of parable about how a love relationship is created and subsequently destroyed. Why does Rosalind invent the imaginary world of Lappin and Lapinova, and why does she continue to play her little game with Ernest long after their honeymoon? The golden wedding party for Ernest's parents is presented in detail as a major but dreaded event in Rosalind's life. Why is it significant that the final episode of the story, the "death" of Lapinova, begins on the anniversary of that night? How are the two events related? How does Lapinova die, and why is it appropriate that Ernest invents this particular fate for her? Why does it simultaneously mark the end of Rosalind's marriage?

*T*hey were married. The wedding march pealed out. The pigeons fluttered. Small boys in Eton jackets threw rice; a fox terrier sauntered across the path; and Ernest Thorburn led his bride to the car through that small inquisitive crowd of complete strangers which always collects in London to enjoy other people's happiness or unhappiness. Certainly he looked handsome and she looked shy. More rice was thrown, and the car moved off.

That was on Tuesday. Now it was Saturday. Rosalind had still to get used to the fact that she was Mrs. Ernest Thorburn. Perhaps she never would get used to the fact that she was Mrs. Ernest Anybody, she thought, as she sat in the bow window of the

hotel looking over the lake to the mountains, and waited for her
husband to come down to breakfast. Ernest was a difficult name to
get used to. It was not the name she would have chosen. She
would have preferred Timothy, Antony, or Peter. He did not look
like Ernest either. The name suggested the Albert Memorial,
mahogany sideboards, steel engravings of the Prince Consort with
his family—her mother-in-law's dining-room in Porchester Terrace
in short.

But here he was. Thank goodness he did not look like Ernest
—no. But what did he look like? She glanced at him sideways.
Well, when he was eating toast he looked like a rabbit. Not that
anyone else would have seen a likeness to a creature so diminutive
and timid in this spruce, muscular young man with the straight
nose, the blue eyes, and the very firm mouth. But that made it all
the more amusing. His nose twitched very slightly when he ate.
So did her pet rabbit's. She kept watching his nose twitch; and then
she had to explain, when he caught her looking at him, why she
laughed.

"It's because you're like a rabbit, Ernest," she said. "Like a
wild rabbit," she added, looking at him. "A hunting rabbit; a King
Rabbit; a rabbit that makes laws for all the other rabbits."

Ernest had no objection to being that kind of rabbit, and since
it amused her to see him twitch his nose—he had never known that
his nose twitched—he twitched it on purpose. And she laughed and
laughed; and he laughed too, so that the maiden ladies and the
fishing man and the Swiss waiter in his greasy black jacket all
guessed right; they were very happy. But how long does such happiness last? they asked themselves; and each answered according
to his own circumstances.

At lunch time, seated on a clump of heather beside the lake,
"Lettuce, rabbit?" said Rosalind, holding out the lettuce that had
been provided to eat with the hard-boiled eggs. "Come and take it
out of my hand," she added, and he stretched out and nibbled the
lettuce and twitched his nose.

"Good rabbit, nice rabbit," she said, patting him, as she used
to pat her tame rabbit at home. But that was absurd. He was not a
tame rabbit, whatever he was. She turned it into French. "Lapin,"
she called him. But whatever he was, he was not a French rabbit.
He was simply and solely English—born at Porchester Terrace,
educated at Rugby; now a clerk in His Majesty's Civil Service. So
she tried "Bunny" next; but that was worse. "Bunny" was someone

plump and soft and comic; he was thin and hard and serious. Still, his nose twitched. "Lappin," she exclaimed suddenly; and gave a little cry as if she had found the very word she looked for.

"Lappin, Lappin, King Lappin," she repeated. It seemed to suit him exactly; he was not Ernest, he was King Lappin. Why? She did not know.

When there was nothing new to talk about on their long solitary walks—and it rained, as everyone had warned them that it would rain; or when they were sitting over the fire in the evening, for it was cold, and the maiden ladies had gone and the fishing man, and the waiter only came if you rang the bell for him, she let her fancy play with the story of the Lappin tribe. Under her hands —she was sewing; he was reading—they became very real, very vivid, very amusing. Ernest put down the paper and helped her. There were the black rabbits and the red; there were the enemy rabbits and the friendly. There were the wood in which they lived and the outlying prairies and the swamp. Above all there was King Lappin, who, far from having only the one trick—that he twitched his nose—became as the days passed an animal of the greatest character; Rosalind was always finding new qualities in him. But above all he was a great hunter.

"And what," said Rosalind, on the last day of the honeymoon, "did the King do today?"

In fact they had been climbing all day; and she had worn a blister on her heel; but she did not mean that.

"Today," said Ernest, twitching his nose as he bit the end off his cigar, "he chased a hare." He paused; struck a match, and twitched again.

"A woman hare," he added.

"A white hare!" Rosalind exclaimed, as if she had been expecting this. "Rather a small hare; silver grey; with big bright eyes?"

"Yes," said Ernest, looking at her as she had looked at him, "a smallish animal; with eyes popping out of her head, and two little front paws dangling." It was exactly how she sat, with her sewing dangling in her hands; and her eyes, that were so big and bright, were certainly a little prominent.

"Ah, Lapinova," Rosalind murmured.

"Is that what she's called?" said Ernest—"the real Rosalind?" He looked at her. He felt very much in love with her.

"Yes; that's what she's called," said Rosalind. "Lapinova." And before they went to bed that night it was all settled. He was King

Lappin; she was Queen Lapinova. They were the opposite of each other; he was bold and determined; she wary and undependable. He ruled over the busy world of rabbits; her world was a desolate, mysterious place, which she ranged mostly by moonlight. All the same, their territories touched; they were King and Queen.

Thus when they came back from their honeymoon they possessed a private world, inhabited, save for the one white hare, entirely by rabbits. No one guessed that there was such a place, and that of course made it all the more amusing. It made them feel, more even than most young married couples, in league together against the rest of the world. Often they looked slyly at each other when people talked about rabbits and woods and traps and shooting. Or they winked furtively across the table when Aunt Mary said that she could never bear to see a hare in a dish—it looked so like a baby: or when John, Ernest's sporting brother, told them what price rabbits were fetching that autumn in Wiltshire, skins and all. Sometimes when they wanted a gamekeeper, or a poacher or a Lord of the Manor, they amused themselves by distributing the parts among their friends. Ernest's mother, Mrs. Reginald Thorburn, for example, fitted the part of the Squire to perfection. But it was all secret—that was the point of it; nobody save themselves knew that such a world existed.

Without that world, how, Rosalind wondered, that winter could she have lived at all? For instance, there was the golden-wedding party, when all the Thorburns assembled at Porchester Terrace to celebrate the fiftieth anniversary of that union which had been so blessed—had it not produced Ernest Thornburn?—and so fruitful—had it not produced nine other sons and daughters into the bargain, many themselves married and also fruitful? She dreaded that party. But it was inevitable. As she walked upstairs she felt bitterly that she was an only child and an orphan at that; a mere drop among all those Thorburns assembled in the great drawing-room with the shiny satin wallpaper and the lustrous family portraits. The living Thorburns much resembled the painted; save that instead of painted lips they had real lips; out of which came jokes; jokes about schoolrooms, and how they had pulled the chair from under the governess; jokes about frogs and how they had put them between the virgin sheets of maiden ladies. As for herself, she had never even made an apple-pie bed. Holding her present in her hand she advanced toward her mother-in-law sumptuous in yellow satin; and toward her father-in-law decorated with a rich yellow carnation. All round them on tables and chairs there were golden tributes, some nestling in cotton wool; others branching resplendent—candlesticks; cigar boxes; chains; each stamped with the goldsmith's proof that it was solid gold, hall-marked, authentic. But her present was only a little pinchbeck box pierced with holes; an old sand caster, an eighteenth-century relic, once used to sprinkle sand over wet ink. Rather a senseless present she felt—in an age of blotting paper; and as she proffered it, she saw in front of her the stubby black handwriting in which her mother-in-law when they were engaged had expressed the hope that "My son will make you happy." No, she was not happy. Not at all happy. She looked at Ernest, straight as a ramrod with a nose like all the noses in the family portraits; a nose that never twitched at all.

Then they went down to dinner. She was half hidden by the great chrysanthemums that curled their red and gold petals into large tight balls. Everything was gold. A gold-edged card with gold initials intertwined recited the list of all the dishes that would be set one after another before them. She dipped her spoon in a plate of clear golden fluid. The raw white fog outside had been turned by the lamps into a golden mesh that blurred the edges of the plates and gave the pineapples a rough golden skin. Only she herself in her white wedding dress peering ahead of her with her prominent eyes seemed insoluble as an icicle.

As the dinner wore on, however, the room grew steamy with heat. Beads of perspiration stood out on the men's foreheads. She felt that her icicle was being turned to water. She was being melted; dispersed; dissolved into nothingness; and would soon faint. Then through the surge in her head and the din in her ears she heard a woman's voice exclaim, "But they breed so!"

The Thorburns—yes; they breed so, she echoed; looking at all the round red faces that seemed doubled in the giddiness that overcame her; and magnified in the gold mist that enhaloed them. "They breed so." Then John bawled:

"Little devils! . . . Shoot 'em! Jump on 'em with big boots! That's the only way to deal with 'em . . . rabbits!"

At that word, that magic word, she revived. Peeping between the chrysanthemums she saw Ernest's nose twitch. It rippled, it ran with successive twitches. And at that a mysterious catastrophe befell the Thorburns. The golden table became a moor with the gorse in full bloom; the din of voices turned to one peal of lark's laughter ringing down from the sky. It was a blue sky—clouds passed slowly. And they had all been changed—the Thorburns. She looked at her father-in-law, a furtive little man with dyed moustaches. His foible was collecting things—seals, enamel boxes, trifles from eighteenth-century dressing tables which he hid in the drawers of his study from his wife. Now she saw him as he was—a poacher, stealing off with his coat bulging with pheasants and partridges to drop them stealthily into a three-legged pot in his smoky little cottage. That was her real father-in-law—a poacher. And Celia, the unmarried daughter, who always nosed out other people's secrets, the little things they wished to hide—she was a white ferret with pink eyes, and a nose clotted with earth from her horrid underground nosings and pokings. Slung round men's shoulders, in a net, and thrust down a hole—it was a pitiable life—Celia's; it was none of her fault. So she saw Celia. And then she looked at her mother-in-law—whom they dubbed the Squire. Flushed, coarse, a bully—she was all that, as she stood returning thanks, but now that Rosalind—that is Lapinova—saw her, she saw behind her the decayed family mansion, the plaster peeling off the walls, and heard her, with a sob in her voice, giving thanks to her children (who hated her) for a world that had ceased to exist. There was a sudden silence. They all stood with their glasses raised; they all drank; then it was over.

"Oh, King Lappin!" she cried as they went home together in the fog, "if your nose hadn't twitched just at that moment, I should have been trapped!"

"But you're safe," said King Lappin, pressing her paw.

"Quite safe," she answered.

And they drove back through the Park, King and Queen of the marsh, of the mist, and of the gorse-scented moor.

Thus time passed; one year; two years of time. And on a winter's night, which happened by a coincidence to be the anniversary of the golden-wedding party—but Mrs. Reginald Thorburn was dead; the house was to let; and there was only a caretaker in residence—Ernest came home from the office. They had a nice little home; half a house above a saddler's shop in South Kensington, not far from the Tube station. It was cold, with fog in the air, and Rosalind was sitting over the fire, sewing.

"What d'you think happened to me today?" she began as soon as he had settled himself down with his legs stretched to the blaze. "I was crossing the stream when—"

"What stream?" Ernest interrupted her.

"The stream at the bottom, where our wood meets the black wood," she explained.

Ernest looked completely blank for a moment.

"What the deuce are you talking about?" he asked.

"My dear Ernest!" she cried in dismay. "King Lappin," she added, dangling her little front paws in the firelight. But his nose did not twitch. Her hands—they turned to hands—clutched the stuff she was holding; her eyes popped half out of her head. It took him five minutes at least to change from Ernest Thorburn to King Lappin; and while she waited she felt a load on the back of her neck, as if somebody were about to wring it. At last he changed to King Lappin; his nose twitched; and they spent the evening roaming the woods much as usual.

But she slept badly. In the middle of the night she woke, feeling as if something strange had happened to her. She was stiff and cold. At last she turned on the light and looked at Ernest lying beside her. He was sound asleep. He snored. But even though he snored, his nose remained perfectly still. It looked as if it had never twitched at all. Was it possible that he was really Ernest; and that she was really married to Ernest? A vision of her mother-in-law's dining-room came before her; and there they sat, she and Ernest, grown old, under the engravings, in front of the sideboard. . . . It was their golden-wedding day. She could not bear it.

"Lappin, King Lappin!" she whispered, and for a moment his nose seemed to twitch of its own accord. But he still slept. "Wake up, Lappin, wake up!" she cried.

Ernest woke; and seeing her sitting bolt upright beside him he asked:

"What's the matter?"

"I thought my rabbit was dead!" she whimpered. Ernest was angry.

"Don't talk such rubbish, Rosalind," he said. "Lie down and go to sleep."

He turned over. In another moment he was sound asleep and snoring.

But she could not sleep. She lay curled up on her side of the bed, like a hare in its form. She had turned out the light, but the street lamp lit the ceiling faintly, and the trees outside made a lacy network over it as if there were a shadowy grove on the ceiling in which she wandered, turning, twisting, in and out, round and round, hunting, being hunted, hearing the bay of hounds and horns; flying, escaping . . . until the maid drew the blinds and brought their early tea.

Next day she could settle to nothing. She seemed to have lost
something. She felt as if her body had shrunk; it had grown small,
and black and hard. Her joints seemed stiff too, and when she
looked in the glass, which she did several times as she wandered
about the flat, her eyes seemed to burst out of her head, like cur-
rants in a bun. The rooms also seemed to have shrunk. Large pieces
of furniture jutted out at odd angles and she found herself knock-
ing against them. At last she put on her hat and went out. She
walked along the Cromwell Road; and every room she passed and
peered into seemed to be a dining-room where people sat eating
under steel engravings, with thick yellow lace curtains, and
mahogany sideboards. At last she reached the Natural History
Museum; she used to like it when she was a child. But the first
thing she saw when she went in was a stuffed hare standing on
sham snow with pink glass eyes. Somehow it made her shiver all
over. Perhaps it would be better when dusk fell. She went home
and sat over the fire, without a light, and tried to imagine that she
was out alone on a moor; and there was a stream rushing; and beyond the stream a dark wood. But she could get no further than the
stream. At last she squatted down on the bank on the wet grass,
and sat crouched in her chair, with her hands dangling empty, and
her eyes glazed, like glass eyes, in the firelight. Then there was the
crack of a gun. . . . She started as if she had been shot. It was
only Ernest, turning his key in the door. She waited, trembling. He
came in and switched on the light. There he stood tall, handsome,
rubbing his hands that were red with cold.

"Sitting in the dark?" he said.

"Oh, Ernest, Ernest!" she cried, starting up in her chair.

"Well, what's up, now?" he asked briskly, warming his hands
at the fire.

"It's Lapinova . . ." she faltered, glancing wildly at him out
of her great startled eyes. "She's gone, Ernest. I've lost her!"

Ernest frowned. He pressed his lips tight together. "Oh, that's
what's up, is it?" he said, smiling rather grimly at his wife. For ten
seconds he stood there, silent; and she waited, feeling hands tight-
ening at the back of her neck.

"Yes," he said at length. "Poor Lapinova . . ." He straightened
his tie at the looking-glass over the mantelpiece.

"Caught in a trap," he said, "killed," and sat down and read
the newspaper.

So that was the end of that marriage.

Bliss

KATHERINE MANSFIELD

*"Bliss" is a story of a woman who experiences a sudden
awakening to life, only to have it prematurely shattered. Bertha
doesn't know how to express the overwhelming sensation within
her because she has never before felt anything passionately. The
irony of the story is that just as she comes to understand the
meaning of her emotion she realizes that it is too late for her to
express it. She discovers bliss in time only to lose it. The pear tree
is described as being in full bloom, without a single bud or faded
petal, and Bertha looks at it three times—before, during, and
after her dinner party. How is she different each time she sees the
tree, and what is the irony implied in each context? What is the
nature of the experience Bertha shares with Miss Fulton?*

Although Bertha Young was thirty she still had moments like this
when she wanted to run instead of walk, to take dancing steps on
and off the pavement, to bowl a hoop, to throw something up in
the air and catch it again, or to stand still and laugh at—nothing—at
nothing, simply.

What can you do if you are thirty and, turning the corner of
your own street, you are overcome, suddenly, by a feeling of bliss—
absolute bliss!—as though you'd suddenly swallowed a bright piece
of that late afternoon sun and it burned in your bosom, sending out
a little shower of sparks into every particle, into every finger and
toe? . . .

Oh, is there no way you can express it without being "drunk

and disorderly"? How idiotic civilization is! Why be given a body if you have to keep it shut up in a case like a rare, rare fiddle?

"No, that about the fiddle is not quite what I mean," she thought, running up the steps and feeling in her bag for the key—she'd forgotten it, as usual—and rattling the letter-box. "It's not what I mean, because—Thank you, Mary,"—she went into the hall. "Is Nurse back?"

"Yes, M'm."

"And has the fruit come?"

"Yes, M'm. Everything's come."

"Bring the fruit up to the dining-room, will you? I'll arrange it before I go upstairs."

It was dusky in the dining-room and quite chilly. But all the same Bertha threw off her coat; she could not bear the tight clasp of it another moment, and the cold air fell on her arms.

But in her bosom there was still that bright glowing place—that shower of little sparks coming from it. It was almost unbearable. She hardly dared to breathe for fear of fanning it higher, and yet she breathed deeply, deeply. She hardly dared to look into the cold mirror—but she did look, and it gave her back a woman, radiant, with smiling, trembling lips, with big, dark eyes and an air of listening, waiting for something . . . divine to happen . . . that she knew must happen . . . infallibly.

Mary brought in the fruit on a tray and with it a glass bowl, and a blue dish, very lovely, with a strange sheen on it as though it had been dipped in milk.

"Shall I turn on the light, M'm?"

"No, thank you. I can see quite well."

There were tangerines and apples stained with strawberry pink. Some yellow pears, smooth as silk, some white grapes covered with a silver bloom and a big cluster of purple ones. These last she had bought to tone in with the new dining-room carpet. Yes, that did sound rather far-fetched and absurd, but it was really why she had bought them. She had thought in the shop: "I must have some purple ones to bring the carpet up to the table." And it had seemed quite sense at the time.

When she had finished with them and had made two pyramids of these bright round shapes, she stood away from the table to get the effect—and it really was most curious. For the dark table seemed to melt into the dusky light and the glass dish and the blue bowl to float in the air. This, of course in her present mood, was so incredibly beautiful. . . . She began to laugh.

"No, no. I'm getting hysterical." And she seized her bag and coat and ran upstairs to the nursery.

Nurse sat at a low table giving Little B her supper after her bath. The baby had on a white flannel gown and a blue woollen jacket, and her dark, fine hair was brushed up into a funny little peak. She looked up when she saw her mother and began to jump.

"Now, my lovey, eat it up like a good girl," said Nurse, setting her lips in a way that Bertha knew, and that meant she had come into the nursery at another wrong moment.

"Has she been good, Nanny?"

"She's been a little sweet all the afternoon," whispered Nanny. "We went to the park and I sat down on a chair and took her out of the pram and a big dog came along and put his head on my knee and she clutched its ear, tugged it. Oh, you should have seen her."

Bertha wanted to ask if it wasn't rather dangerous to let her clutch at a strange dog's ear. But she did not dare to. She stood watching them, her hands by her side, like the poor little girl in front of the rich little girl with the doll.

The baby looked up at her again, stared, and then smiled so charmingly that Bertha couldn't help crying:

"Oh, Nanny, do let me finish giving her her supper while you put the bath things away."

"Well, M'm, she oughtn't to be changed hands while she's eating," said Nanny, still whispering. "It unsettles her; it's very likely to upset her."

How absurd it was. Why have a baby if it has to be kept—not in a case like a rare, rare fiddle—but in another woman's arms?

"Oh, I must!" said she.

Very offended, Nanny handed her over.

"Now, don't excite her after her supper. You know .you do, M'm. And I have such a time with her after!"

Thank heaven! Nanny went out of the room with the bath towels.

"Now I've got you to myself, my little precious," said Bertha, as the baby leaned against her.

She ate delightfully, holding up her lips for the spoon and

then waving her hands. Sometimes she wouldn't let the spoon go; and sometimes, just as Bertha had filled it, she waved it away to the four winds.

When the soup was finished Bertha turned round to the fire. "You're nice—you're very nice!" said she, kissing her warm baby. "I'm fond of you. I like you."

And, indeed, she loved Little B so much—her neck as she bent forward, her exquisite toes as they shone transparent in the firelight—that all her feeling of bliss came back again, and again she didn't know how to express it—what to do with it.

"You're wanted on the telephone," said Nanny, coming back in triumph and seizing *her* Little B.

Down she flew. It was Harry.

"Oh, is that you, Ber? Look here. I'll be late. I'll take a taxi and come along as quickly as I can, but get dinner put back ten minutes—will you? All right?"

"Yes, perfectly. Oh, Harry!"

"Yes?"

What had she to say? She'd nothing to say. She only wanted to get in touch with him for a moment. She couldn't absurdly cry: "Hasn't it been a divine day!"

"What is it?" rapped out the little voice.

"Nothing. *Entendu*," said Bertha, and hung up the receiver, thinking how more than idiotic civilization was.

They had people coming to dinner. The Norman Knights—a very sound couple—he was about to start a theatre, and she was awfully keen on interior decoration, a young man, Eddie Warren, who had just published a little book of poems and whom everybody was asking to dine, and a "find" of Bertha's called Pearl Fulton. What Miss Fulton did, Bertha didn't know. They had met at the club and Bertha had fallen in love with her, as she always did fall in love with beautiful women who had something strange about them.

The provoking thing was that, though they had been about together and met a number of times and really talked, Bertha couldn't yet make her out. Up to a certain point Miss Fulton was rarely, wonderfully frank, but the certain point was there, and beyond that she would not go.

Was there anything beyond it? Harry said "No." Voted her dullish, and "cold like all blond women, with a touch, perhaps, of anemia of the brain." But Bertha wouldn't agree with him; not yct, at any rate.

"No, the way she has of sitting with her head a little on one side, and smiling, has something behind it, Harry, and I must find out what that something is."

"Most likely it's a good stomach," answered Harry.

He made a point of catching Bertha's heels with replies of that kind . . . "liver frozen, my dear girl," or "pure flatulence," or "kidney disease," . . . and so on. For some strange reason Bertha liked this, and almost admired it in him very much.

She went into the drawing-room and lighted the fire; then, picking up the cushions, one by one, that Mary had disposed so carefully, she threw them back on to the chairs and the couches. That made all the difference; the room came alive at once. As she was about to throw the last one she surprised herself by suddenly hugging it to her, passionately, passionately. But it did not put out the fire in her bosom. Oh, on the contrary!

The windows of the drawing-room opened on to a balcony overlooking the garden. At the far end, against the wall, there was a tall, slender pear tree in fullest, richest bloom; it stood perfect, as though becalmed against the jade-green sky. Bertha couldn't help feeling, even from this distance, that it had not a single bud or a faded petal. Down below, in the garden beds, the red and yellow tulips, heavy with flowers, seemed to lean upon the dusk. A grey cat, dragging its belly, crept across the lawn, and a black one, its shadow, trailed after. The sight of them, so intent and so quick, gave Bertha a curious shiver.

"What creepy things cats are!" she stammered, and she turned away from the window and began walking up and down. . . .

How strong the jonquils smelled in the warm room. Too strong? Oh, no. And yet, as though overcome, she flung down on a couch and pressed her hands to her eyes.

"I'm too happy—too happy!" she murmured.

And she seemed to see on her eyelids the lovely pear tree with its wide open blossoms as a symbol of her own life.

Really—really—she had everything. She was young. Harry and she were as much in love as ever, and they got on together splendidly and were really good pals. She had an adorable baby. They didn't have to worry about money. They had this absolutely satisfactory house and garden. And friends—modern, thrilling friends, writers and painters and poets or people keen on social questions—just the kind of friends they wanted. And then there were books, and there was music, and she had found a wonderful little dressmaker, and they were going abroad in the summer, and their new cook made the most superb omelettes. . . .

"I'm absurd! Absurd!" She sat up; but she felt quite dizzy, quite drunk. It must have been the spring.

Yes, it was the spring. Now she was so tired she could not drag herself upstairs to dress.

A white dress, a string of jade beads, green shoes and stockings. It wasn't intentional. She had thought of this scheme hours before she stood at the drawing-room window.

Her petals rustled softly into the hall, and she kissed Mrs. Norman Knight, who was taking off the most amusing orange coat with a procession of black monkeys round the hem and up the fronts.

". . . Why! Why! Why is the middle-class so stodgy—so utterly without a sense of humour! My dear, it's only by a fluke that I am here at all—Norman being the protective fluke. For my darling monkeys so upset the train that it rose to a man and simply ate me with its eyes. Didn't laugh—wasn't amused—that I should have loved. No, just stared—and bored me through and through."

"But the cream of it was," said Norman, pressing a large tortoiseshell-rimmed monocle into his eye, "you don't mind me telling this, Face, do you?" (In their home and among their friends they called each other Face and Mug.) "The cream of it was when she, being full fed, turned to the woman beside her and said: 'Haven't you ever seen a monkey before?' "

"Oh, yes!" Mrs. Norman Knight joined in the laughter. "Wasn't that too absolutely creamy?"

And a funnier thing still was that now her coat was off she did look like a very intelligent monkey—who had even made that yellow silk dress out of scraped banana skins. And her amber earrings; they were like little dangling nuts.

"This is a sad, sad fall!" said Mug, pausing in front of Little B's perambulator. "When the perambulator comes into the hall—" and he waved the rest of the quotation away.

The bell rang. It was lean, pale Eddie Warren (as usual) in a state of acute distress.

"It *is* the right house, *isn't* it?" he pleaded.

"Oh, I think so—I hope so," said Bertha brightly.

"I have had such a *dreadful* experience with a taxi-man; he was *most* sinister. I couldn't get him to *stop*. The *more* I knocked and called the *faster* he went. And *in* the moonlight this *bizarre* figure with the *flattened* head *crouching* over the *lit-tle* wheel. . . ."

He shuddered, taking off an immense white silk scarf. Bertha noticed that his socks were white, too—most charming.

"But how dreadful!" she cried.

"Yes, it really was," said Eddie, following her into the drawing-room. "I saw myself *driving* through Eternity in a *timeless* taxi."

He knew the Norman Knights. In fact, he was going to write a play for N. K. when the theatre scheme came off.

"Well, Warren, how's the play?" said Norman Knight, dropping his monocle and giving his eye a moment in which to rise to the surface before it was screwed down again.

And Mrs. Norman Knight: "Oh, Mr. Warren, what happy socks!"

"I *am* so glad you like them," said he, staring at his feet. "They seem to have got so *much* whiter since the moon rose." And he turned his lean sorrowful young face to Bertha. "There *is* a moon, you know."

She wanted to cry: "I am sure there is—often—often!"

He really was a most attractive person. But so was Face, crouched before the fire in her banana skins, and so was Mug, smoking a cigarette and saying as he flicked the ash: "Why doth the bridegroom tarry?"

"There he is, now."

Bang went the front door open and shut. Harry shouted: "Hullo, you people. Down in five minutes." And they heard him swarm up the stairs. Bertha couldn't help smiling; she knew how he loved doing things at high pressure. What, after all, did an extra five minutes matter? But he would pretend to himself that they mattered beyond measure. And then he would make a great point of coming into the drawing-room, extravagantly cool and collected.

Harry had such a zest for life. Oh, how she appreciated it in him. And his passion for fighting—for seeking in everything that came up against him another test of his power and of his courage—that, too, she understood. Even when it made him just occasionally, to other people, who didn't know him well, a little ridiculous perhaps. . . . For there were moments when he rushed into battle where no battle was. . . . She talked and laughed and positively forgot until he had come in (just as she had imagined) that Pearl Fulton had not turned up.

"I wonder if Miss Fulton has forgotten?"

"I expect so," said Harry. "Is she on the 'phone?"

"Ah! There's a taxi, now." And Bertha smiled with that little air of proprietorship that she always assumed while her women finds were new and mysterious. "She lives in taxis."

"She'll run to fat if she does," said Harry coolly, ringing the bell for dinner. "Frightful danger for blond women."

"Harry—don't," warned Bertha, laughing up at him.

Came another tiny moment, while they waited, laughing and talking, just a trifle too much at their ease, a trifle too unaware. And then Miss Fulton, all in silver, with a silver fillet binding her pale blond hair, came in smiling, her head a little on one side.

"Am I late?"

"No, not at all," said Bertha. "Come along." And she took her arm and they moved into the dining-room.

What was there in the touch of that cool arm that could fan— fan—start blazing—blazing—the fire of bliss that Bertha did not know what to do with?

Miss Fulton did not look at her; but then she seldom did look at people directly. Her heavy eyelids lay upon her eyes and the strange half smile came and went upon her lips as though she lived by listening rather than seeing. But Bertha knew, suddenly, as if the longest, most intimate look had passed between them—as if they had said to each other: "You, too?"—that Pearl Fulton, stirring the beautiful red soup in the grey plate, was feeling just what she was feeling.

And the others? Face and Mug, Eddie and Harry, their spoons rising and falling—dabbing their lips with their napkins, crumbling bread, fiddling with the forks and glasses and talking.

"I met her at the Alpha shore—the weirdest little person. She'd not only cut off her hair, but she seemed to have taken a dreadfully good snip off her legs and arms and her neck and her poor little nose as well."

"Isn't she very *liée* with Michael Oat?"

"The man who wrote *Love in False Teeth?*"

"He wants to write a play for me. One act. One man. Decides to commit suicide. Gives all the reasons why he should and why he shouldn't. And just as he has made up his mind either to do it or not to do it—curtain. Not half a bad idea."

"What's he going to call it—'Stomach Trouble'?"

"I *think* I've come across the *same* idea in a lit-tle French review, *quite* unknown in England."

No, they didn't share it. They were dears—dears—and she loved having them there, at her table, and giving them delicious food and wine. In fact, she longed to tell them how delightful they were, and what a decorative group they made, how they seemed to set one another off and how they reminded her of a play by Tchekof!

Harry was enjoying his dinner. It was part of his—well, not his nature, exactly, and certainly not his pose—his—something or other —to talk about food and to glory in his "shameless passion for the white flesh of the lobster" and "the green of pistachio ices—green and cold like the eyelids of Egyptian dancers."

When he looked up at her and said: "Bertha, this is a very admirable *soufflé!*" she almost could have wept with child-like pleasure.

Oh, why did she feel so tender towards the whole world to-night? Everything was good—was right. All that happened seemed to fill again her brimming cup of bliss.

And still, in the back of her mind, there was the pear tree. It would be silver now, in the light of poor dear Eddie's moon, silver as Miss Fulton, who sat there turning a tangerine in her slender fingers that were so pale a light seemed to come from them.

What she simply couldn't make out—what was miraculous— was how she should have guessed Miss Fulton's mood so exactly and so instantly. For she never doubted for a moment that she was right, and yet what had she to go on? Less than nothing.

"I believe this does happen very, very rarely between women. Never between men," thought Bertha. "But while I am making the coffee in the drawing-room perhaps she will 'give a sign.'"

What she meant by that she did not know, and what would happen after that she could not imagine.

While she thought like this she saw herself talking and laughing. She had to talk because of her desire to laugh.

"I must laugh or die."

But when she noticed Face's funny little habit of tucking something down the front of her bodice—as if she kept a tiny, secret hoard of nuts there, too—Bertha had to dig her nails into her hands —so as not to laugh too much.

It was over at last. And: "Come and see my new coffee machine," said Bertha.

"We only have a new coffee machine once a fortnight," said

Harry. Face took her arm this time; Miss Fulton bent her head and followed after.

The fire had died down in the drawing-room to a red, flickering "nest of baby phoenixes," said Face.

"Don't turn up the light for a moment. It is so lovely." And down she crouched by the fire again. She was always cold . . . "without her little red flannel jacket, of course," thought Bertha.

At that moment Miss Fulton "gave the sign."

"Have you a garden?" said the cool, sleepy voice.

This was so exquisite on her part that all Bertha could do was to obey. She crossed the room, pulled the curtains apart, and opened those long windows.

"There!" she breathed.

And the two women stood side by side looking at the slender, flowering tree. Although it was so still it seemed, like the flame of a candle, to stretch up, to point, to quiver in the bright air, to grow taller and taller as they gazed—almost to touch the rim of the round, silver moon.

How long did they stand there? Both, as it were, caught in that circle of unearthly light, understanding each other perfectly, creatures of another world, and wondering what they were to do in this one with all this blissful treasure that burned in their bosoms and dropped, in silver flowers, from their hair and hands?

For ever—for a moment? And did Miss Fulton murmur. "Yes. Just *that*." Or did Bertha dream it?

Then the light was snapped on and Face made the coffee and Harry said: "My dear Mrs. Knight, don't ask me about my baby. I never see her. I shan't feel the slightest interest in her until she has a lover," and Mug took his eye out of the conservatory for a moment and then put it under glass again and Eddie Warren drank his coffee and set down the cup with a face of anguish as though he had drunk and seen the spider.

"What I want to do is to give the young men a show. I believe London is simply teeming with first-chop, unwritten plays. What I want to say to 'em is: 'Here's the theatre. Fire ahead.'"

"You know, my dear, I am going to decorate a room for the Jacob Nathans. Oh, I am so tempted to do a fried-fish scheme, with the backs of the chairs shaped like frying pans and lovely chip potatoes embroidered all over the curtains."

"The trouble with our young writing men is that they are still too romantic. You can't put out to sea without being seasick and wanting a basin. Well, why won't they have the courage of those basins?"

"A *dreadful* poem about a *girl* who was *violated* by a beggar *without* a nose in a lit-tle wood. . . ."

Miss Fulton sank into the lowest, deepest chair and Harry handed round the cigarettes.

From the way he stood in front of her shaking the silver box and saying abruptly: "Egyptian? Turkish? Virginian? They're all mixed up," Bertha realized that she not only bored him; he really disliked her. And she decided from the way Miss Fulton said: "No, thank you, I won't smoke," that she felt it, too, and was hurt.

"Oh, Harry, don't dislike her. You are quite wrong about her. She's wonderful, wonderful. And, besides, how can you feel so differently about some one who means so much to me. I shall try to tell you when we are in bed tonight what has been happening. What she and I have shared."

At those last words something strange and almost terrifying darted into Bertha's mind. And this something blind and smiling whispered to her: "Soon these people will go. The house will be quiet—quiet. The lights will be out. And you and he will be alone together in the dark room—the warm bed. . . ."

She jumped up from her chair and ran over to the piano.

"What a pity some one does not play!" she cried. "What a pity somebody does not play."

For the first time in her life Bertha Young desired her husband.

Oh, she'd loved him—she'd been in love with him, of course, in every other way, but just not in that way. And, equally, of course, she'd understood that he was different. They'd discussed it so often. It had worried her dreadfully at first to find that she was so cold, but after a time it had not seemed to matter. They were so frank with each other—such good pals. That was the best of being modern.

But now—ardently! ardently! The word ached in her ardent body! Was this what that feeling of bliss had been leading up to? But then—then—

"My dear," said Mrs. Norman Knight, "you know our shame. We are the victims of time and train. We live in Hampstead. It's been so nice."

"I'll come with you into the hall," said Bertha. "I love having you. But you must not miss the last train. That's so awful, isn't it?"

"Have a whisky, Knight, before you go?" called Harry.

"No, thanks, old chap."

Bertha squeezed his hand for that as she shook it.

"Good night, good-bye," she cried from the top step, feeling that this self of hers was taking leave of them for ever.

When she got back into the drawing-room the others were on the move.

". . . Then you can come part of the way in my taxi."

"I shall be *so* thankful *not* to have to face *another* drive *alone* after my *dreadful* experience."

"You can get a taxi at the rank just at the end of the street. You won't have to walk more than a few yards."

"That's comfort. I'll go and put on my coat."

Miss Fulton moved towards the hall and Bertha was following when Harry almost pushed past.

"Let me help you."

Bertha knew that he was repenting his rudeness—she let him go. What a boy he was in some ways—so impulsive—so—simple.

And Eddie and she were left by the fire.

"I *wonder* if you have seen Bilks' *new* poem called *Table d'Hôte*," said Eddie sof·ly. "It's *so* wonderful. In the last Anthology. Have you got a copy? I'd *so* like to *show* it to you. It begins with an *incredibly* beautiful line: 'Why Must it Always be Tomato Soup?' "

"Yes," said Bertha. And she moved noiselessly to a table opposite the drawing-room door and Eddie glided noiselessly after her. She picked up the little book and gave it to him; they had not made a sound.

While he looked it up she turned her head towards the hall. And she saw . . . Harry with Miss Fulton's coat in his arms and Miss Fulton with her back turned to him and her head bent. He tossed the coat away, put his hands on her shoulders and turned her violently to him. His lips said: "I adore you," and Miss Fulton laid her moonbeam fingers on his cheeks and smiled her sleepy smile. Harry's nostrils quivered; his lips curled back in a hideous grin while he whispered: "Tomorrow," and with her eyelids Miss Fulton said: "Yes."

"Here it is," said Eddie. " 'Why Must it Always be Tomato Soup?' It's so *deeply* true, don't you feel? Tomato soup is so *dreadfully* eternal."

"If you prefer," said Harry's voice, very loud, from the hall, "I can 'phone you a cab to come to the door."

"Oh, no. It's not necessary," said Miss Fulton, and she came up to Bertha and gave her the slender fingers to hold.

"Good-bye. Thank you so much."

"Good-bye," said Bertha.

Miss Fulton held her hand a moment longer.

"Your lovely pear tree!" she murmured.

And then she was gone, with Eddie following, like the black cat following the grey cat.

"I'll shut up shop," said Harry, extravagantly cool and collected.

"Your lovely pear tree—pear tree—pear tree!"

Bertha simply ran over to the long windows.

"Oh, what is going to happen now?" she cried.

But the pear tree was as lovely as ever and as full of flower and as still.

Cruel and Barbarous Treatment

MARY McCARTHY

"Cruel and Barbarous Treatment" is a brittle satire on modern marriage. Why does the author designate the characters by the roles they are assigned to play rather than by personal names? The shallow artificiality of the main character is consistent with her self-conscious view of her life as a drama to be acted out rather than felt. She plays from a script that society supplies for all public performances. As the main character learns her part as Mistress, what observations does she make about being engaged and having an affair? As she plays through her role as Unfaithful Wife, what does she see as the function of marriage? As she projects herself into the part of Divorcée, why does she feel it to be the natural step in a sequence that began long before marriage? How does she justify her actions and convince herself at each step that her behavior is appropriate? What additional perspective does her husband add to the story? What is the irony of the title?

She could not bear to hurt her husband. She impressed this on the Young Man, on her confidantes, and finally on her husband himself. The thought of Telling Him actually made her heart turn over in a sudden and sickening way, <u>she said</u>. This was true, and yet she knew that being a potential divorcee was deeply pleasurable in somewhat the same way that being an engaged girl had been. In both cases, there was at first a subterranean courtship, whose significance it was necessary to conceal from outside observers. The concealment of the original, premarital courtship had, however, been a mere superstitious gesture, briefly sustained. It had also been, on the whole, a private secretiveness, not a partnership of silence. One put one's family and one's friends off the track because one was still afraid that the affair might not come out right, might not lead in a clean, direct line to the altar. To confess one's aspirations might be, in the end, to publicize one's failure. Once a solid understanding had been reached, there followed a short intermission of ritual bashfulness, in which both parties awkwardly participated, and then came the Announcement.

But with the extramarital courtship, the deception was prolonged where it had been ephemeral, necessary where it had been frivolous, conspiratorial where it had been lonely. It was, in short, serious where it had been dilettantish. That it was accompanied by feelings of guilt, by sharp and genuine revulsions, only complicated and deepened its delights, by abrading the sensibilities, and by imposing a sense of outlawry and consequent mutual dependence upon the lovers. But what this interlude of deception gave her, above all, she recognized, was an opportunity, unparalleled in her experience, for exercising feelings of superiority over others. For her husband she had, she believed, only sympathy and compunction. She got no fun, she told the Young Man, out of putting horns on her darling's head, and never for a moment, she said, did he appear to her as the comic figure of the cuckolded husband that one saw on the stage. (The Young Man assured her that his own sentiments were equally delicate, that for the wronged man he felt the most profound respect, tinged with consideration.) It was as if by the mere act of betraying her husband, she had adequately bested him; it was supererogatory for her to gloat, and, if she gloated at all, it was over her fine restraint in not-gloating, over the integrity of her moral sense, which allowed her to preserve even while engaged in sinfulness the acute realization of sin and shame. Her overt superiority feelings she reserved for her friends. Lunches and teas, which had been time-killers, matters of routine, now became perilous and dramatic adventures. The Young Man's name was a bright, highly explosive ball which she bounced casually back and forth in these feminine *tête-à-têtes*. She would discuss him in his status of friend of the family, speculate on what girls he might have, attack him or defend him, anatomize him, keeping her eyes clear and impersonal, her voice empty of special emphasis, her manner humorously detached. *While all the time . . . !*

Three times a week or oftener, at lunch or tea, she would let herself tremble thus on the exquisite edge of self-betrayal, involving her companions in a momentous game whose rules and whose risks only she herself knew. The Public Appearances were even more satisfactory. To meet at a friend's house by design and to register surprise, to strike just the right note of young-matronly affection at cocktail parties, to treat him formally as "my escort" at the theater during intermissions—these were triumphs of stage management, more difficult of execution, more nerve-racking than the lunches and teas, because *two* actors were involved. His over-ardent glance must be hastily deflected; his too-self-conscious reading of his lines must be entered in the debit side of her ledger of love, in anticipation of an indulgent accounting in private.

The imperfections of his performance were, indeed, pleasing to her. Not, she thought, because his impetuosities, his gaucheries, demonstrated the sincerity of his passion for her, nor because they proved him a new hand at this game of intrigue, but rather because the high finish of her own acting showed off well in comparison. "I should have gone on the stage," she could tell him gaily, "or been a diplomat's wife or an international spy," while he would admiringly agree. Actually, she doubted whether she could ever have been an actress, acknowledging that she found it more amusing and more gratifying to play herself than to interpret any character conceived by a dramatist. In these private theatricals it was her own many-faceted nature that she put on exhibit, and the audience, in this case unfortunately limited to two, could applaud both her skill of projection and her intrinsic variety. Furthermore, this was a play in which the *donnée* was real, and the penalty for a missed cue or an inopportune entrance was, at first anyway, unthinkable.

She loved him, she knew, for being a bad actor, for his docility in accepting her tender, mock-impatient instruction. Those superiority feelings were fattening not only on the gullibility of her friends, but also on the comic flaws of her lover's character, and on the vulnerability of her lover's position. In this particular hive she was undoubtedly queen bee.

The Public Appearances were not exclusively duets. They sometimes took the form of a trio. On these occasions the studied and benevolent carefulness which she always showed for her husband's feelings served a double purpose. She would affect a conspicuous domesticity, an affectionate conjugal demonstrativeness, would sprinkle her conversation with "Darlings," and punctuate it with pats and squeezes till her husband would visibly expand and her lover plainly and painfully shrink. For the Young Man no retaliation was possible. These endearments of hers were sanctioned by law, usage, and habit; they belonged to her role of wife and could not be condemned or paralleled by a young man who was himself unmarried. They were clear provocations, but they could not be called so, and the Young Man preferred not to speak of them. *But she knew* . . . Though she was aware of the sadistic intention of these displays, she was not ashamed of them, as she was sometimes twistingly ashamed of the hurt she was preparing to inflict on her husband. Partly she felt that they were punishments which the Young Man richly deserved for the wrong he was doing her husband, and that she herself in contriving them was acting, quite fittingly, both as judge and accused. Partly, too, she believed herself justified in playing the fond wife, whatever the damage to her lover's ego, because, in a sense, she actually was a fond wife. She *did* have these feelings, she insisted, whether she was exploiting them or not.

Eventually, however, her reluctance to wound her husband and her solicitude for his pride were overcome by an inner conviction that her love affair must move on to its next preordained stage. The possibilities of the subterranean courtship had been exhausted; it was time for the Announcement. She and the Young Man began to tell each other in a rather breathless and literary style that The Situation Was Impossible, and Things Couldn't Go On This Way Any Longer. The ostensible meaning of these flurried laments was that, under present conditions, they were not seeing enough of each other, that their hours together were too short and their periods of separation too dismal, that the whole business of deception had become morally distasteful to them. Perhaps the Young Man really believed these things; she did not. For the first time, she saw that the virtue of marriage as an institution lay in its public character. Private cohabitation, long continued, was, she concluded, a bore. Whatever the coziness of isolation, the warm delights of having a secret, a love affair finally reached the point where it needed the glare of publicity to revive the interest of its protagonists. Hence, she thought, the engagement parties, the showers, the big church weddings, the presents, the receptions. These were simply socially approved devices by which the lovers got themselves talked about. The gossip value of a divorce and remarriage was obviously far greater than the gossip value of a mere engagement, and she was now ready, indeed hungry, to hear What People Would Say.

The lunches, the teas, the Public Appearances were getting a little flat. It was not, in the end, enough to be a Woman With A Secret, if to one's friends one appeared to be a woman without a secret. The bliss of having a secret required, in short, the consummation of telling it, and she looked forward to the My-dear-I-had-no-idea's, the I-thought-you-and-Tom-were-so-happy-together's, the How-did-you-keep-it-so-dark's with which her intimates would greet her announcement. The audience of two no longer sufficed her; she required a larger stage. She tried it first, a little nervously, on two or three of her closest friends, swearing them to secrecy. "Tom must hear it first from me," she declared. "It would be too terrible for his pride if he found out afterwards that the whole town knew it before he did. So you mustn't tell, even later on, that I told you about this today. I felt I had to talk to someone." After these lunches she would hurry to a phone booth to give the Young Man the gist of the conversation. "She certainly was surprised," she could always say with a little gush of triumph. "But she thinks it's fine." *But did they actually?* She could not be sure. Was it possible that she sensed in these luncheon companions, her dearest friends, a certain reserve, a certain unexpressed judgment?

It was a pity, she reflected, that she was so sensitive to public opinion. "I couldn't really love a man," she murmured to herself once, "if everybody didn't think he was wonderful." Everyone seemed to like the Young Man, of course. *But still . . .* She was getting panicky, she thought. Surely it was only common sense that nobody is admired by everybody. And even if a man were universally despised, would there not be a kind of defiant nobility in loving him in the teeth of the whole world? There would, certainly, but it was a type of heroism that she would scarcely be called upon to practice, for the Young Man was popular, he was invited everywhere, he danced well, his manners were ingratiating, he kept up intellectually. But was he not perhaps *too* amiable, *too* accommodating? Was it for this that her friends seemed silently to criticize him?

At this time a touch of acridity entered into her relations with the Young Man. Her indulgent scoldings had an edge to them now, and it grew increasingly difficult for her to keep her make-believe impatience from becoming real. She would look for dark spots in his character and drill away at them as relentlessly as a dentist at a cavity. A compulsive didacticism possessed her: no truism of his, no cliché, no ineffectual joke could pass the rigidity of her censorship. And, hard as she tried to maintain the character of charming schoolmistress, the Young Man, she saw, was taking alarm. She suspected that, frightened and puzzled, he contemplated flight. She found herself watching him with impersonal interest, speculating as to what course he would take, and she was relieved but faintly disappointed when it became clear that he ascribed her sharpness to the tension of the situation and had decided to stick it out.

The moment had come for her to tell her husband. By this single, cathartic act, she would, she believed, rid herself of the doubts and anxieties that beset her. If her husband were to impugn the Young Man's character, she could answer his accusations and at the same time discount them as arising from jealousy. From her husband, at least, she might expect the favor of an open attack, to which she could respond with the prepared defense that she carried, unspoken, about with her. Further, she had an intense, childlike curiosity as to How Her Husband Would Take It, a curiosity which she disguised for decency's sake as justifiable apprehension. The confidences already imparted to her friends seemed like pale dress rehearsals of the supreme confidence she was about to make. Perhaps it was toward this moment that the whole affair had been tending, for this moment that the whole affair had been designed. This would be the ultimate testing of her husband's love, its final, rounded, quintessential expression. Never, she thought, when you live with a man do you feel the full force of his love. It is gradually rationed out to you in an impure state, compounded with all the other elements of daily existence, so that you are hardly sensible of receiving it. There is no single point at which it is concentrated; it spreads out into the past and the future until it appears as a nearly imperceptible film over the surface of your life. Only face to face with its own annihilation could it show itself wholly, and, once shown, drop into the category of completed experiences.

She was not disappointed. She told him at breakfast in a fashionable restaurant, because, she said, he would be better able to control his feelings in public. When he called at once for the check, she had a spasm of alarm lest in an access of brutality or grief he leave her there alone, conspicuous, and, as it were, unfulfilled. But they walked out of the restaurant together and through the streets, hand in hand, tears streaming "unchecked," she whispered to herself, down their faces. Later they were in the Park, by an artificial lake, watching the ducks swim. The sun was very bright, and she felt a kind of superb pathos in the careful and irrelevant attention they gave to the pastoral scene. This was, she knew, the most profound, the most subtle, the most idyllic experience of her life. All the strings of her nature were, at last, vibrant. She was both doer and sufferer: she inflicted pain and participated in it. And she was, at the same time, physician, for, as she was the weapon that dealt the wound, she was also the balm that could assuage it. Only she could know the hurt that engrossed him, and it was to her that he turned for the sympathy she had ready for him. Finally, though she offered him his discharge slip with one hand, with the other she beckoned him to approach. She was wooing him all over again, but wooing him to a deeper attachment than he had previously experienced, to an unconditional surrender. She was demanding his total understanding of her, his compassion, and his forgiveness. When at last he answered her repeated and agonized I-love-you's by grasping her hand more tightly and saying gently, "I know," she saw that she had won him over. She had drawn him into a truly mystical union. Their marriage was complete.

Afterwards everything was more prosaic. The Young Man had to be telephoned and summoned to a conference à *trois,* a conference, she said, of civilized, intelligent people. The Young Man was a little awkward, even dropped a tear or two, which embarrassed everyone else, but what, after all, she thought, could you expect? He was in a difficult position; his was a thankless part. With her husband behaving so well, indeed, so gallantly, the Young Man could not fail to look a trifle inadequate. The Young Man would have preferred it, of course, if her husband had made a scene, had bullied or threatened her, so that he himself might have acted the chivalrous protector. She, however, did not hold her husband's heroic courtesy against him: in some way, it reflected credit on herself. The Young Man, apparently, was expecting to Carry Her Off, but this she would not allow. "It would be too heartless," she whispered when they were alone for a moment. "We must all go somewhere together."

So the three went out for a drink, and she watched with a sort of desperation her husband's growing abstraction, the more and more perfunctory attention he accorded the conversation she was so bravely sustaining. "He is bored," she thought. "He is going to leave." The prospect of being left alone with the Young Man seemed suddenly unendurable. If her husband were to go now, he would take with him the third dimension that had given the affair depth, and abandon her to a flat and vulgar love scene. Terrified, she wondered whether she had not already prolonged the drama beyond its natural limits, whether the confession in the restaurant and the absolution in the Park had not rounded off the artistic whole, whether the sequel of divorce and remarriage would not, in fact, constitute an anticlimax. Already she sensed that behind her husband's good manners an ironical attitude toward herself had sprung up. Was it possible that he had believed that they would return from the Park and all would continue as before? It was conceivable that her protestations of love had been misleading, and that his enormous tenderness toward her had been based, not on the idea that he was giving her up, but rather on the idea that he was taking her back—with no questions asked. If that were the case, the telephone call, the conference, and the excursion had in his eyes been a monstrous *gaffe*, a breach of sensibility and good taste, for which he would never forgive her. She blushed violently. Looking at him again, she thought he was watching her with an expression which declared: I have found you out: now I know what you are like. For the first time, she felt him utterly alienated.

When he left them she experienced the let-down she had feared but also a kind of relief. She told herself that it was as well that he had cut himself off from her: it made her decision simpler. There was now nothing for her to do but to push the love affair to its conclusion, whatever that might be, and this was probably what she most deeply desired. Had the poignant intimacy of the Park persisted, she might have been tempted to drop the adventure she had begun and return to her routine. But that was, looked at coldly, unthinkable. For if the adventure would seem a little flat after the scene in the Park, the resumption of her marriage would seem even flatter. If the drama of the triangle had been amputated by her confession, the curtain had been brought down with a smack on the drama of wedlock.

And, as it turned out, the drama of the triangle was not quite ended by the superficial rupture of her marriage. Though she had left her husband's apartment and been offered shelter by a confidante, it was still necessary for her to see him every day. There were clothes to be packed, and possessions to be divided, love letters to be reread and mementoes to be wept over in common.

There were occasional passionate, unconsummated embraces; there were endearments and promises. And though her husband's irony remained, it was frequently vulnerable. It was not, as she had at first thought, an armor against her, but merely a sword, out of *Tristan and Isolde,* which lay permanently between them and enforced discretion.

They met often, also, at the houses of friends, for, as she said, "What can I do? I know it's not tactful, but we all know the same people. You can't expect me to give up my friends." These Public Appearances were heightened in interest by the fact that these audiences, unlike the earlier ones, had, as it were, purchased librettos, and were in full possession of the intricacies of the plot. She preferred, she decided, the evening parties to the cocktail parties, for there she could dance alternately with her lover and her husband to the accompaniment of subdued gasps on the part of the bystanders.

This interlude was at the same time festive and heart-rending: her only dull moments were the evenings she spent alone with the Young Man. Unfortunately, the Post-Announcement period was only too plainly an interlude and its very nature demanded that it be followed by something else. She could not preserve her anomalous status indefinitely. It was not decent, and, besides, people would be bored. From the point of view of one's friends, it was all very well to entertain a Triangle as a novelty; to cope with it as a permanent problem was a different matter. Once they had all three got drunk, and there was a scene, and, though everyone talked about it afterwards, her friends were, she thought, a little colder, a little more critical. People began to ask her when she was going to Reno. Furthermore, she noticed that her husband was getting a slight edge in popularity over the Young Man. It was natural, of course, that everyone should feel sorry for him, and be especially nice. *But yet* . . .

When she learned from her husband that he was receiving attentions from members of her own circle, invitations in which she and the Young Man were unaccountably not included, she went at once to the station and bought her ticket. Her good-bye to her husband, which she had privately allocated to her last hours in town, took place prematurely, two days before she was to leave. He was rushing off to what she inwardly feared was a Gay Week End in the country; he had only a few minutes; he wished her a pleasant trip; and he would write, of course. His highball was drained while her glass still stood half full; he sat forward nervously on his chair; and she knew herself to be acting the Ancient Mariner, but her dignity would not allow her to hurry. She hoped that he would miss his train for her, but he did not. He left her sitting in the bar, and that night the Young Man could not, as he put it, do a thing with her. There was nowhere, absolutely nowhere, she said passionately, that she wanted to go, nobody she wanted to see, nothing she wanted to do. "You need a drink," he said with the air of a diagnostician. "A drink," she answered bitterly. "I'm sick of the drinks we've been having. Gin, whisky, rum, what else is there?" He took her into a bar, and she cried, but he bought her a fancy mixed drink, something called a Ramos gin fizz, and she was a little appeased because she had never had one before. Then some friends came in, and they all had another drink together, and she felt better. "There," said the Young Man, on the way home, "don't I know what's good for you? Don't I know how to handle you?" "Yes," she answered in her most humble and feminine tones, but she knew that they had suddenly dropped into a new pattern, that they were no longer the cynosure of a social group, but merely another young couple with an evening to pass, another young couple looking desperately for entertainment, wondering whether to call on a married couple or to drop in somewhere for a drink. This time the Young Man's prescription had worked, but it was pure luck that they had chanced to meet someone they knew. A second or a third time they would scan the faces of the other drinkers in vain, would order a second drink and surreptitiously watch the door, and finally go out alone, with a quite detectable air of being unwanted.

When, a day and a half later, the Young Man came late to take her to the train, and they had to run down the platform to catch it, she found him all at once detestable. He would ride to 125th Street with her, he declared in a burst of gallantry, but she was angry all the way because she was afraid there would be trouble with the conductor. At 125th Street, he stood on the platform blowing kisses to her and shouting something that she could not hear through the glass. She made a gesture of repugnance, but, seeing him flinch, seeing him weak and charming and incompetent, she brought her hand reluctantly to her lips and blew a kiss back. The other passengers were watching, she was aware, and though their looks were doting and not derisive, she felt herself to be humiliated and somehow vulgarized. When the train began to move, and the Young Man began to run down the platform after it, still blowing kisses and shouting alternately, she got up, turned sharply away from the window and walked back to the club car. There she sat down and ordered a whisky and soda.

There were a number of men in the car, who looked up in unison as she gave her order, but, observing that they were all the middle-aged, small-businessmen who "belonged" as inevitably to the club car as the white-coated porter and the leather-bound *Saturday Evening Post,* she paid them no heed. She was now suddenly overcome by a sense of depression and loss that was unprecedented for being in no way dramatic or pleasurable. In the last half-hour she had seen clearly that she would never marry the Young Man, and she found herself looking into an insubstantial future with no signpost to guide her. Almost all women, she thought, when they are girls never believe that they will get married. The terror of spinsterhood hangs over them from adolescence on. Even if they are popular they think that no one really interesting will want them enough to marry them. Even if they get engaged they are afraid that something will go wrong, something will intervene. When they do get married it seems to them a sort of miracle, and, after they have been married for a time, though in retrospect the whole process looks perfectly natural and inevitable, they retain a certain unarticulated pride in the wonder they have performed. Finally, however, the terror of spinsterhood has been so thoroughly exorcised that they forget ever having been haunted by it, and it is at this stage that they contemplate divorce. "How could I have forgotten?" she said to herself and began to wonder what she would do.

She could take an apartment by herself in the Village. She would meet new people. She would entertain. But, she thought, if I have people in for cocktails, there will always come the moment when they have to leave, and I shall be alone and have to pretend to have another engagement in order to save embarrassment. If I have them to dinner, it will be the same thing, but at least I shan't have to pretend to have an engagement. I will give dinners. Then, she thought, there will be the cocktail parties, and, if I go alone, I shall always stay a little too late, hoping that a young man or even a party of people will ask me to dinner. And if I fail, if no one asks me, I shall have the ignominy of walking out alone, trying to look as if I had somewhere to go. Then there will be the evenings at home with a good book when there will be no reason at all for going to bed, and I shall perhaps sit up all night. And the mornings when there will be no point in getting up, and I shall perhaps stay in bed till dinnertime. There will be the dinners in tearooms with other unmarried women, tearooms because women alone look conspicuous and forlorn in good restaurants. And then, she thought, I shall get older.

She would never, she reflected angrily, have taken this step, had she felt that she was burning her bridges behind her. She would never have left one man unless she had had another to take his place. But the Young Man, she now saw, was merely a sort of mirage which she had allowed herself to mistake for an oasis. "If the Man," she muttered, "did not exist, the Moment would create him." This was what had happened to her. She had made herself the victim of an imposture. But, she argued, with an access of cheerfulness, if this were true, if out of the need of a second, a new, husband she had conjured up the figure of one, she had possibly been impelled by unconscious forces to behave more intelligently than appearances would indicate. She was perhaps acting out in a sort of hypnotic trance a ritual whose meaning had not yet been revealed to her, a ritual which required that, first of all, the Husband be eliminated from the cast of characters. Conceivably, she was designed for the role of *femme fatale*, and for such a personage considerations of safety, provisions against loneliness and old age, were not only philistine but irrelevant. She might marry a second, a third, a fourth time, or she might never marry again. But, in any case, for the thrifty bourgeois love insurance, with its daily payments of patience, forbearance, and resignation, she was no longer eligible. She would be, she told herself delightedly, a bad risk.

She was, or soon would be, a Young Divorcee, and the term still carried glamour. Her divorce decree would be a passport conferring on her the status of citizeness of the world. She felt gratitude toward the Young Man for having unwittingly effected her transit into a new life. She looked about her at the other passengers. Later she would talk to them. They would ask, of course, where she was bound; that was the regulation opening move of train conversations. But it was a delicate question what her reply should be. To say "Reno" straight out would be vulgar; it would smack of confidences too cheaply given. Yet to lie, to say "San Francisco," for instance, would be to cheat herself, to minimize her importance, to mislead her interlocutor into believing her an ordinary traveler with a commonplace destination. There must be some middle course which would give information without appearing to do so, which would hint at a *vie galante* yet indicate a barrier of impeccable reserve. It would probably be best, she decided, to say "West" at first, with an air of vagueness and hesitation. Then, when pressed, she might go as far as to say "Nevada." But no farther.

Unmailed, Unwritten Letters

JOYCE CAROL OATES

*This story by Joyce Carol Oates probes the responses of a woman
involved in an affair that she began with guilt and that she
continues with increasing tension. The tone approaches the pitch
of hysteria as the narrator attempts to manage, on the one hand,
a "normal" relationship with her husband and her parents and,
on the other hand, an illicit and bizarre relationship with her
lover and his wife and suicidal child. She mentally composes
letters that fluctuate between insight and insanity. The author
has chosen the details of the letters with care to convey the woman's
sense of inescapable, enveloping chaos. What is the effect, for
example, of the woman's alternating criticism and jealousy of her
lover? Would her problems be solved if she were willing to divorce
her husband and marry her lover? What prevents her from seeking
a divorce? What function does Detroit serve as the setting of the
story, and what effect is created by the many references to
contemporary events? What is the meaning of the context in
which the woman composes the last letter?*

*D*ear Mother and Father,

The weather is lovely here. It rained yesterday. Today the sky
is blue. The trees are changing colors, it is October 20, I have got
to buy some new clothes sometime soon, we've changed dentists,
doctors, everything is lovely here and I hope the same with you.
Greg is working hard as usual. The doctor we took Father to see,
that time he hurt his back visiting here, has died and so we must
change doctors. Dentists also. I want to change dentists because I

can't stand to go back to the same dentist any more. He is too much of a fixed point, a reference point. It is such a chore, changing doctors and dentists.

Why are you so far away in the Southwest? Is there something about the Southwest that lures old people? Do they see images there, shapes in the desert? Holy shapes? Why are you not closer to me, or farther away? In an emergency it would take hours or days for you to get to me. I think of the two of you in the Southwest, I see the highways going off into space and wonder at your courage, so late in life, to take on space. Father had all he could do to manage that big house of yours, and the lawn. Even with workers to help him it was terrifying, all that space, because he owned it. Maybe that was why it terrified him, because he owned it. Out in the Southwest I assume that no one owns anything. Do people even live there? Some people live there, I know. But I think of the Southwest as an optical illusion, sunshine and sand and a mountainous (mountainous?) horizon, with highways perfectly divided by their white center lines, leading off to Mars or the moon, unhurried. And there are animals, the designs of animals, mashed into the highways! The shape of a dog, a dog's pelty shadow, mashed into the hot, hot road—in mid-flight, so to speak, mid-leap, run over again and again by big trucks and retired people seeing America. That vastness would terrify me. I think of you and I think of protoplasm being drawn off into space, out there, out in the West, with no human limits to keep it safe.

Dear Marsha Katz,

Thank you for the flowers, white flowers, but why that delicate hint of death, all that fragrance wasted on someone like myself who is certain to go on living? Why are you pursuing me? Why in secrecy? (I see all the letters you write to your father, don't forget; and you never mention me in them.) Even if your father were my lover, which is not true and cannot be verified, why should you pursue me? Why did you sign the card with the flowers *Trixie?* I don't know anyone named Trixie! How could I know anyone named Trixie? It is a dog's name, a high school cheerleader's name, an aunt's name . . . why do you play these games, why do you pursue me?

Only ten years old, and too young for evil thoughts—do you look in your precocious heart and see only grit, the remains of things, a crippled shadow of a child? Do you see in all this the defeat of your Daughterliness? Do you understand that a Daughter, like a Mistress, must be feminine or all is lost, must keep up the struggle with the demonic touch of matter-of-fact irony that loses us all our men . . . ? I think you have lost, yes. A ten-year-old cannot compete with a thirty-year-old. Send me all the flowers you want. I pick them apart one by one, getting bits of petals under my fingernails, I throw them out before my husband gets home.

Nor did I eat that box of candies you sent. Signed "Uncle Bumble"!

Are you beginning to feel terror at having lost? Your father and I are not lovers, we hardly see each other any more, since last Wednesday and today is Monday, still you've lost because I gather he plans on continuing the divorce proceedings, long distance, and what exactly can a child do about that . . . ? I see all the letters you write him. No secrets. Your Cape Cod sequence was especially charming. I like what you did with that kitten, the kitten that is found dead on the beach! Ah, you clever little girl, even with your I.Q. of uncharted heights, you couldn't quite conceal from your father and me your attempt to make him think 1) the kitten suggests a little girl, namely you 2) its death suggests your pending, possible death, if Father does not return. Ah, how we laughed over that! . . . Well, no, we didn't laugh, he did not laugh, perhaps he did not even understand the trick you were playing . . . your father can be a careless, abrupt man, but things stick in his mind, you know that and so you write of a little white kitten, alive one day and dead the next, so you send me flowers for a funeral parlor, you keep me in your thoughts constantly so that I can feel a tug all the way here in Detroit, all the way from Boston, and I hate it, I hate that invisible pulling, tugging, that witch's touch of yours. . . .

Dear Greg,

We met about this time years ago. It makes me dizzy, it frightens me to think of that meeting. Did so much happen, and yet nothing? Miscarriages, three or four, one loses count, and eight or nine sweet bumbling years—why do I use the word *bumbling*, it isn't a word I would ever use—and yet there is nothing there, if I go to your closet and open the door your clothes tell me as much as you do. You are a good man. A faithful husband. A subdued and excellent husband. The way you handled my parents alone

would show how good you are, how excellent. . . . My friend
X, the one with the daughter said to be a genius and the wife no
one has ever seen, X couldn't handle my parents, couldn't put up
with my father's talk about principles, the Principles of an Orderly
Universe, which he sincerely believes in though he is an intelligent
man. . . . X couldn't handle anything, anyone. He loses patience.
He is vulgar. He watches himself swerve out of control but can't
stop. Once, returning to his car, we found a ticket on the wind-
shield. He snatched it and tore it up, very angry, and then when
he saw my surprise he thought to make a joke of it—pretending
to be tearing it with his teeth, a joke. And he is weak, angry men
are weak. He lets me close doors on him. His face seems to crack
with sorrow, but he lets me walk away, why is he so careless and
weak . . . ?

But I am thinking of us, our first meeting. An overheated
apartment, graduate school . . . a girl in dark stockings, myself,
frightened and eager, trying to be charming in a voice that didn't
carry, a man in a baggy sweater, gentle, intelligent, a little per-
plexed, the two of us gravitating together, fearful of love and
fearful of not loving, of not being loved. . . . So we met. The
evening falls away, years fall away. I count only three miscarriages, really. The fourth a sentimental miscalculation.

My darling,

I am out somewhere, I see a telephone booth on a corner, the
air is windy and too balmy for October. I won't go in the phone
booth. Crushed papers, a beer bottle, a close violent stench. . . .
I walk past it, not thinking of you. I am out of the house so that
you can't call me and so that I need not think of you. Do you talk
to your wife every night, still? Does she weep into your ear? How
many nights have you lain together, you and that woman now
halfway across the country, in Boston, weeping into a telephone?
Have you forgotten all those nights?

Last night I dreamed about you mashed into a highway. More
than dead. I had to wake Greg up, I couldn't stop trembling, I
wanted to tell him of the waste, the waste of joy and love, your
being mashed soundlessly into a road and pounded into a shape
no one would recognize as yours. . . . Your face was gone. What
will happen to me when your face is gone from this world?

I parked the car down here so that I could go shopping at Saks
but I've been walking, I'm almost lost. The streets are dirty. A tin
can lies on the sidewalk, near a vacant lot. Campbell's Tomato

Soup. I am dressed in the suit you like, though it is a little baggy on me, it would be a surprise for someone driving past to see a lady in such a suit bend to pick up a tin can. . . . I pick the can up. The edge is jagged and rusty. No insects inside. Why would insects be inside, why bother with an empty can? Idly I press the edge of the lid against my wrist; it isn't sharp, it makes only a fine white line on my skin, not sharp enough to penetrate the skin.

Dear Greg,

I hear you walking downstairs. You are going outside, out into the back yard. I am tempted, heart pounding, to run to the window and spy on you. But everything is tepid, the universe is dense with molecules, I can't get up. My legs won't move. You said last night, "The Mayor told me to shut up in front of Arthur Grant. He told me to shut up." You were amused and hurt at the same time, while I was furious, wishing you were . . . were someone else, someone who wouldn't be amused and hurt, a good man, a subdued man, but someone else who would tell that bastard to go to hell. I am a wife, jealous for her husband.

Three years you've spent working for the Mayor, His Honor, dodging reporters downtown. Luncheons, sudden trips, press conferences, conferences with committees from angry parts of Detroit, all of Detroit angry, white and black, bustling, ominous. Three years. Now he tells you to shut up. All the lies you told for him, not knowing how to lie with dignity, he tells you to shut up, my body suffers as if on the brink of some terrible final expulsion of our love, some blood-smear of a baby. When a marriage ends, who is left to understand it? No witnesses. No young girl in black stockings, no young man, all those witnesses gone, grown up, moved on, lost.

Too many people know you now, your private life is dwindling. You are dragged back again and again to hearings, commission meetings, secret meetings, desperate meetings, television interviews, interviews with kids from college newspapers. Everyone has a right to know everything! *What Detroit Has Done to Combat Slums. What Detroit Has Done to Prevent Riots,* up-dated to *What Detroit Has Done to Prevent a Recurrence of the 1967 Riot.* You people are rewriting history as fast as history happens. I love you, I suffer for you, I lie here in a paralysis of love, sorrow, density, idleness, lost in my love for you, my shame for having betrayed you. . . . Why should slums be combatted? Once I wept to see photographs of kids playing in garbage heaps, now I weep at crazy sudden visions of my lover's body become only a body, I have no tears left for anyone else, for anything else. Driving in the city I have a sudden vision of my lover dragged along by a stranger's, car, his body somehow caught up under the bumper or the fender and dragged along, bleeding wildly in the street. . . .

My dear husband, betraying you was the most serious act of my life. Far more serious than marrying you. I knew my lover better when he finally became my lover than I knew you when you became my husband. I know him better now than I know you. You and I have lived together for eight years. Smooth coins, coins worn smooth by constant handling. . . . I am a woman trapped in love, in the terror of love. Paralysis of love. Like a great tortoise, trapped in a heavy deathlike shell, a mask of the body pressing the body down to earth. . . . I went for a week without seeing him, an experiment. The experiment failed. No husband can keep his wife's love. So you walk out in the back yard, admiring the leaves, the sky, the flagstone terrace, you are a man whom betrayal would destroy and yet your wife betrayed you, deliberately.

To The Editor:

Anonymously and shyly I want to ask—why are white men so weak, so feeble? The other day I left a friend at his hotel and walked quickly, alone, to my car, and the eyes of black men around me moved onto me with a strange hot perception, seeing everything. They knew, seeing me, what I was. Tension rose through the cracks in the sidewalk. Where are white men who are strong, who see women in this way? The molecules in the air of Detroit are humming. I wish I could take a knife and cut out an important piece of my body, my insides, and hold it up . . . on a street corner, an offering. Then will they let me alone? The black men jostle one another on street corners, out of work and not wanting work, content to stare at me, knowing everything in me, not surprised. My lover, a white man, remains back in the hotel, his head in his hands because I have walked out, but he won't run after me, he won't follow me. *They* follow me. One of them bumped into me, pretending it was an accident. I want to cut up my body, I can't live in this body.

Next door to us a boy is out in his driveway, sitting down, playing a drum. Beating on a drum. Is he crazy? A white boy of about sixteen pounding on a drum. He wants to bring the city down with that drum and I don't blame him. I understand that vicious throbbing.

Dear Marsha Katz,

Thank you for the baby clothes. Keep sending me things, test your imagination. I feel that you are drowning. I sense a tightness in your chest, your throat. Are your eyes leaden with defeat, you ten-year-old wonder? How many lives do children relive at the moment of death?

Dear Mother and Father,

The temperature today is ————. Yesterday at this time, ————. Greg has been very busy as usual with ————, ————, ————. This weekend we must see the ————'s, whom you have met. How is the weather there? How is your vacation? Thank you for the postcard from ————. I had not thought lawns would be green there.

. . . The Mayor will ask all his aides for resignations, signed. Some he will accept and others reject. A kingly man, plump and alcoholic. Divorced. Why can't I tell you about my husband's job, about my life, about anything real? Scandals fall on the head of my husband's boss, reading the paper is torture, yet my husband comes home and talks seriously about the future, about improvements, as if no chaos is waiting. No picketing ADC mothers, no stampede to buy guns, no strangled black babies found in public parks. In the midst of this my husband is clean and untouched, innocent, good. He has dedicated his life to helping others. I love him but cannot stop betraying him, again and again, having reclaimed my life as my own to throw away, to destroy, to lose. My life is my own. I keep on living.

My darling,

It is one-thirty and if you don't call by two, maybe you won't call; I know that you have a seminar from two to four, maybe you won't call; I know that you have a seminar from two to four, maybe you won't call today and everything will end. My heart pounds bitterly, in fear, in anticipation? Your daughter sent me some baby clothes, postmarked Boston. I understand her hatred, but one thing: how much did you tell your wife about me? About my wanting children? You told her you no longer loved her and couldn't live with her, that you loved another woman who could not marry you, but . . . did you tell her this other woman had no children? And what else?

I will get my revenge on you.

I walk through the house in a dream, in a daze. I am sinking slowly through the floor of this expensive house, a married woman in a body grown light as a shell, empty as a shell. My body has no other life in it, only its own. What you discharge in me is not life but despair. I can remember my body having life, holding it. It seemed a trick, a feat that couldn't possibly work: like trying to retain liquid up a reed, turning the reed upside down. The doctor said, "Babies are no trouble. Nothing." But the liquid ran out. All liquid runs out of me. That first week, meeting with you at the Statler, everything ran out of me like blood. I alarmed you, you with your nervous sense of fate, your fear of getting cancer, of having a nervous breakdown. I caused you to say stammering *But what if you get pregnant?* I am not pregnant but I feel a strange tingling of life, a tickling, life at a distance, as if the spirit of your daughter is somehow in me, lodged in me. She sucks at my insides with her pinched jealous lips, wanting blood. My body seeks to discharge her magically.

My dear husband,

I wanted to test being alone. I went downtown to the library, the old library. I walked past the hotel where he and I have met, my lover and I, but we were not meeting today and I was alone, testing myself as a woman alone, a human being alone. The library was filled with old men. Over seventy, dressed in black, with white shirts. Black and white: a reading room of old men, dressed in black and white.

I sat alone at a table. Some of the old men glanced at me. In a dream I began to leaf through a magazine, thinking, *Now I am leafing through a magazine: this is expected.* Why can't I be transformed to something else—to a mask, a shell, a statue? I glance around shyly, trying to gauge the nature of the story I am in. Is it tragic or only sad? The actors in this play all seem to be wearing masks, even I am wearing a mask, I am never naked. My nakedness, with my lover, is a kind of mask—something he sees, something I can't quite believe in. Women who are loved are in perpetual motion, dancing. We dance and men follow to the brink of madness and death, but what of us, the dancers?—when the dancing ends we stand back upon our heels, back upon our heels, dazed and hurt. Beneath the golden cloth on our thighs is flesh, and flesh hurts. Men are not interested in the body, which feels pain, but in the rhythm of the body as it goes about its dance, the body of a woman who cannot stop dancing.

A confession. In Ann Arbor last April, at the symposium, I fell in love with a man. The visiting professor from Boston University— a man with black-rimmed glasses, Jewish, dark-eyed, dark-haired, nervous and arrogant and restless. Drumming his fingers. Smoking too much. (And you, my husband, were sane enough to give up smoking five years ago.) A student stood up in the first row and shouted out something and it was he, my lover, the man who would become my lover, who stood up in turn and shouted something back . . . it all happened so fast, astounding everyone, even the kid who reported for the campus newspaper didn't catch the exchange. How many men could handle a situation like that, being wilder and more profane than a heckler? . . . He was in the group at the party afterward, your friend Bryan's house. All of you talked at once, excited and angry over the outcome of the symposium, nervous at the sense of agitation in the air, the danger, and he and I wandered to the hostess's table, where food was set out. We made pigs of ourselves, eating. He picked out the shrimp and I demurely picked out tiny flakes of dough with miniature asparagus in them. Didn't you notice us? Didn't you notice this dark-browed man with the glasses that kept slipping down his nose, with untidy black hair? We talked. We ate. I could see in his bony knuckles a hunger that would never be satisfied. And I, though I think I am starving slowly to death now, I leaped upon the food as if it were a way of getting at him, of drawing him into me. We talked. We wandered around the house. He looked out a window, drawing a curtain aside, at the early spring snowfall, falling gently outside, and he said that he didn't know why he had come to this part of the country, he was frightened of traveling, of strangers. He said that he was very tired. He seduced me with the slump of his shoulders. And when he turned back to me we entered another stage of the evening, having grown nervous and brittle with each other, the two of us suddenly conscious of being together. My eyes grew hot and searing. I said carelessly that he must come over to Detroit sometime, we could have lunch, and he said at once, "I'd like that very much. . . ." and then paused. Silence.

Later, in the hotel, in the cheap room he rented, he confessed to me that seeing my face had been an experience for him—did he believe in love at first sight, after all? Something so childish? It had been some kind of love, anyway. We talked about our lives, about his wife, about my husband, and then he swung onto another subject, talking about his daughter for forty-five minutes . . . a genius, a ten-year-old prodigy. I am brought low, astounded. I want to cry out to him, *But what about me! Don't stop thinking about me!* At the age of six his daughter was writing poems, tidy little poems, like Blake's. *Like Blake's? Yes.* At the age of eight she was publishing those poems.

No, I don't want to marry him. I'm not going to marry him. What we do to each other is too violent, I don't want it brought into marriage and domesticated, nor do I want him to see me at unflattering times of the day . . . getting up at three in the morning to be sick, a habit of mine. He drinks too much. He reads about the connection between smoking and death, and turns the page of the newspaper quickly. Superstitious, stubborn. In April he had a sore throat, that was why he spoke so hoarsely on the program . . . but a month later he was no better: "I'm afraid of doctors," he said. This is a brilliant man, the father of a brilliant child? We meet nowhere, at an unimaginative point X, in a hotel room, in the anonymous drafts of air from blowers that never stop blowing, the two of us yearning to be one, in this foreign dimension where anything is possible. Only later, hurrying to my car, do I feel resentment and fury at him . . . why doesn't he buy me anything, why doesn't he get a room for us, something permanent? And hatred for him rises in me in long shuddering surges, overwhelming me. I don't want to marry him. Let me admit the worst— anxious not to fall in love with him, I think of not loving him at the very moment he enters me, I think of him already boarding a plane and disappearing from my life, with relief, I think with pity of human beings and this sickness of theirs, this desire for unity. Why this desire for unity, why? We walk out afterward, into the sunshine or into the smog. Obviously we are lovers. Once I saw O'Leary, from the Highway Commission, he nodded and said a brisk hello to me, ignored my friend; obviously we are lovers, anyone could tell. We walked out in the daylight, looking for you. That day, feverish and aching, we were going to tell you everything. He was going to tell his wife everything. But nothing happened . . . we ended up in a cocktail lounge, we calmed down. The air conditioning calmed us. On the street we passed a Negro holding out pamphlets to other Negroes but drawing them back when whites passed. I saw the headline—*Muslim Killed in Miami Beach by Fascist Police.* A well-dressed Negro woman turned down a pamphlet with a toothy, amused smile—none of that junk for her! My lover didn't even notice.

Because he is not my husband I don't worry about him. I worry about my own husband, whom I own. I don't own this man. I am thirty and he is forty-one; to him I am young—what a laugh. I don't worry about his coughing, his drinking (sometimes over the telephone I can hear ice cubes tinkling in a glass—he drinks to get the courage to call me), his loss of weight, his professional standing. He didn't return to his job in Boston, but stayed on here. A strange move. The department at Michigan considered it a coup to get him, this disintegrating, arrogant man, they were willing to pay him well, a man who has already made enemies there. No, I don't worry about him.

On a television program he was moody and verbose, moody and silent by turns. Smokes too much. Someone asked him about the effect of something on something—Vietnam on the presidential election, I think—and he missed subtleties, he sounded distant, vague. Has lost passion for the truth. He has lost his passion for politics, discovering in himself a passion for me. It isn't my fault. On the street he doesn't notice things, he smiles slowly at me, complimenting me, someone brushes against him and he doesn't notice, what am I doing to this man? Lying in his arms I am inspired to hurt him. I say that we will have to give this up, these meetings; too much risk, shame. What about my husband, what about his wife? (A deliberate insult—I know he doesn't love his wife.) I can see at once that I've hurt him, his face shows everything, and as soon as this registers in both of us I am stunned with the injustice of what I've done to him, I must erase it, cancel it out, undo it; I caress his body in desperation. . . . Again and again. A pattern. What do I know about caressing the bodies of men? I've known only two men in my life. My husband and his successor. I have never wanted to love anyone, the strain and risk are too great, yet I have fallen in love for the second time in my life and this time the sensation is terrifying, bitter, violent. It ends the first cycle, supplants all that love, erases all that affection—destroys everything. I stand back dazed, flat on my heels, the dance being over. I will not move on into another marriage. I will die slowly in this marriage rather than come to life in another.

Dear Mrs. Katz,
    I received your letter of October 25 and I can only say
    I don't know how to begin this letter except to tell you
    Your letter is here on my desk. I've read it over again and again

all morning. It is true, yes, that I have made the acquaintance of a man who is evidently your husband, though he has not spoken of you. We met through mutual friends in Ann Arbor and Detroit. Your informant at the University is obviously trying to upset you, for her own reasons. I assume it is a woman—who else would write you such a letter? I know nothing of your personal affairs. Your husband and I have only met a few times, socially. What do you want from me?

And your daughter, tell your daughter to let me alone!

Thank you both for thinking of me. I wish I could be equal to your hatred. But the other day an old associate of my husband's, a bitch of a man, ran into me in the Fisher lobby and said, "What's happened to you—you look terrible! You've lost weight!" He pinched the waist of my dress, drawing it out to show how it hung loose on me, he kept marveling over how thin I am, not releasing me. A balding, pink-faced son of a bitch who has made himself rich by being on the board of supervisors for a county north of here, stuffing himself at the trough. I know all about him. A sub-politician, never elected. But I trust the eyes of these submen, their hot keen perception. Nothing escapes them. "One month ago," he said, "you were a beautiful woman." Nothing in my life has hurt me as much as that remark, *One month ago you were a beautiful woman*. . . .

Were you ever beautiful? He says not. So he used you, he used you up. That isn't my fault. You say in your letter—thank you for typing it, by the way—that I could never understand your husband, his background of mental instability, his weaknesses, his penchant (your word) for blaming other people for his own faults. Why tell me this? He isn't going to be my husband. I have a husband. Why should I betray my husband for yours, your nervous, guilty, hypo-chrondriac husband? The first evening we met, believe it or not, he told me about his *hurts*—people who've hurt him deeply! "The higher you go in a career, the more people take after you, wanting to bring you down," he told me. And listen: "The worst hurt of my life was when my first book came out, and an old professor of mine, a man I had idolized at Columbia, reviewed it. He began by saying, *Bombarded as we are by prophecies in the guise of serious historical research* . . . and my heart was broken." We were at a party but apart from the other people, we ate, he drank, we played a game with each other that made my pulse leap, and certainly my pulse leaped to hear a man, a stranger, speak of his heart being broken—where I come from men don't talk like that! I told him a *hurt* of my own, which I've never told anyone before: "The first time my mother saw my husband, she took me aside and said, *Can't you tell him to stand up straighter?* and my heart was broken. . . ."

And so, with those words, I had already committed adultery, betraying my husband to a stranger.

Does he call you every night? I am jealous of those telephone calls. What if he changes his mind and returns to you, what then? When he went to the Chicago convention I'm sure he telephoned you constantly (he telephoned me only three times, the bastard) and joked to you about his fear of going out into the street. "Jesus, what if somebody smashes in my head, there goes my next book!" he said over the phone, but he wasn't kidding me. I began to cry, imagining him beaten up, bloody, far away from me. Why does he joke like that? Does he joke like that with you?

Dear Mother and Father,

My husband Greg is busy with ————. Doing well. Not fired. Pressure on, pressure off. Played golf with ————. I went to a new doctor yesterday, a woman. I had made an appointment to go to a man but lost my courage, didn't show up. Better a woman. She examined me, she looked at me critically and said, "Why are you trying to starve yourself?" *To keep myself from feeling love, from feeling lust, from feeling anything at all.* I told her I didn't know I was starving myself. I had no appetite. Food sickened me . . . how could I eat? She gave me a vitamin shot that burned me, like fire. Things good for you burn like fire, shot up into you, no escape. You would not like my lover, you would take me aside and say, *Jews are very brilliant and talented, yes, but. . . .*

I am surviving at half-tempo. A crippled waltz tempo. It is only my faith in the flimsiness of love that keeps me going—I know this will end. I've been waiting for it to end since April, having faith. Love can't last. Even lust can't last. I loved my husband and now I do not love him, we never sleep together, that's through. Since he isn't likely to tell you that, I will.

Lloyd Burt came to see my husband the other day, downtown. Eleven in the morning and already drunk. His kid had been stopped in Grosse Pointe, speeding. The girl with him knocked out on pills. *He* had no pills on him, luckily. Do you remember Lloyd? Do you remember any of us? I am your daughter. Do you regret having had a daughter? I do not regret having no children,

not now. Children, more children, children upon children, protoplasm upon protoplasm. . . . Once I thought I couldn't bear to live
without having children, now I can't bear to live at all. I must be
the wife of a man I can't have, I don't even want children from
him. I sit here in my room with my head and body aching with a
lust that has become metaphysical and skeptical and bitter, living
on month after month, cells dividing and heating endlessly. I don't
regret having no children. I don't thank you for having me. No
gratitude in me, nothing. No, I feel no gratitude. I can't feel
gratitude.

My dear husband,

I want to tell you everything. I am in a motel room, I've just
taken a bath. How can I keep a straight face telling you this? Sat
in the bathtub for an hour, not awake, not asleep, the water was
very hot. . . .

I seem to want to tell you something else, about Sally Rodgers.
I am lightheaded, don't be impatient. I met Sally at the airport this
afternoon, she was going to New York, and she saw me with
a man, a stranger to her, the man who is the topic of this letter,
the crucial reason for this letter. . . . Sally came right up to me
and started talking, exclaiming about her bad fortune, her car had
been stolen last week! Then, when she and a friend took her boat
out of the yacht club and docked it at a restaurant on the Detroit
River, she forgot to take the keys out and someone stole her boat!
Twenty thousand dollars' worth of boat, a parting gift from her
ex-husband, pirated away down-river. She wore silver eyelids, silver
stockings, attracting attention not from men but from small children, who stared. My friend, my lover, did not approve of her—
her clanking jewelry made his eye twitch.

I am thirty miles from Detroit. In Detroit the multiplication of
things is too brutal, I think it broke me down. Weak, thin, selfish,
a wreck, I have become oblivious to the deaths of other people.
(Robert Kennedy was murdered since I became this man's mistress, but I had no time to think of him—I put the thought of his
death aside, to think of later. No time now.) Leaving him and walking in Detroit, downtown, on those days we met to make love, I
began to understand what love is. Holding a man between my
thighs, my knees, in my arms, one single man out of all this multiplication of men, this confusion, this din of human beings. So it is
we choose someone. Someone chooses us. I admit that if he did not

love me so much I couldn't love him. It would pass. But a woman has no choice, let a man love her and she must love him, if the man is strong enough. I stopped loving you, I am a criminal. . . . I see myself sinking again and again beneath his body, those heavy shoulders with tufts of dark hair on them, again and again pressing my mouth against his, wanting something from him, betraying you, giving myself up to that throbbing that arises out of my heartbeat and builds to madness and then subsides again, slowly, to become my ordinary heartbeat again, the heartbeat of an ordinary body from which divinity has fled.

Flesh with an insatiable soul. . . .

You would hear in a few weeks, through your innumerable far-flung cronies, that my lover's daughter almost died of aspirin poison, a ten-year-old girl with an I.Q. of about 200. But she didn't die. She took aspirin because her father was leaving her, divorcing her mother. The only gratitude I can feel is for her not having died. . . . My lover, whom you hardly know (he's the man of whom you said that evening, "He certainly can talk!") telephoned me to give me this news, weeping over the phone. A man weeping. A man weeping turns a woman's heart to stone. I told him I would drive out at once, I'd take him to the airport. He had to catch the first plane home and would be on stand-by at the airport. So I drove to Ann Arbor to get him. I felt that we were already married and that passion had raced through us and left us years ago, as soon as I saw him lumbering to the car, a man who has lost weight in the last few months but who carries himself a little clumsily, out of absent-mindedness. He wore a dark suit, rumpled. His necktie pulled away from his throat. A father distraught over his daughter belongs to mythology. . . .

Like married people, like conspirators, like characters in a difficult scene hurrying their lines, uncertain of the meaning of lines . . . "It's very thoughtful of you to do this," he said, and I said, "What else can I do for you? Make telephone calls? Anything?" *Should I go along with you?* So I drive him to the airport. I let him out at the curb, he hesitates, not wanting to go without me. He says, "But aren't you coming in . . . ?" and I see fear in his face. I tell him yes, yes, but I must park the car. This man, so abrupt and insulting in his profession, a master of whining rhetoric, stares at me in bewilderment as if he cannot remember why I have brought him here to let him out at the United Air Lines terminal, why I am eager to drive away. "I can't park here," I tell him sanely, "I'll get a ticket." He respects all minor law; he nods and backs away. It takes me ten minutes to find a parking place. All this time I am sweating in the late October heat, thinking that his daughter is going to win after all, has already won. Shouldn't I just drive home and leave him, put an end to it? A bottle of aspirin was all it took. The tears I might almost shed are not tears of shame or regret but tears of anger—that child has taken my lover from me. That child! I don't cry, I don't allow myself to cry, I drive all the way through a parking lot without finding a place and say to the girl at the booth, who puts her hand out expecting a dime, "But I couldn't find a place! I've driven right through! This isn't fair!" Seeing my hysteria, she relents, opens the gate, lets me through. *Once a beautiful woman,* she is thinking. I try another parking lot.

Inside the terminal, a moment of panic—what if he has already left? Then he hurries to me. I take his arm. He squeezes my hand. Both of us very nervous, agitated. "They told me I can probably make the two-fifteen, can you wait with me?" he says. His face, now so pale, is a handsome man's face gone out of control; a pity to look upon it. In a rush I feel my old love for him, hopeless. I begin to cry. Silently, almost without tears. A girl in a very short skirt passes us with a smile—lovers, at their age! "You're not to blame," he says, very nervous, "she's just a child and didn't know what she was doing—please don't blame yourself! It's my fault—" But a child tried to commit suicide, shouldn't someone cry? I am to blame. She is hurting me across the country. I have tried to expel her from life and she, the baby, the embryo, stirs with a will of her own and chooses death calmly. . . . "But she's going to recover," I say to him for the twentieth time, "isn't she? You're sure of that?" He reassures me. We walk.

The airport is a small city. Outside the plate glass, airplanes rise and sink without effort. Great sucking vacuums of power, enormous wings, windows brilliant with sunlight. We look on unamazed. To us these airplanes are unspectacular. We walk around the little city, walking fast and then slowing down, wandering, holding hands. It is during one of those strange lucky moments that lovers have—he lighting a cigarette—that Sally comes up to us. We are not holding hands at that moment. She talks, bright with attention for my friend, she herself being divorced and not equipped to live without a man. He smiles nervously, ignoring her, watching people hurry by with their luggage. She leaves. We glance at each other, understanding each other. Nothing to say. *My darling! . . .*

Time does not move quickly. I am sweating again, I hope he won't notice, he is staring at me in that way . . . the way that frightens me. I am not equal to your love, I want to tell him. Not equal, not strong enough. I am ashamed. Better for us to say good-by. A child's corpse between us? A few hundred miles away, in Boston, are a woman and a child I have wronged, quite intentionally; aren't these people real? But he stares at me, the magazine covers on a newsstand blur and wink, I feel that everything is becoming a dream and I must get out of here, must escape from him, before it is too late. . . . "I should leave," I tell him. He seems not to hear. He is sick. Not sick; frightened. He shows too much. He takes my hand, caresses it, pleading in silence. A terrible sensation of desire rises in me, surprising me. I don't want to feel desire for him! I don't want to feel it for anyone, I don't want to feel anything at all! I don't want to be drawn to an act of love, or even to think about it; I want freedom, I want the smooth sterility of coins worn out from friendly handling, rubbing together, I want to say good-by to love at the age of thirty, not being strong enough for it. A woman in the act of love feels no joy but only terror, a parody of labor, giving birth. Torture. Heartbeat racing at 160, 180 beats a minute, where is joy in this, what is this deception, this joke. Isn't the body itself a joke?

He leads me somewhere, along a corridor. Doesn't know where he is going. People head toward us with suitcases. A soldier on leave from Vietnam, we don't notice, a Negro woman weeping over another soldier, obviously her son, my lover does not see. A man brushes against me and with exaggerated fear I jump to my lover's side . . . but the man keeps on walking, it is nothing. My lover strokes my damp hand. "You won't. . . . You're not thinking of. . . . What are you thinking of?" he whispers. Everything is open in him, everything. He is not ashamed of the words he says, of his fear, his pleading. No irony in him, this ironic man. And I can hear myself saying that we must put an end to this, it's driving us both crazy and there is no future, nothing ahead of us, but I don't say these words or anything like them. We walk along. I am stunned. I feel a heavy, ugly desire for him, for his body. I want him as I've wanted him many times before, when our lives seemed simpler, when we were both deluded about what we were doing . . . both of us thought, in the beginning, that no one would care if we fell in love . . . not my husband, not his family. I don't know why. Now I want to say good-by to him but nothing comes out, nothing. I am still crying a little. It is not a weapon of mine—it is an admission of defeat. I am not a woman who cries well. Crying is a confession of failure, a giving in. I tell him no, I am not thinking of anything, only of him. I love him. I am not thinking of anything else.

We find ourselves by Gate 10. What meaning has Gate 10 to us? People are lingering by it, obviously a plane has just taken off, a stewardess is shuffling papers together, everything is normal. I sense normality and am drawn to it. We wander on. We come to a doorway, a door held open by a large block of wood. Where does that lead to? A stairway. The stairway is evidently not open. We can see that it leads up to another level, a kind of runway, and though it is not open he takes my hand and leads me to the stairs. In a delirium I follow him, why not? The airport is so crowded that we are alone and anonymous. He kicks the block of wood away, wisely. We are alone. On this stairway—which smells of disinfectant and yet is not very clean—my lover embraces me eagerly, wildly, he kisses me, kisses my damp cheeks, rubs his face against mine. I half-fall, half-sit on the stairs. He begins to groan, or to weep. He presses his face against me, against my breasts, my body. It is like wartime—a battle is going on outside, in the corridor. Hundreds of people! A world of people jostling one another! Here, in a dim stairway, clutching each other, we are oblivious to their deaths. But I want to be good! What have I wanted in my life except to be good? To lead a simple, good, intelligent life? He kisses my knees, my thighs, my stomach. I embrace him against me. Everything has gone wild, I am seared with the desire to be unfaithful to a husband who no longer exists, nothing else matters except this act of unfaithfulness. I feel that I am a character in a story, a plot, who has not understood until now exactly what is going to happen to her. Selfish, eager, we come together and do not breathe, we are good friends and anxious to help each other, I am particularly anxious to help him, my soul is sweated out of me in those two or three minutes that we cling together in love. Then, moving from me, so quickly exhausted, he puts his hands to his face and seems to weep without tears, while I feel my eyelids closing slowly upon the mangled length of my body. . . .

This is a confession but part of it is blacked out. Minutes pass in silence, mysteriously. It is those few minutes that pass after we make love that are most mysterious to me, uncanny. And then we cling to each other again, like people too weak to stand by ourselves; we are sick in our limbs but warm with affection, very good friends, the kind of friends who tell each other only good news. He helps me to my feet. We laugh. Laughter weakens me, he has to hold me, I put my arms firmly around his neck and we kiss, I am ready to give up all my life for him, just to hold him like this. My body is all flesh. There is nothing empty about us, only a close space, what appears to be a stairway in some public place. . . . He draws my hair back from my face, he stares at me. It is obvious that he loves me.

When we return to the public corridor no one has missed us. It is strangely late, after three. This is a surprise, I am really surprised, but my lover is more businesslike and simply asks at the desk—the next plane? to Boston? what chance of his getting on? His skin is almost ruddy with pleasure. I can see what pleasure does to a man. But now I must say good-by, I must leave. He holds my hand. I linger. We talk seriously and quietly in the middle of the great crowded floor about his plans—he will stay in Boston as long as he must, until things are settled; he will see his lawyer; he will talk it over, *talk it over*, with his wife and his daughter, he will not leave until they understand why he has to leave. . . . I want to cry out at him, *Should you come back?* but I can't say anything. Everything in me is a curving to submission, in spite of what you, my husband, have always thought.

Finally . . . he boards a plane at four. I watch him leave. He looks back at me, I wave, the plane taxis out onto the runway and rises . . . no accident, no violent ending. There is nothing violent about us, everything is natural and gentle. Walking along the long corridor I bump into someone, a woman my own age. I am suddenly dizzy. She says, "Are you all right?" I turn away, ashamed. I am on fire! My body is on fire! I feel his semen stirring in my loins, that rush of heat that always makes me pause, staring into the sky or at a wall, at something blank to mirror the blankness in my mind . . . stunned, I feel myself so heavily a body, so lethargic with the aftermath of passion. How did I hope to turn myself into a statue, into the constancy of a soul? No hope. The throbbing in my loins has not yet resolved itself into the throbbing of my heart. A woman does not forget so quickly, nothing lets her forget. I am transparent with heat. I walk on, feeling my heart pound weakly, feeling the moisture between my legs, wondering if I will ever get home. My vision seems blotched. The air—air conditioning—is humming, unreal. It is not alien to me but a part of my own confusion, a long expulsion of my own breath. What do I look like making love? Is my face distorted, am I ugly? Does he see me? Does he judge? Or does he see nothing but beauty, transported in love as I am, helpless?

I can't find the car. Which parking lot? The sun is burning. A man watches me, studies me. I walk fast to show that I know what I'm doing. And if the car is missing, stolen . . . ? I search through my purse, noting how the lining is soiled, ripped. Fifty thousand dollars in the bank and no children and I can't get around to buying a new purse; everything is soiled, ripped, worn out . . . the keys are missing . . . only wadded tissue, a sweetish smell, liquid stiffening on the tissue . . . everything hypnotizes me. . . . I find the keys, my vision swims, I will never get home.

My knees are trembling. There is an ocean of cars here at Metropolitan Airport. Families stride happily to cars, get in, drive away. I wander around, staring. I must find my husband's car in order to get home. . . . I check in my purse again, panicked. No, I haven't lost the keys. I take the keys out of my purse to look at them. The key to the ignition, to the trunk, to the front door of the house. All there. I look around slyly and see, or think I see, a man watching me. He moves behind a car. He is walking away. My body still throbs from the love of another man, I can't concentrate on a stranger, I lose interest and forget what I am afraid of. . . .

The heat gets worse. Thirty, forty, forty-five minutes pass . . . I have given up looking for the car . . . I am not lost, I am still heading home in my imagination, but I have given up looking for the car. I turn terror into logic. I ascend the stairway to the wire-guarded overpass that leads back to the terminal, walking sensibly, and keep on walking until I come to one of the airport motels. I ask them for a room. A single. Why not? Before I can go home I must bathe, I must get the odor of this man out of me, I must clean myself. I take a room, I close the door to the room behind me; alone, I go to the bathroom and run a tubful of water. . . .

And if he doesn't call me from Boston then all is finished, at an end. What good luck, to be free again and alone, the way I am alone in this marvelous empty motel room! the way I am alone in this bathtub, cleansing myself of him, of every cell of him!

My darling,
    You have made me so happy. . . .

A Man and Two Women
DORIS LESSING

*"A Man and Two Women" is a complex story about a woman's
relationship with a young couple after the birth of their first
child. Stella recounts several reasons for her friendship with the
Bradfords, and her evaluation is, among other things, an analysis
of a strong marriage. The newborn baby and the husband's
casual infidelity, however, unsettle the new mother, whose strong
but conflicting emotions threaten both the marriage and the
friendship. Stella observes that Dorothy feels guilty because
her love for the baby constitutes a kind of infidelity to Jack. Is this
a sound diagnosis of her problem? Does it indicate only a
temporary state, or is their marriage in permanent danger? Has
Stella's friendship with them been destroyed during her visit, or
has she acted to preserve it? What insights does Stella gain into
her own marriage?*

Stella's friends the Bradfords had taken a cheap cottage in Essex
for the summer, and she was going down to visit them. She wanted
to see them, but there was no doubt there was something of a let-
down (and for them too) in the English cottage. Last summer Stella
had been wandering with her husband around Italy; had seen the
English couple at a café table, and found them sympathetic. They
all liked each other, and the four went about for some weeks, sharing meals, hotels, trips. Back in London the friendship had not, as
might have been expected, fallen off. Then Stella's husband departed abroad, as he often did, and Stella saw Jack and Dorothy
by herself. There were a great many people she might have seen,
but it was the Bradfords she saw most often, two or three times a

A MAN AND TWO WOMEN   From *A Man and Two Women*. Copyright © 1958,
1962, 1963, by Doris Lessing. Reprinted by permission of Simon and Schuster,
Inc., and Curtis Brown Ltd.

week, at their flat or hers. They were at ease with each other. Why were they? Well, for one thing they were all artists—in different ways. Stella designed wallpapers and materials; she had a name for it.

The Bradfords were real artists. He painted, she drew. They had lived mostly out of England in cheap places around the Mediterranean. Both from the North of England, they had met at art school, married at twenty, had taken flight from England, then returned to it, needing it, then off again: and so on, for years, in the rhythm of so many of their kind, needing, hating, loving England. There had been seasons of real poverty, while they lived on *pasta* or bread or rice, and wine and fruit and sunshine, in Majorca, southern Spain, Italy, North Africa.

A French critic had seen Jack's work, and suddenly he was successful. His show in Paris, then one in London, made money; and now he charged in the hundreds where a year or so ago he charged ten or twenty guineas. This had deepened his contempt for the values of the markets. For a while Stella thought that this was the bond between the Bradfords and herself. They were so very much, as she was, of the new generation of artists (and poets and playwrights and novelists) who had one thing in common, a cool derision about the racket. They were so very unlike (they felt) the older generation with their Societies and their Lunches and their salons and their cliques: their atmosphere of connivance with the snobberies of success. Stella, too, had been successful by a fluke. Not that she did not consider herself talented; it was that others as talented were unfêted, and unbought. When she was with the Bradfords and other fellow spirits, they would talk about the racket, using each other as yardsticks or fellow consciences about how much to give in, what to give, how to use without being used, how to enjoy without becoming dependent on enjoyment.

Of course Dorothy Bradford was not able to talk in quite the same way, since she had not yet been "discovered"; she had not "broken through." A few people with discrimination bought her unusual delicate drawings, which had a strength that was hard to understand unless one knew Dorothy herself. But she was not at all, as Jack was, a great success. There was a strain here, in the marriage, nothing much; it was kept in check by their scorn for their arbitrary rewards of "the racket." But it was there, nevertheless.

Stella's husband had said: "Well, I can understand that, it's like me and you—you're creative, whatever that may mean, I'm just a bloody TV journalist." There was no bitterness in this. He was a good journalist, and besides he sometimes got the chance to make a good small film. All the same, there was that between him and Stella, just as there was between Jack and his wife.

After a time Stella saw something else in her kinship with the couple. It was that the Bradfords had a close bond, bred of having spent so many years together in foreign places, dependent on each other because of their poverty. It had been a real love marriage, one could see it by looking at them. It was now. And Stella's marriage was a real marriage. She understood she enjoyed being with the Bradfords because the two couples were equal in this. Both marriages were those of strong, passionate, talented individuals; they shared a battling quality that strengthened them, not weakened them.

The reason why it had taken Stella so long to understand this was that the Bradfords had made her think about her own marriage, which she was beginning to take for granted, sometimes even found exhausting. She had understood, through them, how lucky she was in her husband; how lucky they all were. No marital miseries; nothing of (what they saw so often in friends) one partner in a marriage victim to the other, resenting the other; no claiming of outsiders as sympathisers or allies in an unequal battle.

There had been a plan for these four people to go off again to Italy or Spain, but then Stella's husband departed, and Dorothy got pregnant. So there was the cottage in Essex instead, a bad second choice, but better, they all felt, to deal with a new baby on home ground, at least for the first year. Stella, telephoned by Jack (on Dorothy's particular insistence, he said), offered and received commiserations on its being only Essex and not Majorca or Italy. She also received sympathy because her husband had been expected back this weekend, but had wired to say he wouldn't be back for another month, probably—there was trouble in Venezuela. Stella wasn't really forlorn; she didn't mind living alone, since she was always supported by knowing her man would be back. Besides, if she herself were offered the chance of a month's "trouble" in Venezuela, she wouldn't hesitate, so it wasn't fair . . . fairness characterised their relationship. All the same, it was nice that she could drop down (or up) to the Bradfords, people with whom she could always be herself, neither more nor less.

She left London at midday by train, armed with food unobtainable in Essex: salamis, cheeses, spices, wine. The sun shone, but it wasn't particularly warm. She hoped there would be heating in the cottage, July or not.

The train was empty. The little station seemed stranded in a green nowhere. She got out, cumbered by bags full of food. A porter and a stationmaster examined, then came to succour her. She was a tallish, fair woman, rather ample; her soft hair, drawn back, escaped in tendrils, and she had great helpless-looking blue eyes. She wore a dress made in one of the materials she had .designed. Enormous green leaves laid hands all over her body, and fluttered about her knees. She stood smiling, accustomed to men running to wait on her, enjoying them enjoying her. She walked with them to the barrier where Jack waited, appreciating the scene. He was a smallish man, compact, dark. He wore a blue-green summer shirt, and smoked a pipe and smiled, watching. The two men delivered her into the hands of the third, and departed, whistling, to their duties.

Jack and Stella kissed, then pressed their cheeks together.

"Food," he said, "food," relieving her of the parcels.

"What's it like here, shopping?"

"Vegetables all right, I suppose."

Jack was still Northern in this: he seemed brusque, to strangers; he wasn't shy, he simply hadn't been brought up to enjoy words. Now he put his arm briefly around Stella's waist, and said: "Marvellous, Stell, marvellous." They walked on, pleased with each other. Stella had with Jack, her husband had with Dorothy, these moments, when they said to each other wordlessly: If I were not married to my husband, if you were not married to your wife, how delightful .it would be to be married to you. These moments were not the least of the pleasures of this four-sided friendship.

"Are you liking it down here?"

"It's what we bargained for."

There was more than his usual shortness in this, and she glanced at him to find him frowning. They were walking to the car, parked under a tree.

"How's the baby?"

"Little bleeder never sleeps, he's wearing us out, but he's fine."

The baby was six weeks old. Having the baby was a definite achievement: getting it safely conceived and born had taken a couple of years. Dorothy, like most independent women, had had divided thoughts about a baby. Besides, she was over thirty and complained she was set in her ways. All this—the difficulties, Dorothy's hesitations—had added up to an atmosphere which Dorothy herself described as "like wondering if some damned horse is going to take the fence." Dorothy would talk, while she was pregnant, in a soft staccato voice: "Perhaps I don't really want a baby at all? Perhaps I'm not fitted to be a mother? Perhaps . . . and if so . . . and how . . . ?"

She said: "Until recently Jack and I were always with people who took it for granted that getting pregnant was a disaster, and now suddenly all the people we know have young children and baby-sitters and . . . perhaps . . . if . . ."

Jack said: "You'll feel better when it's born."

Once Stella had heard him say, after one of Dorothy's long troubled dialogues with herself: "Now that's enough, that's enough, Dorothy." He had silenced her, taking the responsibility.

They reached the car, got in. It was a second-hand job recently bought. "They" (being the press, the enemy generally) "wait for us" (being artists or writers who have made money) "to buy flashy cars." They had discussed it, decided that *not* to buy an expensive car if they felt like it would be allowing themselves to be bullied; but bought a second-hand one after all. Jack wasn't going to give *them* so much satisfaction, apparently.

"Actually we could have walked," he said, as they shot down a narrow lane, "but with these groceries, it's just as well."

"If the baby's giving you a tough time, there can't be much time for cooking." Dorothy was a wonderful cook. But now again there was something in the air as he said: "Food's definitely not too good just now. You can cook supper, Stell, we could do with a good feed."

Now Dorothy hated anyone in her kitchen, except, for certain specified jobs, her husband; and this was surprising.

"The truth is, Dorothy's worn out," he went on, and now Stella understood he was warning her.

"Well, it is tiring," said Stella soothingly.

"You were like that?"

Like that was saying a good deal more than just worn out, or tired, and Stella understood that Jack was really uneasy. She said, plaintively humorous: "You two always expect me to remember things that happened a hundred years ago. Let me think. . . ."

She had been married when she was eighteen, got pregnant at once. Her husband had left her. Soon she had married Philip, who also had a small child from a former marriage. These two children, her daughter, seventeen, his son, twenty, had grown up together.

She remembered herself at nineteen, alone, with a small baby. "Well, I was alone," she said. "That makes a difference. I remember I was exhausted. Yes, I was definitely irritable and unreasonable."

"Yes," said Jack, with a brief reluctant look at her.

"All right, don't worry," she said, replying aloud as she often did to things that Jack had not said aloud.

"Good," he said.

Stella thought of how she had seen Dorothy, in the hospital room, with the new baby. She had sat up in bed, in a pretty bed jacket, the baby beside her in a basket. He was restless. Jack stood between basket and bed, one large hand on his son's stomach. "Now, you just shut up, little bleeder," he had said, as he grumbled. Then he had picked him up, as if he'd been doing it always, held him against his shoulder, and, as Dorothy held her arms out, had put the baby into them. "Want your mother, then? Don't blame you."

That scene, the ease of it, the way the two parents were together, had, for Stella, made nonsense of all the months of Dorothy's self-questioning. As for Dorothy, she had said, parodying the expected words but meaning them: "He's the most beautiful baby ever born. I can't imagine why I didn't have him before."

"There's the cottage," said Jack. Ahead of them was a small labourer's cottage, among full green trees, surrounded by green grass. It was painted white, had four sparkling windows. Next to it a long shed or structure that turned out to be a greenhouse.

"The man grew tomatoes," said Jack. "Fine studio now."

The car came to rest under another tree.

"Can I just drop in to the studio?"

"Help yourself." Stella walked into the long, glass-roofed shed. In London Jack and Dorothy shared a studio. They had shared huts, sheds, any suitable building, all around the Mediterranean. They always worked side by side. Dorothy's end was tidy, exquisite, Jack's lumbered with great canvases, and he worked in a clutter. Now Stella looked to see if this friendly arrangement continued, but as Jack came in behind her he said: "Dorothy's not set herself up yet. I miss her, I can tell you."

The greenhouse was still partly one: trestles with plants stood along the ends. It was lush and warm.

"As hot as hell when the sun's really going, it makes up. And Dorothy brings Paul in sometimes, so he can get used to a decent climate young."

Dorothy came in, at the far end, without the baby. She had recovered her figure. She was a small dark woman, with neat, delicate limbs. Her face was white, with scarlet rather irregular lips, and black glossy brows, a little crooked. So while she was not pretty, she was lively and dramatic-looking. She and Stella had their moments together, when they got pleasure from contrasting their differences, one woman so big and soft and blond, the other so dark and vivacious.

Dorothy came forward through shafts of sunlight, stopped, and said: "Stella, I'm glad you've come." Then forward again, to a few steps off, where she stood looking at them. "You two look good together," she said, frowning. There was something heavy and overemphasized about both statements, and Stella said: "I was wondering what Jack had been up to."

"Very good, I think," said Dorothy, coming to look at the new canvas on the easel. It was of sunlit rocks, brown and smooth, with blue sky, blue water, and people swimming in spangles of light. When Jack was in the South he painted pictures that his wife described as "dirt and grime and misery"—which was how they both described their joint childhood background. When he was in England he painted scenes like these.

"Like it? It's good, isn't it?" said Dorothy.

"Very much," said Stella. She always took pleasure from the contrast between Jack's outward self—the small, self-contained little man who could have vanished in a moment into a crowd of factory workers in, perhaps Manchester, and the sensuous bright pictures like these.

"And you?" asked Stella.

"Having a baby's killed everything creative in me—quite different from being pregnant," said Dorothy, but not complaining of it. She had worked like a demon while she was pregnant.

"Have a heart," said Jack, "he's only just got himself born."

"Well, I don't care," said Dorothy. "That's the funny thing, I *don't* care." She said this flat, indifferent. She seemed to be looking at them both again from a small troubled distance. "You two look good together," she said, and again there was the small jar.

"Well, how about some tea?" said Jack, and Dorothy said at once: "I made it when I heard the car. I thought better inside, it's not really hot in the sun." She led the way out of the greenhouse, her white linen dress dissolving in lozenges of yellow light from the glass panes above, so that Stella was reminded of the white limbs of Jack's swimmers disintegrating under sunlight in his new picture. The work of these two people was always reminding one of each other, or each other's work, and in all kinds of ways: they were so much married, so close.

The time it took to cross the space of rough grass to the door of the little house was enough to show Dorothy was right: it was really chilly in the sun. Inside two electric heaters made up for it. There had been two little rooms downstairs, but they had been knocked into one fine low-ceilinged room, stone-floored, white-washed. A tea table, covered with a purple checked cloth, stood waiting near a window where flowering bushes and trees showed through clean panes. Charming. They adjusted the heaters and arranged themselves so they could admire the English countryside through glass. Stella looked for the baby; Dorothy said: "In the pram at the back." Then she asked: "Did yours cry a lot?"

Stella laughed and said again: "I'll try to remember."

"We expect you to guide and direct, with all your experience," said Jack.

"As far as I can remember, she was a little demon for about three months, for no reason I could see, then suddenly she became civilised."

"Roll on the three months," said Jack.

"Six weeks to go," said Dorothy, handling teacups in a languid indifferent manner Stella found new in her.

"Finding it tough going?"

"I've never felt better in my life," said Dorothy at once, as if being accused.

"You look fine."

She looked a bit tired, nothing much; Stella couldn't see what reason there was for Jack to warn her. Unless he meant the languor, a look of self-absorption? Her vivacity, a friendly aggressiveness that was the expression of her lively intelligence, was dimmed. She sat leaning back in a deep armchair, letting Jack manage things, smiling vaguely.

"I'll bring him in a minute," she remarked, listening to the silence from the sunlit garden at the back.

"Leave him," said Jack. "He's quiet seldom enough. Relax, woman, and have a cigarette."

He lit a cigarette for her, and she took it in the same vague way, and sat breathing out smoke, her eyes half closed.

"Have you heard from Philip?" she asked, not from politeness, but with sudden insistence.

"Of course she has, she got a wire," said Jack.

"I want to know how she feels," said Dorothy. "How do you feel, Stell?" She was listening for the baby all the time.

"Feel about what?"

"About his not coming back."

"But he is coming back, it's only a month," said Stella, and heard, with surprise, that her voice sounded edgy.

"You see?" said Dorothy to Jack, meaning the words, not the edge on them.

At this evidence that she and Philip had been discussed, Stella felt, first, pleasure: because it was pleasurable to be understood by two such good friends; then she felt discomfort, remembering Jack's warning.

"See what?" she asked Dorothy, smiling.

"That's enough now," said Jack to his wife in a flash of stubborn anger, which continued the conversation that had taken place.

Dorothy took direction from her husband, and kept quiet a moment, then seemed impelled to continue: "I've been thinking it must be nice, having your husband go off, then come back. Do you realise Jack and I haven't been separated since we married? That's over ten years. Don't you think there's something awful in two grown people stuck together all the time like Siamese twins?" This ended in a wail of genuine appeal to Stella.

"No, I think it's marvellous."

"But you don't mind being alone so much?"

"It's not *so* much, it's two or three months in a year. Well of course I mind. But I enjoy being alone, really. But I'd enjoy it too if we were together all the time. I envy you two." Stella was surprised to find her eyes wet with self-pity because she had to be without her husband another month.

"And what does he think?" demanded Dorothy. "What does Philip think?"

Stella said: "Well, I think he likes getting away from time to time—yes. He likes intimacy, he enjoys it, but it doesn't come as easily to him as it does to me." She had never said this before because she had never thought about it. She was annoyed with herself that she had had to wait for Dorothy to prompt her. Yet she knew that getting annoyed was what she must not do, with the state Dorothy was in, whatever it was. She glanced at Jack for guidance, but he was determinedly busy on his pipe.

"Well, I'm like Philip," announced Dorothy. "Yes, I'd love it if Jack went off sometimes. I think I'm being stifled being shut up with Jack day and night, year in year out."

"Thanks," said Jack, short but good-humoured.

"No, but I mean it. There's something humiliating about two adult people never for one second out of each other's sight."

"Well," said Jack, "when Paul's a bit bigger, you buzz off for a month or so and you'll appreciate me when you get back."

"It's not that I don't appreciate you, it's not that at all," said Dorothy, insistent, almost strident, apparently fevered with rest-lessness. Her languor had quite gone, and her limbs jerked and moved. And now the baby, as if he had been prompted by his father's mentioning him, let out a cry. Jack got up, forestalling his wife, saying: "I'll get him."

Dorothy sat, listening for her husband's movements with the baby, until he came back, which he did, supporting the infant sprawled against his shoulder with a competent hand. He sat down, let his son slide onto his chest, and said: "There now, you shut up and leave us in peace a bit longer." The baby was looking up into his face with the astonished expression of the newly born, and Dorothy sat smiling at both of them. Stella understood that her restlessness, her repeated curtailed movements, meant that she longed—more, needed—to have the child in her arms, have its body against hers. And Jack seemed to feel this, because Stella could have sworn it was not a conscious decision that made him rise and slide the infant into his wife's arms. Her flesh, her needs, had spoken direct to him without words, and he had risen at once to give her what she wanted. This silent instinctive conversation be-tween husband and wife made Stella miss her own husband vio-lently, and with resentment against fate that kept them apart so often. She ached for Philip.

Meanwhile Dorothy, now the baby was sprawled softly against her chest, the small feet in her hand, seemed to have lapsed into good humour. And Stella, watching, remembered something she really had forgotten: the close, fierce physical tie between herself and her daughter when she had been a tiny baby. She saw this bond in the way Dorothy stroked the small head that trembled on its neck as the baby looked up into his mother's face. Why, she remembered it was like being in love, having a new baby. All kinds of forgotten or unused instincts woke in Stella. She lit a cigarette, took herself in hand; set herself to enjoy the other woman's love affair with her baby instead of envying her.

The sun, dropping into the trees, struck the windowpanes; and there was a dazzle and a flashing of yellow and white light into the room, particularly over Dorothy in her white dress and the baby. Again Stella was reminded of Jack's picture of the white-limbed swimmers in sun-dissolving water. Dorothy shielded the baby's eyes with her hand and remarked dreamily: "This is better than any man, isn't it, Stell? Isn't it better than any man?"

"Well—no," said Stella laughing. "No, not for long."

"If you say so, you should know . . . but I can't imagine ever . . . tell me, Stell, does your Philip have affairs when he's away?"

"For God's sake!" said Jack, angry. But he checked himself. "Yes, I am sure he does."

"Do you mind?" asked Dorothy, loving the baby's feet with her enclosing palm.

And now Stella was forced to remember, to think about having minded, minding, coming to terms, and the ways in which she now did not mind.

"I don't think about it," she said.

"Well, I don't think I'd mind," said Dorothy.

"Thanks for letting me know," said Jack, short despite himself. Then he made himself laugh.

"And you, do you have affairs while Philip's away?"

"Sometimes. Not really."

"Do you know, Jack was unfaithful to me this week," remarked Dorothy, smiling at the baby.

"That's *enough*," said Jack, really angry.

"No it isn't enough, it isn't. Because what's awful is, I don't care."

"Well why should you care, in the circumstances?" Jack turned to Stella. "There's a silly bitch Lady Edith lives across that field. She got all excited, real live artists living down her lane. Well Dorothy was lucky, she had an excuse in the baby, but I had to go to her silly party. Booze flowing in rivers, and the most incredible people—you know. If you read about them in a novel you'd never believe . . . but I can't remember much after about twelve."

"Do you know what happened?" said Dorothy. "I was feeding the baby, it was terribly early. Jack sat straight up in bed and said: 'Jesus, Dorothy, I've just remembered, I screwed that silly bitch Lady Edith on her brocade sofa.' "

Stella laughed. Jack let out a snort of laughter. Dorothy laughed, an unscrupulous chuckle of appreciation. Then she said seriously: "But that's the point, Stella—the thing is, I don't care a tuppenny damn."

"But why should you?" asked Stella.

"But it's the first time he ever has, and surely I should have minded?"

"Don't you be too sure of that," said Jack, energetically puffing his pipe. "Don't be too sure." But it was only for form's sake, and Dorothy knew it, and said: "Surely I should have cared, Stell?"

"No. You'd have cared if you and Jack weren't so marvellous together. Just as I'd care if Philip and I weren't . . ." Tears came running down her face. She let them. These were her good friends; and besides, instinct told her tears weren't a bad thing, with Dorothy in this mood. She said, sniffing: "When Philip gets home, we always have a flaming bloody row in the first day or two, about something unimportant, but what it's really about, and we know it, is that I'm jealous of any affair he's had and vice versa. Then we go to bed and make up." She wept, bitterly, thinking of this happiness, postponed for a month, to be succeeded by the delightful battle of their day-to-day living.

"Oh Stella," said Jack. "Stell . . ." He got up, fished out a handkerchief, dabbed her eyes for her. "There, love, he'll be back soon."

"Yes, I know. It's just that you two are so good together and whenever I'm with you I miss Philip."

"Well, I suppose we're good together?" said Dorothy, sounding surprised. Jack, bending over Stella with his back to his wife, made a warning grimace, then stood up and turned, commanding the situation. "It's nearly six. You'd better feed Paul. Stella's going to cook supper."

"Is she? How nice," said Dorothy. "There's everything in the kitchen, Stella. How lovely to be looked after."

"I'll show you our mansion," said Jack.

Upstairs were two small white rooms. One was the bedroom, with their things and the baby's in it. The other was an overflow room, jammed with stuff. Jack picked up a large leather folder off the spare bed and said: "Look at these, Stell." He stood at the window, back to her, his thumb at work in his pipe bowl, looking into the garden. Stella sat on the bed, opened the folder and at once exclaimed: "When did she do these?"

"The last three months she was pregnant. Never seen anything like it, she just turned them out one after the other."

There were a couple of hundred pencil drawings, all of two bodies in every kind of balance, tension, relationship. The two bodies were Jack's and Dorothy's, mostly unclothed, but not all. The drawings startled, not only because they marked a real jump forward in Dorothy's achievement, but because of their bold sensuousness. They were a kind of chant, or exultation about the marriage. The instinctive closeness, the harmony of Jack and Dorothy, visible in every movement they made towards or away from each other, visible even when they were not together, was celebrated here with a frank, calm triumph.

"Some of them are pretty strong," said Jack, the Northern working-class boy reviving in him for a moment's puritanism.

But Stella laughed, because the prudishness masked pride: some of the drawings were indecent.

In the last few of the series the woman's body was swollen in pregnancy. They showed her trust in her husband, whose body, commanding hers, stood or lay in positions of strength and confidence. In the very last Dorothy stood turned away from her husband, her two hands supporting her big belly, and Jack's hands were protective on her shoulders.

"They are marvellous," said Stella.

"They are, aren't they."

Stella looked, laughing, and with love, towards Jack; for she saw that his showing her the drawings was not only pride in his wife's talent; but that he was using this way of telling Stella not to take Dorothy's mood too seriously. And to cheer himself up. She said, impulsively: "Well that's all right then, isn't it?"

"What? Oh yes, I see what you mean, yes, I think it's all right."

"Do you know what?" said Stella, lowering her voice. "I think Dorothy's guilty because she feels unfaithful to you."

"*What?*"

"No, I mean, with the baby, and that's what it's all about."

He turned to face her, troubled, then slowly smiling. There was the same rich unscrupulous quality of appreciation in that smile as there had been in Dorothy's laugh over her husband and Lady Edith. "You think so?" They laughed together, irrepressibly and loudly.

"What's the joke?" shouted Dorothy.

"I'm laughing because your drawings are so good," shouted Stella.

"Yes, they are, aren't they?" But Dorothy's voice changed to flat incredulity: "The trouble is, I can't imagine how I ever did them, I can't imagine ever being able to do it again."

"Downstairs," said Jack to Stella, and they went down to find Dorothy nursing the baby. He nursed with his whole being, all of him in movement. He was wrestling with the breast, thumping Dorothy's plump pretty breast with his fists. Jack stood looking down at the two of them, grinning. Dorothy reminded Stella of a cat, half closing her yellow eyes to stare over her kittens at work on her side, while she stretched out a paw where claws sheathed and unsheathed themselves, making a small rip-rip-rip on the carpet she lay on.

"You're a savage creature," said Stella, laughing.

Dorothy raised her small vivid face and smiled. "Yes, I am," she said, and looked at the two of them calm, and from a distance, over the head of her energetic baby.

Stella cooked supper in a stone kitchen, with a heater brought by Jack to make it tolerable. She used the good food she had brought with her, taking trouble. It took some time, then the three ate slowly over a big wooden table. The baby was not asleep. He grumbled for some minutes on a cushion on the floor, then his father held him briefly, before passing him over, as he had done earlier, in response to his mother's need to have him close.

"I'm supposed to let him cry," remarked Dorothy. "But why should he? If he were an Arab or an African baby he'd be plastered to my back."

"And very nice too," said Jack. "I think they come out too soon into the light of day, they should just stay inside for about eighteen months, much better all around."

"Have a heart," said Dorothy and Stella together, and they all laughed; but Dorothy added, quite serious: "Yes, I've been thinking so too."

This good nature lasted through the long meal. The light went cool and thin outside; and inside they let the summer dusk deepen, without lamps.

"I've got to go quite soon," said Stella, with regret.

"Oh, no, you've got to stay!" said Dorothy, strident. It was sudden, the return of the woman who made Jack and Dorothy tense themselves to take strain.

"We all thought Philip was coming. The children will be back tomorrow night, they've been on holiday."

"Then stay till tomorrow, I *want* you," said Dorothy, petulant.

"But I can't," said Stella.

"I never thought I'd want another woman around, cooking in my kitchen, looking after me, but I do," said Dorothy, apparently about to cry.

"Well, love, you'll have to put up with me," said Jack.

"Would you mind, Stell?"

"Mind *what?*" asked Stella, cautious.

"Do you find Jack attractive?"

"Very."

"Well I know you do. Jack, do you find Stella attractive?"

"Try me," said Jack, grinning; but at the same time signalling warnings to Stella.

"Well, then!" said Dorothy.

"A *ménage à trois?*" asked Stella laughing. "And how about my Philip? Where does he fit in?"

"Well, if it comes to that, I wouldn't mind Philip myself," said Dorothy, knitting her sharp black brows and frowning.

"I don't blame you," said Stella, thinking of her handsome husband.

"Just for a month, till he comes back," said Dorothy. "I tell you what, we'll abandon this silly cottage, we must have been mad to stick ourselves away in England in the first place. The three of us'll just pack up and go off to Spain or Italy with the baby."

"And what else?" enquired Jack, good-natured at all costs, using his pipe as a safety valve.

"Yes, I've decided I approve of polygamy," announced Dorothy. She had opened her dress and the baby was nursing again, quietly this time, relaxed against her. She stroked his head, softly, softly, while her voice rose and insisted at the other two people: "I never understood it before, but I do now. I'll be the senior wife, and you two can look after me."

"Any other plans?" enquired Jack, angry now. "You just drop in from time to time to watch Stella and me have a go, is that it?

Or are you going to tell us when we can go off and do it, give us your gracious permission?"

"Oh I don't care what you do, that's the point," said Dorothy, sighing, sounding forlorn, however.

Jack and Stella, careful not to look at each other, sat waiting.

"I read something in the newspaper yesterday, it struck me," said Dorothy, conversational. "A man and two women living together—here, in England. They are both his wives, they consider themselves his wives. The senior wife has a baby, and the younger wife sleeps with him—well, that's what it looked like, reading between the lines."

"You'd better stop reading between lines," said Jack. "It's not doing you any good."

"No, I'd like it," insisted Dorothy. "I think our marriages are silly. Africans and people like that, they know better, they've got some sense."

"I can just see you if I did make love to Stella," said Jack.

"Yes!" said Stella, with a short laugh which, against her will, was resentful.

"But I wouldn't mind," said Dorothy, and burst into tears.

"Now, Dorothy, that's enough," said Jack. He got up, took the baby, whose sucking was mechanical now, and said: "Now listen, you're going right upstairs and you're going to sleep. This little stinker's full as a tick, he'll be asleep for hours, that's my bet."

"I don't feel sleepy," said Dorothy, sobbing.

"I'll give you a sleeping pill, then."

Then started a search for sleeping pills. None to be found.

"That's just like us," wailed Dorothy, "we don't even have a sleeping pill in the place. . . . Stella, I wish you'd stay, I really do. Why can't you?"

"Stella's going in just a minute, I'm taking her to the station," said Jack. He poured some Scotch into a glass, handed it to his wife and said: "Now drink that, love, and let's have an end of it. I'm getting fed-up." He sounded fed-up.

Dorothy obediently drank the Scotch, got unsteadily from her chair and went slowly upstairs. "Don't let him cry," she demanded, as she disappeared.

"Oh you silly bitch," he shouted after her. "When have I let him cry? Here, you hold on a minute," he said to Stella, handing her the baby. He ran upstairs.

Stella held the baby. This was almost for the first time, since she sensed how much another woman's holding her child made Dorothy's fierce new possessiveness uneasy. She looked down at the small, sleepy, red face and said softly: "Well, you're causing a lot of trouble, aren't you?"

Jack shouted from upstairs: "Come up a minute, Stell." She went up, with the baby. Dorothy was tucked up in bed, drowsy from the Scotch, the bedside light turned away from her. She looked at the baby, but Jack took it from Stella.

"Jack says I'm a silly bitch," said Dorothy, apologetic, to Stella.

"Well, never mind, you'll feel different soon."

"I suppose so, if you say so. All right, I *am* going to sleep," said Dorothy, in a stubborn, sad little voice. She turned over, away from them. In the last flare of her hysteria she said: "Why don't you two walk to the station together? It's a lovely night."

"We're going to," said Jack, "don't worry."

She let out a weak giggle, but did not turn. Jack carefully deposited the now sleeping baby in the bed, about a foot from Dorothy. Who suddenly wriggled over until her small, defiant white back was in contact with the blanketed bundle that was her son.

Jack raised his eyebrows at Stella: but Stella was looking at mother and baby, the nerves of her memory filling her with sweet warmth. What right had this woman, who was in possession of such delight, to torment her husband, to torment her friend, as she had been doing—what right had she to rely on their decency as she did?

Surprised by these thoughts, she walked away downstairs, and stood at the door into the garden, her eyes shut, holding herself rigid against tears.

She felt a warmth on her bare arm—Jack's hand. She opened her eyes to see him bending towards her, concerned.

"It'd serve Dorothy right if I did drag you off into the bushes. . . ."

"Wouldn't have to drag me," she said; and while the words had the measure of facetiousness the situation demanded, she felt his seriousness envelop them both in danger.

The warmth of his hand slid across her back, and she turned towards him under its pressure. They stood together, cheeks touching, scents of skin and hair mixing with the smells of warmed grass and leaves.

She thought: What is going to happen now will blow Dorothy

and Jack and that baby sky-high; it's the end of my marriage; I'm going to blow everything to bits. There was almost uncontrollable pleasure in it.

She saw Dorothy, Jack, the baby, her husband, the two half-grown children, all dispersed, all spinning downwards through the sky like bits of debris after an explosion.

Jack's mouth was moving along her cheek towards her mouth, dissolving her whole self in delight. She saw, against closed lids, the bundled baby upstairs, and pulled back from the situation, exclaiming energetically: "Damn Dorothy, damn her, damn her, I'd like to kill her. . . ."

And he, exploding into reaction, said in a low furious rage: "Damn you both! I'd like to wring both your bloody necks. . . ."

Their faces were at a foot's distance from each other, their eyes staring hostility. She thought that if she had not had the vision of the helpless baby they would now be in each other's arms—generating tenderness and desire like a couple of dynamos, she said to herself, trembling with dry anger.

"I'm going to miss my train if I don't go," she said.

"I'll get your coat," he said, and went in, leaving her defenseless against the emptiness of the garden.

When he came out, he slid the coat around her without touching her, and said: "Come on, I'll take you by car." He walked away in front of her to the car, and she followed meekly over rough lawn. It really was a lovely night.

3

Success
and
Failure

Birth

ANAÏS NIN

*"Birth" is a semifictionalized excerpt from Volume I of Anaïs Nin's
Diary in which she describes the pain of delivering a stillborn child.
The labor is indeed a life-and-death struggle, but in an inverted
sense. The child who is to be born is already dead, yet the mother
faces death unless she gives birth to it. Ironically, her maternal
instincts to protect and shelter the premature infant inside her
are also suicidal instincts. What is revealed about the narrator's
character during her angry struggle with the doctor? Why does
the author include the conversations of the nurses during the
delivery? What do they contribute to the story? After presenting
the vivid details of the ordeal, the author describes the dead
child. What is the effect of this description?*

"The child," said the doctor, "is dead."

I lay stretched on a table. I had no place on which to rest my
legs. I had to keep them raised. Two nurses leaned over me. In
front of me stood the doctor with the face of a woman and eyes
protruding with anger and fear. For two hours I had been making
violent efforts. The child inside of me was six months old and yet
it was too big for me. I was exhausted, the veins in me were swelling with the strain. I had pushed with my entire being. I had
pushed as if I wanted this child out of my body and hurled into
another world.

"Push, push with all your strength!"

Was I pushing with all my strength? All my strength?

No. A part of me did not want to push out the child. The

doctor knew it. That is why he was angry, mysteriously angry. He knew. A part of me lay passive, did not want to push out anyone, not even this dead fragment of myself, out in the cold, outside of me. All in me which chose to keep, to lull, to embrace, to love, all in me which carried, preserved, and protected, all in me which imprisoned the whole world in its passionate tenderness, this part of me would not thrust out the child, even though it had died in me. Even though it threatened my life, I could not break, tear out, separate, surrender, open and dilate and yield up a fragment of a life like a fragment of the past, this part of me rebelled against pushing out the child, or anyone, out in the cold, to be picked up by strange hands, to be buried in strange places, to be lost, lost, lost. . . . He knew, the doctor. A few hours before he adored me, served me. Now he was angry. And I was angry with a black anger at this part of me which refused to push, to separate, to lose.

"Push! Push! Push with all your strength!"

I pushed with anger, with despair, with frenzy, with the feeling that I would die pushing, as one exhales the last breath, that I would push out everything inside of me, and my soul with all the blood around it, and the sinews with my heart inside of them, choked, and that my body itself would open and smoke would rise, and I would feel the ultimate incision of death.

The nurses leaned over me and they talked to each other while I rested. Then I pushed until I heard my bones cracking, until my veins swelled. I closed my eyes so hard I saw lightning and waves of red and purple. There was a stir in my ears, a beating as if the tympanum would burst. I closed my lips so tightly the blood was trickling. My legs felt enormously heavy, like marble columns, like immense marble columns crushing my body. I was pleading for someone to hold them. The nurse laid her knee on my stomach and shouted: "Push! Push! Push!" Her perspiration fell on me.

The doctor paced up and down angrily, impatiently. "We will be here all night. Three hours now. . . ."

The head was showing, but I had fainted. Everything was blue, then black. The instruments were gleaming before my eyes. Knives sharpened in my ears. Ice and silence. Then I heard voices, first talking too fast for me to understand. A curtain was parted, the voices still tripped over each other, falling fast like a waterfall, with sparks, and cutting into my ears. The table was rolling gently, rolling. The women were lying in the air. Heads. Heads hung where the enormous white bulbs of the lamps were hung. The doctor was still walking, the lamps moved, the heads came near, very near, and the words came more slowly.

They were laughing. One nurse was saying: "When I had my first child I was all ripped to pieces. I had to be sewn up again, and then I had another, and had to be sewn up, and then I had another. . . ."

The other nurse said: "Mine passed like an envelope through a letter box. But afterwards the bag would not come out. The bag would not come out. Out. Out. . . ." Why did they keep repeating themselves? And the lamps turning. And the steps of the doctor very fast, very fast.

"She can't labor any more, at six months nature does not help. She should have another injection."

I felt the needle thrust. The lamps were still. The ice and the blue that was all around came into my veins. My heart beat wildly. The nurses talked: "Now that baby of Mrs. L. last week, who would have thought she was too small, a big woman like that, a big woman like that, a big woman like that. . . ." The words kept turning, as on a disk. They talked, they talked, they talked. . . .

Please hold my legs! Please hold my legs! Please hold my legs! PLEASE HOLD MY LEGS! I am ready again. By throwing my head back I can see the clock. I have been struggling four hours. It would be better to die. Why am I alive and struggling so desperately? I could not remember why I should want to live. I could not remember anything. Everything was blood and pain. I have to push. I have to push. That is a black fixed point in eternity. At the end of a long dark tunnel. I have to push. A voice saying: "Push! Push! Push!" A knee on my stomach and the marble of my legs crushing me and the head so large and I have to push.

Am I pushing or dying? The light up there, the immense round blazing white light is drinking me. It drinks me slowly, inspires me into space. If I do not close my eyes it will drink all of me. I seep upward, in long icy threads, too light, and yet inside there is a fire too, the nerves are twisted, there is no rest from this long tunnel dragging me, or am I pushing myself out of the tunnel, or is the child being pushed out of me, or is the light drinking me. Am I dying? The ice in the veins, the cracking of the bones, this pushing in darkness, with a small shaft of light in the eyes like the edge of a knife, the feeling of a knife cutting the flesh, the flesh somewhere is tearing as if it were burned through by a flame, somewhere my flesh is tearing and the blood is spilling out. I am pushing in the darkness, in utter darkness. I am pushing until my eyes open and I see the doctor holding a long instrument which he swiftly thrusts into me and the pain makes me cry out. A long animal howl. That will make her push, he says to the nurse. But it does not. It paralyzes me with pain. He wants to do it again. I sit up with fury and I shout at him: "Don't you dare do that again, don't you dare!"

The heat of my anger warms me, all the ice and pain are melted in the fury. I have an instinct that what he has done is unnecessary, that he has done it because he is in a rage, because the hands on the clock keep turning, the dawn is coming and the child does not come out, and I am losing strength and the injection does not produce the spasm.

I look at the doctor pacing up and down, or bending to look at the head which is barely showing. He looks baffled, as before a savage mystery, baffled by this struggle. He wants to interfere with his instruments, while I struggle with nature, with myself, with my child and with the meaning I put into it all, with my desire to give and to hold, to keep and to lose, to live and to die. No instrument can help me. His eyes are furious. He would like to take a knife. He has to watch and wait.

I want to remember all the time why I should want to live. I am all pain and no memory. The lamp has ceased drinking me. I am too weary to move even towards the light, or to turn my head and look at the clock. Inside of my body there are fires, there are bruises, the flesh is in pain. The child is not a child, it is a demon strangling me. The demon lies inert at the door of the womb, blocking life, and I cannot rid myself of it.

The nurses begin to talk again. I say: let me alone. I put my two hands on my stomach and very softly, with the tips of my fingers I drum drum drum drum drum drum on my stomach in circles. Around, around, softly, with eyes open in great serenity. The doctor comes near with amazement on his face. The nurses are silent. Drum drum drum drum drum drum in soft circles, soft quiet circles. Like a savage. The mystery. Eyes open, nerves begin to shiver, . . . a mysterious agitation. I hear the ticking of the clock . . . inexorably, separately. The little nerves awake, stir. But my hands are so weary, so weary, they will fall off. The womb is stirring and dilating. Drum drum drum drum drum. I am ready! The nurse presses her knee on my stomach. There is blood in my eyes. A tunnel. I push into this tunnel, I bite my lips and push. There is a fire and flesh ripping and no air. Out of the tunnel! All my blood is spilling out. Push! Push! Push! It is coming! It is coming! It is coming! I feel the slipperiness, the sudden deliverance, the weight is gone. Darkness. I hear voices. I open my eyes. I hear them saying: "It was a little girl. Better not show it to her." All my strength returns. I sit up. The doctor shouts: "Don't sit up!"

"Show me the child!"

"Don't show it," says the nurse, "it will be bad for her." The nurses try to make me lie down. My heart is beating so loud I can hardly hear myself repeating: "Show it to me." The doctor holds it up. It looks dark and small, like a diminutive man. But it is a little girl. It has long eyelashes on its closed eyes, it is perfectly made, and all glistening with the waters of the womb.

Foothold

ELIZABETH BOWEN

*"Foothold" is the story of a woman who finds her comfortable
life devoid of meaning. To fill the emptiness she creates an alter
ego, the ghost of a woman who had lived an equally "contented"
life in the same house a century before. Although Gerard realizes
that Clara is only a symptom of his wife's problem, he persists
in making an issue of the ghost as if it were the cause. What is
the real source of conflict between Janet and Gerard? In what
ways is Thomas qualified to observe the situation dispassionately?
His diagnosis is that a wedge is slowly separating Janet's
"controlled mind" from her "tempered, vivid emotions." How
perceptive is this analysis of Janet's problem? In what way is this
metaphor related to Gerard's idea of a foothold? How have both
men failed Janet, and at what has Clara succeeded?*

"**M**orning!" exclaimed Gerard, standing before the sideboard,
napkin under his arm. "Sleep well? There are kidneys here, had-
dock; if you prefer it, ham and boiled eggs—I don't *see* any boiled
eggs but I suppose they are coming in—did you see Clara?"

Thomas came rather dazedly round the breakfast table.

"He's hardly awake," said Janet. "Don't shout at him, Gerard—
Good morning, Thomas—let him sit down and think."

"*Are* the boiled eggs—?" cried Gerard.

"Yes, of course they are. Can you possibly bear to wait?" She
added, turning to Thomas, "We are very virile at breakfast."

Thomas smiled. He took out his horn-rimmed glasses, polished
them, looked round the dining-room. Janet did things imaginatively;
a subdued, not too buoyant prettiness had been superimposed on

last night's sombre effect; a honey-coloured Italian tablecloth on
the mahogany, vase of brown marigolds, breakfast-china about
the age of the house with a red rim and scattered gold pimpernels.
The firelight pleasantly jiggled, catching the glaze of dishes and
coffee-pot, the copper feet of the "sluggards' joy." The square high
room had, like Janet, a certain grace of proportion.

"I'm glad you don't have blue at breakfast," said Thomas,
unfolding his napkin. "I do hate blue."

"Did he see Clara?" asked Gerard, clattering the dish-lids.
"Do find out if he saw Clara!"

Janet was looking through a pile of letters. She took up each
envelope, slit it open, glanced at the contents and slipped them
inside again unread. This did not suggest indifference; the more
she seemed to like the look of a letter the more quickly she put
it away. She had put on shell-rimmed spectacles for reading, which
completed a curious similarity between her face and Thomas's;
both sensitive and untroubled, with the soft lines of easy living
covering over the harder young lines of eagerness, self-distrust and
a capacity for pain. When Gerard clamoured she raised her
shoulders gently. "Well, did you?" she said at last, without looking
up from her letters.

"I'm afraid Clara's been encouraged away," said Thomas. "I
specially left out some things I thought might intrigue her; a letter
from Antonia, a daguerreotype of my grandmother I brought down
to show you, rather a good new shirt—lavender-coloured. Then I
lay awake some time waiting for her, but your beds are too comfortable. I had—disappointingly—the perfect night! Yet all through
it I never quite forgot; it was like expecting a telephone call."

"If you'd been half a man," said Gerard, "and Clara'd been
half a ghost, you'd have come down this morning shaking all over
with hair bright white, demanding to be sent to the first train."

Janet, sitting tall and reposeful, swept her letters together
with a movement and seemed faintly clouded. "Well, I'm very glad
Thomas isn't trying to go—tell me, why should Antonia's letters
intrigue her? You complained they were rather dull. *I* find them
dull, but then she isn't a woman's woman."

"I just thought the signature ought to suggest an affinity.
Names, you know. Meredith . . . Don't be discouraged, Gerard;
I'm no sort of a test. I've slept in all sorts of places. There seems
to be some sort of extra thick coating between me and anything
other than fleshly."

"*I've* never met her," said Gerard, "but then I'm a coarse man and Clara's essentially feminine. Perhaps something may happen this evening. Try going to bed earlier—it was half-past one when we were putting the lights out. Clara keeps early hours."

"Have you noticed," Janet said composedly, "that one may discuss ghosts quite intelligently, but never any particular ghost without being facetious?"

"—Forgive my being so purely carnal," exclaimed Thomas suddenly, "but this is the most excellent marmalade. Not gelatinous, not slimy. I never get quite the right kind. Does your cook make it?"

He had noticed that here was "a sensitiveness." Thomas proceeded conversationally like the impeccable dentist with an infinitesimally fine instrument, choosing his area, tapping within it nearer and nearer, withdrawing at a suggestion before there had been time for a wince. He specialized in a particular kind of friendship with that eight-limbed, inscrutable, treacherous creature, the happily-married couple; adapting himself closely and lightly to the composite personality. An indifference to, an apparent unconsciousness of, life in some aspects armoured him against embarrassments. As Janet said, he would follow one into one's bedroom without noticing. Yet the too obvious "tact" she said, *was* the literal word for his quality. Thomas was all finger-tips.

Janet slid her chair back noiselessly on the carpet and turned half round to face the fire. "You're so nice and greedy," she said, "I do love having our food appreciated."

"*I* appreciate it," said Gerard. "You know how I always hate staying away with people. I suppose I am absolutely smug. Now that we've come to this house I hate more than ever going up to the office." He got up and stood, tall and broad, looking out of the window. Beyond, between the heavy fall of the curtains, showed the cold garden; the clipped shrubs like patterns in metal, the path going off in a formal perspective to the ascent of some balustraded steps. Beyond the terrace, a parade of trees on a not very remote skyline, the still, cold, evenly-clouded sky.

A few minutes afterwards he reluctantly left them. Janet and Thomas stood at the door and, as the car disappeared at the turn of the drive, Gerard waved good-bye with a backward scoop of the hand. Then they came in again to the fire and Thomas finished his coffee. He observed, "The room seems a good deal smaller. Do you notice that rooms are adaptable?"

"I do feel the house has grown since we've been in it. The rooms seem to take so much longer to get across. I'd no idea we were buying such a large one. I wanted it because it was white, and late Georgian houses are unexigeant, but I promised myself— and everyone else—it was small."

"Had you been counting on Clara, or didn't you know?"

"I was rather surprised. I met her coming out of your room about four o'clock one afternoon in November. Like an idiot I went downstairs and told Gerard."

"Oh—why like an idiot?"

"He came dashing up, very excited—I suppose it was rather exciting—and I came after him. We went into all the rooms, flinging the doors open as quietly and suddenly as we could; we even looked into the cupboards, though she is the last person one could imagine walking into a cupboard. The stupid thing was that I hadn't looked round to see which way she had gone. Gerard was perfectly certain there must be some catch about that chain of doors going through from my room to his and from his down the steps to the landing where there is a bathroom. He kept saying, 'You go round one way and I'll go the other.' While we'd been simply playing the fool I didn't mind, but when he began to be rational I began to be angry and—well ashamed. I said: 'If she's . . . not like us . . . you know perfectly well we can't corner her, and if she should be, we're being simply eccentric and rude.' He said 'Yes, that's all very well, but I'm not going to have that damned woman going in and out of my dressing-room,' and I (thinking 'Supposing she really is a damned woman?') said 'Don't be so silly, she wouldn't be bothered—why should she?' Then the wind went out of our sails altogether. Gerard went downstairs whistling; we had tea rather irritably—didn't say very much and didn't look at each other. We didn't mention Clara again."

"*Is* she often about?"

"Yes—no—I don't know . . . I really *don't* know, Thomas. I am wishing so much, you see, that I'd never begun her—let her in. Gerard takes things up so fearfully. I knew last night when he took that second whisky and put more logs on we would be coming to Clara."

"Ah," said Thomas. "Really. *That* was what you were waiting for. . . ."

"—The sun's trying to come out!" exclaimed Janet. She got up and pushed the curtains further apart. "In an hour or so when I've finished my house things we'll go round the garden. I do like having a garden you haven't seen. We're making two herbaceous borders down to the beech hedge away from the library window. I do think one needs perspective from a library window; it carries on the lines of the shelves."

"Precious, I think," said Thomas, "distinctly precious."

"Yes, I've always wanted to be. . . . The papers are in the library."

Thomas gathered from headlines and a half-column here and there that things were going on very much as he had expected. He felt remote from all this business of living; he was recently back from Spain. He took down Mabbe's *Celestina* and presently pottered out into the hall with his thumb in the book, to wait for Janet. In the hall, he looked at his own reflection in two or three pieces of walnut and noticed a Famille Rose bowl, certainly new, that they must have forgotten last night when they were showing him those other acquisitions. He decided, treading a zig-pattern across them carefully, that the grey and white marble squares of the floor were *good;* he would have bought the house on the strength of them alone. He liked also—Janet was doubtful about it—Gerard's treatment of the square-panelled doors, leaf-green in their moulded white frames in the smooth white wall. The stairs, through a double-doorway, had light coming down them from some landing window like the cold interior light in a Flemish picture. Janet, pausing half-way down to say something to some one above, stood there as if painted, distinct and unreal.

Janet had brought awareness of her surroundings to such a degree that she could seem unconscious up to the very last fraction of time before seeing one, then give the effect with a look that said "Still there?" of having had one a long time "placed" in her mind. He could not imagine her startled, or even looking at anything for the first time. Thinking of Clara's rare vantage point, in November, up by his bedroom door, he said to himself, "I'd give a good deal to have been Clara, that afternoon."

"If you don't really mind coming out," said Janet, "I should put on an overcoat." As he still stood there vaguely she took the book gently away from him and put it down on a table.

"If *I* had a ghost," said Thomas as she helped him into an overcoat, "she should be called 'Celestina.' I like that better than Clara."

"If I have another daughter," said Janet agreeably, "she shall be called Celestina."

They walked briskly through the garden in thin sunshine.

Thomas, who knew a good deal about gardens, became more direct, clipped in his speech and technical. They walked several times up and down the new borders, then away through an arch in the hedge and up some steps to the terrace for a general survey. "Of course," she said, "one works here within limitations. There's a character to be kept—you feel that? One would have had greater scope with an older house or a newer house. All the time there's a point of view to be respected. One can't cut clear away on lines of one's own like at Three Beeches; one more or less modifies. But it contents me absolutely."

"You ought to regret that other garden?"

"I don't, somehow. Of course, the place was quite perfect; it had that kind of limitation—it was too much our own. We felt 'through with it.' I had some qualms about leaving, beforehand; I suppose chiefly moral—you know, we do spoil ourselves!—but afterwards, as far as regret was concerned, never a pang. Also, practically speaking, of course the house *was* getting too small for us. Children at school get into a larger way of living; when they come home for the holidays—"

"I suppose," said Thomas distastefully, "they do take up rather a lot of room."

She looked at him, laughing. "Hard and unsympathetic!"

"Hard and unsympathetic," accepted Thomas complacently. "I don't see where they come in. I don't see the point of them; I think they spoil things. Frankly, Janet, I don't understand about people's children and frankly I'd rather not. . . . You and Gerard seem to slough your two off in a wonderful way. Do you miss them at all?"

"I suppose we—"

"*You,* you in the singular, thou?"

"I suppose," said Janet, "one lives two lives, two states of life. In terms of time, one may live them alternately, but really the rough ends of one phase of one life (always broken off with a certain amount of disturbance) seem to dovetail into the beginning of the next phase of that same life, perhaps months afterwards, so that there never seems to have been a gap. And the same with the other life, waiting the whole time. I suppose the two run parallel."

"Never meeting," said Thomas comfortably. "You see I'm on one and your children are on the other and I want to be quite sure. Promise me: *never* meeting?"

"I don't think ever. But you may be wise, all the same, not to come in the holidays."

They hesitated a moment or two longer on the terrace as though there were more to be said and the place had in some way connected itself with the subject, then came down by the other steps and walked towards the dining-room windows, rather consciously, as though some one were looking out. She wore a leather coat, unbuttoned, falling away from her full straight graceful figure, and a lemon-and-apricot scarf flung round twice so that its fringes hung down on her breast and its folds were dinted in by the soft, still youthful line of her jaw. Academically, Thomas thought her the most attractive woman of his acquaintance: her bodily attraction was modified and her charm increased by the domination of her clear fastidious aloof mind over her body.

He saw her looking up at the house. "I do certainly like your house," he said. "You've inhabited it to a degree I wouldn't have thought possible."

"Thank you so much."

"You're not—seriously, Janet—going to be worried by Clara?"

"My dear, no! She does at least help fill the place."

"You're not finding it empty?"

"Not the house, exactly. It's not . . ." They were walking up and down under the windows. Some unusual difficulty in her thoughts wrinkled her forehead and hardened her face. "You know what I was saying after breakfast about the house having grown since we came in, the rooms stretching? Well, it's not that, but my life—*this* life—seems to have stretched somehow; there's more room in it. Yet it isn't that I've more time—that would be perfectly simple, I'd do more things. You know how rather odious I've always been about *desoeuvrée* women; I've never been able to see how one's day could fail to be full up, it fills itself. There's been the house, the garden, friends, books, music, letters, the car, golf when one felt like it, going up to town rather a lot. Well, I still have all these and there isn't a moment between them. Yet there's more and more room every day. I suppose it must be underneath."

Thomas licked his upper lip thoughtfully. He suggested "Something spiritual, perhaps?" with detachment, diffidence and a certain respect.

"That's what anybody would say," she agreed with equal detachment. "It's just that I'm not comfortable; I always have been comfortable so I don't like it."

"It must be beastly," said Thomas, concerned. "You don't think it may just be perhaps a matter of not quite having settled down here."

"Oh, I've settled down. Settled, I shouldn't be surprised to hear, for life. After all, Thomas, in eight years or so the children will, even from your point of view, really matter. They'll have all sorts of ideas and feelings; they'll be what's called 'adult.' There'll have to be a shifting of accents in this family."

"When they come home for the holidays, what shall you do about Clara?"

"Nothing. Why should I? She won't matter. Not," said Janet quickly, looking along the windows, "that she matters particularly now."

Thomas went up to his room about half-past three and, leaving the door open, changed his shoes thoughtfully after a walk. "I cannot think," he said to himself, "why they keep dogs of that kind when exercising them ceases to be a matter of temperament and becomes a duty." It was the only reflection possible upon the manner of living of Gerard and Janet. His nose and ears, nipped by the wind, thawed painfully in the even warmth of the house. Still with one shoe off he crossed the room on an impulse of sudden interest to study a print (some ruins in the heroic manner) and remained leaning before it in an attitude of reflection, his arms folded under him on the bow-fronted chest-of-drawers. The afternoon light came in through the big window, flooding him with security; he thought from the dogs to Gerard, from Gerard to Janet, whom he could hear moving about in her room with the door open, sliding a drawer softly open and shut. A pause in her movements—while she watched herself in the glass, perhaps, or simply stood looking critically about the room as he'd seen her do when she believed a room to be empty—then she came out, crossed her landing, came down the three steps to his passage and passed his door.

"Hullo, Janet," he said, half turning round; she hesitated a moment, then went on down the passage. At the end there was a hanging-closet (he had blundered into it in mistake for the bathroom); he heard her click the door open and rustle about among the dresses. Still listening, he pulled open a small drawer under his elbow and searched at the back of it, under his ties, for the daguerreotype of his grandmother. Somehow he failed to hear her;

she passed the door again silently; still with a hand at the back of the drawer he called out: "Come in a moment, Janet, I've something to show you," and turned full round quickly, but she had gone.

Sighing, he sat down and put on the other shoe. He washed his hands, flattened his hair with a brush, shook a clean handkerchief out of its folds with a movement of irritation and, taking up the daguerreotype, went out after her. "Janet!" he said aggrievedly.

"Thomas?" said Janet's voice from the hall below.

"*Hul-lo!*"

"I've been shutting the dogs up—poor dears. We'll have tea in the library." She came upstairs to meet him, drawing her gloves off and smiling.

"But you were in—I thought you—oh well, never mind. . . ." He glanced involuntarily towards the door of her room; she looked after him.

"Yes, never mind," she said. They smiled at each other queerly. She put her hand on his arm for a moment urgently, then with a little laugh went up, on upstairs past him and into her room. He had an instinct to follow her, a quick apprehension, but stood there rooted.

"Right-o; all clear," she called after a second.

"Oh, right-o," he answered, and went downstairs.

"By the way," asked Thomas casually, stirring his tea, "does one tell Gerard?"

"As you like, my dear. Don't you think, though, we might talk about *you* this evening? Yesterday we kept drawing on you for admiration and sympathy; you were too wonderful. We never asked you a thing, but what we should love really, what we are burning to do, is to hear about you in Spain."

"I should love to talk about Spain after dinner. Before dinner I'm always a little doubtful about my experiences; they never seem quite so real as other people's; they're either un-solid or dingy. I don't get carried away by them myself, which is so essential. . . . Just one thing: why is she so like you?"

"Oh! . . . did that strike *you?*"

"I never saw her properly, but it was the way you hold yourself. And her step—well, I've never been mistaken about a step

before. And she looked in as she went by, over her shoulder, like
you would."

"Funny. . . . So that was Clara. Nothing's ever like what one
expected, is it?"

"No . . ." said Thomas, following a train of thought. "She
did perhaps seem eagerer and thinner. If I'd thought at all at the
time (which I didn't) I'd have thought—'Something has occurred
to Janet: what? As it was, after she'd been by the second time I
was cross because I thought you shouldn't be too busy to see me.
What do you know about her—facts, I mean?"

"Very little. Her name occurs in some title-deeds. She was a
Clara Skepworth. She married a Mr. Horace Algernon May and
her father seems to have bought her the house as a wedding present. She had four children—they all survived her but none of them
seems to have left descendants—and died a natural death, middle-
aged, about 1850. There seems no reason to think she was not
happy; she was not interesting. Contented women aren't."

This Thomas deprecated. "Isn't that arbitrary?"

"Perhaps," agreed Janet, holding out a hand to the fire. "You
can defend Clara, I shan't. . . . Why should I?"

"How do you know this Clara Skepworth—or May—is your
Clara?"

"I just know," said Janet, gently and a little wearily conclusive
—a manner she must often have used with her children.

Thomas peppered a quarter of muffin with an air of giving it
all his attention. He masked a keen intuition by not looking at
Janet, who sat with her air of composed unconsciousness, perhaps
a shade conscious of being considered. He had the sense here of
a definite exclusion; something was changing her. He had an intuition of some well he had half-divined in her having been tapped,
of some reserve (which had given her that solidity) being drained
away, of a certain sheathed and, till now, hypothetical faculty
being used to exhaustion. He had guessed her capable of an intimacy, something disruptive, something to be driven up like a
wedge, first blade-fine, between the controlled mind and the
tempered, vivid emotions. It would not be a matter of friendship
(the perfectness of his own with her proved it), she was civilized
too deep down, the responses she made were too conscious; nor of
love; she was perfectly mated (yet he believed her feeling for
Gerard so near, to the casual eye, to the springs of her being—to
be largely maternal and sensual).

In revulsion from the trend of his thoughts, he glanced at her, her comfortable beautiful body made the thing ludicrous. "A peevish dead woman where we've failed," he thought, "it's absurd." Gerard and he—he thought how much less humiliating for them both it would have been if she'd taken a lover.

"Gerard ought to be coming in soon." Uneasy, like a watch-dog waking up at the end of a burglary, he glanced at the clock.

"Shall I put the muffins down by the fire again?"

"Why? Oh, no. He doesn't eat tea now, he thinks he is getting fat."

"He's up to time usually, isn't he?"

"Yes—he's sure to be early this evening. I thought I heard the car then, but it was only the wind. It's coming up, isn't it?"

"Yes, lovely of it. Let it howl. (I like the third person impera-tive.)" He shrugged his folded arms up his chest luxuriously and slid down further into his chair. "I like it after tea, it's so physical."

"Isn't it?"

They listened, not for long in vain, for the sound of the car on the drive.

The drawing-room was in dark-yellow shadow with pools of light; Gerard and Janet were standing in front of the fire. Falling from Janet's arms above the elbows, transparent draperies hung down against the firelight. Her head was bent, with a line of light round the hair from a clump of electric candles on the wall above; she was looking into the fire, her arms stretched out, resting her finger-tips on the mantelpiece between the delicate china. Gerard, his fine back square and black to the room, bent with a creak of the shirt-front to kiss the inside of an elbow. Janet's fingers spread out arching themselves on the mantelpiece as though she had found the chord she wanted on an invisible keyboard and were holding it down.

Thomas saw this from across the hall, through an open door, and came on in naturally. His sympathy was so perfect that they might have kissed in his presence; they both turned, smiling, and made room for him in front of the fire.

"Saturday to-morrow," said Gerard, who smelt of verbena soap, "then Sunday. Two days for me here. You've been here all day, Thomas. It doesn't seem fair."

"I helped take the dogs for a walk," said Thomas. "It was muddy, we slid about and got ice-cold and couldn't talk at all because we kept whistling and whistling to the dogs till our mouths got too stiff. What a lot of virtue one acquires in the country by doing unnecessary things. Being arduous, while there are six or eight people working full time to keep one alive in luxury."

"Sorry," said Janet. "I didn't know you hated it. But I'm sure it was good for you."

"I wish you wouldn't both imply," said Thomas, "that I don't know the meaning of work. On Monday, when I get back to town, I'm going to begin my book on monasteries."

"What became of that poem about the Apocalypse?"

"I'm re-writing it," said Thomas with dignity.

"You are the perfect mixture," said Janet, "of Francis Thompson and H. G. Wells."

"There's a dark room in my flat where a man once did photography. In a year, when I'm thirty-five, I shall retire into it and be Proust, and then you will both be sorry."

The butler appeared in the doorway.

"Dinner . . ." said Gerard.

When Janet left them, Gerard and Thomas looked at each other vaguely and wisely between four candles over a pile of fruit. The port completed its second circle. Thomas sipped, remained with lips compressed and, with an expression of inwardness, swallowed.

"Very ni-ice," he said. "*Very* nice."

"That's the one I was telling you—light of course."

"I don't do with that heavy stuff."

"No, you never could, could you . . . I'm putting on weight—notice?"

"Yes," said Thomas placidly. "Oh, well, it's time we began to. One can't fairly expect, my dear Gerard, to *look* ascetic."

"Oh, look here, speak for yourself, you Londoner. I live pretty hard here—take a good deal of exercise. It would be beastly for Janet if one got to look too utterly gross."

"Ever feel it?"

"M-m-m-m—no."

Thomas sketched with his eyebrows an appeal for closer sincerity.

"Well, scarcely ever. Never more than is suitable." He sent round the port. "Had a good day barring the dogs? I daresay you talked a good deal; you made Janet talk well. She is, isn't she—dispassionately—what you'd call rather intelligent?"

"Yes—you proprietary vulgarian."

"Thanks," said Gerard. He cracked two walnuts between his palms and let the shells fall on to his plate with a clatter. "I suppose she showed you everything out of doors? I shall show it you again to-morrow. Her ideas are quite different from mine, I mean about what we're going to do here. I shall have my innings to-morrow. She's keeping the men at those borders when I want them to get started on levelling the two new courts. We've only one now —I suppose she showed it you—which is ridiculous with Michael and Gill growing up. Well, I mean, it *is* ridiculous, isn't it?"

"Entirely," said Thomas. "Don't cramp the children's development; let them have five or six."

"How you do hate our children," said Gerard comfortably.

There ensued a mellowed silence of comprehension. Gerard, his elbows spread wide on the arms of his chair, stretched his legs further under the table and looked at the fire. Thomas pushed his chair sideways and crossed his legs still more comfortably. A log on the fire collapsed and went up in a gush of pale flame.

Thomas was startled to find Gerard's eyes fixed sharply upon him as though in surprise. He half thought that he must have spoken, then that Gerard had spoken. "Yes?" he said.

"Nothing," said Gerard, "I didn't say anything, did I? As a matter of fact I was thinking—*did* you see anything of Clara?"

"If I were you I should drop Clara: I mean as a joke."

There was nothing about Gerard's manner of one who has joked. He smiled grudgingly. "I do work my jokes rather hard. I'm getting to see when their days are numbered by Janet's expression. As a matter of fact, I think *that's* one form of nerves with me; I feel it annoys Janet and I don't seem able to leave it alone. . . . *You* don't think, seriously, there's anything in this thing?"

"I told you this morning I wasn't a test."

"But aren't you?" insisted Gerard, with penetration. "How about since this morning? How do you feel things are—generally?"

"She's an idea of Janet's."

"Half your philosophers would tell me I was an idea of Janet's. I don't care what she is; the thing is, is she getting on Janet's nerves? You know Janet awfully well: do be honest."

"It needs some thinking about. I'd never thought of Janet as a person who *had* nerves."

"I'd like to know one way or the other," said Gerard, "before I start work on those courts."

"My dear fellow—*leave here?*" Such an abysm of simplicity startled Thomas, who thought of his friends for convenience in terms of himself. *He* wouldn't leave here, once established, for anything short of a concrete discomfort, not for the menacing of all the Janets by all the Claras. "I've never seen Janet better," he quickly objected, "looking nicer, more full of things generally. You can't say the place doesn't suit her."

"Oh yes, it suits her all right, I suppose. She's full of—something. I suppose I'm conservative—inside, which is so much worse— I didn't mind moving house, I was keener than she was on coming here. I wanted this place frightfully and I'm absolutely content now we've got it. I've never regretted Three Beeches. But I didn't reckon on one sort of change, and that seems to have happened. I don't even know if it's something minus or something plus. I think where I'm concerned, minus. It's like losing a book in the move, knowing one can't really have lost it, that it must have got into the shelves somewhere, but not being able to trace it."

"Beastly feeling," said Thomas idly, "till one remembers having lent it to some devil who hasn't given it back."

Gerard looked at him sharply, a look like a gasp. Then his eyes dropped, his face relaxed from haggardness into a set, heavy expression that held a mixture of pride and resentment at his own impenetrability, his toughness. Thomas knew the expression of old; when it appeared in the course of an argument he was accustomed to drop the argument with an "Oh well, I don't know. I daresay you are right." Gerard now raised his glass, frowned expressively at it and put it down again. He said: "I must be fearfully fatuous; I always feel things are so permanent."

Thomas didn't know what to say; he liked Gerard chiefly because he *was* fatuous.

"She's seeing too much of this ghost," continued Gerard. "She wouldn't if things were all right with her. I can't talk about delusions and doctors and things because she's as healthy as I am, obviously, and rather saner. I daresay this thing's *here* all right; from the way you don't answer my question I gather you've been seeing it too."

"To be exact," said Thomas, "somebody walked past my door this afternoon who turned out not to be Janet, though I'd have sworn at the time it was."

"Tell Janet?"

"Yes."

Gerard looked up for a moment and searched his face. "Didn't you wonder," he said, "why she couldn't be natural about it? I remember she and you and I talking rot about ghosts at Three Beeches, and she said she'd love to induct one here. The first time she came down and told me about Clara I thought she thought it fun. I suppose I was rather a hearty idiot; I rushed upstairs and started a kind of rat-hunt. I thought it amused her; when I found it didn't I had rather a shock. . . . Things must be changing, or how can this Clara business have got a foothold? It *has* got a foothold—I worry a good bit when we're alone but we never discuss it, then directly somebody's here something tweaks me on to it and every time I try and be funny something gets worse. . . . Oh, I don't know—I daresay I'm wrong." Gerard dived for his napkin; he reappeared shame-faced. "Wash this out," he said; "I've been talking through my hat. That's the effect of you, Thomas. It's not that you're so damned sympathetic, but you're so damned *un*sympathetic in such a provocative way." He got up. "Come on," he said; "let's come on out of here."

Thomas got up unwillingly; he longed to define all this. Risking a failure in tact he put forward. "What you're getting at is: all this is a matter of foothold?"

"Oh, I suppose so," Gerard agreed non-committally. "Let's wash that out, anyway. Do let's come on out of here."

Thomas talked about Spain. "I can't think why we don't go there," cried Janet. "We never seem to go anywhere; we don't travel enough. You seem so much completer and riper, Thomas, since you've seen Granada. Do go on."

"Quite sure I don't bore you?" said Thomas, elated.

"Get on," said Gerard impatiently. "Don't stop and preen yourself. And, Janet, don't you keep on interrupting him. Let him get on."

Thomas got on. He did require (as he'd told Janet) to gather momentum. Without, he was apt to be hampered by the intense, complacent modesty of the over-subjective; earlier in a day Spain refused to be detached from himself, he seemed to have made it. Now Spain imposed a control on him, selecting his language; words came less from him than through him, he heard them go by in a flow of ingenuous rapture.

Gerard and Janet were under the same domination. The three produced in each other, in talking, a curious sense of equality, of being equally related. Thomas concentrated a sporadic but power-ful feeling for "home" into these triangular contacts. He was an infrequent visitor, here as with other friends, but could produce when present a feeling of continuity, of uninterruptedness. . . . It was here as though there had always been Thomas. The quiet room round them, secure from the whining wind, with its shadowy lacquer, its shades like great parchment cups pouring down light, the straight, almost palpable fall of heavy gold curtains to carpet, "came together" in this peculiar intimacy as though it had lived a long time warm in their common memory. While he talked, it remained in suspension.

"O-oh," sighed Janet and looked round, when he had finished, as though they had all come back from a journey.

"I suppose," said Gerard, "we are unenterprising. Are we?"

"A little," conceded Thomas, still rather exalted, nursing one foot on a knee.

"Let's go abroad to-morrow!"

"You know," exclaimed Janet, "you know, Gerard, you'd sim-ply hate it!" She made a gesture of limitation. "We're rooted here."

"Of course, there's one thing: if you hadn't both got this faculty for being rooted it wouldn't be the same thing to come and see you. I do hate 'service-flat people'; I never know any."

They all sighed, shifted their attitudes; sinking a little deeper into the big chairs. Thomas, aware almost with ecstasy of their three comfortable bodies, exclaimed: "Would we ever really have known each other before there was this kind of chair? I've a theory that absolute comfort runs round the circle to the same point as asceticism. It wears the material veil pretty thin."

Janet raised her arms, looked at them idly and dropped them again: "What material veil?" she said foolishly.

Nobody answered.

"Janet's sleepy," said Gerard, "she can't keep awake unless she does all the talking herself. She's not one of your women who listen."

"I wasn't sleepy till now. I think it's the wind. Listen to it."

"To-morrow, Janet, I'm going to show Thomas where those courts are to be. He says you didn't."

"Thomas has no opinion about tennis-courts; he'd agree with anyone. He really was intelligent about my borders."

"Yes, I really was. You see, Gerard, tennis doesn't really affect me much. Pat-ball's my game." Thomas lay back, looking through half-shut eyes at the wavering streaming flames. "Clara's a dream," he thought. "Janet and I played at her. Gerard's a sick man." He wanted to stretch sideways, touch Janet's bare arm and say to them both: "There's just *this,* just this: weren't we all overwrought?"

Gerard, tenacity showing itself in his attitude, was sticking to something. He turned from one to the other eagerly. "All the same," he said, "tennis courts or no tennis courts, why shouldn't we both, quite soon, go abroad?"

"Exactly," said Thomas, encouraging.

"Because I don't want to," said Janet. "Just like that."

"Oh. . . . Tired?"

"Yes, tired-ish—with no disrespect to Thomas. I've had a wonderful day, but I *am* tired. Suppose it's the wind."

"You said that before."

She got up out of the depths of her chair, gathering up her draperies that slipped and clung to the cushions like cobwebs with perverse independence. "Oh!" she cried. "*Sleepy!*" and flung her arms over her head.

"But you shatter our evening," cried Thomas, looking up at her brilliance, then rising incredulous.

"Then you won't be too late," she said heartlessly. "Don't be too late!" She went across to the door like a sleepy cat. "Goodnight, my dear Thomas." After she closed the door they stood listening, though there was nothing to hear.

Their evening was not shattered, but it was cracked finely and irreparably. There was a false ring to it, never loud but an undertone. Gerard was uneasy; he got up after a minute or two and opened the door again. "Don't you feel the room a bit hot?" he said. "I'd open a window but the wind fidgets the curtains so. That's the only thing that gets on what nerves I have got, the sound of a curtain fidgeting; in and out, in and out, like somebody puffing and blowing."

"Beastly," said Thomas. "I never open a window." If he had been host he'd have invited Gerard to stop prowling and sit down, but one couldn't ask a man—even Gerard—to stop prowling about his own drawing-room when the prowling had just *that* "tone." So Thomas leant back rather exaggeratedly and sent up pacific smoke-wreaths.

"You look sleepy too," said Gerard with some irritation. "Shall we all go to bed?"

"Oh, just as you like, my dear fellow. I'll take up a book with me—"

"—No, don't let's," said Gerard, and sat down abruptly.

The wind subsided during the next half-hour and silences, a kind of surprised stillness, spaced out their talk. Gerard fidgeted with the decanters; half-way through a glass of whisky he got up again and stood undecided. "Look here," he said, "there's something I forgot to ask Janet. Somebody's sent her a message and I must get the answer telephoned through to-morrow, first thing. I'll go up for a moment before she's asleep."

"Do," agreed Thomas, taking up *Vogue.*

Gerard, going out, hesitated rather portentously about shutting the drawing-room door and finally shut it. Thomas twitched an eyebrow but didn't look up from *Vogue,* which he went through intelligently from cover to cover. He remained looking for some time at a coloured advertisement of complexion soap at the end, then, as Gerard hadn't come back, got up to look for *Celestina,* where Janet had left it out in the hall. He crossed the hall soundlessly, avoiding the marble, stepping from rug to rug; with a hand put out for the *Celestina* he halted and stood still.

Gerard stood at the foot of the stairs, through the double doors, looking up, holding on to the banisters. Thomas looked at him, then in some confusion stepped back into the drawing-room. He had a shock; he wished he hadn't seen Gerard's face. "What on earth was he listening for? . . . Why didn't he hear me? . . . I don't believe he's been up at all." He took some more whisky and stood by the fire, waiting, his glass in his hand.

Quickly and noisily Gerard came in. "She's asleep; it was no good."

"Pity," said Thomas; "you ought to have gone up sooner." They did not look at each other.

Thomas waited about—a social gesture purely, for he had the strongest possible feeling of not being wanted—while Gerard put out the downstair lights. Gerard wandered from one switch to another indeterminately, fumbling with wrong ones as though the whole lighting system were unfamiliar. Thomas couldn't make out if he were unwilling that either of them should go up, or whether he wanted Thomas to go up without him. "I'll be going on up," he said finally.

"Oh! Right you are."

"I'll try not to wake Janet."

"Oh, nothing wakes Janet—make as much noise as you like." He went up, his feet made a baffled, unreal sound on the smoothly carpeted stairs. The landing was—by some oversight—all in darkness. Away down the passage, firelight through his bedroom door came out across the carpet and up the wall. He watched—for Clara was somewhere, certainly—to see if anyone would step out across the bar of firelight. Nobody came. "She may be in there," he thought. Lovely to find her in there by the fire, like Janet.

Gerard turned out the last light in the hall and came groping up after him. "Sorry!" he said. "You'll find the switch of the landing outside Janet's door." Thomas groped along the wall till he touched the door-panels. Left or right?—he didn't know, his fingers pattered over them softly.

"Oh Clara," came Janet's quiet voice from inside, ". . . I can't bear it. How could you bear it? The sickening loneliness. . . . Listen, Clara . . ."

He heard Gerard's breathing; Gerard there three steps below him, listening also.

"Damn you, Gerard," said Thomas sharply and noisily. "*I* can't find this thing. I'm lost entirely. Why did you put those lights out?"

See How They Run

MARY ELIZABETH VROMAN

*However sentimental this story may be, "See How They Run"
describes the ingenuity and sheer stamina required of a good
teacher. And teaching is (presumably because it deals with
children) one of the few careers traditionally sanctioned for the
woman who seeks challenge and fulfillment outside the home.
It also illustrates the ambivalence with which an intelligent
woman carries out her responsibilities in an imperfect system.
What does Jane learn, for example, from the other teachers at her
school and from the experience of having to discipline C. T.?
How important is it that Jane is a black woman? How pertinent
are the details given about her previous school and about the kind
of students at her present one? How relevant is her relationship
with Paul to her sense of herself as a teacher?*

A bell rang. Jane Richards squared the sheaf of records decisively
in the large manila folder, placed it in the right-hand corner of her
desk, and stood up. The chatter of young voices subsided, and
forty-three small faces looked solemnly and curiously at the slight
young figure before them. The bell stopped ringing.

I wonder if they're as scared of me as I am of them. She smiled
brightly.

"Good morning, children, I am Miss Richards." As if they
don't know—the door of the third-grade room had a neat new sign
pasted above it with her name in bold black capitals; and anyway,
a new teacher's name is the first thing that children find out about
on the first day of school. Nevertheless she wrote it for their benefit
in large white letters on the blackboard.

"I hope we will all be happy working and playing together this year." Now why does that sound so trite? "As I call the roll will you please stand, so that I may get to know you as soon as possible, and if you like to you may tell me something about yourselves, how old you are, where you live, what your parents do, and perhaps something about what you did during the summer."

Seated, she checked the names carefully. "Booker T. Adams."

Booker stood, gangling and stoop-shouldered: he began to recite tiredly. "My name is Booker T. Adams, I'se ten years old." Shades of Uncle Tom! "I live on Painter's Path." He paused, the look he gave her was tinged with something very akin to contempt. "I didn't do nothing in the summer," he said deliberately.

"Thank you, Booker." Her voice was even. "George Allen." Must remember to correct that stoop. . . . Where is Painter's Path? . . . How to go about correcting those speech defects? . . . Go easy, Jane, don't antagonize them. . . . They're clean enough, but this is the first day. . . . How can one teacher do any kind of job with a load of forty-three? . . . Thank heaven the building is modern and well built even though it is overcrowded, not like some I've seen—no potbellied stove.

"Sarahlene Clover Babcock." Where do these names come from? . . . Up from slavery. . . . How high is up? Jane smothered a sudden desire to giggle. Outside she was calm and poised and smiling. Clearly she called the names, listening with interest, making a note here and there, making no corrections—not yet.

She experienced a moment of brief inward satisfaction: I'm doing very well, this is what is expected of me. . . . Orientation to Teaching. . . . Miss Murray's voice beat a distant tattoo in her memory. Miss Murray with the Junoesque figure and the moon face. . . . "The ideal teacher personality is one which, combining in itself all the most desirable qualities, expresses itself with quiet assurance in its endeavor to mold the personalities of the students in the most desirable patterns." . . . Dear dull Miss Murray.

She made mental estimates of the class. What a cross section of my people they represent, she thought. Here and there signs of evident poverty, here and there children of obviously well-to-do parents.

"My name is Rachel Veronica Smith. I am nine years old. I live at Six-oh-seven Fairview Avenue. My father is a Methodist minister. My mother is a housewife. I have two sisters and one brother. Last summer Mother and Daddy took us all to New York to visit

my Aunt Jen. We saw lots of wonderful things. There are millions
and millions of people in New York. One day we went on a ferry-
boat all the way up the Hudson River—that's a great big river
as wide across as this town, and—"

The children listened wide-eyed. Jane listened carefully. *She
speaks good English. Healthy, erect, and even perhaps a little
smug. Immaculately well dressed from the smoothly braided hair,
with two perky bows, to the shiny brown oxfords. . . . Bless you,
Rachel, I'm so glad to have you.*

"—and the buildings are all very tall, some of them nearly
reach the sky."

"Haw-haw"—this from Booker, cynically.

"Well, they are too." Rachel swung around, fire in her eyes
and insistence in every line of her round, compact body.

"Ain't no building as tall as the sky, is dere, Miz Richards?"

*Crisis No. 1. Jane chose her answer carefully. As high as the
sky . . . mustn't turn this into a lesson in science . . . all in due
time.* "The sky is a long way out, Booker, but the buildings in New
York are very tall indeed. Rachel was only trying to show you how
very tall they are. In fact, the tallest building in the whole world is
in New York City."

"They call it the Empire State Building," interrupted Rachel,
heady with her new knowledge and Jane's corroboration.

Booker wasn't through. "You been dere, Miz Richards?"

"Yes, Booker, many times. Someday I shall tell you more about
it. Maybe Rachel will help me. Is there anything you'd like to add,
Rachel?"

"I would like to say that we are glad you are our new teacher,
Miss Richards." Carefully she sat down, spreading her skirt with
her plump hands, her smile angelic.

*Now I'll bet me a quarter her reverend father told her to say
that.* "Thank you, Rachel."

The roll call continued. . . . *Tanya, slight and pinched, with
the toes showing through the very white sneakers, the darned and
faded but clean blue dress, the gentle voice like a tinkling bell, and
the beautiful sensitive face. . . . Boyd and Lloyd, identical in their
starched overalls, and the slightly vacant look. . . . Marjorie Lee,
all of twelve years old, the well-developed body moving restlessly
in the childish dress, the eyes too wise, the voice too high. . . . Joe
Louis, the intelligence in the brilliant black eyes gleaming above
the threadbare clothes. Lives of great men all remind us*—Well, I

have them all . . . Frederick Douglass, Franklin Delano, Abraham Lincoln, Booker T., Joe Louis, George Washington. . . . What a great burden you bear, little people, heirs to all your parents' still-born dreams of greatness. I must not fail you. The last name on the list . . . C. T. Young. Jane paused, small lines creasing her fore-head. She checked the list again.

"C. T., what is your name? I only have your initials on my list."

"Dat's all my name, C. T. Young."

"No, dear, I mean what does C. T. stand for? Is it Charles or Clarence?"

"No'm, jest C. T."

"But I can't put that in my register, dear."

Abruptly Jane rose and went to the next room. Rather timidly she waited to speak to Miss Nelson, the second-grade teacher, who had the formidable record of having taught all of sixteen years. Miss Nelson was large and smiling.

"May I help you, dear?"

"Yes, please. It's about C. T. Young. I believe you had him last year."

"Yes, and the year before that. You'll have him two years too."

"Oh? Well, I was wondering what name you registered him under. All the information I have is C. T. Young."

"That's all there is, honey. Lots of these children only have initials."

"You mean . . . can't something be done about it?"

"What?" Miss Nelson was still smiling, but clearly impatient.

"I . . . well . . . thank you." Jane left quickly.

Back in Room 3 the children were growing restless. Deftly Jane passed out the rating tests and gave instructions. Then she called C. T. to her. He was as small as an eight-year-old, and hungry-looking, with enormous guileless eyes and a beautifully shaped head.

"How many years did you stay in the second grade, C. T.?"

"Two."

"And in the first?"

"Two."

"How old are you?"

" 'Leven."

"When will you be twelve?"

"Nex' month."

And they didn't care . . . nobody ever cared enough about one small boy to give him a name.

"You are a very lucky little boy, C. T. Most people have to take the name somebody gave them whether they like it or not, but you can choose your very own."

"Yeah?" The dark eyes were belligerent. "My father named me C. T. after hisself, Miz Richards, an' dat's my name."

Jane felt unreasonably irritated. "How many children are there in your family, C. T.?"

" 'Leven."

"How many are there younger than you?" she asked.

"Seven."

Very gently, "Did you have your breakfast this morning, dear?"

The small figure in the too-large trousers and the too-small shirt drew itself up to full height. "Yes'm, I had fried chicken, and rice, and coffee, and rolls, and oranges too."

Oh, you poor darling. You poor proud lying darling. Is that what you'd like for breakfast?

She asked, "Do you like school, C. T.?"

"Yes'm," he told her suspiciously.

She leafed through the pile of records. "Your record says you haven't been coming to school very regularly. Why?"

"I dunno."

"Did you ever bring a lunch?"

"No'm, I eats such a big breakfast, I doan git hungry at lunch-time."

"Children need to eat lunch to help them grow tall and strong, C. T. So from now on you'll eat lunch in the lunchroom"—an afterthought: Perhaps it's important to make him think I believe him— "and from now on maybe you'd better not eat such a big breakfast."

Decisively she wrote his name at the top of what she knew to be an already too large list. "Only those in absolute necessity," she had been told by Mr. Johnson, the kindly, harrassed principal. "We'd like to feed them all, so many are underfed, but we just don't have the money." Well, this was absolute necessity if she ever saw it.

"What does your father do, C. T.?"

"He work at dat big factory cross-town, he make plenty money, Miz Richards." The record said "Unemployed."

"Would you like to be named Charles Thomas?"

The expressive eyes darkened, but the voice was quiet. "No'm."

"Very well." Thoughtfully Jane opened the register; she wrote firmly C. T. Young.

October is a witching month in the Southern United States.

The richness of the golds and reds and browns of the trees forms an enchanted filigree through which the lilting voices of children at play seem to float, embodied like so many nymphs of Pan.

Jane had played a fast-and-furious game of tag with her class and now she sat quietly under the gnarled old oak, watching the tireless play, feeling the magic of the sun through the leaves warmly dappling her skin, the soft breeze on the nape of her neck like a lover's hands, and her own drowsy lethargy. Paul, Paul my darling . . . how long for us now? She had worshiped Paul Carlyle since they were freshmen together. On graduation day he had slipped the small circlet of diamonds on her finger. . . . "A teacher's salary is small, Jane. Maybe we'll be lucky enough to get work together, then in a year or so we can be married. Wait for me, darling, wait for me!"

But in a year or so Paul had gone to war, and Jane went out alone to teach. . . . Lansing Creek—one year . . . the leaky roof, the potbellied stove, the water from the well. . . . Maryweather Point—two years . . . the tight-lipped spinster principal with the small, vicious soul. . . . Three hard lonely years and then she had been lucky.

The superintendent had praised her. "You have done good work, Miss—ah—Jane. This year you are to be placed at Centertown High—that is, of course, if you care to accept the position."

Jane had caught her breath. Centertown was the largest and best equipped of all the schools in the county, only ten miles from home and Paul—for Paul had come home, older, quieter, but still Paul. He was teaching now more than a hundred miles away, but they went home every other weekend to their families and each other. . . . "Next summer you'll be Mrs. Paul Carlyle, darling. It's hard for us to be apart so much. I guess we'll have to be for a long time till I can afford to support you. But, sweet, these little tykes need us so badly." He had held her close, rubbing the nape of the neck under the soft curls. "We have a big job, those of us who teach," he had told her, "a never-ending and often thankless job, Jane, to supply the needs of these kids who lack so much." Dear, warm, big, strong, gentle Paul.

They wrote each other long letters, sharing plans and problems. She wrote him about C. T. "I've adopted him, darling. He's so pathetic and so determined to prove that he's not. He learns nothing at all, but I can't let myself believe that he's stupid, so I keep trying."

"Miz Richards, please, ma'am." Tanya's beautiful amber eyes sought hers timidly. Her brown curls were tangled from playing, her cheeks a bright red under the tightly stretched olive skin. The elbows jutted awkwardly out of the sleeves of the limp cotton dress, which could not conceal the finely chiseled bones in their pitiable fleshlessness. As always when she looked at her, Jane thought, What a beautiful child! So unlike the dark, gaunt, morose mother, and the dumpy, pasty-faced father who had visited her that first week. A fairy's changeling. You'll make a lovely angel to grace the throne of God, Tanya! Now what made me think of that?

"Please, ma'am, I'se sick."

Gently Jane drew her down beside her. She felt the parchment skin, noted the unnaturally bright eyes. Oh, dear God, she's burning up! "Do you hurt anywhere, Tanya?"

"My head, ma'am and I'se so tired." Without warning she began to cry.

"How far do you live, Tanya?"

"Two miles."

"You walk to school?"

"Yes'm."

"Do any of your brothers have a bicycle?"

"No'm."

"Rachel!" Bless you for always being there when I need you. "Hurry, dear, to the office and ask Mr. Johnson please to send a big boy with a bicycle to take Tanya home. She's sick."

Rachel ran.

"Hush now, dear, we'll get some cool water, and then you'll be home in a little while. Did you feel sick this morning?"

"Yes'm, but Mot Dear sent me to school anyway. She said I just wanted to play hooky." Keep smiling, Jane. Poor, ambitious, well-meaning parents, made bitter at the seeming futility of dreaming dreams for this lovely child . . . willing her to rise above the drabness of your own meager existence . . . too angry with life to see that what she needs most is your love and care and right now medical attention.

Jane bathed the child's forehead with cool water at the fountain. Do the white schools have a clinic? I must ask Paul. Do they have a lounge or a couch where they can lay one wee sick head? Is there anywhere in this town free medical service for one small child . . . born black?

The boy with the bicycle came. "Take care of her now, ride

slowly and carefully, and take her straight home. . . . Keep the newspaper over your head, Tanya, to keep out the sun, and tell your parents to call the doctor." But she knew they wouldn't because they couldn't.

The next day Jane went to see Tanya.

"She's sho' nuff sick, Miz Richards," the mother said. "She's always been a puny child, but this time she's took real bad, throat's all raw, talk all out her haid las' night. I been using a poultice and some herb brew but she ain't got no better."

"Have you called a doctor, Mrs. Fulton?"

"No'm, we cain't afford it, an' Jake, he doan believe in doctors nohow."

Jane waited till the tide of high bright anger welling in her heart and beating in her brain had subsided. When she spoke her voice was deceptively gentle. "Mrs. Fulton, Tanya is a very sick little girl. She is your only little girl. If you love her, I advise you to have a doctor for her, for if you don't . . . Tanya may die."

The wail that issued from the thin figure seemed to have no part in reality.

Jane spoke hurriedly. "Look, I'm going into town, I'll send a doctor out. Don't worry about paying him. We can see about that later." Impulsively she put her arms around the taut, motionless shoulders. "Don't you worry, honey, it's going to be all right."

There was a kindliness in the doctor's weather-beaten face that warmed Jane's heart, but his voice was brusque. "You sick, girl? Well?"

"No, sir. I'm not sick." What long sequence of events has caused even the best of you to look on even the best of us as menials? "I am a teacher at Centertown High. There's a little girl in my class who is very ill. Her parents are very poor. I came to see if you would please go to see her."

He looked at her, amused.

"Of course I'll pay the bill, Doctor," she added hastily.

"In that case . . . well . . . where does she live?"

Jane told him. "I think it's diphtheria, Doctor."

He raised his eyebrows. "Why?"

Jane sat erect. Don't be afraid, Jane! You're as good a teacher as he is a doctor, and you made an A in that course in childhood diseases. "High fever, restlessness, sore throat, headache, croupy cough, delirium. It could, of course, be tonsillitis or scarlet fever, but that cough—well, I'm only guessing, of course," she finished lamely.

"Humph." The doctor's face was expressionless. "Well, we'll see. Have your other children been inoculated?"

"Yes, sir. Doctor, if the parents ask, please tell them that the school is paying for your services."

This time he was wide-eyed.

The lie haunted her. She spoke to the other teachers about it the next day at recess.

"She's really very sick, maybe you'd like to help?"

Mary Winters, the sixth-grade teacher, was the first to speak. "Richards, I'd like to help, but I've got three kids of my own, and so you see how it is?"

Jane saw.

"Trouble with you, Richards, is you're too emotional." This from Nelson. "When you've taught as many years as I have, my dear, you'll learn not to bang your head against a stone wall. It may sound hardhearted to you, but one just can't worry about one child more or less when one has nearly fifty."

The pain in the back of her eyes grew more insistent. "I can," she said.

"I'll help, Jane," said Marilyn Andrews, breathless, bouncy, newlywed Marilyn.

"Here's two bucks. It's all I've got, but nothing's plenty for me." Her laughter pealed echoing down the hall.

"I've got a dollar, Richards"—this from mousy, severe, little Miss Mitchell—"though I'm not sure I agree with you."

"Why don't you ask the high-school faculty?" said Marilyn. "Better still, take it up in teachers' meeting."

"Mr. Johnson has enough to worry about now," snapped Nelson. Why, she's mad, thought Jane, mad because I'm trying to give a helpless little tyke a chance to live, and because Marilyn and Mitchell helped.

The bell rang. Wordlessly Jane turned away. She watched the children troop in noisily, an ancient nursery rhyme running through her head:

> *Three blind mice,*
> *three blind mice,*
> *See how they run,*
> *see how they run,*
> *They all ran after*
> *the farmer's wife,*
> *She cut off their tails*
> *with a carving knife.*

> *Did you ever see*
>   *such a sight in your life*
> *As three blind mice?*

Only this time it was forty-three mice. Jane giggled. Why, I'm hysterical, she thought in surprise. The mice thought the sweet-smelling farmer's wife might have bread and a wee bit of cheese to offer poor blind mice; but the farmer's wife didn't like poor, hungry, dirty blind mice. So she cut off their tails. Then they couldn't run any more, only wobble. What happened then? Maybe they starved, those that didn't bleed to death. Running round in circles. Running where, little mice?

She talked to the high-school faculty, and Mr. Johnson. All together, she got eight dollars.

The following week she received a letter from the doctor:

Dear Miss Richards:

I am happy to inform you that Tanya is greatly improved, and with careful nursing will be well enough in about eight weeks to return to school. She is very frail, however, and will require special care. I have made three visits to her home. In view of the peculiar circumstances, I am donating my services. The cost of the medicines, however, amounts to the sum of fifteen dollars. I am referring this to you as you requested. What a beautiful child!

Yours sincerely,
Jonathan H. Sinclair, M.D.

P.S. She had diphtheria.

Bless you forever and ever, Jonathan H. Sinclair, M.D. For all your long Southern heritage, "a man's a man for a' that . . . and a' that!"

Her heart was light that night when she wrote to Paul. Later she made plans in the darkness. You'll be well and fat by Christmas, Tanya, and you'll be a lovely angel in my pageant. . . . I must get the children to save pennies. . . . We'll send you milk and oranges and eggs, and we'll make funny little get-well cards to keep you happy.

But by Christmas Tanya was dead!

The voice from the dark figure was quiet, even monotonous. "Jake an' me, we always work so hard, Miz Richards. We didn't neither one have no schooling much when we was married—our folks never had much money, but we was happy. Jake, he tenant farm. I tuk in washing—we plan to save and buy a little house and farm of our own someday. Den the children come. Six boys, Miz Richards—all in a hurry. We both want the boys to finish school, mabbe go to college. We try not to keep them out to work the farm, but sometimes we have to. Then come Tanya. Just like a little yellow rose she was, Miz Richards, all pink and gold . . . and her voice like a silver bell. We think when she grow up an' finish school she take voice lessons—be like Marian Anderson. We think mabbe by then the boys would be old enough to help. I was kinda feared for her when she get sick, but then she start to get better. She was doing so well, Miz Richards. Den it get cold, an' the fire so hard to keep all night long, an' eben the newspapers in the cracks doan keep the win' out, an' I give her all my kivvers; but one night she jest tuk to shivering an' talking all out of her haid—sat right up in bed, she did. She call your name onc't or twice, Miz Richards, then she say, 'Mot Dear, does Jesus love me like Miz Richards say in Sunday school?' I say, 'Yes, honey.' She say, 'Effen I die will I see Jesus?' I say, 'Yes, honey, but you ain't gwine die.' But she did, Miz Richards . . . jest smiled an' laid down—jest smiled an' laid down."

It is terrible to see such hopeless resignation in such tearless eyes. . . . One little mouse stopped running. . . . You'll make a lovely angel to grace the throne of God, Tanya!

Jane did not go to the funeral. Nelson and Rogers sat in the first pew. Everyone on the faculty contributed to a beautiful wreath. Jane preferred not to think about that.

C. T. brought a lovely potted rose to her the next day. "Miz Richards, ma'am, do you think this is pretty enough to go on Tanya's grave?"

"Where did you get it, C. T.?"

"I stole it out Miz Adams's front yard, right out of that li'l glass house she got there. The door was open, Miz Richards, she got plenty, she won't miss this li'l one."

You queer little bundle of truth and lies. What do I do now? Seeing the tears blinking back in the anxious eyes, she said gently, "Yes, C. T., the rose is nearly as beautiful as Tanya is now. She will like that very much."

"You mean she will know I put it there, Miz Richards? She ain't daid at all?"

"Maybe she'll know, C. T. You see, nothing that is beautiful ever dies as long as we remember it."

So you loved Tanya, little mouse? The memory of her beauty is yours to keep now forever and always, my darling. Those things money can't buy. They've all been trying, but your tail isn't off yet, is it, brat? Not by a long shot. Suddenly she laughed aloud.

He looked at her wonderingly. "What you laughing at, Miz Richards?"

"I'm laughing because I'm happy, C. T.," and she hugged him.

Christmas with its pageantry and splendor came and went. Back from the holidays, Jane had an oral English lesson.

"We'll take this period to let you tell about your holidays, children."

On the weekends that Jane stayed in Centertown she visited different churches, and taught in the Sunday schools when she was asked. She had tried to impress on the children the reasons for giving at Christmastime. In class they had talked about things they could make for gifts, and ways they could save money to buy them. Now she stood by the window, listening attentively, reaping the fruits of her labors.

"I got a bicycle and a catcher's mitt."

"We all went to a party and had ice cream and cake."

"I got—"

"I got—"

"I got—"

Score one goose egg for Jane. She was suddenly very tired. "It's your turn, C. T." Dear God, please don't let him lie too much. He tears my heart. The children never laugh. It's funny how polite they are to C. T. even when they know he's lying. Even that day when Boyd and Lloyd told how they had seen him take food out of the garbage cans in front of the restaurant, and he said he was taking it to some poor hungry children, they didn't laugh. Sometimes children have a great deal more insight than grownups.

C. T. was talking. "I didn't get nothin' for Christmas, because Mamma was sick, but I worked all that week before for Mr. Bondel what owns the store on Main Street. I ran errands an' swep' up an' he give me three dollars, and so I bought Mamma a real pretty handkerchief an' a comb, an' I bought my father a tie pin, paid a big ole fifty cents for it too . . . an' I bought my sisters an' brothers some candy an' gum an' I bought me this whistle. Course I got what you give us, Miz Richards" (she had given each a small gift) "an' Mamma's white lady give us a whole crate of oranges, an' Miz Smith what live nex' door give me a pair of socks. Mamma she was so happy she made a cake with eggs an' butter an' everything; an' then we ate it an' had a good time."

Rachel spoke wonderingly. "Didn't Santa Claus bring you anything at all?"

C. T. was the epitome of scorn. "Ain't no Santa Claus," he said and sat down.

Jane quelled the age-old third-grade controversy absently, for her heart was singing. C. T. . . . . C. T., son of my own heart, you are the bright new hope of a doubtful world, and the gay new song of a race unconquered. Of them all—Sarahlene, sole heir to the charming stucco home on the hill, all fitted for gracious living; George, whose father is a contractor; Rachel, the minister's daughter; Angela, who has just inherited ten thousand dollars—of all of them who got, you, my dirty little vagabond, who have never owned a coat in your life, because you say you don't get cold; you, out of your nothing, found something to give, and in the dignity of giving found that it was not so important to receive. . . . Christ Child, look down in blessing on one small child made in Your image and born black!

Jane had problems. Sometimes it was difficult to maintain discipline with forty-two children. Busy as she kept them, there were always some not busy enough. There was the conference with Mr. Johnson.

"Miss Richards, you are doing fine work here, but sometimes your room is a little . . . well—ah—well, to say the least, noisy. You are new here, but we have always maintained a record of having fine discipline here at this school. People have said that it used to be hard to tell whether or not there were children in the building. We have always been proud of that. Now take Miss Nelson. She is an excellent disciplinarian." He smiled. "Maybe if you ask her she will give you her secret. Do not be too proud to accept help from anyone who can give it, Miss Richards."

"No, sir, thank you, sir, I'll do my best to improve, sir." Ah, you dear, well-meaning, shortsighted, round, busy little man. Why are you not more concerned about how much the children have grown and learned in these past four months than you are about how much noise they make? I know Miss Nelson's secret. Spare not the rod and spoil not the child. Is that what you want me to do? Paralyze these kids with fear so that they will be afraid to move? afraid to question? afraid to grow? Why is it so fine for people not to know there are children in the building? Wasn't the building built for children? In her room Jane locked the door against the sound of the playing children, put her head on the desk, and cried.

Jane acceded to tradition and administered one whipping docilely enough, as though used to it; but the sneer in his eyes that had almost gone returned to haunt them. Jane's heart misgave her. From now on I positively refuse to impose my will on any of these poor children by reason of my greater strength. So she had abandoned the rod in favor of any other means she could find. They did not always work.

There was a never-ending drive for funds. Jane had a passion for perfection. Plays, dances, concerts, bazaars, suppers, parties followed one on another in staggering succession.

"Look here, Richards," Nelson told her one day, "it's true that we need a new piano, and that science equipment, but, honey, these drives in a colored school are like the poor: with us always. It doesn't make too much difference if Suzy forgets her lines, or if the ice cream is a little lumpy. Cooperation is fine, but the way you tear into things you won't last long."

"For once in her life Nelson's right, Jane," Elise told her later. "I can understand how intense you are because I used to be like that; but, pet, Negro teachers have always had to work harder than any others and till recently have always got paid less, so for our own health's sake we have to let up wherever possible. Believe me, honey, if you don't learn to take it easy, you're going to get sick."

Jane did. Measles!

"Oh, no," she wailed, "not in my old age!" But she was glad of the rest. Lying in her own bed at home, she realized how very tired she was.

Paul came to see her that weekend and sat by her bed, and read aloud to her the old classic poems they both loved so well. They listened to their favorite radio programs. Paul's presence was warm and comforting. Jane was reluctant to go back to work.

What to do about C. T. was a question that daily loomed larger in Jane's consciousness. Watching Joe Louis's brilliant development was a thing of joy, and Jane was hard pressed to find enough outlets for his amazing abilities. Jeanette Allen was running a close second, and even Booker, so long a problem, was beginning to grasp fundamentals, but C. T. remained static.

"I always stays two years in a grade, Miz Richards," he told her blandly. "I does better the second year.

"I don't keer." His voice had been cheerful. Maybe he really is slow, Jane thought. But one day something happened to make her change her mind.

C. T. was possessed of an unusually strong tendency to protect those he considered to be poor or weak. He took little Johnny Armstrong, who sat beside him in class, under his wing. Johnny was nearsighted and nondescript, his one outstanding feature being his hero-worship of C. T. Johnny was a plodder. Hard as he tried, he made slow progress at best.

The struggle with multiplication tables was a difficult one, in spite of all the little games Jane devised to make them easier for the children. On this particular day there was the uneven hum of little voices trying to memorize. Johnny and C. T. were having a whispered conversation about snakes.

Clearly Jane heard C. T.'s elaboration. "Man, my father caught a moccasin long as that blackboard, I guess, an' I held him while he was live right back of his ugly head—so."

Swiftly Jane crossed the room. "C. T. and Johnny, you are supposed to be learning your tables. The period is nearly up and you haven't even begun to study. Furthermore, in more than five months you haven't even learned the two-times table. Now you will both stay in at the first recess to learn it, and every day after this until you do."

Maybe I should make up some problems about snakes, Jane mused, but they'd be too ridiculous. . . . Two nests of four snakes —Oh, well, I'll see how they do at recess. Her heart smote her at the sight of the two little figures at their desks, listening wistfully to the sound of the children at play, but she busied herself and pretended not to notice them. Then she heard C. T.'s voice:

"Lissen, man, these tables is easy if you really want to learn them. Now see here. Two times one is two. Two times two is four. Two times three is six. If you forgit, all you got to do is add two like she said."

"Sho' nuff, man?"

"Sho'. Say them with me . . . two times one—" Obediently Johnny began to recite. Five minutes later they came to her. "We's ready, Miz Richards."

"Very well. Johnny, you may begin."

"Two times one is two. Two times two is four. Two times three is. . . . Two times three is—"

"Six," prompted C. T.

In sweat and pain, Johnny managed to stumble through the two-times table with C. T.'s help.

"That's very poor, Johnny, but you may go for today. Tomorrow I shall expect you to have it letter perfect. Now it's your turn, C. T."

C. T.'s performance was a fair rival to Joe Louis's. Suspiciously she took him through in random order.

"Two times nine?"

"Eighteen."

"Two times four?"

"Eight."

"Two times seven?"

"Fourteen."

"C. T., you could have done this long ago. Why didn't you?"

"I dunno. . . . May I go to play now, Miz Richards?"

"Yes, C. T. Now learn your three-times table for me tomorrow."

But he didn't, not that day or the day after that or the day after that. . . . Why doesn't he? Is it that he doesn't want to? Maybe if I were as ragged and deprived as he I wouldn't want to learn either.

Jane took C. T. to town and bought him a shirt, a sweater, a pair of dungarees, some underwear, a pair of shoes and a pair of socks. Then she sent him to the barber to get his hair cut. She gave him the money so he could pay for the articles himself and figure up the change. She instructed him to take a bath before putting on his new clothes, and told him not to tell anyone but his parents that she had bought them.

The next morning the class was in a dither.

"You seen C. T.?"

"Oh, boy, ain't he sharp!"

"C. T., where'd you get them new clothes?"

"Oh, man, I can wear new clothes any time I feel like it, but I can't be bothered with being a fancypants all the time like you guys."

C. T. strutted in new confidence, but his work didn't improve.

Spring came in its virginal green gladness and the children chafed for the out-of-doors. Jane took them out as much as possible on nature studies and excursions.

C. T. was growing more and more mischievous, and his influence began to spread throughout the class. Daily his droll wit became more and more edged with impudence. Jane was at her wit's end.

"You let that child get away with too much, Richards," Nelson told her. "What he needs is a good hiding."

One day Jane kept certain of the class in at the first recess to do neglected homework, C. T. among them. She left the room briefly. When she returned C. T. was gone.

"Where is C. T.?" she asked.

"He went out to play, Miz Richards. He said couldn't no ole teacher keep him in when he didn't want to stay."

Out on the playground C. T. was standing in a swing gently swaying to and fro, surrounded by a group of admiring youngsters. He was holding forth.

"I gets tired of stayin' in all the time. She doan pick on nobody but me, an' today I put my foot down. 'From now on,' I say, 'I ain't never goin' to stay in, Miz Richards.' Then I walks out." He was enjoying himself immensely. Then he saw her.

"You will come with me, C. T." She was quite calm except for the telltale veins throbbing in her forehead.

"I ain't comin'." The sudden fright in his eyes was veiled quickly by a nonchalant belligerence. He rocked the swing gently.

She repeated, "Come with me, C. T."

The children watched breathlessly.

"I done told you I ain't comin', Miz Richards." His voice was patient as though explaining to a child. "I ain't . . . comin' . . . a . . . damn . . . tall!"

Jane moved quickly, wrenching the small but surprisingly strong figure from the swing. Then she bore him bodily, kicking and screaming, to the building.

The children relaxed, and began to giggle. "Oh boy! Is he goin' to catch it!" they told one another.

Panting, she held him, still struggling, by the scruff of his collar before the group of teachers gathered in Marilyn's room. "All right, now you tell me what to do with him!" she demanded. "I've tried everything." The tears were close behind her eyes.

"What'd he do?" Nelson asked.

Briefly she told them.

"Have you talked to his parents?"

"Three times I've had conferences with them. They say to beat him."

"That, my friend, is what you ought to do. Now he never

acted like that with me. If you'll let me handle him, I'll show you how to put a brat like that in his place."

"Go ahead," Jane said wearily.

Nelson left the room, and returned with a narrow but sturdy leather thong. "Now, C. T."—she was smiling, tapping the strap in her open left palm—"go to your room and do what Miss Richards told you to."

"I ain't gonna, an' you can't make me." He sat down with absurd dignity at a desk.

Still smiling, Miss Nelson stood over him. The strap descended without warning across the bony shoulders in the thin shirt. The whip became a dancing demon, a thing possessed, bearing no relation to the hand that held it. The shrieks grew louder. Jane closed her eyes against the blurred fury of a singing lash, a small boy's terror and a smiling face.

Miss Nelson was not tired. "Well, C. T.?"

"I won't, Yer can kill me but I won't!"

The sounds began again. Red welts began to show across the small arms and through the clinging sweat-drenched shirt.

"Now will you go to your room?"

Sobbing and conquered, C. T. went. The seated children stared curiously at the little procession. Jane dismissed them.

In his seat C. T. found pencil and paper.

"What's he supposed to do, Richards?" Jane told her.

"All right, now write!"

C. T. stared at Nelson through swollen lids, a curious smile curving his lips. Jane knew suddenly that come hell or high water, C. T. would not write. I mustn't interfere. Please, God, don't let her hurt him too badly. Where have I failed so miserably? . . . Forgive us our trespasses. The singing whip and the shrieks became a symphony from hell. Suddenly Jane hated the smiling face with an almost unbearable hatred. She spoke, her voice like cold steel.

"That's enough, Nelson."

The noise stopped.

"He's in no condition to write now anyway."

C. T. stood up. "I hate you. I hate you all. You're mean and I hate you." Then he ran. No one followed him. Run, little mouse! They avoided each other's eyes.

"Well, there you are," Nelson said as she walked away. Jane never found out what she meant by that.

The next day C. T. did not come to school. The day after that he brought Jane the fatal homework, neatly and painstakingly done, and a bunch of wild flowers. Before the bell rang, the children surrounded him. He was beaming.

"Did you tell yer folks you got a whipping, C. T.?"

"Naw! I'd 'a' only got another."

"Where were you yesterday?"

"Went fishin'. Caught me six cats long as your haid, Sambo."

Jane buried her face in the sweet-smelling flowers. Oh, my brat, my wonderful resilient brat. They'll never get your tail, will they?

It was seven weeks till the end of term, when C. T. brought Jane a model wooden boat.

Jane stared at it. "Did you make this? It's beautiful, C. T."

"Oh, I make them all the time . . . an' airplanes an' houses too. I do 'em in my spare time," he finished airily.

"Where do you get the models, C. T.?" she asked.

"I copies them from pictures in the magazine."

Right under my nose . . . right there all the time, she thought wonderingly. "C. T., would you like to build things when you grow up? Real houses and ships and planes?"

"Reckon I could, Miz Richards," he said confidently.

The excitement was growing in her.

"Look, C. T. You aren't going to do any lessons at all for the rest of the year. You're going to build ships and houses and airplanes and anything else you want to."

"I am huh?" He grinned. "Well, I guess I wasn't goin' to get promoted nohow."

"Of course if you want to build them the way they really are, you might have to do a little measuring, and maybe learn to spell the names of the parts you want to order. All the best contractors have to know things like that, you know."

"Say, I'm gonna have real fun, huh? I always said lessons wussent no good nohow. Pop say too much study eats out yer brains anyway."

The days went by. Jane ran a race with time. The instructions from the model companies arrived. Jane burned the midnight oil planning each day's work.

Learn to spell the following words: ship, sail, steamer—boat, anchor, airplane wing, fly.

Write a letter to the lumber company, ordering some lumber.

The floor of our model house is ten inches long. Multiply the length by the width and you'll find the area of the floor in square inches.

Read the story of Columbus and his voyages.

Our plane arrives in Paris in twenty-eight hours. Paris is the capital city of a country named France across the Atlantic Ocean.

Long ago sailors told time by the sun and the stars. Now, the earth goes around the sun—

Work and pray, Jane, work and pray!

C. T. learned. Some things vicariously, some things directly. When he found that he needed multiplication to plan his models to scale, he learned to multiply. In three weeks he had mastered simple division.

Jane bought beautifully illustrated stories about ships and planes. He learned to read.

He wrote for and received his own materials.

Jane exulted.

The last day! Forty-two faces waiting anxiously for report cards. Jane spoke to them briefly, praising them collectively, and admonishing them to obey the safety rules during the holidays. Then she passed out the report cards.

As she smiled at each childish face, she thought, I've been wrong. The long arm of circumstance, environment and heredity is the farmer's wife that seeks to mow you down, and all of us who touch your lives are in some way responsible for how successful she is. But you aren't mice, my darlings. Mice are hated, hunted pests. You are normal, lovable children. The knife of the farmer's wife is double-edged for you, because you are Negro children, born mostly in poverty. But you are wonderful children, nevertheless, for you wear the bright protective cloak of laughter, the strong shield of courage, and the intelligence of children everywhere. Some few of you may indeed become as the mice—but most of you shall find your way to stand fine and tall in the annals of man. There's a bright new tomorrow ahead. For every one of us whose job it is to help you grow that is insensitive and unworthy, there are hundreds who daily work that you may grow straight and whole. If it were not so, our world could not long endure.

She handed C. T. his card.

"Thank you, ma'm."

"Aren't you going to open it?"

He opened it dutifully. When he looked up his eyes were wide with disbelief. "You didn't make no mistake?"

"No mistake, C. T. You're promoted. You've caught up enough to go to the fourth grade next year."

She dismissed the children. They were a swarm of bees released from a hive. "'By, Miss Richards." . . . "Happy holidays, Miss Richards."

C. T. was the last to go.

"Well, C. T.?"

"Miz Richards, you remember what you said about a name being important?"

"Yes, C. T."

"Well, I talked to Mamma, and she said if I wanted a name it would be all right, and she'd go to the courthouse about it."

"What name have you chosen, C. T.?" she asked.

"Christopher Turner Young."

"That's a nice name, Christopher," she said gravely.

"Sho' nuff, Miz Richards?"

"Sure enough, C. T."

"Miz Richards, you know what?"

"What, dear?"

"I love you."

She kissed him swiftly before he ran to catch his classmates.

She stood at the window and watched the running, skipping figures, followed by the bold mimic shadows. I'm coming home, Paul. I'm leaving my forty-two children, and Tanya there on the hill. My work with them is finished now. The laughter bubbled up in her throat. But Paul, oh Paul. See how straight they run!

Short Story
Focus - not as much.

One Summer

MARY LAVIN

*"One Summer" presents the transformation of a woman into a
spinster and explores on several levels the irony of that fate.
Vera's attachment to her father is a crippling dependency that
deprives her of any identity except as his daughter. As a result of
an incident in her childhood, Vera believes her only value lies in
the fact that her father values her. Although Alan offers a chance
for real fulfillment, she lacks both the confidence and the will to
free herself for him. Her father's hostility toward Alan is a
terrible source of conflict for Vera. Is her father motivated only
by a jealous desire to prevent her marriage? Is Alan justified in
delivering an ultimatum to Vera? Why is her decision to remain
at home inevitable? How does Vera's relationship with her father
change during his fatal illness, and how does Rita effect that
change? What is the function of the friendship between Rita and
Lily, the maid? What is the bitter irony of her father's dying words?*

Australia image

Above the wind and the rain Vera called her goodbyes to him
again from the pier edge, as the steel hawsers splashed back into
the water and the ship eased out from the North Wall. If there was
an answering message, she did not hear it in a blast from the fun-
nel. And in the mist she was not, in fact, certain that the figure to
whom she waved was Alan. A few minutes later and there was no
distinguishing anything. Only the portholes shone. Even then she
did not leave the pier. She sat in the car till the last speck of light
was quenched in waves of darkness.

It was late when she reached home. When she got out to open
the field gate, she could see through the trees that the light was

ONE SUMMER From *The New Yorker*, September 11, 1965. Reprinted by permission; © 1965 The New Yorker Magazine, Inc.

out in her father's room. A light burned in the maid's room, but as the car swept up to the front steps this light was put out. Lily in all likelihood thought that she'd been jilted. Vera sighed. Cramped, cold, and worn out, she went to her room. In a few minutes, she was in a dead sleep. Was it any wonder she heard nothing during the night? It was getting on for morning when Lily ran in and shook her awake. An awful moaning was coming from her father's room.

"God, Miss, I think he's dying!"

"Stop it!" Vera said sharply. Yet her mind fastened on the girl's hysterical words. If they were true, how badly she'd been served by time! Alan was no farther than Liverpool. It would be hours yet before he boarded the Orcades.

Her father moaned again. Shamed by her thoughts, she sprang up and ran across the landing. "Oh, Father, what's wrong?" she cried.

But from the door she could tell by a strange strength in his stare that he could not speak. Those glaring eyes seemed all of him alive. Spread-eagled on the bed, as if flung from a great height, he lay inert. Then the pain caught him up again and he was once more gathered into a living mass. Putting her arms under him, she tried to drag him to a sitting position, but he gave her such a bitter look she let him fall back. Oh, why had she gone defiantly to bed without going in to him! He might have been lying awake in the dark, as miserable as herself. "Don't be angry with me, Father!" she cried. As if she were at fault, not him! Then she turned on Lily. "Stop that nonsense," she said, "and go for the doctor."

Lily was frantically running around, filling hot-water bottles and forcing brandy between his lips. She had lights burning everywhere. Even out in the yard a light streamed unnaturally into the fields of dawn. "Oh, Miss, I hate to leave him," she said. "Wouldn't you go? You'd be no time going in the car!"

But Vera shook her head. It wasn't to have him die without her that she'd given up Alan. So Lily pedaled off in the grayness and the wet.

Standing back out of range of her father's angry eyes, Vera stared helplessly at him. The first onslaught of pain was over and he lay in a sheet of sweat. Yet it seemed an age until the doctor's car came up the drive, with Lily sitting up importantly beside the old man on the front seat, her bike strapped to the back. Vera ran down to meet them.

"Sounds like a blockage," the old doctor said as he got out of the car. "Don't worry. We'll do all we can!"

Indeed, his presence had helped already, and as they went in to her father he managed a few words. "What's wrong with me, Doctor?" he whispered.

The doctor turned down the bedclothes. "Tell me, have you been dosing yourself?" he demanded.

Vera went limp with relief. So it was that! As long as she could remember, he was always dosing himself. "Cleans you out!" he'd say when she protested, and defiantly he'd pour himself another spoon of the concoction of cascara and treacle that he called blackjack. Turning eagerly, she was about to tell the doctor when a look from her father silenced her.

But Lily spoke up. "I told him he'd blast the insides out of himself, Doctor, but he wouldn't heed me."

The doctor nodded gloomily.

"It was that made him throw up, too!" the girl said.

"When was that?" Vera asked sharply.

"He was always at it." The girl spoke as if she felt doubted. "You could hear him all over the house." She shuddered.

Vera put her hands to her face.

"That's enough!" the doctor said to Lily. He turned to Vera. "I'll give him something to ease him," he said, in a low voice, "but I'm afraid it's a blockage all right. We'll have to get him away to Dublin." He patted her shoulder. "Don't worry, we'll do our best," he said kindly, but later, when they were going downstairs, he looked more keenly at her. "You should get some sleep," he said. "You look exhausted. Let the girl sit up with him for what's left of the night."

"Oh, but she must be jaded," Vera said.

"What matter—she's young!" said the doctor.

Through the great high window on the landing, they could see the doctor's battered car looming indistinctly in the morning mist, and as they went out onto the glittering granite steps Lily came toward them, half wheeling, half carrying the bicycle. Like the gravel under her feet, her cheeks were freshened and brightened by the damp. The stress of the night had left no mark on her.

"What did I tell you?" the doctor cried, his own eyes brightening. "This one doesn't need any sleep! She's fitter far than you to stay up!"

Intermittently through the past hours, Vera's mind had guiltily traveled after Alan. At one minute, she thought yes, she would write to him. At the next, she thought no. It was like the moments she stood on the dark pier and watched the light of the ship that carried him away from her; it came and went several times in the sea mist before she knew finally that it was engulfed. Now, in the cold air of dawn, she came to a decision. "I can't lie down, Doctor," she said firmly. "I have an important letter to write."

The doctor looked oddly at her. "Well, we all have our own anodyne," he said, and he got into the car. "I'll call later, when I've got in touch with the hospital. Don't be blaming yourself! He must already have had some discomfort to go taking those doses."

To satisfy him, she nodded her head. But all he knew about was the blackjack and the retching. What about the black moods of the past year, and the black looks, and the fits of black, black silence? Was her father not already then gravely ill? Filled with remorse, she ran upstairs.

He was lying as they left him. He was staring up at the ceiling. "Do I have to go to hospital?" he asked.

Had he heard what the doctor said? Or was he only trying to find out? "Are you frightened, Father?" she asked him.

"No!" he said decisively. "As long as it's not what I dreaded."

She knew, of course, what he feared. But that was all she knew. The word blockage—so familiar, so domestic a word—had up to that moment almost reassured her. But was it, in fact, a euphemism for his fear? She grew rigid with resolve. If so, he must not know—ever! Then, at the thought that she might not have been there to protect him, her breath caught. Others would have cared for him and been kind—Lily had already shown amazing tenderness—but who except her would protect him from a word? It was little things like this that Alan would never understand.

Her face must have given her thoughts away, because the glare had appeared again in her father's eyes. "When is that fellow going?" he asked.

Was it possible he did not know? "But he's gone, Father!" She was so eager to reassure him she made it sound as if Alan's going was something joyous. "That's where I was last night—seeing him off at the boat!"

If he was relieved, he was too clever to show it. Instead, he shifted his position. "I knew he was no good," he said.

Sick as he was, she could not stand for that. "You know why he went!" she cried. And she had the satisfaction of seeing his eyes falter.

"I shouldn't have said that," he said, humbly enough. "You've been a good daughter to me, Vera—always." Their eyes met then, and met with love. "You won't regret it," he said.

And immediately her heart filled up with feeling for him until, as when she was a child, it was deep with love. Reaching out, she put her hand on his, and weakly he raised his other hand, placing it over hers again. It reminded her of a game they used to play when she was a child. "Do you remember, Father? 'Hot hands'?"

He nodded, and tears came to his eyes. But they were happy tears, and after a few minutes his lids closed as if he might sleep. Gently, she drew her hand away.

What miracles of love he had performed when she was little. He made it seem that to be motherless was to be privileged. When he called for her after school, his spare male figure stood out among the floppy mothers and set her, too, apart. A plain child, his love gave her sparkle. But as the years went by, his care and caution were sometimes excessive and set too high a price upon her company. Oftener and oftener, her classmates left her out of their pranks and their larking. Then, if her father found out, he'd spring up with his black eyes flashing. "Never mind," he'd cry. "I'll take you!"

There was one winter when the lake behind the schoolhouse froze and a sliding party was hastily organized. As usual, she was not included, but he saw the others going past, and, as usual, he sprang up as if to a challenge. "We'll show them!" he cried. "Wait!" And he dashed upstairs to an old leather chest that stood, always locked, on the landing. She'd never seen it opened. Its depths were as unknown to her as his life before she'd been born into it. But she was hardly surprised when he drew out an ancient pair of skates. Within a minute, it seemed, they were at the lakeside, where they found her classmates gathered, timidly trying out the ice. Running a little way out across it and holding up one foot, they slid along as far as their own momentum carried them. Her father pushed his way to the edge of the ice, put on the skates, and, with a laugh, sped away like a bird. Out into the middle of the lake he went, and for the next few minutes he held all eyes with the capers he cut. Then, taking wing again, he was suddenly back on the shore. "Get down on your hunkers," he ordered her, and, bending, he tied her feet together with her own shoelaces. Then he took a piece of rope from his pocket and tied one end around her middle and the other around his own. In the blink of an eye, he was flying over the ice again—only this time it was on her all eyes were centered, as she swayed to and fro behind him, in a kind of splendid redundance, like a tassel on the end of a gorgeous cord, or the tuft on the tail of a lion.

The next day, the lake cracked like glass and everyone said they could have been killed—both of them. Her father only laughed. "What matter!" he said. "We'd have gone together!"

She stared in amazement. Ordinarily, he was obsessed for her safety. In the evenings, after he'd heard her tables and her catechism, he used to put her through a catechism of his own:

"What would you do if you were chased by a bull?"

"Take off my coat and throw it over his horns."

"If your clothes took fire?"

"Roll on the ground."

"If you were caught in a thunderstorm?"

"Lie flat."

"If you got lost?"

"Stand still in one spot."

His litany, however, could not make provision for everything. Once, she nearly broke her neck. She was climbing on the roof of a shed when her foot slipped. Except that he was in the yard and quick enough to reach out and catch her, she would have been killed. It was the first time she saw him fly into a rage. Marching her ahead of him into the house and up the stairs to the landing, he once more opened the leather chest. This time he took out a small revolver wrapped in a length of black calico. "Do you see this?" he asked. "Well, if anything happened to you, do you want to know what I'd do?" He put the barrel to his head and pulled the trigger. The sound of the empty clack was the most terrifying sound she had ever heard.

But he'd gone too far. He had shown her more than her value; he had shown her where it lay—in his own eyes. From that hour, her confidence diminished. Shy and distant always, she became more so. And when she was of an age to go to dances, she got very few invitations. Even then, her father was full of eagerness to escort her himself. "It's a good thing your old father can still pick up his heels," he'd say. But one day she found him appraising her. "You'd have been better-looking if you'd taken after your mother," he said. "But don't mind. You may be better off in the long run. I'd never have got anywhere if I hadn't learned to stand alone!"

It was the first time he had ever mentioned her mother, and

she was so surprised she didn't at once take in the fact that he was speaking of her single state as if it were final. She was only twenty-three or twenty-four at the time. And he made similar remarks over the years. "What will you do when I'm taken from you?" he asked shortly after her thirtieth birthday, but they laughed at the thought of a thing so remote. He threw back his head. "Nature takes care of everything!" he cried. "Let's hope you'll have me as long as you need me."

Ironically, it was that year she met Alan. They met in a public library in Dublin. She'd already seen him a few times when one day they arrived together at the library door shortly before it was opened. "I've seen you before," he said. "I always notice people who are alone. I find myself wondering if, like myself, they dislike their fellow-men." She laughed, but he reproved her. "I'm serious," he said. "I hate the common herd."

After that, whenever they met they exchanged a few words, and if they were leaving at the same time he saw her to her car. Once or twice when she hadn't the car, he walked to the bus with her. He was a solicitor, attached to an office in Dublin. He was interested to learn that she lived in the country. "I should have known," he said. "It accounts for a certain distinction about you."

It seemed a great compliment. Another day, he said something still more preposterously flattering. "If I were not so set against marriage," he said, "you're the girl I'd marry."

It was like a declaration! Her happiness was so blinding she hardly cared that when she told her father, his response was—to say the least of it—tepid. "Wait till you meet him, Father," she said.

The meeting was a failure. Her father even made bones about giving her the car to meet the bus at Ross Cross. He turned on her savagely when she asked for the keys. "Why hasn't he got a car of his own?" he said. "He must be a poor kind of solicitor!"

"There's no need of a car in a city practice, Father," she said, trying to bolster things up.

Her father looked up at the sky. "Can't he walk, then?" he asked. "It's a nice fine day. Is there something the matter with him?" But he threw the car keys to her.

"Be nice to him, Father, For my sake!" she pleaded before she drove away.

And when they arrived back, he was civil enough. The trouble was that Alan didn't take to *him!* And her father saw that. "I can see why you needed the car," he muttered. "He's a delicate-looking article."

"Oh, what a cruel thing to say!" she cried. "About a stranger, too!"

His eyes bored into her. "If you take my advice, you'll keep him that way. I'd pity the woman that'll marry him. He'll die young and leave her with a houseful of brats."

"Don't worry, Father," she said bitterly. "After today, I don't expect I'll see him again."

But she did—more often. Alan came down again and again, doggedly ignoring her father's rudeness. "Don't think I'm thick-skinned, though, Vera," he said one afternoon, "but I will not let him—or anyone—interfere in my life." It was another of the oblique remarks that she took to presage happiness.

But obliquity was catching. Her father, too, seemed to become obscure. He spoke again about her mother. "If she hadn't married me, she might be alive today!" he said morosely.

He'd never told her the cause of her mother's death, but she knew it had happened shortly after her own birth and was probably connected with it. Aware of a strong undertow in the conversation, she picked her words with care, "She made her own choice, didn't she?"

"Don't talk like a fool," he said.

At that she lost her temper. "Oh, what's the matter, Father?" she cried. "Do you want to stop me marrying?"

He evaded her eyes. "I don't see any signs of that happening," he said. "That fellow is no more bent on marriage than I am!"

"Is it Alan?" His words stupefied her.

"Has he asked you to marry him?" he demanded.

She stared. If never explicit of proposal, *all* Alan's words had seemed to hold promise. They could not have been uttered by any man who did not feel himself deeply committed! Yet on them, in one instant, a huge doubt was cast.

"Well?" her father insisted. "Has he?"

"I don't see why I should tell you," she said, trembling to think of the anger her words would provoke. "It's my own business." When he said nothing at all and she was at last compelled to look at him, however, she saw with a shock that the rage in his eyes was a rage of pity.

And suddenly she realized his dilemma. For the first time, he'd come up against something he could not get for her—something that, if it was to be got at all, could be got only by herself. "Don't worry, Father," she said. "It'll work out all right in the end. You'll see."

From that day, there was a change in his attitude. "Is that fellow worried about money, do you think?" he asked once. "I never see his name in the papers. He mustn't do much court work. Of course," he said meditatively, "small court cases don't pay well —it's sales and leaseholds that pay. Conveyances! That's what the big solicitors make their money on." It was almost comical to see the interest he began to take in the legal column of the newspapers. "How much commission do you think he'd get on the sale of a good farm—say, a farm about this size?" he asked one day.

Unnerved by his question, she answered coldly. "Why? Are you going to sell?"

"No," he said, "but I might buy. And if I did, I could give that fellow the carriage of sale!"

Her heart softened. "Oh, Father, you don't want any more responsibility at your age!"

"Land is a safe investment at any time," he said soberly.

"Tell me," he said affably to Alan the next time they saw him, "are you any judge of land? There's an outfarm at Ross Cross that I was thinking of buying."

"But haven't you enough land, sir?" Alan said, and it seemed to Vera that he looked questioningly at them both.

Her father noticed nothing. "It's not a big farm, mind you," he said. "It's only forty acres. It mightn't be worth your while having anything to do with it."

"Oh, well, one must creep before one walks," Alan said quietly. "I'll be glad to act for you, sir." He'd got the point!

"Well said!" her father cried, slapping his thigh in delight. His good humor was doubled. "Come down one day next week and we'll walk the land." Behind Alan's back, he winked at Vera.

When the day came for them to look at the land, though, her father was moody and irritable. "This fellow can't have much to do if he can waste a whole day coming down here," he said as they drove to the bus.

"He's coming down on business, isn't he?" she cried hotly.

"He'd want to be hard up to call this business! It's not much wonder he hasn't a car!"

She let the taunt pass, because she had just been thinking that if Alan did have a car they could live down here and be near her father. Would that be at the back of her father's mind, too? Then she saw the bus coming down the hill. "Here it is!" she cried, tumbling out of the car. She could see Alan standing out on the step, and she ran to meet him.

But Alan was not looking at her. "Where's your father?" he asked.

She turned around. Her father was still sitting in the car—black and silent, looking twice his bulk. "There's something wrong!" she cried, and she ran back. Meeting the bus was a pastime with her father. Always early, he'd prance up and down the road, fairly dancing with impatience, denouncing the bus for late! At no time else did one get such a sense of his leashed energy.

"Oh, hurry, Alan!" she cried. But before they reached him he'd got stiffly out. And on the road he looked more normal, except that there was something unpleasant in the way he dispensed with a greeting. He trudged up the side road till they came to a lane, into which he turned without a word.

Looking doubtfully at each other, Vera and Alan followed. The lane was long. As they walked, Alan chatted casually about the weather and the countryside. Her father's black mood appeared to be lifting. Then, as they were about to climb over the locked gate that led into the farm, his face darkened again and he pointed to Alan's feet. "What kind of shoes are those for going through fields?" he demanded.

Alan said nothing. He just got over the gate and plunged into the long grass in his fine shoes.

After a short pause, her father, too, got over the gate. But on the other side he immediately turned up the collar of his coat and shoved his hands into his pockets as if to imply that he had little interest in what was going on. When they were scarcely halfway across the first field, he came to a stand. "Well? What do you think of it?" he asked, turning to Alan.

"I haven't seen enough of it to form any opinion," Alan said coldly.

He began to walk on, but her father didn't stir. "I have!" he said. "It doesn't take *me* long to make up my mind!"

"What are we to understand by that?" Alan asked. "That it's good? Or that it's bad?"

"There's no such thing as bad land hereabouts," her father said. "There are other things to be considered, though," he added.

Miserably, Vera looked from one of them to the other. She could not bear the strain of waiting for Alan to speak. "There's no house on it, for one thing!" she said, not caring if she blundered.

Both men stared at her—her father with a glance that applauded, Alan with one she could not read. "Does that matter?" Alan asked. It was to her father he spoke, not her. "What is the need for a house on an outfarm?" His voice was so disengaged that Vera shivered.

Her father turned on his heel and walked away.

An appalling feeling of humiliation came over Vera. She would have stumbled after her father if Alan had not laid his hand on her arm. "Let me handle this, Vera," he said crisply. "I told you I must do things in my own way, not in his." But the expression on his face as he looked after her father was one of compassion. "I'm sorry for him," he said. "I know how he feels." He turned back to her. "But there are times when a man must put himself first. Will I be able to make *you* see that, though?"

She was too worried to extract any sweetness from what his question implied. "We must be kind to him, Alan," she said.

He nodded. "I suppose there's no use in us all being unhappy," he said.

Her father had reached the gate and climbed over it. "Is he going to go off without us?" she cried.

"Let him if he likes," Alan said. "We can walk. Sooner or later, we'll have to talk things out!"

"Oh, later then—later!" she said, and she ran after her father, but the coarse grass entangled her feet like seaweed and impeded her at every step.

The drive home was accomplished in heavy silence. And at the house things were no better. Her father seemed unable to stay in the same room with them. He kept going in and out. And when Lily put a meal on the table, he stood up from it three or four times and went out without explanation or apology. His absence was as oppressive as his presence.

Vera could not keep her mind on anything Alan said.

"I'd better go back on an early bus, I think," Alan said at last, and miserably she agreed it might be best.

"I'll drive you to the Cross," she said.

"Don't bother, Vera," he said. "I'd prefer to walk. It's a lovely evening anyway. Why don't you come with me? Take your bike. I'll wheel it along, and you can cycle back."

It was only March and early in the month, but the daffodils were out on either side of the drive. As they walked by them, the massed flower heads shone like a lake of light. "Who planted them?" Alan asked idly.

"My mother—I think," said Vera.

Alan turned. "You think?"

"He never mentions her, you know. Someone else told me." They walked on. "It must be strange to know nothing about her. Do you imagine they got on well?"

Vera shrugged. But they both stopped and looked back.

"She must have had a great feeling for flowers, anyway," Alan said. "I never saw so many daffodils."

"Oh, I daresay they've spread a lot since they were put down," Vera said. Her mind was not on them, but Alan still stood looking at them meditatively. They'd spread into the pastures, indeed, where many of them were trampled and broken by the cattle, and far off, in the very middle of the field, there were a few stragglers. Like convent girls in a convent park, these stragglers wandered two by two.

"I suppose you love this place," he said.

"Wouldn't anyone?" she cried.

"I suppose so," he said reluctantly. Then, just as they came to the big gates, he exclaimed, "Now, *there's* a marvelous sight! Look!" He pointed westward to where, clear of the trees, the sky burned like a sea of flame. "Do you know what I like about that? I like it because it's the same the world over. It belongs to everyone—and to no one!" ~~Sunset positive - Ukra sunset death~~

But she wasn't listening. "Oh, did you see?" she cried. As they started upward, a late-returning bird had flown between them and the sky, and for an instant, pierced by the flaming rays, all but its core was burned away, utterly consumed.

He'd seen it. "Wasn't it extraordinary?" he said. "Like a glass bird. You could see right through it. Wings, feathers—all gone."

"All but its heart," Vera said softly.

For a minute, he only stared at her. "Oh, Vera," he said then, and, bending, he kissed her. "I wanted to do that ever since we were out in the fields. And I wanted to say something, only I felt your father was listening, even when he was out of the room. Listening to our thoughts! He doesn't want any more land—I know what he had in mind!" But when her face reddened, he caught her to him. "I'm not blaming him, Vera. But I can't stand him meddling. If we are to get married, it must be on my terms and no one else's." He paused. "Not even yours! It's bad enough that I can't do without you!"

"Oh, Alan!" she cried. The grudging way he said it did not take one whit from her joy.

But he was intent on making his meaning clear. "Some men want to marry," he said. "They're only waiting to meet the right woman. But there are others—like me—who hate the thought of it. They are forced into it by meeting a woman they cannot live without."

"Do you really feel that way about me, Alan?" she asked timidly.

"Yes," he said. "But I can't share you. It's me or him. Oh, Vera, can't you see our situation? You've let him become so engrossed in you that his whole life has gone. Not that I care about him! But I can't stand by and see you consumed, too."

"Oh, Alan, you're exaggerating," she said. But she didn't know whom she was defending, herself or her father. "What can I do?" she asked helplessly.

"You can come away with me," he said peremptorily. "In fact, that's what we've got to do—for a few years, anyway."

"You know I can't do that!" she cried. "And where would we go?"

His face darkened. "I knew that would be your attitude. Well, let me tell you something. I am going anyway, to Australia—with or without you."

For a minute, her mind blurred. "When?"

"This summer!"

"Well, we can't discuss it now." Her voice was weary.

"Why not?"

She felt cornered. "There are so many things to be considered," she said vaguely.

"The trouble with you is that you've lost all sense of your identity," he said. "Both of you. Do you know what I think? If it weren't for you hanging around his neck all the time, he might have married again. He might do so yet if you'd get out of the way! There's more to life than seeing one generation into the world or another out of it! I bet if you left him he'd be married within a year. Oh, Vera! Can't you see that without you he might begin to live again?"

It was such an entirely new prospect that opened before her, her head reeled. "What if he got ill?"

"Is it *that* man? He's as fit as an ox. He might see us both down

Sickness
extended in *euphor*
194 *Success and Failure* *parallel*

yet!" Then, as they heard the sound of the bus, he took her arm and shook her. "Think it over," he said.

Oh, how quick upon his heels the irony of that last conversation was brought home! "As fit as an ox." The words were hardly bearable now, Alan should not be left in ignorance of what had happened—it would not be fair to her father. It was, however, several days before Vera got a chance to write her letter. And when at last she began it, the top of the page bore the address of a Dublin hospital.

Dear Alan:

 I write to tell you that my father is ill. Oh, Alan, he is very, very ill—so bad, indeed, that I might have written to tell you, knowing you would be sad for him, apart from any consideration of how his illness might affect us. It was on the very night you sailed the pain first struck him. I feel sure that, like me, you will think that very strange. And I hope you will think that fact a sufficient reason for my writing. Anyway, I cannot believe that you meant us to drop completely out of each other's existence. Do you realize that I do not even know in what part of Australia you intend to settle? And that if I do not post this letter in time to reach you at Gibraltar or Aden, I may quite literally lose sight of you forever?

 To return to Father, it now appears that he must have been ailing for some time—all winter, perhaps. I can't help an ache at my heart when I think that if we had had more patience matters might now be very different for us. Not that I am blaming you, dear, or thinking that you should not have gone, for although there can be no mistaking that Father's ailment is fatal, nevertheless his illness may be long and painfully drawn out. Poor, poor Father. I suppose in a way my reaction to your going has been altered by these new circumstances. Perhaps now you can see there was something to be said for my remaining behind. In spite of all the happiness I have forfeited, I am glad—oh, so glad—that I, too, am not at this moment thousands of miles away. You will hardly believe me, Alan, but, all things considered, I can almost say I am happy. Our parting no longer seems so senseless as it did the night you left.

 I am, of course, doing everything I can for him, but the fact is that very little can be done. He is to have a small exploratory operation, but the disease may well be too advanced for much to be done. At his age, an operation is always a risk, but the doctors see no reason for thinking he will not get through it. His heart, they say, is as strong as the heart of a young man.

I should tell you that I do not really expect a reply, although I am nearly miserable enough to crave any crumb of comfort! Quite frankly, at times I cannot believe you are really gone. I will leave it to you, dear.

VERA

P.S. I did not stick down the envelope when I realized in how short a time I would have the surgeon's opinion. Things are as I feared. It is now only a question of time. However, there is a further operation advised, not so much in the hope of prolonging his life as of making what is left of it more comfortable. I have given my consent. After that, we will be going home—by ambulance, of course. You can imagine how I hate breaking that news to him. We will have to bring back a nurse, too—which is another thing he will resent. But I will do my best to get a pleasant and agreeable girl. Thank God I am here. But oh, Alan, it would give me some solace to think that at last you may see my point? Perhaps I will expect a line from you after all—just a line. And although I don't suppose your letter will in any way alter anything in our situation, I cannot for all that hide the eagerness with which I will look for it.

V

The second operation was successful only in that the patient got over it. The pain was bought off, but at the price of new discomfort.

"I didn't realize he'd be so helpless," Vera said to the nurse as they waited for the ambulance that was to take them home. "He'll hate being carried down on a stretcher."

"He's a lucky man it's not in his coffin," the nurse said practically.

Vera stared at her. She had not, in the end, been able to pick and choose her nurse. She had to take the first one that came to hand. Indeed, she had hardly glanced at her in the hospital, and even when they got into the ambulance she was only aware of how much room the creature took up; she was the big, hefty sort, who sat firmly planted down, with her feet apart. Her face wasn't bad, although her skin was thick and the big brown eyes seemed lacking in expression. But there was one point in her favor—the sick man had taken to her.

"What is your first name, Nurse?" he asked.

And when she said it was Rita, he started to call her that. It was extremely distasteful to Vera.

The ambulance had to go very slow, and the journey seemed as if it would never end. "Is it far more?" the nurse kept asking. And once, when they went over a hump in the road, she snapped at Vera, "You shouldn't have moved him!"

"We're nearly there, Nurse," Vera said, ignoring the criticism.

The nurse shrugged. "I wouldn't answer for him if there's another jolt like that!"

"Mind would he hear you!" Vera whispered, and at the next lurch she said fiercely, "I'd rather he'd die on the way home than in a hospital, anyway!" Over the patient's head, their eyes met hostilely.

When at last they got home, however, and Lily came flying down the steps, all warmth and good will, the nurse brightened considerably.

"Upsy-daisy!" Lily cried, as the stretcher listed and tilted on its way up the stairs. And what might have been an ordeal was made to seem almost a lark.

"She'd make a great ward maid," Rita said, looking after her when the patient was finally settled in his bed. "Had she any previous experience of nursing, I wonder?"

"None whatever!" Vera cried, disclaiming the compliment to Lily as if it had been paid to her, and, feeling that the occasion asked for an answering zest, she called after Lily, who was going down to make a cup of tea, "Put two extra cups on the tray, Lily! We'll all have some."

But the nurse hurried out. "Put mine on a separate tray, please," she countermanded. And she turned to Vera. "Our regulations strictly forbid us to eat in the sickroom. I'd advise you not to do so, either."

Vera reddened with annoyance. "Just one cup extra, so, Lily," she said.

The sad thing was that her father didn't seem to appreciate her attention. "Where is *she* having hers?" he asked. "Oughtn't you to keep her company?"

"I don't think she cares particularly for my company," Vera said.

But he misunderstood her. "Oh, she will. She will!" he said. "Give her time."

Irritated beyond words, Vera gulped down her tea and went

out again to where, on the landing, the nurse was standing with her cup in her hand, leaning down over the banisters. She was staring at the old prints on the wall. The house had made some impression, Vera was glad to see. "They're Malton prints," she said proudly. She let her own glance travel with pleasure around the white medallioned walls and the wide stone staircase that poured down between the iron banisters like a mountain cataract.

The nurse's voice broke in on her. "A bit of a rookery, isn't it?" she said. And she turned and looked out of the landing window at the flat fields. "It must be bleak in bad weather. Lonely, too, I'd say. Or are you used to it?"

Bleak! Lonely! Did that mean the creature might not stay? Vera stared out of the window. The tangled shrubs stripped of leaves were twisted with strands of barbed briar. A stranger might think it a prison.

"Oh, it doesn't matter to me," the nurse said. "I'm only here for a while, but how do you stick it?" A faint curiosity showed for the first time in her eyes. "I don't suppose you'll stay on here, will you—afterward, I mean?" she said, and she nodded toward the door of the sickroom.

Vera said nothing. Then she became aware of a deep resentment. Why should this woman assume that but for her father she would be alone in the world? On a reckless impulse, she faced around, "I may be going out to Australia," she flashed. The next minute, she would have given anything to take back those words. It didn't make her feel any better that the nurse made nothing out of her lie.

"You've people out there, I suppose?" she said. "I've people out there myself. They're always writing and asking me out. I might go sometime, too, but I'd never settle down there." Her expression changed. "I have other plans!"

Vera stared. There was a kind of smirk in the woman's eyes. A fellow—that was it! Involuntarily, she glanced at the nurse's left hand.

But Rita laughed and spread out her bare hands. "We're not allowed to wear jewelry on duty!" She laughed. "A ring above all! Bad for the morale of the patients! Oh, you may not think it," she said, as Vera raised her eyebrows, "but it's a fact. You'd be surprised how it depresses them." She nodded toward the sickroom. "At any age!"

"How ridiculous!" Vera said. Yet almost at once Alan's words came to her mind. Oh, but when those words were said her father was well. And anyway, sick or well, was it likely that a big lump like this would strike a spark in her father? "I think you overestimate my father's capacities," she said. "And now, if you'll excuse me, there are a few things I have to discuss with him—confidentially."

The nurse drew herself up. "He's not able for much," she said warningly. But at that moment Lily's voice came up from below in a snatch of song. "I'll tell you what!" Rita said more humanly, and she caught up the tray. "I'll take this down and give that girl instructions about the meals. I'm dying for a smoke." For a big girl, she went down the stairs at a good lick! She was probably younger than she looked.

When Vera went in to her father, he looked up. "Oh, is it you!" he said, obviously disappointed.

"Yes, it's me," she said flatly. "Are you comfortable, Father? Will I fix your pillows?"

"No!" Impatiently, he put out his hand. "Leave them! She'll do them. She has a knack."

"Well, I should hope so! It's part of her training. I don't think we should leave everything to her, all the same," she said. "Is there nothing you'd like *me* to do?"

He was lying back, looking up at the ceiling, but he glanced around the room. "You could get her a chair," he said. He frowned at the hard bentwood chair beside his bed. "She ought to have a big armchair. Where did you put her, anyway?"

"Up beside Lily," she said dully.

"Isn't it dark up there under the roof?" He didn't actually frown, but she could see he was dissatisfied. And then he said something outrageous. "Why didn't you give her your room?"

"I gave her the room Lily had got ready for her," she said tartly, but under his stare she weakened. "It would have been an awful job to move out all my things."

"You'd have time to do it now while she's downstairs," he said, so casual it was almost sly.

But from below at that moment came the sound of laughter. "I think it would be a great mistake to move her away from Lily," she said. "They seem to be getting on famously."

"She'd be nearer to me if she was in your room."

"You seem to forget, Father, that what would be an advantage to you might not be one to her. She's not a night nurse, you know.

To convenience her during the day seems quite unnecessary. We *are* paying her, after all!" But she was sorry she'd mentioned money. "Please let me fix your pillows, Father?" she said.

He waved her hand away again. "Leave them," he said. And he looked up at her cunningly. "That's part of what we're paying her for, isn't it? How much is her salary, anyway?"

Oh, why had she brought up the subject! "That's my worry, Father," she said. Before he went into the hospital, he had arranged for her to have a power of attorney. Once or twice, he questioned her as to how she was managing, but only in a vague way, and gradually she had taken full responsibility. As his sole heir anyway, she felt it was virtually her own money she was spending. "Her wages are not much, really they're not," she lied. "And she's well worth every penny we pay her, isn't she?" She forced out the words.

It was sad to see how readily he lent himself to her deception. "We're very lucky to get a girl like her," he said. "What's keeping her, I wonder."

"She'll be up in a minute, I'm sure, Father," she said, but she couldn't resist giving him a dig. "I don't think we should grudge her any time she spends below. It's lonely here, you know, and neither you nor I have much to offer her!"

"That's true," he said, but lukewarmly. Then he spoke with a burst of his old energy. "What are you waiting for? Why don't you get that chair?" He closed his eyes. "I'll try and get some sleep," he said. "I want to save my strength all I can."

Save it for what? For that nurse, she supposed. Dejectedly, she left him. And when, as she went out onto the landing, there was another peal of laughter from below, the tears came into her eyes. All at once it seemed to Vera that in her own home there was no place for her. She was not wanted upstairs or down. And then the kitchen door opened and she heard footsteps in the hall below. Hastily, she dried her eyes as Rita came to the foot of the stairs.

"Oh, there you are," the nurse said.

Was it imagination, or did the nurse look up at her with a more lively interest? But then, the nurse looked more interesting to Vera —less lumpy and heavy. Her big brown eyes, like berries that had ripened, were warmer, softer. And as she came up the stairs two at a time, she was smiling. Halfway up, she stopped. Her hands were behind her back. "Which hand will you have?" she called out gaily.

A letter!

"Lily forgot to give this to you in all the fuss," she said. "A little bird told me you were expecting it." So they *had* been talking about her! But not disparagingly.

Filled with joy, Vera took the letter. "Thank you." She said it so earnestly that Rita laughed.

"You'd think I wrote it," she said. "Off with you now and read it."

Vera was warmed by her friendliness. But when she went into her room and sat down on her bed, her heart went chill with apprehension. Supposing he was angry with her for having written! That his letter might not be a reply to hers at all simply did not occur to her—not until she was halfway down the first page.

Dear Vera:

I won't try to tell you how I felt when the boat sailed. But it isn't to blame you that I write. Far from it, Vera. And I know that if you were here with me now I could imagine no greater happiness, because apart altogether from my own feelings of emptiness and desolation the voyage itself promises to be very enjoyable. We left London . . .

At this point she stopped. And as she realized he hadn't got her letter her hands began to tremble. He, too, could not endure a total severance! Her eyes flew back to the close-written page.

I must tell you a funny thing. Today on the promenade deck I saw a young woman seemingly—like myself—alone. And oh Vera, she was so like you!—it was uncanny, really. For a moment I was mad enough to think it was you—that you'd thrown your scruples to the winds and followed me. As if you would! Truly, though, Vera, the likeness in profile anyway was remarkable. When she turned around, I could see, of course, she was much rounder in the face than you, although there was still something about her eyes and the shape of her forehead and even the way she wore her hair, that almost broke my heart. You should have seen the look she gave me, though, when she caught me staring at her. I suppose I should have done the civilized thing and explained myself to her. I'll have to do so if I meet her again, which is likely enough, I suppose. The passenger list is small for a ship of this tonnage.

Do you know that we traveled at 17 knots yesterday and 18 knots today? But these bulletins can mean little to you! Why do I tell you about them, you may ask. Ah, but then why am I writing this letter at all? I can hear you saying I have not the courage of my convictions. And you are right. Our decision to make a clean break was the only sane one. But do not blame me too much. I promise I will try hard not to transgress again. Let us regard this as another farewell. Goodbye and God bless you. Give my respects to your father. I hope he is well.

ALAN

She put down the letter. Two farewells! As if one was not bad enough. Well! By now he would have got her letter. She'd have another communication from him soon—a cablegram, perhaps. And for the rest of the voyage he need not feel so bereft. How well she knew the poignancy of the moment when that strange woman reminded him of her. She herself a dozen times had fancied some hurrying stranger in the streets to be him, only to find that, close up, there would be no vestige of likeness and what seemed a concession of memory would turn out to be an ugly trick of the eye. But oh, if that woman had in fact been her! For a long time she sat on her bed thinking of him, but although there was a chance that now she might, after all, be joining him out there in Australia someday, her sadness was not lessened. A forfeit had been paid—that voyage out with him.

But what was going on outside on the landing? For some time, she had been aware of noises—pushings and shovings—and now the two girls were running down the stairs, giggling. She opened her door. The door of the sickroom was open, and she could see her father lying on his side, facing the wall. At her step, he turned around. "Where were you?" he asked crossly. "They had to do everything themselves!"

Then she saw that the big wardrobe in which his clothes had been kept was gone, and in its place was a moth-eaten red plush armchair that used to be in Lily's room. The pictures had been taken down, too.

"Well, what do you think of it?" he asked, thawing a bit because he was himself so pleased.

"It's nice and airy certainly, Father," she said cautiously. Did he not see that it was the appurtenances of life that had been taken away? The bareness of the room depressed her.

"She's going to take up the carpet tomorrow," he said, "and Lily's going to scrub the floor. I'll be cool for the summer."

Involuntarily, she glanced out of the window. An east wind had driven across the land all week and blackened the early blossoms. "Summer is still a long way off, I'm afraid," she said, and in her voice there must have been a latent bitterness, because he looked at her sharply.

He reached out and caught her hand. "Do you ever hear from him?" he asked.

"Is it Alan?" she asked stupidly. The name had not been uttered by either of them since the day he'd insinuated that she'd been let down. She hesitated. "I had a letter some time ago, Father," she said.

"I knew you would," he said quietly. "He'll want you to go out to him one of these days. That will be the next thing!"

To her astonishment, she saw that the expression on his face was one of satisfaction.

"Mark my words," he said. "You'll be going out there someday." He meant when he'd be dead! But how nicely he'd settled things in his own regard. "What do you think yourself?" he asked, and his eyes were fixed on her insistently.

She ought to be glad that he was not a prey to remorse—that his mind was at ease about her. But she could only shrug. "Who knows!" she said, and turned away.

"That's right," he said, lost in his complacency. "There's no knowing what is in store for us."

The bareness of the room was depressing, and she made an excuse to leave him.

If life had ebbed from the sickroom, however, the rest of the house teemed with it. Lily and Rita had only to be together down in the kitchen for five minutes and the din was deafening. Rita was so different from what Vera had first taken her to be. She was so cheerful and so gay! As time went on, she gave a hand with everything—peeling potatoes, scraping vegetables, drying up dishes. Prodigal of herself in all directions, she helped Vera, too, mending torn linen, darning, and even doing a bit of dressmaking on the side. Her effect on Lily was extraordinary. The girl went about her work in a whirl, giddily doing chores for everyone. One day, she washed the doctor's car when he was upstairs!

It was with the patient, though, that Rita had her greatest success. Vera blushed to remember the suspicions she had had on the first day. It was true that Rita flirted with him, but this was soon understood by all of them to be a kind of charity. It helped him to keep up appearances in spite of his steady deterioration. To Vera's amazement, Rita brought out a foppishness in him of which she herself had never imagined him capable, though she sometimes wondered if he might not be voluntarily lending himself to the blandishments, playing a part in a kind of ritual. There was about the sickroom at times the blended gaiety and gloom of carnival.

One day, a strange thought crossed Vera's mind. She had tried in the past, without success, to imagine what it would be like to be married to Alan. Now, listening to the happy babble in the house and seeing day run into day, purposeful and busy, she began to think that if she were married and had children, this, perhaps, was what her life would be like. To lovers, love might seem an isolated place, shutting them in and shutting out the world, but channeled into marriage would it not quickly become a populous place from which in time another generation would have to seek an escape? Vera smiled at her thoughts. Her life for the moment was certainly a good substitute for marriage! In spite of the shadow of death, the house was very happy. She herself was so happy that she was hardly surprised one afternoon when there was a knock on the door and she opened to the postman. The letter. It had come.

Like the last, this letter was long. It was not written on ship's paper, however, but bore the letterhead of a hotel in Gibraltar. And this time Vera knew immediately that it was not a reply to hers. Before she had read a line, some of the good went out of it for her.

Dear Vera:

As you can see, I am writing this in the Grand Hotel, Gibraltar; on the veranda, as a matter of fact. I am going on one of the excursions arranged by the ship's officers, and as it happens I have had an unexpected wait. But I am running on—I must explain myself a bit further.

I really should have begun by telling you my reason for writing a second time. I'm sure you did not expect a letter, although this morning when I saw the mail bags on the deck it crossed my own mind that there might have been one from you—oh, just a word of good will, Vera, nothing more, but I would have appreciated it. As it happened, we did not get our mail. Can you imagine, the launch that took us ashore was the same one that brought the passenger mail aboard a few minutes earlier! So that, as we were carried away, we had the frustration of seeing the sacks being dragged into the purser's office for sorting.

The letter rambled on and on. Oh, it was too much! Then, at the bottom of a page, a few words leaped out at her:

. . . and so it may yet be that, in spite of everything, it will *be to you that I will owe my life's happiness. And that, Vera, is why I write to you in such haste. I want to give you a hint of what I dare to presume may be in store for me. And I want you to know how much I hope that for you, too, the same happiness is in store, of which the happiness we had together may have been only a foreshadowing.*

Bewildered, she turned back. Then, beside herself, she skipped through the first pages.

You will remember how we often spoke of destiny? It certainly does seem now that there was, after all, a strange concatenation of events in my life. Not only did I, in a way, initially undertake this voyage because of you, and most certainly because of you at the time I did, but it was a likeness to you that first drew my attention to Mary. That is her name: Mary Seward, the girl I told you about in my other letter. It is for her I'm waiting here in the hotel at this moment.

When I ran into her on deck the day after my last letter to you, and we got into chat, I cannot tell you how much I was struck by several small resemblances between you. In no time at all I was telling her about you. I found her so understanding. It was the beginning of our friendship. And now it seems that there is to be more in it for us than mere friendship. How strange to think you and I knew each other for so long, and Mary and I have just flown into each other's lives while both of us, as she put it rather beautifully, were "on the wing."

When things are settled, I will write to you again. And if I am not mistaken, Mary will want to write to you, too. She told me last night how very conscious she was of the part you played in our lives. She said she would like to thank you. In spite of the distance that divides us, it is my hope that you two will be friends.

But I must stop. I see her coming. We will have to hurry, as we must be back on the Orcades *at 10:45* P.M. *In haste, but with affectionate remembrance,*

ALAN

Affectionate remembrance! It was like a line on a mortuary card. As for that sentimental rubbish from the other woman, that hurt most of all.

Oh, it was so humiliating! And what would Lily and Rita think? Vera sprang to her feet. But as she stood staring down at the miserable pages, her heart froze at a sound from her father's room. "Oh God, what is that?" she said out loud. Headlong, she ran onto the landing. Although low, those sounds had filled the house, and ahead of her Rita and Lily had raced up the stairs and were with her father. Rita was bending over the bed, and Lily was on her knees, mopping up the floor. "What is the matter?" Vera cried.

Her father was almost entirely out of the bed, leaning forward in a position so grotesque that, combined with the way they were holding him, it made it seem as if he were trying to swim, or to fly. He was retching violently. And as the black bile poured out of him, it seemed that by its force he, too, was splayed out over the side of the bed. "Vera!" he gasped as their eyes met. Do you see now for what it was that I saved my strength, those eyes seemed to ask.

As suddenly as it started, the retching stopped. And where before he seemed to have been flung forward, now he seemed to be flung back, his gaze transfixed.

Rita, as white as a sheet, straightened up. Her face was wet with sweat. "Another minute and he would have been gone! He shouldn't have been left alone."

"Is he dying?" Vera cried hysterically, trying to push past her to get to the bed.

"Oh, not at all; he's all right now," Rita said impatiently. "We got to him in time."

Vera was shaking. "What does it mean?" she cried.

Rita swung around. "I'll tell you what it means," she said callously. "It means that you'll have to get a night nurse right away! Where would we be if this happened during the night? He could have choked!"

Vera's face reddened. "Wouldn't I have heard him?" she cried.

"You didn't hear him in broad daylight, did you?" Rita said. She wiped her hair back from her face. "A nice kettle of fish that would have been—for me, I mean. We should have had one from the start, I suppose, but I was sparing you."

"There was no need for that!" The tears came into Vera's eyes. When had she been niggling?

Rita had the grace to be ashamed at least. "It's not that I'd mind getting up at night," she said. "But if I lost my sleep too often I'd be no use to you or to him. Good will isn't enough in nursing," she added awkardly.

"I understand, Nurse," Vera said. It took an effort to be polite.

"I hope you do." Rita looked more contrite every minute. "I want to give him an injection," she said. "I'll have to go upstairs to my room for a new needle. Will you stay with him while I prepare it?" As she went out of the room, she looked back. "There wasn't bad news in your letter, was there?" she asked.

The letter? A thousand years could have passed since she'd read it. Alan and his bride-to-be had shrunk to specks on a very far horizon. Even the pain they'd inflicted had been deadened. "Not really," she said quickly.

But Rita's eyes probed her through and through. "A little misunderstanding, I expect!" she said lightly. She went out.

Vera moved over to the bed. Her father was conscious again. She bent and kissed his forehead. Wasn't he all she had in the world now? She had a great longing to unburden herself to him, to tell him about her heartbreak.

But Rita was back. "Well! A nice fright you gave us!" she said briskly as she came in the door. "Why didn't you call someone? Shame on you!" Across the bed, she winked at Vera. Then, bending down, she smiled into the sick man's eyes and her voice was soft and cajoling. "I'm only joking," she said. "It was *our* fault. We shouldn't have left you alone. But it won't happen again. We can promise you that! We're going to get someone to sit up with you and keep you company, even at night. Won't that be nice?" When he looked taken aback, she gave him a playful nudge. "We'd have had one long ago, only we couldn't find anyone fetching enough for you!"

For a moment, her father seemed to hesitate, and then, playing his part, he tried to smile. "How about a blonde this time?" he whispered.

"Come, now. I can't have talk like that," Rita said. "I'll be getting jealous."

"Oh, you'll always be my first love, Nurse," he said, but it made Vera sad to hear that he had given Rita back her formal title.

It wasn't easy to get another nurse, with the summer coming on. After several trips to the phone in the village post office with no success, Rita said desperately, "I wonder if we ought to try for a nurse attendant. All we need really is someone to sit with him at night. And I know one who's free—a very reliable person. We were on a case together before. She's an old dear."

"Oh, she's old?" Vera was doubtful at once.

"She's fairly old," Rita said, "there's no denying it. But she's very efficient. She's had enough experience, God knows!" And here it seemed she could not help laughing. Vera felt she might have been less unfeeling.

Next day, however, when the old nurse stepped out of the taxi at the door, Vera's own first impulse was to laugh. She looked a million years old. How would her father take this? It took them five minutes to get her up the steps, and once inside she didn't seem to have a glimmer about direction; several times they found her going the wrong way along a corridor, or looking for the patient's room on the wrong landing. It was nearly eleven that first night before they'd got her ready for her duties of the night. She'd be almost as much trouble as the patient, Vera thought uneasily as she said good night to her. She herself was having a cup of cocoa in the kitchen with Rita and Lily before they, too, went to bed. "How can she be competent to mind a sick man at this rate?" she asked.

Rita looked both serious and sympathetic. "Don't let that worry you," she said. "Your father likes her! And that's the important thing, isn't it?"

It was true that the sick man did seem to like the old woman. Was it, perhaps, that the efforts of gallantry had been a strain? Did he welcome the peace the old creature brought with her? There was certainly a new quiet in the sickroom. He often dozed when the two of them were together. Going into the room once, it crossed Vera's mind that the old woman, too—no less than her patient— was waiting for her last end. Her few words were uttered in so soft a voice they could not be heard outside the door, and when she moved around the room she made no sound in the old felt slippers she wore. As time passed, it even seemed that the whole house was becoming muted.

Rita and Lily were gay as ever, but, freer now to leave the house, they worked off their excess vitality in bicycle rides and an occasional dance in the village. And once or twice when they had been out late, the old lady made Rita lie in next morning. "I can rest as well in a chair as a bed," she said placidly. And, indeed, the big plush armchair was as big as a bed for her small, shrunken body. "Anyway, I'll soon have enough sleep," she said once, and it was impossible to tell whether she spoke humorously or otherwise.

"She sleeps on her feet, I think," Lily said. "Like a bird on a branch."

"All the same, I don't want to trade on her good will," Rita said.

And yet it was inevitable that they did—all of them, even Vera. One day, she let Rita persuade her to go for a spin on the bike with her. "You're in the house too much," Rita said. "You need to get out in the air."

"Take sandwiches with you," Lily urged. "Make a day of it."

It was not yet the real summer, but this was a day such as seldom comes even in summer. The sun shone down as they rode along between the hedges, already thickening with leaf and bud, and they laughed and talked as happily as if they were one as young and carefree as the other. Rita took her hands off the handle-bars and pedaled along whistling like a messenger boy. They stopped for lunch on a long, treeless stretch of road where the banks were high but softly mounded and the ditches shallow and dry. Throwing down her bike, Rita clambered up on the bank and sat down.

"Are you sure the grass isn't damp?" Vera asked, feeling it.

"Are you mad!" Rita cried. "It hasn't rained for days!"

But they had no sooner settled themselves and taken out their packages of food than rain splashed on the greaseproof paper. By the time they had got to their feet, it was pouring. "Oh, where will we shelter?" Vera cried, looking up and down the treeless road.

"Come along!" Rita cried, jumping up on her bicycle. "It's hardly worth our while sheltering at all." Already they were soaking.

"Look, there's a clump of trees ahead," Vera said, but a few moments later, when they reached it, Rita didn't stop.

"Let's keep going," she said. "We can change our clothes when we get back. I love the rain." Throwing back her head, she held her face up to it. Just then, the sky was split with lightning.

"Oh, my God! Did you see that?" Vera cried. Her words were drowned in a long peal of thunder.

"Oh, it's miles away," Rita said indifferently, although a second peal had volleyed over their heads.

"We can't go on!" Vera cried.

But there seemed to be a devil in Rita. "Why not?" she called back, and her voice was almost buried under the cataracts of sound.

To be heard, Vera had to draw abreast of her. "It's terribly dangerous!" she shouted. "Especially on a bike! Steel attracts lightning."

"Nonsense! We're safer on the bikes than anywhere! Aren't the tires rubber?"

In any case, the clump of trees was far behind. Keeping abreast, they careered along, while to either side of them the darkening countryside was lashed with light. Shrinking down over the handlebars, Vera didn't dare to raise her head, but Rita, standing on the pedals, rose up and down with them and stared out over the transfigured landscape. "Isn't it wonderful?"

"I'm scared!" Vera screamed.

Rita threw her a scathing glance. "Stay, then," she said. "I'm going on. Anyway, I've got to get back to my patient. A nice thing it would be if he hopped the twig while I was skulking in a ditch!"

In her fright, Vera's foot slipped off the pedal and she almost fell. "You don't really mean that?" she cried.

"Oh, for heaven's sake, don't take me up on every word I utter," Rita yelled crossly. "It's just that you never can tell with any case!"

As if her father was only a "case" to her! "Oh, let's get back quick!" Vera cried, and with a new spurt she shot ahead. Up to then, obscurely she'd felt that the blades of light as they scythed across the tops of the hedges would not dip to find her if she crouched low enough over the handlebars. But now she, too, stood up on the pedals and pressed them down with all her might. She, too, stared out over the fields; in that eerie light they were as strange as the fields of the moon. Trees and bushes even on the farthest rim of the sky were suddenly brought so close their branches switched her eyeballs. Near and far were one. Then around a bend in the road the white gable of a cottage came in sight. It seemed to rear up out of nowhere. And up its walls went their shadows, hers and Rita's, riding like furies. "Look at us, Rita!" she cried. "We're like death riders in a circus!"

Then there was another flash, and a second cottage rose up out of the earth. The walls this time were rosy pink, but to Vera it seemed that they were in flames. The whole world was in flames.

Even Rita was startled. "My God, that gave me a fright!" she cried, acknowledging with a grimace that perhaps, after all, death could have been riding with them.

When they got back at last, they could see Lily's white face pressed to the window, and as they flung down their bikes she threw open the door for them and ran back, not daring to stand in the doorway.

"How's my father?" Vera cried.

Lily grinned. "He slept through it!" she said. "The old girl, too. I might as well have been all alone. I was scared stiff. And look! I got stung by a wasp!" She held up her arm. It was red and swollen. "And what do you suppose! There's a nest of them under the kitchen window—in the grass. I nearly stood in it!" She laughed.

Rita was the one who was cross. "You'll have to do something about that!" she said sharply to Vera. "There's your father to think of! If we managed to get him out in the sun for a few hours, it would be a nice thing to have him stung to death!"

Bewildered, Vera looked at her. How could she have him dying one minute and out in the sun the next!

Vera went upstairs. Her father was still asleep. So after she changed her clothes, she ran down again. Rita and Lily were sitting at the kitchen table. They exchanged a very odd glance, but Rita immediately drew her into the conversation. "I was just saying to Lily here that those thunderstorms are usually a sign of good weather—summer storms."

"But it's only May," Vera said instinctively.

"Nearly June!" Rita said.

"And those wasps!" Lily cried. "They're a sign of summer." But she looked guilty. "Of course, this fine weather could be just a flash in the pan."

Rita gave her a quelling glance. "This could well be all the good weather we'll get. I've made that mistake too often—spent May and June watching out for the good weather and July and August finding out it was over."

They were thinking of their holidays! Vera's face must have given her consternation away to them.

"Of course, I'd never take my holiday in the middle of a case," Rita said quickly. "That is, not if the end was in sight. There is this to be considered, though. If I were to take my holiday now, while your father's condition is fairly stable, I'd be back when you really need me."

"At the end, you mean?" Vera said quietly.

"Oh, the end could be easy enough," Rita said airily. "But he might go into a coma. You might like to have me here then! All things considered, I really think I ought to go while the going is good. And the great thing is that you won't need anyone to replace me. I sounded out the old girl and she said that if you put a cot in your father's room she could easily manage singlehanded. It isn't everyone would do it, mind you. Oh, wasn't it a godsend it was her we got! She's as good as two people rolled into one!"

So it was already settled. Vera's heart sank. How false had been her feeling of solidarity with them. These girls had their private lives, which at all costs they would safeguard from inter-ference.

Yet when the day came for Rita to leave, her concern was genuine. "Do you think you'll be all right without me?" she asked anxiously, for about the twentieth time. There was a car calling for her, and they were standing on the steps, waiting to see her off.

"Her fellow," Lily whispered to Vera.

But Rita was uneasy and restless. "The wasp's nest!" she cried. "We forgot it! Oh, perhaps I oughtn't to go at all! Not that I really think your father will ever stir out-of-doors again, but there's the old girl to consider! What if she got stung?" She wrung her hands.

"Don't worry," Vera said placatingly. "I'll attend to it at once—tomorrow!"

"But how? That's the whole point. It may not be as easy as you think."

"What about tar?" Lily cried. "We could pour it into the nest!"

Rita shook her head. "Too hard to handle. You have to heat it. It's very dangerous. But you could set fire to it, perhaps, with petrol—"

"Not petrol so near the house!" Vera cried. "The whole place could go!"

Rita bit her lip in vexation, but all at once her face lit up. "Wait!" she cried. "Have you a gun? You could fire a shot into it—at close range! But can you handle a gun?"

"I'm sure I could manage," Vera said.

"Well, then, there's no more to worry about." Leaning forward, Rita strained to see the road through the trees. "Here he is," she said as she saw a car. "I told him I'd meet him at the gate," and, catching up her bag, she gave them both a quick kiss and ran down the steps. "Goodbye," she called back. "Goodbye."

Looking after her, Vera felt curiously bereft. She looked at Lily.

"Well, that's that!" Lily said, and she turned and went back into the house.

Had the sun gone? Had the birds stopped singing? It was hardly possible that one person's absence could make itself felt so immediately. Yet before the week ended, the house was like a tomb. Certainly the kitchen became one. The leaves of the trees had thickened and the shrubs grown dense, and although the upper rooms were above the level of their shade, the lower part of the house was sometimes as dark by day as if evening had prematurely fallen. One afternoon, when Vera went down to make a pot of tea, it gave her a shock to see two birds that were chasing each other dash in one window and out the other, as if, indeed, the house was a deserted place.

And then, one afternoon while Vera was upstairs mending a sheet, the silence of the house was shattered. Voices. Like a twitter of birds, only louder and more inconsequential. Unmistakably, she heard Rita's laugh. Throwing the sheet aside, she ran down the stairs.

"Oh, there you are!" Rita cried gaily. She ran forward and kissed Vera. "I was just telling Lily here that I got bored in Dublin and hopped on a bike and came over to see how you were getting on! Talk of a busman's holiday! But how are you? And how," she added quickly, as an afterthought, "is your father? I must go up and see him before I leave. Not that I can stay long," she said, glancing at her watch. Then she laughed. "What I'm dying to know is how you're getting on with her nibs?"

"Oh, she's been very good and very kind," Vera said sincerely.

Lily, too, was full of praise. But she giggled. "She's a howl, really," she said. "I never stopped laughing since you left!"

Vera looked at her with astonishment. When had all this hilarity taken place?

"Oh, I didn't let on to you," Lily said, "but she was going to leave several times, only I got around her to stay. There was one time she had her bags all packed, ready for off. She thought she was in a madhouse!" Lily was spluttering with laughter, and Rita joined in. "It was that day, you remember"—she turned to Vera—

"she was just having a cup of tea when you walked in with the master's gun in your hand!"

"Oh, Lily!" Rita squealed. "Don't tell me!"

"Wait!" Lily begged. "I've been dying to tell someone. 'I thought it was the closed season!' the poor old thing said. 'Oh,' says you, 'I'm only going out in the garden to shoot a few wasps'!"

"Oh, no!" Rita screamed. Laughing, the two girls sank onto the kitchen chairs, their feet sprawled out in front of them.

"To think I never noticed a thing!" Vera said so sadly that Rita was sobered.

"Ah, you were too anxious about your father," she said kindly. "You didn't tell me how he is! Ought I go up to him, or might it only disturb him?"

A week earlier, there would have been no question, but all of a sudden Vera had misgivings. "Would you like me to tell him you're here and see what he says?" she said, after a minute. And without waiting for an answer, she slipped upstairs.

In the sickroom, the windows were thrown up, and the whole room was filled with a myriad of small sweet summer sounds—the hum of insects and the songs of birds. As Vera went softly in, there was a whir of wings as the swallows under the eaves swooped back and forth from their nests. The old nurse and her patient were both awake, but although they were not speaking, Vera felt as if she were intruding. It was as if they were communicating in some way beyond her understanding. How could she ever have been so mistaken as to think that life had ebbed from this room? Dying, too, was a part of life. For a minute, she stood unobserved in the doorway. When she heard footsteps on the stairs, she stepped back quickly, closing the door.

But not before Rita had seen into the room. "Oh, what a change there is in him!" she whispered. Gently, she put her hand on Vera's arm. "It looks to me as if he's near the end." But, seeing Vera start, she spoke sternly. "You're lucky, you know—the end is going to be very easy." Then, drawing Vera toward the stairs, she went down a few steps. "It's funny the way things work out, isn't it? We only thought of that old woman as a stopgap, and now it looks as if it was God who sent her to you. I don't think you'll need me back at all," she said firmly.

"Oh, Rita!" Vera cried. "We couldn't do without you!"

But Rita shook her head. "It's not my business, I suppose," she said, "and I don't know how you're fixed with regard to money, but there's never any sense in throwing it away."

"The money doesn't matter," Vera said in a flat voice.

Rita looked censoriously at her. "You'd be surprised what a financial drain it can be," she said. "A death in the family, I mean. And coming after a long illness!" She threw up her hands. "When it's all over, there's an avalanche of bills. I've seen people *crushed* by them. Yes, *crushed.*"

"Oh, Rita," Vera cried, putting out her hands, "I can't bear to think of the house without you! And what will Lily do?"

"A pity about Lily!" Rita said. "She'll be getting married on you one of these days. She can live on the thought of it! And as for you—won't you be going out to Australia?"

It was a long time since Alan had been referred to, and Vera had begun to think Rita and Lily both suspected that there was something wrong.

But Rita's face was guileless. "It's a pity," she said. "It's not— God forgive me—that I grudge your father his last days, but it seems a pity that the summer is passing. Ah, well, it's only one summer."

Vera looked at her. She was so strong and young. One summer more or less would indeed matter little to her. Unable to bear her secret any longer, she said in a low voice, "I may not be going out at all."

But Rita missed her meaning. "Oh, is he coming back?" she asked. "I can well believe it. I know lots of people who didn't like it out there. Still, it's a pity you didn't have the trip!" She yawned. "Oh, I'm jaded," she said. "I was at a dance last night. Late hours kill me." Then she looked at her watch. "I'd better be off," she said.

In the days that followed, it became clear to Vera that her father was dying at last. His small world was shrinking smaller still. In the beginning of his illness, when there was a noise downstairs or in the yard he'd sometimes ask them not to slam doors or let things fall, but after a time when there was a noise he'd only look startled and his eyes would dilate as if with fear. It was as if the world outside the bedroom had become a foreign, a forgotten, world. Now sudden sounds in the sickroom gave him a start. His world had narrowed down to the bed on which he lay, and his face seemed to wear a habitual look of surprise. At first, Vera thought it was that he could not believe the pass to which he had been brought, but slowly she came to realize that it was the old life of health and normality in which he could not believe. When a light went on, he was startled. When a chair was moved, he started. When Lily brought his tray, he was startled, and yet again when she bent to take it from him. And once when Vera herself went into his room, he seemed to find her presence so startling she had to protest.

"Where did you think I was, Father?" she cried. Was it possible that deep down he did not trust in the finality of her break with Alan? Did he imagine she had deserted him, after all? In that moment, she made up her mind to tell him the truth. And so one day when she was sitting with him while the old nurse was taking a doze, she said quietly, "There's something I never told you, Father—about Alan. He's gone out of my life for good."

Weak as he was, he was able to hide his immediate reaction. Then he turned and looked at her. "What matter!" he said dully.

Stung, she was about to move away, when she was struck by the depths of pity in his eyes. It was not the rage of pity of long ago; it was a pity that embraced them both. And he did not need to explain it. She knew what it was—what matter anything when all comes to this in the end!

Then he took her hand. "What does your mother's loss matter now to me?" he said sadly. "And someday it will be the same with you."

It seemed a strange and unreal analogy—this analogy between her and her dead mother—and yet it was valid, she supposed. A silence fell as they pondered their separate aspects of the same thought.

"Vera, do you think there's any meeting in the next life?" he asked suddenly.

Taken aback, she said, "I don't know, Father." Not for years had she given the matter thought.

"Because I don't," he said vehemently. "When they dig the black hole and put you down in it, that's the end of you."

"Oh, no!" Her heart cried out against the thought of his facing into that nothingness and that nowhere. "Of course there's a hereafter!" she cried. "Otherwise, what would be the meaning of love?"

Weak tears came into his eyes. "Do you really believe that, Vera?" he said.

Partly lying and, like himself, partly wanting to believe, she nodded.

He closed his eyes. "It would make up for everything!" he said, almost under his breath. Then he opened his eyes wide. "Just to see her! Just to see her!"

Vera's own eyes widened. "Who are you talking about?"

"Your mother," he said, and he looked surprised. "Who else!"

Natural History

CONSTANCE URDANG

*"Natural History" presents a rare portrait of a woman whose
maturity and intelligence enable her to cope successfully with the
complexities of life. The selection consists of a series of prose
episodes that describe a variety of characters, ideas, and events.
A unifying element is the narrator's awareness of herself as a
woman. In her words, to be a woman is to feel "the tension between
the race and the individual." How is this tension manifested in the
narrator as well as in the other women whom she knows? As she
deals with her husband, children, mother, and friends, what roles
does she see herself playing and how do they both contribute to
and deprive her of an individual identity? How does the fact that
she is a writer, concerned with the process of fiction, influence her
relationships with others? How does her career affect her sense
of fulfillment? What is the significance of the title?*

Svake baba viestica
. . . cette insupportable ligneé de femmes auteurs . . .
This volume consists chiefly in
anecdotes of Americans who won out smiling
—advt. by Holt, 1908
My petti-skirt hath a scallop. Mayhap that will help thy
history.—Patience Worth

Ardis called last night. She is disappointed when I answer the
phone instead of Jim. She sounds tired; world-weary, she'd put it.
Nothing new. Same old catalogue of disasters. She is going to leave
St. Louis. For the millionth time, I wonder why anyone stays in

St. Louis. It is so ugly, and the climate is atrocious; it's one of those provincial cities from which everything always seems to be happening someplace else. Sometimes I find myself staring at the full-color photographs of the heather-covered hills and foaming lochs of Scotland or the Hebrides that they use to advertise scotch whisky in the magazines, stupefied all over again to think that real people actually live there, surrounded by such views & vistas every day of their lives, while we, like the great gray mass of mankind, stay stuck in the great gray mass of this ugly city. But if I stare long enough I can put myself inside somebody who feels himself imprisoned by the lochs and the heather, alone and isolated enough to be living on another planet, even farther from the great centers where everything is happening than St. Louis. I know how that person feels, because I think I used to feel that way sometimes (less than an hour by commuter train from Grand Central!) when I lay on the beach or on the dry hot grass at the top of what used to be Slater's hill, contemplating "New York"—the idea of New York—as I lay there half stupefied with sun and the smells of salt water and cut grass.

—But of course, for Ardis it's a different matter. She feels, *instinctively*, as the circulating-library novelists, and Ardis herself, would say (and for once I agree with her, no other word could describe so expressively what passes for a thought-process when the question of what to do about her life floats to the surface of her consciousness), that the time has come for her to take some sort of action. This time, taking a new lover will not be enough. This time, simply drifting with the tide (or her own inertia) won't be enough. Or, rather, if—out of apprehensiveness or inertia, or because of some external accident, like meeting a new man or having the child get sick—she does not take action immediately, then she will not have done away with the necessity for taking action, but simply have postponed the date.

Not a novel. A series of images in the form of prose episodes. Their meaning, if any, to emerge when at the end one can look back to try and make out the "significant patterns . . . as a man sees from a plane the track of a Roman road under crops and chicken runs" (Joyce Cary).

A long poem written not in, but by means of, prose. Its techniques that of the poem. The substance, prose. Or,

Where more commonly the poem consists of single words and

images, the projected poem to consist of clumps, accretions, blocks of words, and episodes.

Instead of using simple metaphors, use narrative sequences as metaphors. People, situations, as metaphors. (Not symbols!)

Emotional impact to implode, as in a poem, rather than empathy, antipathy, etc., as in a novel.

"When electrons become old-fashioned/My sister-in-law put one on her piano"—this refers to Ann (I must remember to call her Anya) having arranged on her (prim, upright) piano a tintype of her great-grandmother next to a photograph of Roy, my father, and myself, taken (probably) in 1935 or '36. The great-grandmother resembles a painted wooden doll from Russia or Poland, its serene rigid features delineated with sharp, sure strokes, painted black hair dipping demurely from a center part. Behind the gentle convexity of that brow, that looks so smooth as to have been lacquered, what thoughts and feelings must have "struggled toward inchoate expression"; pogroms in those days, life a terrible and precarious thing. As now.

Great-grandmother of Ann (Anya), you are planted like a sturdy little tree on top of the piano, not smiling, exactly, but with an expression of expectant acceptance on your face of a carved wooden doll.

—And next to her, on the wooden porch steps at the beach house, sits my father in his ankle-high sneakers, white with black edging and a zipper up the front, half-turned to look at Roy, cherubic, plump, and sullen on the step above, his hair silky and tangled down to his earlobes, while I sit slightly apart but complacent of my centrality in this family grouping; a big silk moiré hair-ribbon perched like an enormous butterfly on the left side of my head. Behind us, the screen door bulges imperceptibly toward the camera, slightly out of focus, with its shadowy revelations and concealments.

At a hosiery counter in Stix, Baer, and Fuller, my mother said to me (and I was already 38 years old), "I suppose you could wear these, you have such big legs."

I looked at my mother, in my mind's eye contemplating my legs, of which I have always been rather vain, and meditated on love, the maternal instinct, and the threat of hatching an alien egg in one's own nest. I've always known, of course, since I reached my full height, that I was much taller than Mother or Father; Roy is taller still, but somehow in a man this seems perfectly fitting, and his height doesn't throw all their proportions out of whack, the way mine seems to in the snapshot somebody once took of the three of us. But what a shock—to come suddenly on the realization that Mother was conscious of it too, and that to her *I*, pumped full of milk, orange juice, and cod-liver oil, weighed, measured, examined, tested in every particular as the seasons changed and recurred, was the one whose proportions were out of whack.

How will I like it, when my daughters are revealed as giantesses? Will that make me a pygmy?

What right has Lola to appear in the guise of earth-mother—an enormous maternal figure, four months gone, trailed by five or six little girls—? To arrive in subzero weather, towed into St. Louis because her car broke down on the highway—without a stick of furniture or a place to lay their heads?

Saturday afternoon they arrived. Sunday she looked for an apartment, and before supper she phoned to tell us she found one, a third-floor walk-up on Leland. But—the landlady was clearly suspicious of her with her little girls and no furniture and out-of-town car, and followed her to the phone booth, demanding an extra month's rent money, cash, as security. When Lola couldn't produce it she kept following them down the street, a mute husband for support, babbling an incoherent, half-Yiddish story that the apartment, "as a matter of fact," had already been rented to someone else "by my sister-in-law, in the morning." So Lola surged forth into Sunday night to find another place, and she did find one.

But by the time we received them, early Monday, they had slept on the floor in freezing drafts all night, and, "It won't do, we have to find a better place," begun the search anew. Also, the baby had a cough, diarrhoea, and fever. Lola took for the night a hotel room where at least they will be warm and have beds to sleep on, and found a third apartment, first floor, two bedrooms, stove and refrigerator, newly papered and painted. It sounded too good to be true, but I cringed when I heard Lola assuring the landlord over our phone that the children are very quiet and the baby never cries. Anyhow, she took it, she is permitted to rent it, she has it.

So—on Wednesday they will move in. We gave them a bed and four chairs we've been storing in the basement, the old red dresser, an electric heater, and some baby things. Roy and Ann gave them a studio couch and their old dining-room table. Eddie gave them a rollaway bed. Lola washed walls and scrubbed floors all day. She was to come and pick up the rest of the furniture on Thursday, but phoned to say the car had broken down again . . .

The point is, here is Lola, Earth-Goddess (unlikely as it seems). Her second husband was "an older man—the whole thing was a Tragic Mistake," says Lola; the new baby, due in July, is not his; Lola is enormous already. She says of Chuck, the husband we knew, that he is married now to his Boyhood Sweetheart (who had turned him down shortly before Lola married him), and that on thinking it over it seems to her that she and her marriage to Chuck were really only Obstacles to the course of True Love in Chuck's True Story. She says her own True Story was nothing to do with Chuck at all. The capitals are all Lola's. Her redeeming feature: that ability to stand back and observe her own flounderings in the emotional swamp where she has struggled since puberty, and to characterize them, with uncanny exactitude, in terms of the tabloids and cheap magazines which she devours in the intervals of reading Kafka and Nietzsche. In the fall she intends to marry again. This Len, a boy of twenty, is the father of her unborn child. The other children all call him "Daddy" already, she told Ann; as far as the children are concerned, he is their real father.

Meanwhile, she cooks, washes, irons and mends, scrubs, folds diapers, makes formula, and keeps her appointments at the maternity clinic. She is a true nest-builder, making curtains, buying chairs and pictures at Mrs. Borrow's or the Salvation Army store.

Mrs. Borrow as the fairy godmother who invests the ordinary objects of our undistinguished life with the glamour of romance. How is the magic accomplished? By taking them from their normal context,

lifting them out of the banal living-room where they have existed secretly for years (only nobody looked at them), and setting them down in new juxtapositions,

or no juxtapositions

she compels our attention to the object,

and

the object becomes beautiful.

But Mrs. Borrow is not Picasso. When Picasso says, "I take a vase and with it I make a woman," he speaks literally; it is the prerogative of genius; it is not a replica or an imitation of a woman he makes: "I take the old metaphor, make it work in the opposite direction and give it a new lease on life." He is a great artist, he creates things, he makes a new kind of woman out of the old cliché ("People have said for ages that a woman's hips are shaped like a vase. It's no longer poetic; it's become a cliché. I take a vase, and . . ."). How many Picasso women are walking around in the streets at this very minute, women who could not have existed before Picasso imagined them. Plenty of them never having heard of him, or, even if they've heard the name, never having seen the originals which they themselves imitate.

So, Picasso creates; Mrs. Borrow does not. And yet, Mrs. Borrow sees, and her vision animates. Like Picasso, she sees with the eye of love. Not namby-pamby, ooey-gooey, slick-paper love. And not the collector's greedy, destructive love. Hers is for the humanity that created, and prizes, and still adheres in the object.

Mrs. Borrow, who owns the shop, is ensconced in the late 19th century at the rear, behind—in this weather—a little gas stove —surely she belongs in a novel: "a frowsy little junkshop in a slummy quarter of the town.

". . . The tiny interior of the shop was in fact uncomfortably full, but there was almost nothing in it of the slightest value. The floor space was very restricted because all round the walls were stacked innumerable dusty picture frames. In the window there were trays of nuts and bolts, tarnished watches that did not even pretend to be in going order, and other miscellaneous rubbish. Only on a small table in the corner was there a litter of odds and ends— lacquered snuff-boxes, agate brooches, and the like—which looked as though they might include something interesting . . ." *who wrote that?* Why, George Orwell did, in *Nineteen Eighty-Four,* and he had never set foot in St. Louis, but still he described the place in his book 30 years ago exactly as it is in real life! today.

Mrs. Borrow is a Homely Philosopher—she would be flattered by the designation.

"I'm just so tired of all this plastic and chrome," she says seriously. "All the new things seem so much alike to me, I get so tired! and it seems there are a lot of people who feel the same way, that's why they come here."

Why do Anya and I go there? There's nothing there of value, no surprise in the clutter that you can buy for a quarter and sell for $25, no hidden treasure in the attic. And yet these dusty shelves of chipped crockery, lidless sugar bowls, undistinguished brown custard cups, dented metal candy-boxes, hand mirrors on whose tarnished silver backs someone else's initials are lavishly entwined, souvenir spoons, nutmeg graters, cracked teacups and pitchers, draw me like so many magnets. The books you pick up in Mrs. Borrow's shop have a heady smell of mildew and dust, although they are not even old; she sells them for a dime. Leafing through them, one after another, it occurs to me that often the ones I am most strongly drawn to are the same books that stood through so many damp summers in the glass-fronted bookcase in the beach house. Books by authors you never study in school, books nobody ever talks about, with torn backs and stained bindings, books that persist (maybe) only in the stacks of the local branch library, where nobody ever takes them out. And the furniture at Mrs. Borrow's— some of it she has stripped and refinished, rickety little side tables and washstands, wooden chairs that need re-caning, footstools and benches and chests of no particular period, all scarred and marred with the signs of honorable use. Where does she find them all? We have never asked her, but surely she doesn't buy up auction lots, like other junkshop keepers; we feel that every eggcup, every crazed tureen, rungless stool, chipped picture frame, was chosen for itself alone.

Once I bought there a little golden Holy Grail. It wasn't till I got it home that I realized it was only a toothpick holder from a cheap restaurant.

"Roy is feeling optimistic": After a long evening with Roy and Anya, Jim tells me that Roy has told him that at Palomar they have seen the Blue Light.

"What does that mean?" I *enquire nervously* (well, even without irony, perhaps there is some little nervousness in the question; even if the thing isn't to happen for a thousand years or so I find I'm not ready for, or reconciled to, a final thumbs-down verdict on the universe).

"Why, that the universe is not eternally decaying," says Jim.

"Oh," I say, "you mean Roy is feeling optimistic." Then I say, "It occurs to me that that is a completely *feminine* response."

Jim says, "Yes."

Woman. Difficult to accept role of being one, because state of being *female* (defined as embodiment of life force) seems to be incompatible with being a rational (intellectual?) socio-political-economic *individual*. Also, paradoxically, women in their insistence on seeing each case separately, their reluctance to generalize/categorize/abstract, seem more bent on individuality than men (because they have to fight harder to achieve it?). Don't enter argument about whether or not women should take "jobs outside the home" or bake bread; not a question of should or ought; matter of jobs, when not a question of economic necessity, has become a question of tastes, predilections, as some prefer an evening at the ballet, others a basketball game. Society gives or withholds penalties here, and problem of being a woman goes deeper than the merely social (societal). Attitudes (women's, men's) toward such a question heavily dependent on society's view; in society where it's unheard-of for a woman to take a job, that simply isn't one of the possibilities open. But even in our society today, where it is possible for women to work in practically any field, difference between sexes has not been eliminated. O.K.—vive la difference!

Question remains, exactly what *is* the difference? The tension between the race and the individual. Women feel it, men don't.

We think Jim's mother has an affinity for what's broken. When we gave her a new toaster, she "didn't need it"; yet I overheard her say to the children, "I'm a poor girl, I don't have a nice toaster like yours at home," and when she saw ours (it hasn't worked for months; I took it down to an electrical repair shop on Olive Street and instead of an estimate for fixing it the man offered to buy it for a dollar and a half—alas, I was too proud to accept)—we told her it's broken—she said she wanted it.

The catalogue of calamity is endless. She's like Ardis; if you know someone who got sick from a wasp sting, she knows somebody who died of one.

Before Jane was born, she unearthed a feeble-minded relative (child of Muriel's half-sister) to worry about: "They always *said* they dropped her on her head—they said she wasn't born that way—but how do I know if I should believe them? And that other child—a can opener fell in his eye and he lost the sight of it . . ." as if that too might mark the dreaming foetus.

Part of the letter from Chuck: ". . . I can understand your silence. For years now, ever since Lola and I separated, I've been writing to all my friends, acquaintances, and enemies, begging desperately for help, pity, comfort, new plans and self-deceptions. You had only to wait, you knew, before hearing from me that everything was changed, that (something) was out and God-knows-what was in: a job in publishing, joining the Navy, becoming a beachcomber—a hair-dresser—a chest of drawers. . . ."

It must have been put at once, out of a kind of delicacy of feeling, into this drawer where I've now found it, still unanswered.

Pat turns up. She wants to talk. She says Eddie is going to Chicago, he really is going—on Sunday. She will keep the apartment until the end of the month. But she doesn't know if she should go to Chicago or not. I say, "What are the alternatives?"

"That's just it," she says, "there aren't any."

"No, no," I say, "there are always alternatives."

In the midst of our strenuous preparations for dinner Sunday evening, Ardis arrives—hooting, honking, fluting, hugging us interchangeably, breathless: "I heard your book is out! Marvelous! How marvelous!"—and then, sotto voce, "Will you look at Deedee's dress, she and I've had a fight about it already, I wanted to sew up those slits in the sides—aren't I silly—" She is looking a trifle feverish, her complexion is bad, her hair is too long and fastened back behind her ears with bobby pins.

It wasn't until I was sixteen that I became aware of what must always have been the split, the crack, the gulf between the two irreconcilable halves of my world. Ilya Ehrenburg, writing about his impressions of Berlin in the '20s:

". . . seemed unreal. Big-bosomed Valkyries stonily supported the facades of houses as before. The lifts worked, but there was hunger and cold in the flats. The conductor courteously helped the Geheimrat's wife out of the tramcar. . . . Catastrophe assumed the guise of prosperity . . . sight in shop windows of pink and blue dickeys as substitutes for shirts that had become too expensive; the dickeys were a sign . . . if not of prosperity, at least of respectability. In the Josti café where I sometimes went, the wishy-washy so-called Mocha was served in metal coffee-pots with a little glove on the handle to prevent the customer from burning his fingers. Sweet cakes were made of frostbitten potatoes. As before, the Berliners smoked cigars labelled Havana or Brazilian, though in fact they were made of cabbage leaves steeped in nicotine. All was orderly, pleasant, almost as it had been under the Kaiser. . . .

"The artificial limbs of war cripples did not creak, empty sleeves were pinned up with safety-pins. Men whose faces had been scorched by flame-throwers wore large black spectacles. The lost war took care to camouflage itself as it roamed the streets. . . .

". . . audiences . . . were hungry for the semblance of suffering, brutal cruelty, tragic endings. I once happened to be present at the shooting of one film of this kind. The heroine's father tried to wall her up, her lover lashed her with a whip, she threw herself out of a seventh-floor window while the hero hanged himself . . . with what rapture pale, skinny adolescents watched the screen when rats gnawed a man to death or a venomous snake bit a lovely girl. . . .

"Everything was colossal: prices, abuse, despair."

What so disturbs me about this view of Berlin: that this is what Fraülein came to us from.

Fraülein, her scrubbed, forthright face, her athletic body, her shy, romantic (hidden) soul.

The healthy, scrubbed boys and girls who sang the *Wanderlieder,* were the Hitler Jugend. The magical city of Unter den Linden and the legendary Brandenburger Tor that meant music and history—were "Berlin with its long depressing streets." The Black Forest, with its spotted toadstools, cuckoo clocks, witches, and woodcutters: "the first shots of the fascists."

She herself, no student of political science, must have had cloudy intimations of something wrong ("colossal: prices, abuse, despair"), for she and her friend, Lilli, had themselves sung *Nun adee, du mein' lieb' Heimatland,* and traveled the long, long way to our apartment on Riverside Drive. Never to return, never to see again parents, sisters, brothers, friends, lovers until many years later, in another world, after the war. And yet never did she breathe a word of it—her own despair—to us. (And our own childhood, in the midst of the depression, strikes, unemployment, men selling apples on our own street corner, was somehow insulated from these things; is childhood per se self-insulating? Thinking about it now it seems impossible to have remained untouched, immune to the contagion of its hysteria. Asleep—in a cocoon of self-absorption.)

What about Fraülein herself, the vulnerable self? Her voyage away from the witches and woodcutters and Sans Souci ("it means, *without any cares*") to Riverside Drive, Sutton Place, and Clearwater, Florida? I can only speculate and invent. Lilli, with her flat pale face and glasses, their Thursday afternoons closeted together, then her solitary departure into a mental hospital—and after that?— since now I know that such a story doesn't end with the simple closing and locking of a door?

> THEN (from the *Imaginary Poems*)
> While I was a mermaid, swimming
> Down there in the perfect musical silence
> Where everything is green
> They killed my boy-husband
> The one I would have married
> And lived in a hollow pumpkin
>
> My grandfather, they marched you quickstep
> Into the ovens   My sisters
> Oh my sisters and brothers, I did not come up
> Out of the water to save you I stayed
> Under the silent ceiling in my jade rooms
> My rooms of sapphire, opal, and emerald

. . . from this, I suppose, they will deduce that I am a German Jew, refugee, brought to the United States as a child, whose grandfather did not survive a concentration camp ("quickstep/ Into the ovens"), etc., etc. Not a word of which, of course, is true; I was born in New York City, on West 74th St. to be exact, and both my grandfathers had been dead for years before my birth, one of them died of tuberculosis in 1895 and the other (I think) of influenza in the great epidemic of World War I. The (private) hospital where I was born has been torn down and a large, formerly luxury (but now gently decaying) apartment house put up in its place.

However it is true that for many years I was a mermaid.

Contemplating the central problem of fiction. How to distill the True (Truth?) from the fictional. What is true? What is fictional? I sit down to tell what I said to Jim (or Ardis, Pat, Mother, etc.) yesterday, or what they said to me, and it comes out on the page altogether (but *how?*) different. A sea change, into something rich and strange. Let alone trying to put down what something really looks like—Jim, Eddie, etc.—even an egg or a chair.

Mrs. Borrow, drawn from life. But would she recognize herself? I mean, the way one recognizes oneself in a mirror, without hesitation, without thought? (More complicated—think of the experiments in which people didn't recognize themselves, walking with their heads in paper bags, or profiles or back views—a matter of having to learn to accept visually a view one seldom gets of oneself while having it constantly of other people?) Does one always recognize oneself in a mirror, even face to face, unless one is expecting to see oneself there? Might Mrs. Borrow—the hypothetical Mrs. Borrow—not only not recognize "herself" as drawn by me, but actually identify some other character as herself? Would that mean that she "sees" herself as I see that other character—for example, Lola? Or Ardis? She herself knowing more about the Lolesque or Ardisian side of herself than I do?

Look at what happens to Mother, who both is and isn't herself, to Charlotte, to "me." And yet, I haven't set out to distort, to "invent." The act of writing (or reading?) has itself transformed them (us) into fictions.

Need a character not myself, who can think thoughts and have opinions about abstract or theoretical matters, or even about politics, art, morals (what else is there?). Because in the book, myself oughtn't to express opinions—reader should have to deduce my (myself's) views on generalities (appearance and reality, yesterday and today, man and woman, age and youth, *usw.*) from my particular reactions to particular people and their particular situations.

Pat turns up again this warm afternoon, having walked over from school. She has heard from Eddie—no, he's not going to stay in Chicago after all, he just went up to see the agency man and ask him whether he thought Eddie ought to relocate in Chicago. Last night when he phoned he said the man said that while his *work* is fine and his *record* is good, there are *so many*—

"—What is he going to do?" I ask.

"I don't know," says Pat. "The thing is, could he make enough money?"

I say, "How would you feel about staying in St. Louis? If you got married? Would you mind?"

"No, I wouldn't mind," she says slowly in her rather high-pitched serious voice. "I'd get a job I guess."

Shortly afterward she bursts out—but quietly, Pat is a quiet girl—"No, I don't think I want to get married now, anyhow, not right away, no."

The newest issue of *Woman's Day* (on Ann's coffee table) has in it a piece on anti-matter: ". . . a massive atom smasher to prove that when an atom is created its opposite is also created . . . anti-atom . . . anti-matter makes conceivable the existence of anti-stars, anti-galaxies and anti-planets . . ." a trifle girlish, but oddly reminiscent, as stated, of the Zen idea of the existence of nothing—non-being.

On the grimy wall of an apartment house at the corner of Fort Washington Ave. and 160th St., Washington Heights, New York, N.Y., someone wrote,

"Here died baby pigeon born June."

To come riding out of the middle west. Backward, away from the frontier which relentlessly pushes on into the sunset, the frontier now consisting of garbage disposal units, automatic dishwashers, whole-house air-conditioning, color television, a Honda and two cars in every garage, and a Cessna for the affluent. It occurs to me that the persistent images of "back" East and "out" West have validity not only historically but in the very motion of the earth itself (our mother). It's literally always later here and earlier there: time runs out sooner in New York than in St. Louis, one hour's difference by the clock—and it's even later (than you think) in Europe, the shades of night already falling fast *back there* while America still basks on the shadowless plains of noon—

Well then, the paint everywhere is peeling, the ceilings are precarious; on the day of our arrival a piece of kitchen ceiling 3 ft. in diameter lay in a heap of plaster-fragments on the floor. Windows won't open, doors won't close; furniture in every room is propped up with paperback books. Everything seems to be peeling, dropping off, disintegrating; cracks in the paint, in the walls, in the stone on the outside of the apartment house. Around the corner we have the Holy Ghost Miracle Revival, Three Services Daily, Bring all the Sick. On the marquee of what used to be the Rio Theater, where the gritty gray dust still blows up Broadway, swirling around your nylons and getting in your eyes:

The Blind See
The Deaf Hear
The Lame Walk
Prayer for Sick Nightly.

The apartment: triple locks on the door, an extra key for the downstairs door that opens into the gloomy, green-tiled lobby, and double locks on the windows; the windows in the unused bedroom that used to be Jim's, and in the dining-room, have been nailed shut; meanwhile Jim's mother says she is cold, always cold. In the huge, inconvenient kitchen we rummage for utensils; she won't tell us where anything is; using the oven or the ironing board requires endless preliminaries, removing the stacks of pots, pans, and pot covers, unused from one end of the year to the next, that nest in the (unused) oven, or the ranks of mops, brooms, brushes, cleaning rags, and dustpans from the crowded broom closet to get at the ironing board, an old-fashioned padded wooden board without legs, that has to be balanced between the stove and the cluttered kitchen table before you can use it; everything in the apartment is like that, propped up by clutter. The closets are packed tight. Brim-full. She wants to give us an enormous old samovar; there is Russian writing on the base; before you can boil water in it you must light a charcoal fire. Somewhere in one of the closets is an ancient waffle-iron; do we want it? Oh, how she wishes she could move, but how can she? How could she *live* in a smaller place? The piano alone—

I ask if she ever plays the (baby grand) piano; the smile appears, the wistful 3-cornered smile I have seen reflected on my daughter Jane's face—her painted lips are thin above the tiny chin, between the chubby jowls—

"No, no, not for years and years," she says tragically.

"Then why keep it?"

"It was Mother's."

"But, well—yes," I say, "couldn't you maybe give it to someone who would play it, use it?"

She gives me a stern glance. "Do you realize, my dear, how much that piano is *worth?*"

On the piano, a piano-scarf; a framed, tinted photograph of Jim, aged seven, with his brother and a long-dead dog; of the grandchildren; a dusty candy-dish; the samovar; a calendar from one of the neighborhood banks; a bottle of orange pills; and a shopping bag containing 5 yo-yos, 3 harmonicas, a game of Chinese Checkers, and a toy weaving set.

Domination of things. "A man murdered by his furniture." Magical properties of things. Things famous men have owned, used, touched: George Washington slept here. One step from an original holograph manuscript. What do we hope for when we sleep where George Washington slept? Sweet dreams? Why do they (we) visit, daily, Kennedy's, Stalin's, Napoleon's, tomb? "Here lies one whose name was writ in water." Why do collectors collect (book-collectors, autograph collectors, collectors of paintings, old clocks, demitasse-cups, souvenir spoons, coins, stamps, Sandwich glass, Audubon prints, music boxes, player piano rolls)? Is it an enormous effort of the public imagination—to try and extend oneself, a consciousness-expanding mechanism, a trying to feel oneself into the great ones' shoes? An act of piety? A wishing that the brush or pen laid down by the great will spring magically to life in our hands? Strength from eating the lion's heart, the enemy's liver.

Virtue inhering in objects. Apart from value, intrinsic or extrinsic.

From a short novel by Anna Holmes: "She came from Nebraska where she sang in the choir and read books about woman's role as a homemaker but she was born out of the nobility too, out of their momentary desires—the Archduke of Austria and one of his laundry women."

Which is to say, for "Nebraska," read New Jersey, Ohio, Kansas, Montana, Texas, Oklahoma, Pennsylvania, Maine, Rhode Island, Connecticut, Indiana, Illinois, Georgia, Florida, Alabama, Louisiana, Mississippi, Missouri, New York, Vermont, New Hampshire, Wyoming, Wisconsin, Idaho, Iowa, Oregon, Massachusetts, Washington, North Dakota, South Dakota, Arkansas, Maryland, Delaware, Virginia, Kentucky, West Virginia, Tennessee, North Carolina, South Carolina, Arizona, New Mexico, Minnesota, Michigan, Colorado, Nevada, California, Utah, the District of Columbia, and Alaska (but not Hawaii).

For "sang in the choir," read attended PTA meetings, played bridge, drank Coca-Cola, celebrated her wedding anniversary, studied political science, deplored juvenile delinquency, took piano lessons, addressed envelopes for the League of Women Voters, wrote thank-you notes, bought Defense Bonds, believed in Planned Parenthood, knew how to knit one, purl one, and etcetera.

For "the Archduke of Austria," read the Sheik of Araby, Prince of Ruritania, Prince Charming, Prince Matchabelli, Emperor of Cathay, -of Ice Cream, King of the Castle, King Kong, Enrico Caruso, President John F. Kennedy, Clark Gable, Cardinal Spellman, and/or Ringo Starr & Frankie Avalon.

Query: Why is it that one can never write about "love," "being in love," "a love affair" without sounding like a third-rate sob sister in the yellow press writing for frustrated housewives? How few books there have been that can make the reader feel what the character feels (characters feel). Neither the clinical nor the cynical, the sly nor the dry, the romantic, frantic, nor the—

What secret? Perhaps simply having the patience to dwell, in prose, on the beloved object as patiently, insatiably, tenaciously, and inexorably as the actual lover does—dotes!—on the actual beloved. Never to say, for example, "insatiable embraces"; the eye skims that phrase in a fraction of a fraction of the time it would take for the briefest and least passionate of kisses.

Ardis: the evening when, sitting in our dining-room and nibbling pretzel sticks, she counts on her fingers the number of men she has been to bed with in the past five years: "If Deedee ever found out—eight affairs—in five years? It would ruin her—she would hate me—what would she think of me—I couldn't do it—"

The divided sensibility that can, first, convince itself that every time she goes to bed with a man it's an affair, and that each affair is a grand passion; second, that there's *nothing wrong* (her italics) with going to bed with anyone she pleases, and, simultaneously, express *genuine horror* (my italics) as she adds up what she's been doing—along with a (suppressed?) *frisson* of delight at her own promiscuity, along with renewed protestations of her lack of promiscuity. Her ardent romantic loves. Disappointments. Tragic Denouements. Betrayals.

What Mrs. Dietz said, amid the hollyhocks and peonies: "When I used to go into people's houses to do the housework, *as* I did for Mr. Dietz before I *became* Mrs. Dietz, I remember when I first went to the professor where I stayed for seventeen-and-a-half years, and when he interviewed me for the job he said, 'Do you smoke?'

" 'No,' I said.

" 'Do you drink?'

" 'No,' I said.

" 'Do you have gentlemen callers?'

" 'No, I haven't *dated* since my husband left me in 1932,' I said.

" 'Well,' he said. 'If I ever catch you smoking, or drinking, or entertaining men friends, in my house, I will throw you out in two seconds flat,' he said.

"One day a girl friend of mine came to see me; she was someone I used to know years before and I hadn't seen her in a very long time when I walked into a restaurant and there she was, working as a waitress. After she left that time, the professor said to me,

" 'Minnie, how well do you know that girl?'

" 'I don't know much about her, but I used to know her,' I answered.

" 'Minnie,' the professor said, 'I don't think she is the kind of girl for you. I don't think you should see her any more, or spend any time with her. That girl is no better than she should be.' "

And Mrs. Dietz turned to me (amid the hollyhocks) and said, "How do men *know* these things? How do they *know* about a girl?"

"He could have been wrong, about her," I suggested.

"*Oh* no, *he* wasn't wrong! Not about her!" Mrs. Dietz triumphantly rejoined. "Why, he was absolutely right. One time I went over to her place, where she was living, and there she was with a man friend. They said they were going out for a drink and invited me to come along. 'Come on, Minnie, just for one drink,' they said, and they wouldn't listen when I said I had to be getting back to the house. So I said to myself, 'Here you are, and you can't get away from them, Minnie, so you have to join them. But remember, walk the straight path, look neither to the right nor to the left, and do not drink any intoxicating liquors.' So I went along with them, and we went to a tavern, and they ordered drinks, and they asked me what I wanted, and I said, 'A coke.' So that was all right. And then they went to another place, and met an ex-jockey who was a friend of theirs, and they paired me off with him—me, who was always so particular about who I went with! And he was telling me about the Underworld.

"When they decided to go home this ex-jockey took my girl

friend home first and then he took me in his car and he parked in front of the professor's house—I have to laugh, the lady across the street was watching at her upstairs window and she heard everything he said, because the next day she said to the girl who worked next door, 'Who was Mrs. Dietz out with last night, May?' (only of course my name wasn't Mrs. Dietz at that time), and May said, 'Oh, I know Mrs. Dietz never *dates*, she doesn't go out with men since her husband left her in 1932. It must have been her son she was with,' and the lady said, 'Oh no, that I can tell you, it was not her son talking to her in that car!'

" 'You let me out,' I said to him, 'let me out of this car right here and now or I shall scream so loud that every soul on the block will come running out and you will be arrested by the police.' So he said, 'Oh well, if you're going to be that way,' and he let me out.

"But do you know, when I got back into the house and into my own room, I got down on my knees next to the bed and I gave thanks that I was a good Christian girl, and for my dear, dear parents who gave me a good Christian upbringing and taught me to know right from wrong, for I said to myself, 'Tonight I have seen how the other half of the world lives, and there, but for the grace of God, go I.' "

Lola says she has bought a TV set. A small one, portable, at Sears. She says last time there was something she wanted to see, the political conventions or something, she rented a set. So this time she thought she would buy one and watch what she wanted to and then return it, it would be cheaper than renting one, she wouldn't have to pay anything. But when she had had it around for a few days she sort of liked it and decided to keep it. "It isn't obtrusive, and they have some good programs on the educational channels."

I tell Lola about Jim's involvement in the obscene-book case— she asks, in her habitual ingenuous way which always seems to me (falsely, I think) to cloak some pointed and penetrating intention, "Have you read the book?"

I am at once on the defensive, saying, well, not exactly, yes, but not thoroughly, not carefully, I just skimmed through it, it really isn't worth careful reading I thought—finally I say, "Have you?"

She says, "No."

In this same vein, I am defensive about my handling of my children (read *house, husband, work, life*) in Lola's presence—because the bland, ingenuous (watching) look seems always to cloak some secret, weighing, judging, penetrating Observer; in actuality, I don't believe this is the case, it's more a trick of vision, a mannerism—a nervous tic—like her involuntary eye-blinking, and the odd pursing and stretching of her mouth—so noticeable and even comic when they all appeared, waifs & strays, on the doorstep in February—by now the tics and mannerisms have receded for me again so I don't even notice them any more, and even forget that they exist and what they are (must be) silently saying about the interior life and arrangements of this soul—

Lola says, "Bess is on vacation from school this week. I thought it was last week, and kept her home for a few days before I noticed the other children going back and forth, and called up the school, and sure enough, it was the wrong week."

How can I put Lola in the novel? She has bared her soul to me, all unsuspecting that I'm itching to get my hands on a pencil. And I have asked her questions, shamelessly, simply because I want to write down her answers. "We have to train the children not to be sentimental and self-pitying, like Most People, we must sweep away the cobwebs," says Lola blandly, waving her large, bare arms in inconclusive sweeping movements, while her nose twitches rabbitlike and her eye involuntarily blinks.

I have been disturbed by part of Bea's letter, that goes, "Wow! Something must have happened to Eddie. He has paid his child support since being under a court order. It is indeed unfortunate, but, well, I suppose it takes a man-made law to make one fulfill his natural duty. I used to like to think that Eddie couldn't pay because of lack of employment, etc., but his air trips to New York and Chicago seem to dispel that theory . . ."

Poor Bea, I think, she sounds as if she is turning into a shrew, into one of those divorced women who (yes) never does remarry, but instead grows more stringy and embittered and tired day by day, feeling the terrible weight of the child increase, fed as it is on venom and resentment, wasp poison, spider bites. Not that she isn't right. And Eddie—he can convince himself that black is white, if it's to his (real or imagined) advantage, between tonight and tomorrow morning.

He can convince himself that he's sending exorbitant sums to Bea. That there's nothing incongruous in his buying a car or a TV set, flying to New Orleans, etc., etc., while at the same time protesting his desperate lack of cash. He can believe, simultaneously, in his utter and continuing bankruptcy—and in the imminence of a job that will pay him $35,000. And he can believe that he's got to leave St. Louis and go to L.A.—forgetting that he's been to L.A., and the reason he returned to St. Louis was that everyone he saw there told him he ought to go back.

Marriage is for the race. More than merely a social (societal) institution; the institution of marriage a societal structuring of the race's need to perpetuate itself. Romantic love is for the individual. The dreadful confusion in our society between romantic love and marriage.

Woman (the female principle) is emblematic of the race. The race cannot die. Man is individual. "An" individual? "The" individual? Man-as-individual is free to die. The individual is free to die.

The female spider devours the male after mating.

"The artificial coital equipment was created by radio-physicists. The penises are plastic and were developed with the same optics as plate glass. Cold-light illumination allows observation and recording without distortion. . . . The equipment is powered electrically."

(Masters & Johnson, *Human Sexual Response*, on the Best Seller list all over the U.S. for so-and-so many months now.)

Remember the awful agonies of ordinary people; remember Cara: "I've had nine months of resentment"—the picture (imagined) of her joyless life, the living-room picked up, dusted, vacuum-cleaned; the little girls in starched, ironed dresses skipping off to their painting, dancing, music lessons—their joyless camping trip: "It was an ordeal for me, of course, but they enjoyed it"—clambering up a muddy, mosquito-infested hill in search of wildflowers—"all the other children were dancing to rock'n'roll on their transistor radios, it was horrible, horrible"—one month later, a baby boy.

"After you have one, people start telling you it's so wonderful—I've never liked any of my friends' little boys—oh, maybe one or two—but they're so loud, dirty; rude, hard to toilet-train—"

In the nightmare hospital where the ceiling fell down in the corridor: "Luckily the babies were all in the rooms—after the plaster dust settled they covered up the babies with plastic and took them back to the nursery."

To think of the sheer physical stamina required (by herself) of this dried-up skin-and-bones prim-mouthed female creature—her carefully waved hair, her little pale eyes behind her glasses, her fur (mink?) cape—is staggering. And still up nightly for the 2 A.M. feeding.

Without love.

Ardis, are you listening? You middle-aged Juliet!—unscarred and unwrinkled by all the scarifying experience of your once-upon-a-time disastrous marriage and monotonously repetitious "love affairs"—perpetual adolescent virgin ("Thrill me!") despite the ins and outs of all those tumbled beds—what is it you expect from this (never-to-be) perfect marriage of yours? You sit there pious as a pupil at Sunday school, repeating, "Marriage isn't easy, you have to *work hard* to make it work."

—What can you possibly mean by that?

Do you understand why the old women cry at weddings?

"Trouble is—I was born in the wrong century," Eddie says truculently. "Wrong century and wrong place."

"Which century would you prefer?" I ask—idly.

He pauses. Twirls the drink in his hand (maybe?). Pours it down his throat. Says, "Oh—19th—16th—"

Says, "—in a court, anyway. I think I belong in a court—royalty. Some sort of royalty—I'm sure that's what I should have been."

Part of a letter from Charlotte: "I remember your grandmother telling me all about these streets on the lower east side—Hester, Essex, Clinton, East Broadway, Henry St. where Aunt Lucy was born, Chatham Square, etc. Of course, most of it is entirely different now—huge apartment houses with playground areas—but there are still enough traces of the old way of living to make it interesting. I can't wait to walk down the street where the pushcarts still are. I remember we used to go with my father every Saturday evening to buy eggs in 10-dozen lots, butter, cheese, smoked fish, and to eat baked sweet potatoes while we walked. Every cart had flares that were always blowing in the wind and

the faces of the people all seemed eerie lit up by the flickering
flames. I can still see them. . . ."

Mother—what a splendid figure as she debouched from the
cross-country bus—in her brown pin-stripe flannel suit with its
beige ribbon-knit blouse and blue neck scarf, her large floppy-
brimmed blue hat, her necklace, gloves, leather bag, and elegant
legs! Into the steamy, sticky, sordid, rubbishy heat of the June
night at the Trailways Bus Depot, St. Louis, its stink of carbolic,
its floor stippled and lumpy with the accretion of years of chewing
gum, its crumpled candy wrappers, gum wrappers, cigarette packages, hillbilly farmers, citified young Negro girls, sloppy young
white housewives in slacks, hair in curlers, carrying the too-heavy
sleeping baby while a couple of wide-awake kids are grabbing
at their legs.

If he could see her, I think Father would be pleased at my
mother's way with a shopping bag—that symbol of (to me) untidy
housewifery, slatternliness, and disorderly conduct—the invincible
elegance of her ankle above the well- and neatly-shod foot, the
firm grip of the two gloved hands on the stout twine handles, the
interior of the bag organized with as much determination as I
remember (falsely?) her own household, where I grew up, to have
been—

Is there actually anything of truth in this picture? My Portrait
of Mother (arrangement in black and white) . . .

The other side of the "remember Cara" coin: Cara's husband,
ejected from Cara's bed, his own woman's, picked up by the police
on suspicion of soliciting in a public lavatory, the whole fortunately
hushed up, hurried past, smoothed over—

Returning to the problem of fiction. Query: How do people
"recognize" themselves anyhow? Through labels. If one were to
describe a "character" as having such-and-such a name, profession,
a house on thus-and-so street, so many children, these political
views, that nationality, wearing glasses or dentures or a wooden
leg—then, of course, if one had a friend with precisely those attributes one would assume he "was" that character. So—if I write
that my husband's name is Jim, he is a poet, etc., etc., Jim will

recognize himself and all our friends will recognize him. What if I change his name? My husband's name is Kurt, he is an accountant. Can I go on writing about the real Jim, the poet, as Kurt, the accountant? Or have I, by changing those two attributes, actually created a new person? Kurt, the accountant, has problems poets don't have. Kurt and I have 2 children, both boys, and we live in a modern efficiency apartment. Can this still be Jim and me?

Or Ardis. If I change her name to Leslie, is she still Ardis? What about Mother, who has already changed her own name from Marya to Marilyn? What remains of Eddie if his name becomes Charles and he turns into a government-surplus dealer with a French girl friend instead of Pat? Is Lola still Lola if I call her Yvette? If I add or subtract a husband or two, tinker with the children's ages and sexes, move her to Detroit or Albany?

Must St. Louis itself go? Ought I to familiarize myself with the streets and neighborhoods, flora and fauna, of Cleveland, Ohio, or Omaha, Nebr.?

The terrible ignominy of old age. Loss of dignity. Dependence. Ineffectuality—to which is added, ineffectuality to protest.

Must not confuse old age, its characteristics, with the characteristics of particular old people; remember Jim's Spanish proverb, "A young bastard turns into an old bastard."

Anecdote about Somerset Maugham at 80, "There are also many advantages to being old"—dash dash—long, painful pause—"I am trying to think what they are—"

To be an old woman writing the oral history of St. Louis et de l'Univers, as the hotel signs say in France and Switzerland. Being neither elegant—like Dietrich—nor can I to this day put up my hair in a French roll. Fearing that in my old age I'll neither dance the tango in a green sequined sheath (slit to the knee) in some dark little Latin-American bar under the slowly-revolving ceiling fan, nor—like Josephine Herbst—wear red sneakers in Woodstock, N.Y.

Let me be Mother Seagull, then, and study to translate all their caw-cawings.

With what pertinacity life persists in imitating art—even to its forms and techniques, the modes of the age; in ours, when art is

formless, or perhaps circular or spiral in shape, the spectacle of
   Ardis, who resolves her problem by not resolving it,
   Lola, in whose life the pattern repeats like wallpaper,
   Eddie, who will never "go to Chicago and get rich,"
   Pat, who will never marry Eddie or go to Chicago, etc.;
consider the 19th century, when every story either had a happy
ending, or the heroine died of consumption and the hero became
a Hero—in jungle, bush, or veldt—when things really happened,
or seemed to, "by pluck and luck"—no wonder we all suffer from
an ineradicable nostalgia, not for Eden, but for the good old un-
speakable days when the rich were rich, men were men, and
children worked in the coal mines up to their waists in water,
sixteen hours a day . . .

   The beach house. The place, which is the same (no?), is
utterly changed. For example, the wooden steps leading up to the
front screen door where my father and Roy and I sat in the photograph on Anya's piano—they are gone. In their place rears up a set
of concrete stairs with a metal hand rail. The elderberry bushes,
they're gone, of course, and even the tree that Arthur liked so much.
"It was always interfering with the telephone wires."
   In spite of concrete, and the heavy overstuffed furniture moved
from the New York apartment to replace the old wicker and canvas,
the house retains, inside, an inconclusive, unfinished air. Who lives
here? The sunny rooms have a musty smell. Upstairs, the bedrooms—
the plaster has been painted gay, irrelevant pinks, greens, yellows—
are full of ghosts. Beds and dressers have been shifted from room
to room, nothing is precisely the way it was. But ghosts, ghosts
everywhere, intruding among the bobby pins, earrings, boxes of
face powder, and snapshots of someone else's grandchildren. The
house resists time; it refuses to grow old gracefully. Instead, it
suffers patching-up. Holes in the plaster, crumbling of the stucco,
missing shingles: patched up. In the big, bare, grassy back yard
the rusty hammock still creaks, waits. The new neighbors in the
(new) house next door drive a Mercedes. What do they make of
this scowling, glowering, cranky old house? We are visitors here.
We pull into the weedy driveway and out again.
   The place "I loved more than anyplace else in the world . . ."

   "This was the building where Mr. Dawson had killed a man
for peeing in the hall. I remember being afraid to go downstairs

the morning after Mr. Dawson had busted that man's head open with a baseball bat. I could still see blood all over the hall. This was the building where somebody was always shooting out the windows in the hall. . . . This was the building that I loved more than anyplace else in the world . . ." (Claude Brown).

Ann has made an astounding statement. The conversation is about Ezra Pound, his saying in an interview that his entire life has been a mistake, that he was mistaken all the time—a repudiation that seems to us tragic, at the threshold of death, at the close of a life so filled with controversy and position-taking. The men continue discussing the ins and outs of it; meanwhile, Ann, under her breath, remarks that she thinks this is the way most people feel at the end of their lives. I think I haven't, can't have, heard right, or else that surely she meant something else, so I say, "You mean you think *most people* in old age believe their whole lives to have been a mistake?"

"Yes," she says brightly, "I do. Because even if they have been 'successful,' success is something always in the future when you're younger, but when you are old everything is in the past and nothing is in the future, and so you feel that you have failed."

It was Mother's mother, my own Grandma, who said to me, as she lay propped up in bed in the nursing home on Valentine Avenue in her ninety-third year, that if she had it to do all over again, she didn't think she would have married "that man," my grandfather. "I didn't really like him, but I was such a young girl, I didn't know I could say, No."

I don't mean to frighten Mother, and yet it occurs to me that I can hardly do anything else. My youngest daughter's vision of life, in the course of which she, who is now small, will grow big, while we, who are now big, will grow small, is devastating in the accuracy of its metaphor. (I think there are also primitive peoples who believe this.)

" 'You frighten me, you do,' her mother murmurs to the formidable daughter at her bedside."—from a review of Simone de Beauvoir's book, *A Very Easy Death*.

With what a familiar twinge do I remember my own feelings as a child about Grandma. It wasn't a matter of simple liking or disliking. I simply could not understand how that old woman, inhabitant of a different world that scarcely impinged on mine, to whom—as I sensed—I was no more *myself*, a person, an individuality, than a kitten or a butterfly is an individuality, could ever have been in the same relation to my mother as my mother was to me.

Mother never could forgive my father's mother for taking to her bed, wandering in her mind, failing to recognize us, and finally, dying! at the age of eighty-four. She feels it was a weakness, a flaw, basically a defect of character, a giving-in to one's baser self. There's no way to convince her that Grandmother's loss of memory and her inability to concentrate were symptoms of a disease brought on by old age; for one thing, she refuses (now as then) to admit the existence of old age. And so she persistently believes that this condition existed for lack of a determined effort of will on Grandmother's part.

"Why, *my* mother—your other Grandma—was much older than that, why, she was over ninety when she died, and she knew every one of us when we walked in, right up to the last night."

And Grandmother—now no one can know her, now she is dead. That cranky old woman, embittered, lonely, probably in pain most of the time; even the ones who loved her (we) laughed and whispered about her "solitary drinking" when she took a bottle of wine upstairs and hid it—kept it—in her closet. Now I think of her in the damp, chilly, flimsily constructed house; alone; her eyesight is failing; she can't knit or crochet or embroider any more; when she reads, Edgar Wallace or E. Phillips Oppenheim or some other thriller they brought her on the commuter train from New York, she holds the book three inches from her nose; when she sits and watches TV in a scratchy overstuffed chair, waiting for them to come home or for a phone call from Charlotte, she sits hunched right up to the flickering gray tube; even when radiators and an oil furnace have been installed the house seems to me in winter to be chilly and comfortless—I no longer begrudge her, if I ever did! the bottle of wine and the surreptitious, warming, comforting little nips.

So tall, so straight and unbending; like a tree. With her sparse salt-and-pepper hair braided around her head like a coronet, her sharp, little, bright eyes, so dark a brown behind the thick bifocals that they appear to be black, as she rolls out the dough for a fruit pie and cuts it and lays it neatly in the pie pan, singing meanwhile.

"Darling, I am grow-ing o-old,

Silver threads among the gold," and I eat the apple peelings and smell the other pies already baking in the oven and the other smells steaming gustily from pots bubbling on the two stoves, warmed and lulled and comforted.

"Yet, my darling, you will be-ee,

Always young and fair to me."

On that broad, flat, and uncompromising bosom, whether covered by the print percale (smelling faintly of mildew—was it?) of a house dress or the sober navy blue of a rayon two-piece ensemble, dress and jacket, she wore always a large, oval cameo brooch; Charlotte wears it now. Her skirts were never more than eight inches above the ankle, she never went sleeveless, There is a photograph somebody snapped on the beach once, which shows her fully clothed, including the cameo brooch, ungainly in midflight, one arm outstretched, one foot in the air, trying to get away from the eye of the camera; Uncle, in his black one-piece bathing-suit with the round holes cut out under the arms, is smiling and holding her by the other arm; in the background are shadowy, bathing suited figures, all smiling, all laughing, conspiring to make her one of them.

Does each generation seem to itself a diminution of the preceding one? Who could ever approach in size those looming giants of our childhood? The paradox being, that in terms of actual measurements we have outstripped them all, are taller and heavier not only than our parents and grandparents (those little old people), but the soldiers of the Civil War, both North and South, if one can judge by their uniforms; the Knights of the Round Table, judging by their armor; the Pharaohs themselves, judging by their mummy-cases—and so on, all the way back to Adam and Eve dining on apple and quince in a Lilliputian garden.

Pat in New York: she meets us at the Museum of Modern Art. Her New York Museum-of-Modern-Art self is the same as her St. Louis self; she wears tennis shoes and a skirt and blouse, a kerchief tied on her head, and walks sturdily among the Giacomettis. She is worried about her parents, she says, they are going to sell their big house and move into an apartment; "I think my father has been losing a lot of money," she says with a little nervous laugh.

This is the father who, in Eddie's eyes, is the rich man; the stingy man; the man who lives in the big house that Eddie has always wanted to live in, and whose daughter Eddie has finally succeeded in laying—both privately and publicly; the mean, despicable peasant-father, the boor-father, from whom it is actually a service, a duty, to take money, since "we" want it for good purposes, like maybe buying books or records, while he wants it only because it's money, and when he has it he hardly knows what to do with it, except possibly make more money—

"My father is in terrible shape," Pat says. "He drinks all the time, I think my mother should join one of those AA groups that helps you deal with an alcoholic in the family, he really is in an awful shape and she doesn't know what to do." Her light, nervous laugh flutters through the quiet, she waves her hands in an inconclusive—a half-gesture. "The one I really feel sorry for is my sister, it's my youngest sister, she has to stay home with both of them and she hates it, she told me, 'You don't know what it's been like.' "

Pat says, "I think what I'll do is look for a job and work in New York for a year. I'll be lonely, but I couldn't stand to have Eddie here—you know he threatened—he said he would come. But what could he do in New York without money—without a job, without any friends or a place to stay? I told him, I wouldn't see him, if he did come."

She is wistful, looking at us sidelong out of her tilted eyes. "I still have to go out there, you know, and get my things—I left all my things in the apartment. I thought I'd look for a job first, and go out there after I'd got one. I'm kind of scared to go—scared of seeing him—" She laughs nervously, apologetically. "I wish there were some other way of doing it, getting my things I mean—I don't care about the furniture or anything, but I left most of my clothes, too. Nobody else could collect them for me—I'm just putting it off, I guess. I guess I know I really ought to go now, now that I've made up my mind I'm not going back to Eddie."

I think of Eddie the last time we saw him, stout and perspiring below his classic statue's face, his hyacinthine locks—no money coming in to pay for fixing the car, which still lay, crippled, in the street in front of the apartment building which is scheduled to be torn down by Urban Ren~ val in two weeks.

What is a "novel of ideas"? Whose ideas? Generally, not the author's—rather, the political, philosophical, moral ideas "going around" (like a virus infection) at the time. I'd like to write a novel of my ideas.

The "idea" of the plastic bomb—which I don't in the least even pretend to understand, I don't have the faintest practical notion of what it is, how it works, what it looks like, what sets it off—fascinates me like the idea of evil itself. As if there now exists in the world a substance—pliable, tensile, infinitely malleable, able to take any color, shape, texture, capable of aping any other substance in the world—which, while appearing entirely innocent (like its truly innocent original) is in actuality totally lethal. As if the universe has now actually become (by man's own hand) what the aborigines always believed it was: infinitely treacherous, governed by the unreadable laws of inscrutable, irrational forces which can only be propitiated (vainly), never dominated or manipulated or understood—

The situation for the novel: involved in the trial, in another state, of another man—the dark brother—the doppelgänger—the son who seeks the father—emotionally and psychologically, the protagonist is called to testify in a trial of a book for obscenity. The obscenity trial ends in a conviction, for still another young man (innocent, except technically; he works in a bookstore where the book is for sale). The unexpectedly harsh sentence—30 days in jail plus a $600 fine—will be appealed and, probably, reversed. The machinery of the law. The ignorance and stupidity of the judge. His prejudices. The prosecution lawyer loses his temper. Bickering between the judge and the prosecutor, who are essentially in sympathy. Political implications: rightists versus liberals. Moral implications: immorality of "morality's" defenders, honest morality of the defenders of the "obscene" book. The parade of experts: professors of literature, of sociology; ministers, aldermen, guardians of public decency, etc. The lumpish jury: "It was impossible to know what they were thinking." Almost a hundred per cent illiterate. How it's all like Dickens, happening all over again nearly a century later. How it's comic, but the future of the innocent young man, who will have a prison record for the rest of his life unless the sentence is reversed, is involved. Eggheads versus Real People; Just Folks; the man-in-the-street, adjudged, in this state (Missouri) as competent to recognize "obscenity" as any expert. The judge's vacillation on allowing expert testimony.

—The other trial, for possession of narcotics (meaning pot), the real subject matter, dark counterpoint. Ends in suspended sentence (recurrently persistent symbolism of legal terminology—as if we don't all anyhow live under a suspended sentence).

Protagonist: Jim; accused: Eddie; victim: possibly Lola? Change sex, not important—she could be working in a bookstore.

Assisting at (in the French sense) the Veiled Prophet parade, I am seized by a combination of extreme ennui and intolerable excitement—I find tears coming to my eyes at the very oom-pah-pah of a high school tuba. The emotion has nothing to do with the "meaning" of the parade (it has none), it is engendered by the parade itself, in all its gaudy trappings and loud boom-booms. Puffs of smoke from the exploding firecrackers appear white against the navy-blue sky; the arc lights are blue; a Roman candle— "Aaaah!" moans the crowd; it's every carnival, every fiesta, every Mardi Gras in the world. Rolled into one. Ranks of blue-uniformed policemen on foot, on motorcycles, two-by-two in automobiles, followed by eight mounted, costumed men—what they wear represents no particular nationality or century, it is "the idea of" fancy dress, tunics, swords, breastplates, and plumed helmets—an endless interim during which it seems unlikely that anything will ever move. While all the children, for whose sakes all the adults are (presumably) here, squabble among themselves, complain to their mothers that they have to go to the bathroom, that they're hungry, tired, somebody is pushing them, they want a balloon, some popcorn, crackerjack—at last the parade gets underway. The Veiled Prophet himself, preceded by two men carrying acetylene torches— then the Queen of Love and Beauty ("Oooh, isn't she beautiful!" all the little girls say, "I want to be her"; a gum-chewing matron to her friend, "How do they really pick her?" "It's a matter of money, honey, whose family is willing to spend the most," gum-chewing friend replies. "Well, this one cernly has more pep than the one they had last year"), preceded by more torches, then bands, floats, bands, floats—the children have quieted down and are waving to the masked figures or clapping in time to the bands.

A metaphor for life: to stand, simultaneously bored and enthralled, before a totally meaningless spectacle? In such a context, what is "bored"? "Enthralled"? "Ennui"? "Excitement"? The importance of ritual. Ceremony. Order in chaos. The Pope in Yankee Stadium. Etc.

Or—a World of Love and Beauty. Where the nuns have exchanged their habits for tailored suits, and order is imposed on chaos from within.

A grievous vision is declared unto me: the treacherous dealer dealeth treacherously, and the spoiler spoileth (Isaiah 21:2): not pessimism, rather what you might call the qualified optimism of Sartre, when he says, ". . . what people reproach us with is not, after all, our pessimism, but the sternness of our optimism. . . ." If, as he also says, "the coward makes himself cowardly, the hero makes himself heroic; and . . . there is always a possibility for the coward to give up cowardice and for the hero to stop being a hero," then the treacherous dealer can give up dealing treacherously, the spoiler give up spoiling. He who isn't a treacherous dealer doesn't deal treacherously. He who doesn't deal treacherously isn't a treacherous dealer. Sartre: "Therefore, you can see that there is a possibility of creating a human community. . . ."

For the past year or so, Mother has taken to sending the children wildly unsuitable presents she finds in the dime stores. To the little boys she sends novelty tie racks, or games of Imp so shoddily made of plastic that one piece is missing by the time the package arrives; the little girls receive plastic rain-hats, imitation gold mesh change purses, and made-in-Japan doll tea sets already minus a cup or saucer (and sure to be without a lid for the sugar bowl); the baby gets tiny dolls with open-and-shut eyes, whose arms and legs she wrenches off at once, or a box of beads as tiny as seed pearls to string. Boxes of heavily perfumed soap shaped like gardenias or footballs. A package of cookies in letter shapes is (naturally) delivered smashed into crumbs. The puzzle is that she finds it worth the postage to send these cheap, usually worthless things (she believes the postage in general to be exorbitant). The impulse behind the packages is clear; what isn't clear is how she comes to choose these particular objects, which I would have expected her to consider cheap, ugly, and badly made.

On second thought, I think she does consider them cheap, ugly, and etc., but it's quite possible that she thinks I, who am so alien to her, with inexplicable likes and dislikes, will like these things.

My daughter Jane has found—already—an unworthy object for her love: a child called Ursula. Ursula, who is an unconscionable little liar, swings her thick blonde braid behind her back and demurely regards the floor when spoken to by an adult; she lives down the block. She is a Catholic, and instructs the children on Sin. Such a bare-faced little scoundrel, she tilts up her blank, innocent little kisser with its blank, bleak blue eyes, announcing,

"It's a sin on your soul if you tell a lie."

And Jane, who is tormented by these problems and by the fickleness of Ursula, comes home muttering, ". . . a sin on your soul . . ."

Eddie, saying in a loud, careless voice (but not looking at me), "I spoke to Pat last night on the telephone . . . you know she's gone, she went home to see her folks, to New York . . . Say, how much do you think it would cost to live in Mexico now? I thought maybe Pat and I . . . I was talking to Pat about it last night . . ."

He doesn't realize that he scared her, how he scared her, with his rough talk about her father, whom she loves, and how his accusing her of having been brought up "soft," of never having had it hard, like him, was to her simply accusing, convicting, and declaring her guilty of being herself—of being. As if he intended to make the rest of her life an expiation, a punishment, for her whole existence—for the crime of her existence.

"*You* weren't poor! *You* didn't suffer!" Finally, "You aren't *me!* That's the crime for which I'm punishing you, and for which you must continue to be punished." That's what she felt he was saying to her, when he said, "You'll have to work—all the rest of your life—if you stay with me—no more money from Daddy—no more clothes from Peck & Peck—you'll have to get a job—you'll have to—"

As soon as I begin moving away from St. Louis, it reinvests itself with all the glamour of the Other.

Becomes—perversely—in its ineffable ordinariness, its middle-classness, crassness, provinciality, and dullness—exotic. The flatland, unrelieved, shadowless, fertile, stretching to a distant round horizon like the ocean's—even it acquires mystery. The people, in the very resoluteness of their refusal to be "different," become alien. The flat drawled vowels of their speech, which I so dislike, become foreign, with all the fascination of the foreign, distant, unknown.

Fields planted to corn or soybeans as far as the horizon; silos, farmhouses isolated under that enormous shallow sky, sheltering under a clump of trees—the only trees for miles, except perhaps for a straggle that serves as a windbreak along the creek.

The wide straight featureless six-lane highways littered along the edge with beer cans—detritus of midwestern debauch: these too take on again the sinister compelling drama I ascribed to them when first I traveled here.

Exotic to me, child of the bastard, metropolitan east coast, the way Deerslayer! and the Last of the Mohicans! were to the young Berliners of Fraülein's youth.

Statistics on suicide reinforce the revelations of questionnaires-in-depth: married men are "happiest."

And why not? How many (per hundred, or is it per 1,000) men want to be "free to die"?

You would not need to explain to the young bullfighter that wanting to be free to die is not the same as wanting to die.

A piece in the paper on the wood ibis, which by next year would have been extinct, according to the ecologists, due to repeated floods, droughts, tornadoes, and typhoons, which have repeatedly destroyed its nests and eggs: an employee of the Wildlife Service, traveling over its nesting grounds in the Great Dismal Swamp or wherever, reports that in spite of the fact that, this year as last, its eggs have been destroyed, the wood ibis have returned to the swamp and laid a second set of eggs; and that, although the normal count is approx. three eggs per nest, he saw five eggs in most nests.

Mother, along with all the other old ladies, lives in a world of manufactured calamities; Ethel telling her, at the start of her annual journey to St. Louis, "Oh, *don't* go by way of Queens Boulevard!" (like that old joke—and *it* was about an old lady, too, although we always took it as a joke on the provincialism of the Boston Brahmins—about going to California from Boston by way of Belmont).

So I said (to Mother in the jolting car en route from Lambert-St. Louis Airport to our house), "Why didn't she want you to go by way of Queens Boulevard?"

And Mother replied, "Because she said that this year the

traffic there is terrible—really terrible. She said I would never get to the airport on time if the taxi went on Queens Boulevard! But I asked Roy if the traffic was so bad and he said, Nonsense, it isn't any worse than last year, and to leave it up to the cab driver."

She pleated and unpleated her taupe leather gloves, bestowing polite, non-committal looks meanwhile on the undistinguished suburban scenery as it jounced by.

Similarly, another occasion (we are standing in the kitchen, and I am thinking about dinner)—Mother bursts out, "One day I came home with a big bundle and I opened the door of the apartment, and then I went in and hung up my coat and put away the bundle, and I couldn't find my one glove anywhere! I hunted high and low. So finally I went downstairs and told the doorman that if anybody found a glove it was mine. And then I went back upstairs—and there was my glove in my coat pocket."

Or,

The exploding doll. Which seems to me to embody some sort of dreadful fable for our time, our America. What I don't know is exactly how it's significant, or how it should be—can be—interpreted: the radio news commentator remarks that a warning has been issued to all those who have received children's dolls as gifts from Vietnam; the dolls are said to be booby-trapped. Three days later there is a news report in the paper to the effect that the scare about Vietnamese dolls was a false alarm, there are no explosives set to go off when an American child picks up a doll to play with:

"Hundreds of dolls were checked out across the country today, but not one was loaded with Viet Cong explosives.

"Rumor said American servicemen in Vietnam were unwittingly mailing home booby-trapped dolls as gifts. . . .

"The dolls were described as about 15 inches high, handmade, and beautifully dressed.

"Fears that they might be dangerous apparently stemmed from accounts in letters from American servicemen, telling of buddies being injured by exploding dolls. Third Army Headquarters at Fort McPherson, Ga., said it knew of no American serviceman being injured in that manner." —from the *St. Louis Post-Dispatch*

If dreams while asleep are clues to the deeply buried problems and preoccupations of the dreamer, what is it this particularly ugly collective dream of ours is warning us about?

"America can break your heart."

Why the use of that most personal of pronouns, "I," has always seemed to me so inexpressibly touching: at some truly buried level of consciousness I conceive of man as so infinitesimal a part of the universe that personal self-aggrandizement on the part of any one individual can't be anything but touching. My belief so fundamental a part of my conception of the universe that it never occurred to me that it was a function of my own attitudes; it appeared/appears to me in the form of a *donnée*, as self-evident to the experience of my senses as God's existence was to Descartes.

(If (on the other hand) one accepts the Judeo-Christian view that man is, *nolens-volens*, in effect the center of the universe, then of course the repeated use of that word, "I," becomes repugnant.)

Lola calls. She says, Your friend who had all those babies and had varicose veins, did she ever have an operation? I say Yes, she did. Lola says, When did she have it? In between babies or after the last one? After the last one, I say. Lola says, I wonder why she didn't have it in between. I say, Are yours bothering you? Yes, says Lola, these doctors here seem to take them very seriously, they're always asking me about them. And it gets so hot, wearing these awful elastic stockings and bandages. I say, Do the doctors say you should have an operation? Yes, she says, after this baby is born. But in between they always disappear, you can't even see where they are. How would they know which ones to cut out if you can't even see them?

I laugh, and say, "Well, that would be their problem, not yours."

"Oh," says Lola, "I wouldn't mind any of it if I could stay in bed all day, or lie on sofa."

She says she wants to have lots more babies after this one.

In an interview in a woman's magazine, the young bullfighter says, "I think that when a man is married he is no longer free to die . . . and so he can't go on fighting the bulls up close, not close the way I do. But I want to fight the bull up close. . . ."

Assuming that it really was the young bullfighter who said it, and not the interviewer, what deep reserves of mother-wit inform his peasant blood.

"Art is also a 'hazardous occupation,' but no one attempts to safeguard poets or artists; it is generally overlooked that, by the

very character of their profession, a scratch may prove mortal."
—Said Ehrenburg, in his *Memoirs*.

What I see happening to (going askew in) Mother is exactly
mirrored in what is happening in her handwriting; it starts out
looking just as it always did, reassuringly so, the same round, self-
assured, determined, regular characters, until gradually it appears
to be in more and more of a hurry, the letters lean further to the
right, the crossbars don't quite hit the *t*'s, the *a*'s and *o*'s are either
open and slack or choked tight shut; and simultaneously there is an
elusive change in the sense of what she is writing (or in what I am
reading—are they always the same?). In spite of her dutiful references to each of the children by name, and her messages of affectionate remembrance, I have the feeling that she has lost track of
to whom it is she is writing: she has forgotten, briefly, that she is
writing to *me*. Perhaps some semi-abstract daughter still exists in
her mind; she knows she has a daughter, she continues to feel all
the necessary maternal feelings toward this daughter, but she has
quite lost sight of me; I remain, vague, the daughter she might
have had, the daughter she did have, but she has lost myself.

Nothing is ever exactly as one has imagined—remembered?—it:
Charlotte's house. The place is weedy and overgrown; the driveway—its pebbles fight a losing battle against the green that springs
up everywhere, forcing its way upward through the stones. From
the road, the house itself is invisible. The old path leading to the
front gate has disappeared, covered over with high grass and
brambles; the gate, unpainted, sags dumbly open on its hinges, all
that can be seen is the gray slate roof, looking more like a natural
outcropping of slate than part of a man-made building. Everywhere
the weeds and brambles have taken over, nothing has been cut
back, nothing pruned or lopped off, nothing mowed, clipped, or
trimmed. In the woods, dead branches lie where they fell, or
hang, broken, from the trees where they grew. Inside the house,
what a clutter of forgotten objects, piled carelessly in corners and
closets, basement cupboards, laundry rooms, and attics; the old
dolls' house, stripped of its shingles and paint, its wallpaper peeling off and painted over, the glass of its windows long since poked
out, the electric lights so lovingly installed by that long-ago father
(my father!) torn out, and nothing left but tiny empty sockets and

dangling wires—ruined as it is, it has kept its magic for the children, they play with it for hours, arranging stones and bits of wood in the destroyed rooms. Even an old enameled pail turns up, with a lid. On the coffee table in front of the fireplace, Grandmother's brass samovar is ensconced, polished, handsome: "Mother had it electrified, years ago; it used to require charcoal—"

Somehow a natural decay, a decline not foreign or inimical to nature and the natural order, an upwelling or outpouring of fertility, even prodigality, to give the lie to the sterility of the surgically barren woman. That one: if ever a woman was born to mother a brood, it was she. And she has, in fact, mothered several— down, now, to the third generation, children, animals, and flowers— with a fine impartiality. And yet. Does the cruel canker gnaw? —they aren't mine, not out of my body, always they are some other woman's (the enemy's)?

To think that I was thirty-five years old before I realized that many (most?) people see not only you, and "other people," but also themselves, in two dimensions.

If they work as a waitress, or a supermarket cashier, dentist's assistant, professor, shoe salesman, when they think of themselves they think, "Waitress." "Supermarket cashier." "Dentist's assistant." "Professor." "Shoe salesman." Or mother of five. Retired civil servant. War veteran. Program chairman of the League of Women Voters. So naturally they see you and other people in the same way; no denigration intended. No malice.

Similarly, "I am an orphan." "Widow." "Alcoholic." "Shoplifter." "Diabetic." "Good Christian." "Accused." "Birdwatcher." "Responsible citizen."

And if their love deserts them, "Jilted." Appropriately, "Bilked." "Robbed." "Mutilated." "Ruined." "Bankrupt." "Raped!"

I took comfort at this time from what I had read someplace about Buddha, that at the age of 29, in accordance with a prophecy that had been made at the time of his conception, he saw a sick man, an old man, and a corpse, and realized for the first time that sickness, old age, and death were also part of life.

The contrapuntal visits from Pat and Eddie: like—depending on whether you viewed it as comedy or tragedy—a French farce, with fugitive lovers hiding under beds and escaping through doors concealed in closets, one running down the fire-stairs while another rode up in the elevator—or a pas de deux in which one partner was perpetually missing, a sad ballet of the passing of love and the essential solitariness of the heart. A dead-serious game of hide-and-seek, in which he looks for her while trying to escape from himself, while she, avoiding him, tries to confront herself instead.

Pat would telephone, "Hi, I'm in town, and I'd like to come up for a while . . ." she would sit on our borrowed chintz, kicking off her shoes and tucking her feet up under her, after the children had all gone to bed, and tell us about the phone calls, which she would hang up on as soon as she recognized the voice, the special delivery letters she tore up unread. "I really don't want to see him, can't he understand that? I have to have some time by myself, to think about things." It would get later and later, she would sip ice-water and finally stay the night, sleeping on the extra bed in one of the children's rooms, to their great delight when they woke up in the morning and found her.

"Oh, it's keen! Pat's here!" they would shout, as if she had mysteriously materialized and taken shape there under the sheet during the night. I often wondered why they liked her, she seldom paid any attention to them or permitted them to breach the formidable wall of her reserve. In the morning she would pin up her hair into its intricate pattern, drink a glass of juice, put on her shoes, and go.

Or, alternatively, Eddie—announced by the peremptory shrill buzz of the doorbell in the late, hot afternoon, when Jim was still locked away working and the apartment simply couldn't contain all the children, they seemed to be swarming and clustering and clotting everywhere. One of the older ones would rush to the door—"Oooh, it's Eddie! How keen!" And he would stand, sheepish and perspiring in the kitchen doorway, drinking his beer from a can and passing it around for sips to all of them.

After dinner, when they were finally asleep, he'd say casually to Jim or me, "Have you heard from Pat? I tried to call her the other day, but they always say she isn't there . . . I *know* she's there . . ."

"Well, Eddie," I'd say, "I guess she doesn't want to see you now, I don't think she wants to see anybody. Don't you think you should leave her alone and give her a chance to make up her mind about what she wants to do?"

"I'm giving her a chance, I want her to make up her mind by

herself," Eddie would say, "I just don't see why they always say she's out, I'm sure she wouldn't refuse to talk to me. What I don't understand is, I'm sure if I could just see her, we could talk it over."

So he and Jim would play some of the Mingus and Coltrane records and finish the six-packs in the refrigerator and watch the late-late movie, and in the morning the children would shout, "Oh, how keen! Eddie's here!" and jump on his bed until he'd get up and wrestle with them, and when I took them off to the park and the grocery store and Jim locked himself up with the tapes and the piano, he'd doze off on the chintz until it was time to go out after some more beer.

Sometimes when Pat turned up on an evening right after one of Eddie's visits, one of us would say, "Eddie was just here yesterday," and she would give her breathless, rather nervous little laugh, saying, "How is he?" for politeness' sake, perhaps, and tell us how her aunt has set up a job interview for her, for tomorrow.

According to Dr. L., the statistics on the relative number of suicides in groups of married men versus single men are meaningless, because the group "single men" is already a group of deviates in our society, simply through being unmarried. "Marriage is the normal state, so to remain unmarried marks them as deviates, and there is no need to express surprise at a high incidence of suicide in a group which has already demonstrated its alienation from society." Thus Dr. L.

"Deviance . . . is a creation of the public imagination."
—Howard Becker, author of *Outsiders: Studies in the Sociology of Deviance.*

It is after 10, almost 10:30, a foggy Wednesday evening; I am about to go up to bed. The doorbell rings. "Who's *that?*"—Ardis.

"What have you been doing this evening—to bring yourself to this neighborhood at this hour?"

"Oh well, gallivanting," she pouts prankishly. She comes in, ensconces herself on the sofa where Jim has been desultorily examining the newspaper. She is looking well, rather taut around the cheekbones, her hair pulled back tightly and done high in a knot behind.

"Do you know—can you guess—how much I weigh, now?" she

confides—"A hundred and fifty-six! Imagine! But I think I'll keep my unAmerican figure, my saftig European figure, because look at my face, if I lost twenty pounds, I'd look like a skull."

She is wearing a fur-trimmed suede coat, stiletto heels, a "little black dress"; where can she have been?

"I've made a decision; I've finally come to a decision," Ardis announces. "I'm going to leave St. Louis. Definitely. Leave." Pause. "I can't stand it—I should never have come back."

Jim, who tells me later that he always knew she would be back this fall in spite of last spring's protestations (and how astonished she, Ardis, has been, to find that Pat and Eddie have actually gone for good, are really no longer here in St. Louis)—"Of course I knew, she had to come back no matter what she said, she's like a yo-yo, it's her parents—and their money—and Deedee, that pull her back to St. Louis, like a yo-yo on a string"—says nothing.

And I am sitting there, thinking, suddenly dismal, that she never will go, never. Ten years from now I can see her, sitting on someone else's sofa, insisting that she *must* leave, she— Because I did believe her last spring when she quit her job and gave up her apartment and sold all her furniture and said, "I'm not coming back." ("Where are you going? Ardis, what are you going to do when the summer is over, Ardis?" I remember asking, at the same time motherly and ingenuous—as it must have seemed to her.)

"I don't know where I'll go, what I'll do, I don't know, I can't think beyond the summer—if he—" and my heart sank even then, understanding that what she meant, what she was really doing was not making any decision, not taking any stand about herself or her life, but simply launching herself into thin air, the thin blue air of if-he-gets-his-divorce, and if-he-asks-me-to-marry-him, refusing to see what we see so plainly, that there will be no divorce, no marriage, no he and she.

What keeps me quiet is remembering my own experience with Paul. How I loathed my smugly, if not necessarily happily, married friends who so tiresomely repeated, "But how's it going to end? Is he going to marry you? What are you going to do?" Because I knew, and I didn't want to know. Like Ardis. Because it wasn't, by that time, a matter of marriage, or even "love"; rather, a kind of addiction ("state of being given up to some habit, practice, or pursuit"), a symbiotic relationship ("symbiosis, n., *Biol.* the living together of two species of organisms: a term usually restricted to cases in which the union of the two . . . is not disadvantageous to either, or is advantageous or necessary to both, as the case of the fungus and alga which together make up the lichen") rapidly deteriorating, becoming more and more of an emotional drain, a slow seepage and leaking away of all vestiges of self, individuality, separate entity, personal identity.

How I raged against Paul, I remember, that one particular gray, revealing morning in the motel outside Boston (or was it Winston-Salem, or Scranton? by the end, we'd had scenes in all three), accusing him of using me, of having changed me into a mere sexual object: "a public convenience! That's what I am, a public convenience, reserved for your own private use—" *how* he tried to shut me up! He must have thought I was turning into a virago, a shrew, all he most abhorred and feared in a woman.

What he had done, though, was not what I accused him of; his own beloved image of himself forbade him to choose as a sexual object a woman who was merely a sexual object, and he more than I would strive zealously to preserve all that wasn't specifically sexual in our relationship. But he had robbed me, nevertheless, stolen myself away from me, giving nothing of himself—his real self—in return. Changed me, short-changed me, so how could I face the rest of my life without him? The days—endless gray days that had turned into mere interludes of waiting for his call—

So, remembering—not Paul, but myself—I do understand Ardis.

Again, life imitating art. ("Life." "Art.") The people who conceive not only of others—their friends, acquaintances, neighbors, relatives, the faces they recognize from newspaper photos and out of the pages of *Life,* mailmen, delivery boys, bus drivers, nurses, doctors, doormen, ushers in movie houses, etc., etc.—but of themselves as two dimensional. "Flat as a paper doll." I find them astonishing! How astonishing I find them. Not including in this group these who prefer to play—and stay—in the shallows of their personalities (where I include, perhaps, Roy—many, many).

Let me pursue this.

Moments in music when the desire to cry out, "Verweile doch . . ." is unbearably strong; one example, *La Forza del Destino,* Act III. Like crying out to a lover, "Don't stop . . ." while at the very moment of crying out, the moment is already past. But *why should* Faust find only one such moment, and be damned for it? In Real Life, now, the dirty dishes are still piled in the sink, the dirty linen still to be washed, in spite of music, love, and all the rest.

While the child is falling—what then?

The mother reports she left the child unattended for only a minute; when she came back she found the kitchen window open and the child lying on the ground below.

I remember the week before Charles was born, when the baby fell out of the window of the apartment house opposite: sirens. Fire engines. Police cars. Ambulance. Processions: the mother, carrying the body of the motionless child. Followed by a silent chorus of neighbors, police, firemen, ambulance attendants.

The sequel, in which the child recovers (a miracle!) and, after many weeks in the hospital, is returned home, whence he emerges through the door of the apartment house, indistinguishable from the other children who live in the building.

Autumn. Dry yellow or brown leaves somersaulting over the gray sidewalks.

A quick-as-a-wink premonition of disaster.

It is so obvious that I can hardly believe I didn't realize it sooner—without being told. Not physically obvious; it won't (wouldn't) be that for a long time. But in the inevitable, inexorable course of events—of course. How blind and stupid I've been. Pat is pregnant. Of course!

She is concerned, quiet, determined. Not alarmed. She won't have the baby. She won't tell Eddie. "I had to tell someone, though—I had to tell you."

She has a friend who knows a doctor—knows of a doctor— "He'll do it—the abortion—for three hundred dollars. Cash. In advance." She smiles slightly; it has an ugly ring to it, and yet it is a good, kind thing for him to do, and dreadfully risky.

"At this stage, there's no real danger for me, it's early enough."

She suspected last month that there was something wrong, and this month she was sure; two missed periods, and retching into the bathroom basin every morning when she brushed her teeth. Otherwise she feels fine, and the extra ounce or two she has put on are, if anything, becoming, her face is fuller, she has lost the taut look around her eyes.

"My friend made the appointment for me—it's next Tuesday."

From Fraülein's letter: ". . . my day starts at 5 A.M., and after Joseph has gone to work I have my second breakfast, listen to some good Music, watch Nature, the Sunrise, my little feathered friends finding their breakfast, and read for a little while. Then after that my children start coming, mothers who go to work leave their children with me twice a week for the day. We have a grand time together, it still gives me pleasure to take walks, teach, and play games, before you know it the day is gone. I do hope I have given the children a love for Nature, Animals, and that life has many beautiful things in store for them, when they grow up, to look for the things in life that are worthwhile living for. . . . I have sent you a book from East Berlin, behind the iron curtain, which a friend of mine I have known since childhood sent to me. It shows you that in spite of everything, there is still a part of you that can lift you above hate, greed, envy, cruelty, misery if you know how to find it in yourself, your true self. My friend has always been a wonderful person, helping others . . . has gone through terrible things, but never lost her spirit and the hope that there will come a better life for everybody on earth. . . . Warmest greetings to you all, most of all your dear children. . . ."

I find myself at a shoe sale in Famous-Barr's basement in Clayton with Lola; we stand picking up shoes and putting them down again.

"These are pretty," Lola says, holding up a pair. "Why don't you try them on?" She reaches them over to me. I take off one shoe and slide my foot into one of these.

"Quite Elizabethan," says Lola, sounding pleased. "Becoming, really. It looks like you. Why don't you buy these?"

I am a trifle surprised at her enthusiasm; thoughtfully I study my foot in russet suede. It suddenly occurs to me to wonder, what is Lola's picture of me? How does she see me, really? "Elizabethan"— rather quaint? Not of the real—this particular—world, certainly not of this century (although for that matter we are in an Eliza-bethan era—but surely Lola's mind doesn't work along those lines). A simple peasant wife, brewing simples and waiting for the bread to rise (a rôle I myself occasionally find appealing)? A court lady? A sort of bluestocking—like a secular abbess, perhaps? Or—more simply—a 20th century female with a penchant for slightly out-landish clothing (have I?)?

I think I must be a character—very likely even "a character" in Lola's novel.

In any case, I'll take the shoes.

Impelled by this decision, I buy another pair as well, quite unlike my usual style, but Lola seems to be satisfied with them as being "in character." I find myself intently observing my own feet, as if by looking at them I will be able to understand what is in Lola's mind.

The windows of the new junkshop are identical with those of Mrs. Borrow's, even to the bust of the Indian set up on a rickety table; it is almost embarrassing, we hesitate to enter, expecting to see her double emerging from the same back regions. But when we do go in, there is a young man in glasses and a fringe of beard sitting near the back in a rocking chair. The place is small and not crowded (well, after all, it has only been open for two weeks). But to see these things set out on tables, in all seriousness, as if a buyer will come in—maybe this afternoon—and pay 75¢ for a used milk-bottle—it is laughable. Besides, everything is overpriced. What can the young man be thinking of? Here among second-hand kitchen forks and imitation-leather cigarette boxes is a white-enameled urinal. We see a tin tray advertising Coca-Cola; a young lady in a yellow gown reaches out to us with a refreshing glassful; how does it happen that all over St. Louis this same yellow-gowned lady appears in all the junkshops this week? In tiny letters the legend reads, Copyright 1938. Aha. She is a Period Piece. Who sends out the word, "Unload trays advertising Coca-Cola, circa 1938, in St. Louis this week"? Last week I saw none of these trays. Over on a shelf against the wall stand two plastic peanuts on needle-thin legs, wearing top hats, each about three inches tall; I recognize a set of "Mr. Planters" salt-and-pepper shakers, circa what? Here on the floor is a foot-locker with a broken lock: "an old Army trunk," the young man calls it. Jim says he must have bought up some assorted lots of junk and then taken out what he thought were the most likely pieces, washed them, dusted them, even polished and painted them, and set them out on his tables and shelves with all confidence to wait for their buyers. But who will buy that glass milk-bottle?

"Well," I say to Jim triumphantly, "Ann, Anya might . . . yes, why not, if she felt like it . . ."

Mother, on the other hand, never liked junkshops, even in (more socially acceptable) disguise—"Another one! Look, more *antiques!*" she would cry out to the New England hills; even when her friends took courses in Interior Decorating and became knowledgeable about period furniture she couldn't bring herself to pronounce the word without a sniff of derision, and when the object under scrutiny is scratched or cracked her response is simple incredulity at anybody's desire to preserve, let alone admire, it. "What is it, an *antique?*" she enquires, heavily ironic, before a chipped gravy-boat . . .

It's all of a piece, this feeling of hers, with her refusal to admit the approach, the inevitability, and the ravages of old age. As she values youth, she values newness. As she values health, one's own teeth, and the absence of gray hairs, she values a glossy surface and mirrorlike impenetrability. It's a preoccupation with appearance (vs. reality) deeper than at first appears; the gesture becomes magical, the look of youth becomes youth itself, and finally appearance becomes artifice, and whatever the buried reality beneath the artificially contrived surface, it vanishes, it no longer (did it ever?) exists—and what of it?

(Writing about his own mother, Norbert Wiener remarked that to her, and to many others of her generation and background, "respectability is a pearl beyond price. . . . The . . . injunction to avoid even the appearance of evil is interpreted as an injunction to avoid the appearance of evil and vulgarity far more than evil and vulgarity themselves." So: if age is an evil, even if it can't be avoided, the appearance of age can; and if youth can't be indefinitely prolonged, the appearance of youth can, and why shouldn't the appearance be taken for the reality?)

Or—to look at it from another side—her dislike for things-with-a-past is all of a piece with her rejection of her own past. How she would like to have sprung full-grown from her own forehead! Her ideal—in tune with the national ideal of her generation—the self-made man: how she would love to have been entirely her own creation, her own woman. How much deeper this craving is in her than her more practical sisters' simple desire for suffrage, equal rights, and escape from the kitchen. Part of it, the original impelling source, shame at being a "greenhorn"? Rejecting her background—and thus her "heritage"—altogether.

My Esau-mother, who long ago sold her birthright for a mess of pottage, USA.

When I watch the children fighting among themselves (thinking themselves unwatched), attending to their private urgent business, in which Jim and I are simply irrelevant, unwelcome intrusions, interruptions, I wonder—where could they possibly have sprung from?

As if I were a primitive woman, attributing these incredible fruits to some supernatural source, a being that secretly inhabits some cave on which I unwittingly trespassed, or against whom I neglected to take the prescribed precautions. At such times, the fact that they once grew inside my own body seems entirely irrelevant, the more so since the helpless, half-blind, puny, yowling things that they wrapped in blankets and that tried to suck my milk don't exist any more.

Instead, these fierce, rude children who have taken over the house, hardly leaving me a corner of my own mind into which I can crawl and be alone with my thoughts—

One day Charlotte said, "Such a strange feeling as I sat today on the beach—there I could see some children in bathing-suits, playing in the water, and a mother sitting on the sand, and the mother was you, and the children were your children, but for a minute it seemed as though the mother was Marilyn, your mother, and the children were her children—the water still looks the same, and the beach is the same, the sand and the rocks and the shells—and the trees along the shoreline are the same, the new houses are cunningly hidden in shrubbery and trees so you don't really see them—it suddenly seemed as if—as if nothing was real. As if nothing that had ever happened to me was real. It was frightening—frightening. As if nothing had ever happened at all—"

How frightening it is, but we must not let it frighten us. In the spot where the big old white wooden house stood, with its wide, open veranda, its apple trees, grape arbor, lawn, graveled drive, spiky iron fence, gate, and etcetera, they have laid concrete for a parking lot and built a supermarket. Also, people have been born and others have died, wars have started and finished, whole eras of history have come to an end—it will be in the history books—and we have sent ships to the moon: what isn't frightening?

Two-dimensional view of oneself probably the healthy view—what does the other lead to, but *de facto* schizophrenia?

Those of us who are born out of the momentary desires of the Archduke of Austria and one of his laundry women—who are kings, queens, gods, saints, martyrs, and martians in disguise, where is our place in the Great Society?

(À propos of Eddie, really): How we never do choose whom we love. If we chose, surely we'd choose the "best"—strongest, most attractive, intelligent, trustworthy, earnest—at the very least, those who come closest to embodying those positive qualities we value most highly—

I'm no adolescent, mooing and moping about truelove, my hero!, Junemoon, and romance—

I'm talking about our intimate involvements with people like Eddie, or Ardis. Such hurtful bonds; those people force us to suffer their suffering, and we acquiesce. I often wonder why we do it; I'm not at all sure we even like them. But then, liking is a more or less rational exercise. This sort of intimacy isn't rational; it's neither desired nor sought for; it's like walking into the woods, where each step is "only" one more step, and we can still find our way back to the safety of the path quite easily, until suddenly we stop short and look around and discover ourselves lost.

What I mean is—why do *I* have to have bad dreams about Eddie? I resent it.

It has occurred to me to wonder, with some seriousness, whether Pat-and-Eddie, Ardis, Lola aren't, perhaps, simply different facets (faces?) of myself, like those multiple personalities that turn up from time to time in the form of case studies in psychological journals (or in the form of thrillers in paperback). When I get them in proper focus I certainly can see myself in each of them— something of myself in each of them—myself in something of each of them.

Pat—fighting to be herself, a unique and particular individual, resenting and struggling against the all-but-irresistible undertow created by the combined forces of her own femininity (life-force? female principle?) and both the deeper and the more superficial requirements of society (demanding perpetuation of the race and the social structure on the one hand, conformity and "acceptable behavior" on the other—behavior acceptable in terms of what society would insist she be, une jeune fille bien elevée) . . .

Ardis—wanting above all to be rid of the responsibility for being an individual, to lose her individuality in a kind of corporate entity she labels "marriage"—a "married couple"—in which she will acquire a new identity (since she has no respect for her own) as half of a pair . . .

Lola—fulfilled primarily in her self-created role of earth-mother, the endlessly fruitful, generous, all-encompassing one, whose passions are tidal rather than inflammable, whose "individuality" is all but totally submerged in the vast, sluggish ocean out of which the first struggling forms of independent living forms clawed and scrabbled their painful way thousands of years ago . . .

Does this mean that they, Pat, Ardis, and Lola, *don't really exist?* Am I having all these telephone conversations with myself? Are all their assignations, children, and escapes, my own?

It turns out, according to an advertisement for some scientific journal that appears in *The New Republic,* that Roy has been quite wrong about the Blue Light. In fact, whatever it is they have in fact seen at Palomar apparently means the opposite (if I am interpreting the advertisement correctly) of what Roy said it meant. So that only the incorrigible Romantics (like Roy) can continue to be optimistic, which they (we) will persist in doing, in the face of the evidence. And—let Jim laugh—I was right in my interpretation of Roy's statement. After all.

Ardis phones. She wants to know whether I've heard—"Of course I know you've heard about Eddie and Pat breaking up . . . it's bad, isn't it?" she asks. "What can you do—what do you do— when someone you know, someone you care about, is suffering?" Her voice trembles, falls, rises again. "What does Pat think—how does she feel—after all, they were so close—living together all those months—" then, "Poor, poor Eddie, that's all I can think, he's been in such a bad state and he was trying to do something about it, he had *sought help—*" suddenly this phrase from the language of Public Relations astounds my ears. But to Ardis, naturally it's simply a phrase like all the rest, she goes rapidly on.

It has got so I think I can tell when Ardis is lying, from the sound of her voice; there is a higher pitch, an increased or increasing breathiness, a more rapid delivery. Once I challenged her on some statement I was pretty sure was a lie, and she backed down at once. Usually, though, I'm not cruel enough to put the challenge direct, and she simply backs away when the questions get too pointed. Several times she has taken refuge (as I myself have never had the temerity to do) behind a simple, "I'd really rather not—if you don't mind—rather not talk about it."

She did this the last time I asked about Tony, what I thought was an innocuous question about whether she'd heard from him lately. After all, she had kept calling us to ask if we'd had any letters, and whether we knew his address. Which we did not. I do wonder, occasionally, what has happened to Tony, where he is and what he's doing; at one point, Ardis told Eddie (I remember) that she believed he got his divorce. Anything is possible, in sober fact, and he might be anywhere from St. Louis to Vietnam (although no, I don't think so); either of the alternatives would explain Ardis' reluctance to talk about him.

Have I finally spotted the secret, the key which unlocks the (mysterious) heart of the mystery of Ardis?

"She had . . . persuaded herself that love, that marvelous thing which had hitherto been like a great rosy-plumaged bird soaring in the splendors of poetic skies . . . at last within her grasp . . . tried to imagine just what was meant, in life, by the words 'bliss,' 'passion,' and 'rapture'—words that had seemed so beautiful to her in books . . . all the while, she was waiting for something to happen. Like a sailor in distress, she kept casting desperate glances over the solitary waste of the horizon. . . . Spring came again. She found it hard to breathe. . . ."

"Mme. Bovary, c'est moi!" (Steegmuller translation)—no need to change as much as a comma. Not that one can blame her, our society still instills in young girls that same notion of waiting for something to happen to oneself, la belle au bois dormante—

Neither Emma nor Ardis remained a young girl, but experience taught them nothing. As Henry James, even, saw, "she [he meant Emma] does these things . . . while remaining absorbed in the romantic vision, and she remains absorbed in the romantic vision (even) while . . . rolling in the dust. . . ."

Is it Ardis' fate to remain—like so much in this age of the manqué—a Romantic-manquée?

After all, I suppose not. She belongs right in there with her sisters, Pat and Lola—and let me add myself to the list, sisters all— if anything, a Romantic-too-much-with-us. All of us do "these things . . . while remaining absorbed in the romantic vision," and we remain absorbed in the romantic vision while rolling in the dust, even if our own age would put it more crudely.

And yet—she has amputated a part of herself, if we measure her against the ideal whole woman, contemplate her as Compleat

Woman: she has made herself into a purely physical/emotional creature, all instinct and ardor. Without intellect, moral responsibility, or integrity; those aspects of "the human" she has lopped off.

Lola, similarly maimed by self-inflicted mutilations—the Heavenly Cow, the mooing muse . . .

And Pat, who clings desperately to her personal integrity, having realized—at the very last minute—that once that goes, "everything must go" . . .

As for myself—

To Mother, who changed her name to Marilyn as soon as she possibly could (when was it, I wonder, when she registered for Junior High?), having to be known as "Marya" all her life would have seemed the worst sort of punishment. The name, in its foreignness and oddity—and, yes, old-fashionedness, seeming to her to label her as foreign, odd, and old-fashioned, instead of the wholesome, modern American girl she so yearned to be. I'm sure Grandma didn't object to the change; how mysterious all her American daughters must have seemed to her, if she permitted herself (or had the time) to observe them at all.

Contrast here with Roy's wife Ann, that is, Anya. The world in which Anya moves finds the foreign, odd, and old-fashioned "interesting." (Anya loves "antiques," rummages in junkshops, keeps souvenirs, saves old letters.) Given a perfectly good American name like "Ann," she has deliberately chosen to label herself "Anya" after a long-dead great-grandmother, and put jam in her tea.

It's clearly at that level of their personalities that both Mother and Anya really live: the level at which they so clearly stand in complete opposition to each other. To Mother, Anya's choices must seem wilfully perverse. To Anya, Mother's disapproval seems, simply, arbitrary. Superficially, they have much in common: their interest in music, their relationships with Roy, their refusal to remain primarily housewives, and insistence on having "careers." I suppose Anya "explains" Mother's hostility to herself as a mother's refusal to give up her son to his wife, but I think she's wrong. It's even deeper than that, it goes back to the unyielding core of selfhood in each of them that has nothing to do with other people but concerns the self's whole stance vis-à-vis the world.

Charlotte must not be permitted! to become bitter in old age. Possibly there's a danger in pinning one's trust, as she has done,

entirely in personal relationships—in making personal relationships
one's chief, if not only, value; when the individuals die, as they
must one day, when the only thing in life (persons) one valued is
dead, it must be as if value itself is dead, and there is indeed nothing left . . .

Rather,

> Thinking of all the grains of sand in the universe,
> Whose number is finite, although we may not be able to count to it,
> I think I must build my house on those sands.

Or, E. M. Forster wrote, "the confidence-trick is the work
of man; the want-of-confidence trick is the work of the devil"—
something like that.

Mrs. Borrow as the principle of health, the life-principle in
what's broken (by ordinary life), junk, trash—the life-giving principle that holds the junk, rubbish, whatever you call it, of ordinary
life together—so that *things* (objects) don't overwhelm her, she is
not destroyed or even ruled by things, but always maintains control over them. Female principle? Charlotte too: health-giving, life-
giving, in the midst of apparently lifeless, discarded debris of life.

Opposite: the mother-in-law, whose affinity for what's broken
is because she recognizes in it a reflection of her own maimed self.

What is the source of my own attraction toward these things?

Lola's baby, another girl, arrived last month, according to a
birth announcement that has been following us all over the country. In the same mail, a delayed letter from Ann, who had written,
"I've been to visit Lola in the hospital, where, as you've probably
heard, her newest girl has been born. A very pretty baby, like all
the others. Lola seems relieved to have it all over with and to be
getting back to her usual size, and is going ahead with her placid
preparations for the wedding—between feedings. . . ."

In the grand scheme of things, it almost certainly doesn't make
any difference whether the Lolas mother girls or boys, but I can't
help thinking that now there are on this earth that many more
female creatures faced with the necessity of clambering, clawing
their way, out of that slough of femininity where their mother still
flounders, occasionally finding a foothold and crying out, on the
strength of that, for help—then sliding, sinking back under again,

where the cry becomes a gulp, a sigh, a gurgle. A popular dance tune.

Another glimpse into the future. Myself done up in a Hallowe'en mask of wrinkles, wigged, rouged, toothless, in the crystal ball of a hotel fingerbowl. Mother is telling me about the new cook at The Willows, where she has spent the summer.

"Last year they had a good cook, but that one left and the one they got was terrible. The meat was so tough—I couldn't eat it. And the desserts—on the menu they looked lovely but when you ordered it they brought stale cake in some kind of sticky sauce."

She opens her handbag and rummages in it for what she calls "a tissue." Finding one, she dabs at her nose with it and goes on.

"But what I *don't like* is Belle Gordon saying the food is so good. Because it isn't good, it was awful! Last summer it wasn't so bad, but this new cook—nobody could think he was good. And every day I would sit there across from Mrs. Gordon and she told me she thought the food at The Willows is excellent. Excellent!"

She sniffs. I suggest that maybe Mrs. Gordon has good teeth (Mother is willing to admit her teeth aren't so good) and so maybe the meat didn't seem as tough to her as it did to Mother. Mother sniffs again.

"Good teeth!" she says. "Her teeth are worse than mine, worse by far. That was another thing she did—when they brought tough meat, I would send mine back. 'Take this back,' I would say to the waitress—it wasn't her fault, of course, most of them are college girls you know, working during their vacations—'I can't chew it, but it needn't be wasted. It's too tough for me,' I would say. 'There may be some here who can eat it.' But Belle Gordon wouldn't send hers back, no, she would sit there chewing and chewing until you'd get tired watching her. I don't know how she could chew so long! And then she took the piece of meat out of her mouth with her fork and she would put it on the edge of her plate. 'I don't know what you mean, there isn't a thing wrong with the food here, Marilyn,' she would say to me, and by the end of the meal there would be all the pieces of chewed gray meat in a circle around the edge of her plate."

A tune very popular these past few weeks that nudges me to think of Ardis, its plangent melody and lyrics sweetly sad: farewell, my love, some day, somewhere we'll meet again: *that* same old tune. I am pricked by it into wondering where she is and what she is doing, for she has actually gone away, she has left St. Louis, farewell her love, and what is to become of her?

Deedee, too; I think of the two of them in Ibiza, which I have never seen and so am free to imagine; they can climb side by side to the top of the hill and turn their faces toward the ocean—the setting sun—cinematic. And after that, what will they do? As if the supreme effort of will of Ardis' life consisted of lifting herself (and Deedee) out of St. Louis, a gesture without a sequel. As if from now on nothing more will be required of her but to lean back in her seat and await the ending—happy? or sweetly sad?

But—let me remind myself—Ardis is a real person, not a figment—no bundle of rags and wires to be tossed back into the closet when I've finished with her.

Dear lady,
Poetry can do nothing for you. Perhaps you are one of those
Who might benefit from a diet of molecules.

Will people read my book and recognize in it the doorman of their apartment house, resemblance to actual people either living or dead? If so, it will almost certainly be the wrong house.

If somewhere there existed a master key to the *roman à clef*.

If fictions had feet (legs, torsos, breasts, arms, hands, faces, secrets, moustaches, earrings, headaches).

When I ask you to describe an egg, it isn't because I am hungry.

It is easier to put people in boxes than in books.

Yes, well—if today's tourists can be taken to see the Dostoyevsky neighborhood—his house, the courtyard of the old woman moneylender killed by Raskolnikov, the canal where he disposed of the ax, to say nothing of, on the banks of the Volga, the house where Natasha found Prince Andrey dying, and, in Cracow, Doktor Faust's study, his alembics, and the mark of Mephistopheles' foot—
           why can't Eddie and Pat have lived in an apartment on Enright, since torn down, and Lola and her children have tried to rent apartments on practically every street in the Delmar Loop?

Suddenly I'm reading Fraülein's letter as an "explanation"; it seems to answer so many questions about why?—and how?—about what I've called the "split" in my world, the co-existence of the elves and the Nazis in the Black Forest. It was no accident, no ignorance of world affairs, no nursery innocence that produced the intimate atmosphere of my childhood; she did it, she was the Good Fairy, she was the Good German:

"I do hope . . . given the children a liking for nature . . . and that life has many beautiful things in store for them, . . . when they grow up, to look for the things in life that are worthwhile living for . . . in spite of everything . . . a part of you that can lift you above hate, greed, envy, cruelty, misery . . . find that in yourself . . . hope there will come a better life for everybody on earth. . . ."

All the old echoes are set ringing with those honest, earnest phrases, their awkward syntax; there is in them an *echt-Deutsch*, rather, an *echt*-human quality of dignity with sentiment; I seem to see her clearly for the first time since we parted on a New York street-corner when I was fourteen. And in the photograph—that blurred, rather dumpy figure in the round hat, its galoshes firmly planted in the sun-streaked snow—yes, I can recognize it, it is she, twenty-five years later those honest, uncompromising blue eyes (blinking shut against the sun) are looking directly at me, here, all the way from Eighth Avenue and Fifty-seventh Street, although if we had one day passed each other on Delmar Boulevard I would probably not have given this woman a second glance, never suspecting her to be—a countess, yes!—of the true nobility. Royalty, Eddie.

Hans Richter wrote about Schwitters, ". . . every tram-ticket, every envelope, cheese wrapper, or cigar-band, together with old shoe soles or shoe-laces, wire, feathers, dishcloths—everything that had been thrown away—all this he loved, and restored to an honored place in life by means of his art." And someone has added, in a newspaper column, ". . . his tokens still work. Printed with words of another language, making puns that mean nothing to us because the frame of reference is a half-century past, they work because Schwitters was not an artist playing with rubbish—he was an artist making rubbish into art. The rubbish remains itself, proclaiming its commonness; art remains itself, manifesting its assimilative capacities. . . ."

Taking it backwards, consider: "the rubbish remains itself"—

itself, yes, a shoe-lace remains a shoe-lace, a cigar-band a cigar-band; Schwitters is no quick-change artist who twists a shoe-lace (for example) into a likeness of General de Gaulle, when he might have done it so much more quickly with a pencil; nor is he a suburban housewife who, with the help of her eleven-year-old daughter, makes plaques to hang on your wall by pressing thousands of varicolored seeds into plasticine. But—the dictionary defines "rubbish" as "1. waste or refuse material; debris; litter 2. worthless stuff; trash . . ." and Schwitters' shoe-laces and cigar-bands aren't any of these, for, far from being discarded, they are preserved. The rubbish does not remain itself; the rubbish is changed into not-rubbish; art (or Schwitters) has shown us a shoe-lace for the first time, a used shoe-lace, not a new one, he has forced us to *look* at it.

Consider: ". . . and restored to an honored place in life . . ." not quite, it's only in art that shoe-laces have an honored place; change the verb to "awarded."

". . . all this he loved . . ." here is the secret, here is the key! (*Why didn't I think of that?*) Key words: all; loved. Yes, all. Yes, loved.

Schwitters, Picasso, and Mrs. Borrow. Too bad that Mrs. Borrow would (almost certainly) see nothing "artistic" in Schwitters, only a pig-headed anti-aesthetic whim.

The day before yesterday I drove down Enright. A new world. Nothing remains as I remember it. Urban Renewal has been at work during the months we stayed away—not that this should be such a surprise, after all it was more than two years ago that they set up an office on Delmar and announced their plans, and we all voted "Yes" when they set up the voting-machine. What makes the shock and disturbance—and I can see how this feeling would be the same after an air-raid or fire—is the bland, impervious look of the vacant lots created by the demolition of buildings ("In the enormous twilight/Of the demolition of buildings . . ." but this isn't yet twilight, it's clear morning sunlight decorating every leaf and grass-blade, the hard yellowish clay, the white and purple clover, shepherd's purse, ragweed, chicory, fleabane and—now that autumn is here—goldenrod); there are no gaping holes, no actual rubble, no junk- or rubbish-heaps, only these quiet building lots. They must have looked like this before the apartments were built at all, raked smooth, without qualities.

Now the whole two-block stretch is leveled. Some buildings

still stand, shaded by the same plane trees whose leaves cast spotted shade on the spring sidewalks, whose blotched trunks march like scabrous sentinels along the curving pavement. Empty shells, held erect by their network of ivy. Tenanted, tenantless? Others are halfway torn down, window-openings with the look of ruined arches, doorways without doors, walls without roofs, rooms without floors; somehow these aren't so disconcerting as the empty building lots in their late-season bloom.

And the house where Eddie lived in Pat's apartment, that's gone, vanished, disparu. Nothing but flat blue sky roofing over the alley. No more echoing stairway twisting up to the third floor, gray and damp: "Shit" scrawled for emphasis on the plaster wall. And the dark unmysterious rooms, looking out on the dark street— no more. The furniture and personal belongings long since moved out; now the very walls, floors, and ceilings have disappeared.

Pat herself—gone. No more do these pavements take the print of her feet. And Eddie—gone, gone. Even Ardis and Deedee, Lola and the little girls.

Around the corner, on the boulevard, they are tearing down the shops and business blocks. Gone, Mrs. Fischbein's Delicatessen and Dairy. Gone, the kosher butcher and the Mound City Nut Company, Katz Real Estate, Rexall Drugs, Hotel and Motel Supplies Inc., F. James Optometrist, Mme. Adele Modiste, Ethel's Beauty Salon. Rubble and bricks, beams and boards, without even the token courtesy of a fence around the destroyed site. In the plate-glass windows of the shoe store: Removal Sale! As Is! Everything Must Go.

4

Triumph
and
Death

Satire Parody → look for clues

Revelation

FLANNERY O'CONNOR

Although she smugly considers herself "a respectable, hard-working, church-going woman" whose access to heaven seems assured, Mrs. Turpin has an apocalyptic vision that threatens her with damnation. She sees the insignificance of her virtues and the grievousness of her sins: the bigotry, hypocrisy, and pride that made her angrily challenge God's omnipotence. When God answers her, Mrs. Turpin stands "as if she were absorbing some abysmal life-giving knowledge." What is the meaning of this paradoxical phrase? Why does her religious experience occur while she is hosing down her pigs? Is it meant to suggest that she is damned like "a wart hog from hell," or is that message only a warning to her? The girl in the doctor's office is named Mary Grace. What does this detail indicate about her role in the story? What is the meaning of Mrs. Turpin's revelation?

The doctor's waiting room, which was very small, was almost full when the Turpins entered and Mrs. Turpin, who was very large, made it look even smaller by her presence. She stood looming at the head of the magazine table set in the center of it, a living demonstration that the room was inadequate and ridiculous. Her little bright black eyes took in all the patients as she sized up the seating situation. There was one vacant chair and a place on the sofa occupied by a blond child in a dirty blue romper who should have been told to move over and make room for the lady. He was five or six, but Mrs. Turpin saw at once that no one was going to tell him to move over. He was slumped down in the seat, his arms idle at his sides and his eyes idle in his head; his nose ran unchecked.

Mrs. Turpin put a firm hand on Claud's shoulder and said in a voice that included anyone who wanted to listen, "Claud, you sit in that chair there," and gave him a push down into the vacant one. Claud was florid and bald and sturdy, somewhat shorter than Mrs. Turpin, but he sat down as if he were accustomed to doing what she told him to.

Mrs. Turpin remained standing. The only man in the room besides Claud was a lean stringy old fellow with a rusty hand spread out on each knee, whose eyes were closed as if he were asleep or dead or pretending to be so as not to get up and offer her his seat. Her gaze settled agreeably on a well-dressed grey-haired lady whose eyes met hers and whose expression said: if that child belonged to me, he would have some manners and move over—there's plenty of room there for you and him too.

Claud looked up with a sigh and made as if to rise.

"Sit down," Mrs. Turpin said. "You know you're not supposed to stand on that leg. He has an ulcer on his leg," she explained.

Claud lifted his foot onto the magazine table and rolled his trouser leg up to reveal a purple swelling on a plump marble-white calf.

"My!" the pleasant lady said. "How did you do that?"

"A cow kicked him," Mrs. Turpin said.

"Goodness!" said the lady.

Claud rolled his trouser leg down.

"Maybe the little boy would move over," the lady suggested, but the child did not stir.

"Somebody will be leaving in a minute," Mrs. Turpin said. She could not understand why a doctor—with as much money as they made charging five dollars a day to just stick their head in the hospital door and look at you—couldn't afford a decent-sized waiting room. This one was hardly bigger than a garage. The table was cluttered with limp-looking magazines and at one end of it there was a big green glass ash tray full of cigaret butts and cotton wads with little blood spots on them. If she had had anything to do with the running of the place, that would have been emptied every so often. There were no chairs against the wall at the head of the room. It had a rectangular-shaped panel in it that permitted a view of the office where the nurse came and went and the secretary listened to the radio. A plastic fern in a gold pot sat in the opening and trailed its fronds down almost to the floor. The radio was softly playing gospel music.

Just then the inner door opened and a nurse with the highest stack of yellow hair Mrs. Turpin had ever seen put her face in the crack and called for the next patient. The woman sitting beside Claud grasped the two arms of her chair and hoisted herself up; she pulled her dress free from her legs and lumbered through the door where the nurse had disappeared.

Mrs. Turpin eased into the vacant chair, which held her tight as a corset. "I wish I could reduce," she said, and rolled her eyes and gave a comic sigh.

"Oh, *you* aren't fat," the stylish lady said.

"Ooooo I am too," Mrs. Turpin said. "Claud he eats all he wants to and never weighs over one hundred and seventy-five pounds, but me I just look at something good to eat and I gain some weight," and her stomach and shoulders shook with laughter. "You can eat all you want to, can't you, Claud?" she asked, turning to him.

Claud only grinned.

"Well, as long as you have such a good disposition," the stylish lady said, "I don't think it makes a bit of difference what size you are. You just can't beat a good disposition."

Next to her was a fat girl of eighteen or nineteen, scowling into a thick blue book which Mrs. Turpin saw was entitled *Human Development*. The girl raised her head and directed her scowl at Mrs. Turpin as if she did not like her looks. She appeared annoyed that anyone should speak while she tried to read. The poor girl's face was blue with acne and Mrs. Turpin thought how pitiful it was to have a face like that at that age. She gave the girl a friendly smile but the girl only scowled the harder. Mrs. Turpin herself was fat but she had always had good skin, and, though she was forty-seven years old, there was not a wrinkle in her face except around her eyes from laughing too much.

Next to the ugly girl was the child, still in exactly the same position, and next to him was a thin leathery old woman in a cotton print dress. She and Claud had three sacks of chicken feed in their pump house that was in the same print. She had seen from the first that the child belonged with the old woman. She could tell by the way they sat—kind of vacant and white-trashy, as if they would sit there until Doomsday if nobody called and told them to get up. And at right angles but next to the well-dressed pleasant lady was a lank-faced woman who was certainly the child's mother. She had on a yellow sweat shirt and wine-colored slacks, both gritty-looking, and the rims of her lips were stained with snuff. Her dirty yellow hair was tied behind with a little piece of red paper ribbon. Worse than niggers any day, Mrs. Turpin thought.

The gospel hymn playing was, "When I looked up and He looked down," and Mrs. Turpin, who knew it, supplied the last line mentally, "And wona these days I know I'll we-eara crown."

Without appearing to, Mrs. Turpin always noticed people's feet. The well-dressed lady had on red and grey suede shoes to match her dress. Mrs. Turpin had on her good black patent leather pumps. The ugly girl had on Girl Scout shoes and heavy socks. The old woman had on tennis shoes and the white-trashy mother had on what appeared to be bedroom slippers, black straw with gold braid threaded through them—exactly what you would have expected her to have on.

Sometimes at night when she couldn't go to sleep, Mrs. Turpin would occupy herself with the question of who she would have chosen to be if she couldn't have been herself. If Jesus had said to her before he made her, "There's only two places available for you. You can either be a nigger or white-trash," what would she have said? "Please, Jesus, please," she would have said, "just let me wait until there's another place available," and he would have said, "No, you have to go right now and I have only those two places so make up your mind." She would have wiggled and squirmed and begged and pleaded but it would have been no use and finally she would have said, "All right, make me a nigger then—but that don't mean a trashy one." And he would have made her a neat clean respectable Negro woman, herself but black.

Next to the child's mother was a red-headed youngish woman, reading one of the magazines and working a piece of chewing gum, hell for leather, as Claud would say. Mrs. Turpin could not see the woman's feet. She was not white-trash, just common. Sometimes Mrs. Turpin occupied herself at night naming the classes of people. On the bottom of the heap were most colored people, not the kind she would have been if she had been one, but most of them; then next to them—not above, just away from—were the white-trash; then above them were the home-owners, and above them the home-and-land owners, to which she and Claud belonged. Above she and Claud were people with a lot of money and much bigger houses and much more land. But here the complexity of it would begin to bear in on her, for some of the people with a lot of money were common and ought to be below she and Claud and some of the people who had good blood had lost their money and had to rent and then there were colored people who owned their homes and land as well. There was a colored dentist in town who had two red Lincolns and a swimming pool and a farm with registered white-face cattle on it. Usually by the time she had fallen asleep all the classes of people were moiling and roiling around in her head, and she would dream they were all crammed in together in a box car, being ridden off to be put in a gas oven.

"That's a beautiful clock," she said and nodded to her right. It was a big wall clock, the face encased in a brass sunburst.

"Yes, it's very pretty," the stylish lady said agreeably. "And right on the dot too," she added, glancing at her watch.

The ugly girl beside her cast an eye upward at the clock, smirked, then looked directly at Mrs. Turpin and smirked again. Then she returned her eyes to her book. She was obviously the lady's daughter because, although they didn't look anything alike as to disposition, they both had the same shape of face and the same blue eyes. On the lady they sparkled pleasantly but in the girl's seared face they appeared alternately to smolder and to blaze.

What if Jesus had said, "All right, you can be white-trash or a nigger or ugly"!

Mrs. Turpin felt an awful pity for the girl, though she thought it was one thing to be ugly and another to act ugly.

The woman with the snuff-stained lips turned around in her chair and looked up at the clock. Then she turned back and appeared to look a little to the side of Mrs. Turpin. There was a cast in one of her eyes. "You want to know wher you can get you one of themther clocks?" she asked in a loud voice.

"No, I already have a nice clock," Mrs. Turpin said. Once somebody like her got a leg in the conversation, she would be all over it.

"You can get you one with green stamps," the woman said. "That's most likely wher he got hisn. Save you up enough, you can get you most anythang. I got me some joo'ry."

Ought to have got you a wash rag and some soap, Mrs. Turpin thought.

"I get contour sheets with mine," the pleasant lady said.

The daughter slammed her book shut. She looked straight in front of her, directly through Mrs. Turpin and on through the yellow curtain and the plate glass window which made the wall behind her. The girl's eyes seemed lit all of a sudden with a peculiar light, an unnatural light like night road signs give. Mrs. Turpin turned her head to see if there was anything going on outside that she should see, but she could not see anything. Figures passing cast only a pale shadow through the curtain. There was no reason the girl should single her out for her ugly looks.

"Miss Finley," the nurse said, cracking the door. The gum-chewing woman got up and passed in front of her and Claud and went into the office. She had on red high-heeled shoes.

Directly across the table, the ugly girl's eyes were fixed on Mrs. Turpin as if she had some very special reason for disliking her.

"This is wonderful weather, isn't it?" the girl's mother said.

"It's good weather for cotton if you can get the niggers to pick it," Mrs. Turpin said, "but niggers don't want to pick cotton any more. You can't get the white folks to pick it and now you can't get the niggers—because they got to be right up there with the white folks."

"They gonna *try* anyways," the white-trash woman said, leaning forward.

"Do you have one of those cotton-picking machines?" the pleasant lady asked.

"No," Mrs. Turpin said, "they leave half the cotton in the field. We don't have much cotton anyway. If you want to make it farming now, you have to have a little of everything. We got a couple of acres of cotton and a few hogs and chickens and just enough white-face that Claud can look after them himself."

"One thang I don't want," the white-trash woman said, wiping her mouth with the back of her hand. "Hogs. Nasty stinking things, a-gruntin and a-rootin all over the place."

Mrs. Turpin gave her the merest edge of her attention. "Our hogs are not dirty and they don't stink," she said. "They're cleaner than some children I've seen. Their feet never touch the ground. We have a pig-parlor—that's where you raise them on concrete," she explained to the pleasant lady, "and Claud scoots them down with the hose every afternoon and washes off the floor." Cleaner by far than that child right there, she thought. Poor nasty little thing. He had not moved except to put the thumb of his dirty hand into his mouth.

The woman turned her face away from Mrs. Turpin. "I know I wouldn't scoot down no hog with no hose," she said to the wall.

You wouldn't have no hog to scoot down, Mrs. Turpin said to herself.

"A-gruntin and a-rootin and a-groanin," the woman muttered.

"We got a little of everything," Mrs. Turpin said to the pleasant lady. "It's no use in having more than you can handle yourself with help like it is. We found enough niggers to pick our cotton this year but Claud he has to go after them and take them home again in the evening. They can't walk that half a mile. No they can't. I tell you," she said and laughed merrily, "I sure am tired of buttering up niggers, but you got to love em if you want em to work for you. When they come in the morning, I run out and I say, 'Hi yawl this morning?' and when Claud drives them off to the field I just wave to beat the band and they just wave back." And she waved her hand rapidly to illustrate.

"Like you read out of the same book," the lady said, showing she understood perfectly.

"Child, yes," Mrs. Turpin said. "And when they come in from the field, I run out with a bucket of icewater. That's the way it's going to be from now on," she said. "You may as well face it."

"One thang I know," the white-trash woman said. "Two thangs I ain't going to do: love no niggers or scoot down no hog with no hose." And she let out a bark of contempt.

The look that Mrs. Turpin and the pleasant lady exchanged indicated they both understood that you had to *have* certain things before you could *know* certain things. But every time Mrs. Turpin exchanged a look with the lady, she was aware that the ugly girl's peculiar eyes were still on her, and she had trouble bringing her attention back to the conversation.

"When you got something," she said, "you got to look after it." And when you ain't got a thing but breath and britches, she added to herself, you can afford to come to town every morning and just sit on the Court House coping and spit.

A grotesque revolving shadow passed across the curtain behind her and was thrown palely on the opposite wall. Then a bicycle clattered down against the outside of the building. The door opened and a colored boy glided in with a tray from the drug store. It had two large red and white paper cups on it with tops on them. He was a tall, very black boy in discolored white pants and a green nylon shirt. He was chewing gum slowly, as if to music. He set the tray down in the office opening next to the fern and stuck his head through to look for the secretary. She was not in there. He rested his arms on the ledge and waited, his narrow bottom stuck out, swaying slowly to the left and right. He raised a hand over his head and scratched the base of his skull.

"You see that button there, boy?" Mrs. Turpin said. "You can punch that and she'll come. She's probably in the back somewhere."

"Is that right?" the boy said agreeably, as if he had never seen the button before. He leaned to the right and put his finger on it. "She sometime out," he said and twisted around to face his audience, his elbows behind him on the counter. The nurse appeared and he twisted back again. She handed him a dollar and he rooted in his pocket and made the change and counted it out to her. She gave him fifteen cents for a tip and he went out with the empty tray. The heavy door swung to slowly and closed at length with the sound of suction. For a moment no one spoke.

"They ought to send all them niggers back to Africa," the white-trash woman said. "That's wher they come from in the first place."

"Oh, I couldn't do without my good colored friends," the pleasant lady said.

"There's a heap of things worse than a nigger," Mrs. Turpin agreed. "It's all kinds of them just like it's all kinds of us."

"Yes, and it takes all kinds to make the world go round," the lady said in her musical voice.

As she said it, the raw-complexioned girl snapped her teeth together. Her lower lip turned downwards and inside out, revealing the pale pink inside of her mouth. After a second it rolled back up. It was the ugliest face Mrs. Turpin had ever seen anyone make and for a moment she was certain that the girl had made it at her. She was looking at her as if she had known and disliked her all her life—all of Mrs. Turpin's life, it seemed too, not just all the girl's life. Why, girl, I don't even know you, Mrs. Turpin said silently.

She forced her attention back to the discussion. "It wouldn't be practical to send them back to Africa," she said. "They wouldn't want to go. They got it too good here."

"Wouldn't be what they wanted—if I had anythang to do with it," the woman said.

"It wouldn't be a way in the world you could get all the niggers back over there," Mrs. Turpin said. "They'd be hiding out and lying down and turning sick on you and wailing and hollering and raring and pitching. It wouldn't be a way in the world to get them over there."

"They got over here," the trashy woman said. "Get back like they got over."

"It wasn't so many of them then," Mrs. Turpin explained.

The woman looked at Mrs. Turpin as if here was an idiot indeed but Mrs. Turpin was not bothered by the look, considering where it came from.

"Nooo," she said, "they're going to stay here where they can go to New York and marry white folks and improve their color. That's what they all want to do, every one of them, improve their color."

"You know what comes of that, don't you?" Claud asked.

"No, Claud, what?" Mrs. Turpin said.

Claud's eyes twinkled. "White-faced niggers," he said with never a smile.

Everybody in the office laughed except the white-trash and the ugly girl. The girl gripped the book in her lap with white fingers. The trashy woman looked around her from face to face as if she thought they were all idiots. The old woman in the feed sack dress continued to gaze expressionless across the floor at the high-top shoes of the man opposite her, the one who had been pretending to be asleep when the Turpins came in. He was laughing heartily, his hands still spread out on his knees. The child had fallen to the side and was lying now almost face down in the old woman's lap.

While they recovered from their laughter, the nasal chorus on the radio kept the room from silence.

> You go to blank blank
> And I'll go to mine
> But we'll all blank along
> To-geth-ther,
> And all along the blank
> We'll hep eachother out
> Smile-ling in any kind of
> Weath-ther!

Mrs. Turpin didn't catch every word but she caught enough to agree with the spirit of the song and it turned her thoughts sober. To help anybody out that needed it was her philosophy of life. She never spared herself when she found somebody in need, whether they were white or black, trash or decent. And of all she had to be thankful for, she was most thankful that this was so. If Jesus had said, "You can be high society and have all the money you want and be thin and svelte-like, but you can't be a good woman with it," she would have had to say, "Well don't make me that then. Make me a good woman and it don't matter what else, how fat or how ugly or how poor!" Her heart rose. He had not made her a nigger or white-trash or ugly! He had made her herself and given her a little of everything. Jesus, thank you! she said. Thank you thank you thank you! Whenever she counted her blessings she felt as buoyant as if she weighed one hundred and twenty-five pounds instead of one hundred and eighty.

"What's wrong with your little boy?" the pleasant lady asked the white-trashy woman.

"He has a ulcer," the woman said proudly. "He ain't give me a minute's peace since he was born. Him and her are just alike," she said, nodding at the old woman, who was running her leathery fingers through the child's pale hair. "Look like I can't get nothing down them two but Co' Cola and candy."

That's all you try to get down em, Mrs. Turpin said to herself. Too lazy to light the fire. There was nothing you could tell her about people like them that she didn't know already. And it was not just that they didn't have anything. Because if you gave them everything, in two weeks it would all be broken or filthy or they would have chopped it up for lightwood. She knew all this from her own experience. Help them you must, but help them you couldn't.

All at once the ugly girl turned her lips inside out again. Her eyes were fixed like two drills on Mrs. Turpin. This time there was no mistaking that there was something urgent behind them.

Girl, Mrs. Turpin exclaimed silently, I haven't done a thing to you! The girl might be confusing her with somebody else. There was no need to sit by and let herself be intimidated. "You must be in college," she said boldly, looking directly at the girl. "I see you reading a book there."

The girl continued to stare and pointedly did not answer.

Her mother blushed at this rudeness. "The lady asked you a question, Mary Grace," she said under her breath.

"I have ears," Mary Grace said.

The poor mother blushed again. "Mary Grace goes to Wellesley College," she explained. She twisted one of the buttons on her dress. "In Massachusetts," she added with a grimace. "And in the summer she just keeps right on studying. Just reads all the time, a real book worm. She's done real well at Wellesley; she's taking English and Math and History and Psychology and Social Studies," she rattled on, "and I think it's too much. I think she ought to get out and have fun."

The girl looked as if she would like to hurl them all through the plate glass window.

"Way up north," Mrs. Turpin murmured and thought, well, it hasn't done much for her manners.

"I'd almost rather to have him sick," the white-trash woman said, wrenching the attention back to herself. "He's so mean when he ain't. Look like some children just take natural to meanness. It's some gets bad when they get sick but he was the opposite. Took sick and turned good. He don't give me no trouble now. It's me waitin to see the doctor," she said.

If I was going to send anybody back to Africa, Mrs. Turpin thought, it would be your kind, woman. "Yes, indeed," she said aloud, but looking up at the ceiling, "it's a heap of things worse than a nigger." And dirtier than a hog, she added to herself.

"I think people with bad dispositions are more to be pitied than anyone on earth," the pleasant lady said in a voice that was decidedly thin.

"I thank the Lord he has blessed me with a good one," Mrs. Turpin said. "The day has never dawned that I couldn't find something to laugh at."

"Not since she married me anyways," Claud said with a comical straight face.

Everybody laughed except the girl and the white-trash.

Mrs. Turpin's stomach shook. "He's such a caution," she said, "that I can't help but laugh at him."

The girl made a loud ugly noise through her teeth.

Her mother's mouth grew thin and tight. "I think the worst thing in the world," she said, "is an ungrateful person. To have everything and not appreciate it. I know a girl," she said, "who has parents who would give her anything, a little brother who loves her dearly, who is getting a good education, who wears the best clothes, but who can never say a kind word to anyone, who never smiles, who just criticizes and complains all day long."

"Is she too old to paddle?" Claud asked.

The girl's face was almost purple.

"Yes," the lady said, "I'm afraid there's nothing to do but leave her to her folly. Some day she'll wake up and it'll be too late."

"It never hurt anyone to smile," Mrs. Turpin said. "It just makes you feel better all over."

"Of course," the lady said sadly, "but there are just some people you can't tell anything to. They can't take criticism."

"If it's one thing I am," Mrs. Turpin said with feeling, "it's grateful. When I think who all I could have been besides myself and what all I got, a little of everything, and a good disposition besides, I just feel like shouting, 'Thank you, Jesus, for making everything the way it is!' It could have been different!" For one thing, somebody else could have got Claud. At the thought of this, she was flooded with gratitude and a terrible pang of joy ran through her. "Oh thank you, Jesus, Jesus, thank you!" she cried aloud.

The book struck her directly over her left eye. It struck almost at the same instant that she realized the girl was about to hurl it. Before she could utter a sound, the raw face came crashing across the table toward her, howling. The girl's fingers sank like clamps into the soft flesh of her neck. She heard the mother cry out and Claud shout, "Whoa!" There was an instant when she was certain that she was about to be in an earthquake.

All at once her vision narrowed and she saw everything as if it were happening in a small room far away, or as if she were looking at it through the wrong end of a telescope. Claud's face crumpled and fell out of sight. The nurse ran in, then out, then in again. Then the gangling figure of the doctor rushed out of the inner door. Magazines flew this way and that as the table turned over. The girl fell with a thud and Mrs. Turpin's vision suddenly reversed itself and she saw everything large instead of small. The eyes of the white-trashy woman were staring hugely at the floor. There the girl, held down on one side by the nurse and on the other by her mother, was wrenching and turning in their grasp. The doctor was kneeling astride her, trying to hold her arm down. He managed after a second to sink a long needle into it.

Mrs. Turpin felt entirely hollow except for her heart which swung from side to side as if it were agitated in a great empty drum of flesh.

"Somebody that's not busy call for the ambulance," the doctor said in the off-hand voice young doctors adopt for terrible occasions.

Mrs. Turpin could not have moved a finger. The old man who had been sitting next to her skipped nimbly into the office and made the call, for the secretary still seemed to be gone.

"Claud!" Mrs. Turpin called.

He was not in his chair. She knew she must jump up and find him but she felt like some one trying to catch a train in a dream, when everything moves in slow motion and the faster you try to run the slower you go.

"Here I am," a suffocated voice, very unlike Claud's, said.

He was doubled up in the corner on the floor, pale as paper, holding his leg. She wanted to get up and go to him but she could not move. Instead, her gaze was drawn slowly downward to the churning face on the floor, which she could see over the doctor's shoulder.

The girl's eyes stopped rolling and focused on her. They seemed a much lighter blue than before, as if a door that had been tightly closed behind them was now open to admit light and air.

Mrs. Turpin's head cleared and her power of motion returned. She leaned forward until she was looking directly into the fierce brilliant eyes. There was no doubt in her mind that the girl did know her, knew her in some intense and personal way, beyond time and place and condition. "What you got to say to me?" she asked hoarsely and held her breath, waiting, as for a revelation.

The girl raised her head. Her gaze locked with Mrs. Turpin's. "Go back to hell where you came from, you old wart hog," she whispered. Her voice was low but clear. Her eyes burned for a moment as if she saw with pleasure that her message had struck its target.

Mrs. Turpin sank back in her chair.

After a moment the girl's eyes closed and she turned her head wearily to the side.

The doctor rose and handed the nurse the empty syringe. He leaned over and put both hands for a moment on the mother's shoulders, which were shaking. She was sitting on the floor, her lips pressed together, holding Mary Grace's hand in her lap. The girl's fingers were gripped like a baby's around her thumb. "Go on to the hospital," he said. "I'll call and make the arrangements."

"Now let's see that neck," he said in a jovial voice to Mrs. Turpin. IIe began to inspect her neck with his first two fingers. Two little moon-shaped lines like pink fish bones were indented over her windpipe. There was the beginning of an angry red swelling above her eye. His fingers passed over this also.

"Lea' me be," she said thickly and shook him off. "See about Claud. She kicked him."

"I'll see about him in a minute," he said and felt her pulse. He was a thin grey-haired man, given to pleasantries. "Go home and have yourself a vacation the rest of the day," he said and patted her on the shoulder.

Quit your pattin me, Mrs. Turpin growled to herself.

"And put an ice pack over that eye," he said. Then he went and squatted down beside Claud and looked at his leg. After a moment he pulled him up and Claud limped after him into the office.

Until the ambulance came, the only sounds in the room were

the tremulous moans of the girl's mother, who continued to sit on the floor. The white-trash woman did not take her eyes off the girl. Mrs. Turpin looked straight ahead at nothing. Presently the ambulance drew up, a long dark shadow, behind the curtain. The attendants came in and set the stretcher down beside the girl and lifted her expertly onto it and carried her out. The nurse helped the mother gather up her things. The shadow of the ambulance moved silently away and the nurse came back in the office.

"That ther girl is going to be a lunatic, ain't she?" the white-trash woman asked the nurse, but the nurse kept on to the back and never answered her.

"Yes, she's going to be a lunatic," the white-trash woman said to the rest of them.

"Po' critter," the old woman murmured. The child's face was still in her lap. His eyes looked idly out over her knees. He had not moved during the disturbance except to draw one leg up under him.

"I thank Gawd," the white-trash woman said fervently, "I ain't a lunatic."

Claud came limping out and the Turpins went home.

As their pick-up truck turned into their own dirt road and made the crest of the hill, Mrs. Turpin gripped the window ledge and looked out suspiciously. The land sloped gracefully down through a field dotted with lavender weeds and at the start of the rise their small yellow frame house, with its little flower beds spread out around it like a fancy apron, sat primly in its accustomed place between two giant hickory trees. She would not have been startled to see a burnt wound between two blackened chimneys.

Neither of them felt like eating so they put on their house clothes and lowered the shade in the bedroom and lay down, Claud with his leg on a pillow and herself with a damp washcloth over her eye. The instant she was flat on her back, the image of a razor-backed hog with warts on its face and horns coming out behind its ears snorted into her head. She moaned, a low quiet moan.

"I am not," she said tearfully, "a wart hog. From hell." But the denial had no force. The girl's eyes and her words, even the tone of her voice, low but clear, directed only to her, brooked no repudiation. She had been singled out for the message, though there was trash in the room to whom it might justly have been applied. The full force of this fact struck her only now. There was a woman there who was neglecting her own child but she had been overlooked. The message had been given to Ruby Turpin, a respectable, hard-working, church-going woman. The tears dried. Her eyes began to burn instead with wrath.

She rose on her elbow and the washcloth fell into her hand. Claud was lying on his back, snoring. She wanted to tell him what the girl had said. At the same time, she did not wish to put the image of herself as a wart hog from hell into his mind.

"Hey, Claud," she muttered and pushed his shoulder.

Claud opened one pale baby blue eye.

She looked into it warily. He did not think about anything. He just went his way.

"Wha, whasit?" he said and closed the eye again.

"Nothing," she said. "Does your leg pain you?"

"Hurts like hell," Claud said.

"It'll quit terreckly," she said and lay back down. In a moment Claud was snoring again. For the rest of the afternoon they lay there. Claud slept. She scowled at the ceiling. Occasionally she raised her fist and made a small stabbing motion over her chest as if she was defending her innocence to invisible guests who were like the comforters of Job, reasonable-seeming but wrong.

About five-thirty Claud stirred. "Got to go after those niggers," he sighed, not moving.

She was looking straight up as if there were unintelligible handwriting on the ceiling. The protuberance over her eye had turned a greenish-blue. "Listen here," she said.

"What?"

"Kiss me."

Claud leaned over and kissed her loudly on the mouth. He pinched her side and their hands interlocked. Her expression of ferocious concentration did not change. Claud got up, groaning and growling, and limped off. She continued to study the ceiling.

She did not get up until she heard the pick-up truck coming back with the Negroes. Then she rose and thrust her feet in her brown oxfords, which she did not bother to lace, and stumped out onto the back porch and got her red plastic bucket. She emptied a tray of ice cubes into it and filled it half full of water and went out into the back yard. Every afternoon after Claud brought the hands in, one of the boys helped him put out hay and the rest waited in the back of the truck until he was ready to take them home. The truck was parked in the shade under one of the hickory trees.

"Hi yawl this evening?" Mrs. Turpin asked grimly, appearing with the bucket and the dipper. There were three women and a boy in the truck.

"Us doin nicely," the oldest woman said. "Hi you doin?" and her gaze stuck immediately on the dark lump on Mrs. Turpin's forehead. "You done fell down, ain't you?" she asked in a solicitous voice. The old woman was dark and almost toothless. She had on an old felt hat of Claud's set back on her head. The other two women were younger and lighter and they both had new bright green sun hats. One of them had hers on her head; the other had taken hers off and the boy was grinning beneath it.

Mrs. Turpin set the bucket down on the floor of the truck. "Yawl hep yourselves," she said. She looked around to make sure Claud had gone. "No. I didn't fall down," she said, folding her arms. "It was something worse than that."

"Ain't nothing bad happen to you!" the old woman said. She said it as if they all knew that Mrs. Turpin was protected in some special way by Divine Providence. "You just had you a little fall."

"We were in town at the doctor's office for where the cow kicked Mr. Turpin," Mrs. Turpin said in a flat tone that indicated they could leave off their foolishness. "And there was this girl there. A big fat girl with her face all broke out. I could look at that girl and tell she was peculiar but I couldn't tell how. And me and her mama were just talking and going along and all of a sudden WHAM! She throws this big book she was reading at me and . . ."

"Naw!" the old woman cried out.

"And then she jumps over the table and commences to choke me."

"Naw!" they all exclaimed, "naw!"

"Hi come she do that?" the old woman asked. "What ail her?"

Mrs. Turpin only glared in front of her.

"Somethin ail her," the old woman said.

"They carried her off in an ambulance," Mrs. Turpin continued, "but before she went she was rolling on the floor and they were trying to hold her down to give her a shot and she said something to me." She paused. "You know what she said to me?"

"What she say?" they asked.

"She said," Mrs. Turpin began, and stopped, her face very dark and heavy. The sun was getting whiter and whiter, blanching the sky overhead so that the leaves of the hickory tree were black in the face of it. She could not bring forth the words. "Something real ugly," she muttered.

"She sho shouldn't said nothin ugly to you," the old woman said. "You so sweet. You the sweetest lady I know."

"She pretty too," the one with the hat on said.

"And stout," the other one said. "I never knowed no sweeter white lady."

"That's the truth befo' Jesus," the old woman said. "Amen! You des as sweet and pretty as you can be."

Mrs. Turpin knew just exactly how much Negro flattery was worth and it added to her rage. "She said," she began again and finished this time with a fierce rush of breath, "that I was an old wart hog from hell."

There was an astounded silence.

"Where she at?" the youngest woman cried in a piercing voice. "Lemme see her. I'll kill her!"

"I'll kill her with you!" the other one cried.

"She b'long in the sylum," the old woman said emphatically. "You the sweetest white lady I know."

"She pretty too," the other two said. "Stout as she can be and sweet. Jesus satisfied with her!"

"Deed he is," the old woman declared.

Idiots! Mrs. Turpin growled to herself. You could never say anything intelligent to a nigger. You could talk at them but not with them. "Yawl ain't drunk your water," she said shortly. "Leave the bucket in the truck when you're finished with it. I got more to do than just stand around and pass the time of day," and she moved off and into the house.

She stood for a moment in the middle of the kitchen. The dark protuberance over her eye looked like a miniature tornado cloud which might any moment sweep across the horizon of her brow. Her lower lip protruded dangerously. She squared' her massive shoulders. Then she marched into the front of the house and out the side door and started down the road to the pig parlor. She had the look of a woman going single-handed, weaponless, into battle.

The sun was a deep yellow now like a harvest moon and was riding westward very fast over the far tree line as if it meant to reach the hogs before she did. The road was rutted and she kicked several good-sized stones out of her path as she strode along. The pig parlor was on a little knoll at the end of a lane that ran off from the side of the barn. It was a square of concrete as large as a small room, with a board fence about four feet high around it. The concrete floor sloped slightly so that the hog wash could drain off into a trench where it was carried to the field for fertilizer. Claud was standing on the outside, on the edge of the concrete, hanging onto the top board, hosing down the floor inside. The hose was connected to the faucet of a water trough nearby.

Mrs. Turpin climbed up beside him and glowered down at the hogs inside. There were seven long-snouted bristly shoats in it—tan with liver-colored spots—and an old sow a few weeks off from farrowing. She was lying on her side grunting. The shoats were running about shaking themselves like idiot children, their little slit pig eyes searching the floor for anything left. She had read that pigs were the most intelligent animal. She doubted it. They were supposed to be smarter than dogs. There had even been a pig astronaut. He had performed his assignment perfectly but died of a heart attack afterwards because they left him in his electric suit, sitting upright throughout his examination when naturally a hog should be on all fours.

A-gruntin and a-rootin and a-groanin.

"Gimme that hose," she said, yanking it away from Claud. "Go on and carry them niggers home and then get off that leg."

"You look like you might have swallowed a mad dog," Claud observed, but he got down and limped off. He paid no attention to her humors.

Until he was out of earshot, Mrs. Turpin stood on the side of the pen, holding the hose and pointing the stream of water at the hind quarters of any shoat that looked as if it might try to lie down. When he had had time to get over the hill, she turned her head slightly and her wrathful eyes scanned the path. He was nowhere in sight. She turned back again and seemed to gather herself up. Her shoulders rose and she drew in her breath.

"What do you send me a message like that for?" she said in a low fierce voice, barely above a whisper but with the force of a shout in its concentrated fury. "How am I a hog and me both? How am I saved and from hell too?" Her free fist was knotted and with the other she gripped the hose, blindly pointing the stream of water in and out of the eye of the old sow whose outraged squeal she did not hear.

The pig parlor commanded a view of the back pasture where their twenty beef cows were gathered around the hay-bales Claud and the boy had put out. The freshly cut pasture sloped down to the highway. Across it was their cotton field and beyond that a dark green dusty wood which they owned as well. The sun was behind the wood, very red, looking over the paling of trees like a farmer inspecting his own hogs.

"Why me?" she rumbled. "It's no trash around here, black or white, that I haven't given to. And break my back to the bone every day working. And do for the church."

She appeared to be the right size woman to command the arena before her. "How am I a hog?" she demanded. "Exactly how am I like them?" and she jabbed the stream of water at the shoats. "There was plenty of trash there. It didn't have to be me.

"If you like trash better, go get yourself some trash then," she railed. "You could have made me trash. Or a nigger. If trash is what you wanted why didn't you make me trash?" She shook her fist with the hose in it and a watery snake appeared momentarily in the air. "I could quit working and take it easy and be filthy," she growled. "Lounge about the sidewalks all day drinking root beer. Dip snuff and spit in every puddle and have it all over my face. I could be nasty.

"Or you could have made me a nigger. It's too late for me to be a nigger," she said with deep sarcasm, "but I could act like one. Lay down in the middle of the road and stop traffic. Roll on the ground."

In the deepening light everything was taking on a mysterious hue. The pasture was growing a peculiar glassy green and the streak of highway had turned lavender. She braced herself for a final assault and this time her voice rolled out over the pasture. "Go on," she yelled, "call me a hog! Call me a hog again. From hell. Call me a wart hog from hell. Put that bottom rail on top. There'll still be a top and bottom!"

A garbled echo returned to her.

A final surge of fury shook her and she roared, "Who do you think you are?"

The color of everything, field and crimson sky, burned for a moment with a transparent intensity. The question carried over the pasture and across the highway and the cotton field and returned to her clearly like an answer from beyond the wood.

She opened her mouth but no sound came out of it.

A tiny truck, Claud's, appeared on the highway, heading rapidly out of sight. Its gears scraped thinly. It looked like a child's toy. At any moment a bigger truck might smash into it and scatter Claud's and the niggers' brains all over the road.

Mrs. Turpin stood there, her gaze fixed on the highway, all her muscles rigid, until in five or six minutes the truck reappeared, returning. She waited until it had had time to turn into their own road. Then like a monumental statue coming to life, she bent her head slowly and gazed, as if through the very heart of mystery, down into the pig parlor at the hogs. They had settled all in one corner around the old sow who was grunting softly. A red glow suffused them. They appeared to pant with a secret life.

Until the sun slipped finally behind the tree line, Mrs. Turpin remained there with her gaze bent to them as if she were absorbing some abysmal life-giving knowledge. At last she lifted her head. There was only a purple streak in the sky, cutting through a field of crimson and leading, like an extension of the highway, into the descending dusk. She raised her hands from the side of the pen in a gesture hieratic and profound. A visionary light settled in her eyes. She saw the streak as a vast swinging bridge extending upward from the earth through a field of living fire. Upon it a vast horde of souls were rumbling toward heaven. There were whole companies of white-trash, clean for the first time in their lives, and bands of black niggers in white robes, and battalions of freaks and lunatics shouting and clapping and leaping like frogs. And bringing up the end of the procession was a tribe of people whom she recognized at once as those who, like herself and Claud, had always had a little of everything and the God-given wit to use it right. She leaned forward to observe them closer. They were marching behind the others with great dignity, accountable as they had always been for good order and common sense and respectable behavior. They alone were on key. Yet she could see by their shocked and altered faces that even their virtues were being burned away. She lowered her hands and gripped the rail of the hog pen, her eyes small but fixed unblinkingly on what lay ahead. In a moment the vision faded but she remained where she was, immobile.

At length she got down and turned off the faucet and made her slow way on the darkening path to the house. In the woods around her the invisible cricket choruses had struck up, but what she heard were the voices of the souls climbing upward into the starry field and shouting hallelujah.

The Jilting of Granny Weatherall

KATHERINE ANNE PORTER

*This story focuses on the moment of an old woman's death at the
same time that it provides a view of her past life—its hardships
and its joys. On the surface Granny Weatherall has lived fully and
can take satisfaction in her accomplishments: a husband, children,
a home, hard work, and piety. Beneath the surface, however, she
has committed a sin that means her damnation. She cannot keep
from remembering one day in her past, the day she was jilted by
the only man she ever loved. This contrast between appearances
and inner reality is reflected in Granny Weatherall's attitudes about
herself as a wife, mother, and widow. How do her feelings about
her children vary during the course of the monologue? In what
perspective does she recall her husband, and how does that
image differ from the way she thinks of George? Why does the
mere memory of him evoke a vision of hell? What is the nature of
her sin, and what do her final words reveal about her entire life?
What is the irony of her name?*

She flicked her wrist neatly out of Doctor Harry's pudgy careful
fingers and pulled the sheet up to her chin. The brat ought to be in
knee breeches. Doctoring around the country with spectacles on
his nose! "Get along now, take your schoolbooks and go. There's
nothing wrong with me."

Doctor Harry spread a warm paw like a cushion on her forehead where the forked green vein danced and made her eyelids
twitch. "Now, now, be a good girl, and we'll have you up in no
time."

"That's no way to speak to a woman nearly eighty years old just because she's down. I'd have you respect your elders, young man."

"Well, Missy, excuse me." Doctor Harry patted her cheek. "But I've got to warn you, haven't I? You're a marvel, but you must be careful or you're going to be good and sorry."

"Don't tell me what I'm going to be. I'm on my feet now, morally speaking. It's Cornelia. I had to go to bed to get rid of her."

Her bones felt loose, and floated around in her skin, and Doctor Harry floated like a balloon around the foot of the bed. He floated and pulled down his waistcoat and swung his glasses on a cord. "Well, stay where you are, it certainly can't hurt you."

"Get along and doctor your sick," said Granny Weatherall. "Leave a well woman alone. I'll call for you when I want you. . . . Where were you forty years ago when I pulled through milk-leg and double pneumonia? You weren't even born. Don't let Cornelia lead you on," she shouted, because Doctor Harry appeared to float up to the ceiling and out. "I pay my own bills, and I don't throw my money away on nonsense!"

She meant to wave good-by, but it was too much trouble. Her eyes closed of themselves, it was like a dark curtain drawn around the bed. The pillow rose and floated under her, pleasant as a hammock in a light wind. She listened to the leaves rustling outside the window. No, somebody was swishing newspapers: no, Cornelia and Doctor Harry were whispering together. She leaped broad awake, thinking they whispered in her ear.

"She was never like this, *never* like this!" "Well, what can we expect?" "Yes, eighty years old. . . ."

Well, and what if she was? She still had ears. It was like Cornelia to whisper around doors. She always kept things secret in such a public way. She was always being tactful and kind. Cornelia was dutiful; that was the trouble with her. Dutiful and good: "So good and dutiful," said Granny, "that I'd like to spank her." She saw herself spanking Cornelia and making a fine job of it.

"What'd you say, Mother?"

Granny felt her face tying up in hard knots.

"Can't a body think, I'd like to know?"

"I thought you might want something."

"I do. I want a lot of things. First off, go away and don't whisper."

She lay and drowsed, hoping in her sleep that the children

would keep out and let her rest a minute. It had been a long day. Not that she was tired. It was always pleasant to snatch a minute now and then. There was always so much to be done, let me see: tomorrow.

Tomorrow was far away and there was nothing to trouble about. Things were finished somehow when the time came; thank God there was always a little margin over for peace: then a person could spread out the plan of life and tuck in the edges orderly. It was good to have everything clean and folded away, with the hair brushes and tonic bottles sitting straight on the white embroidered linen: the day started without fuss and the pantry shelves laid out with rows of jelly glasses and brown jugs and white stone-china jars with blue whirligigs and words painted on them: coffee, tea, sugar, ginger, cinnamon, allspice: and the bronze clock with the lion on top nicely dusted off. The dust that lion could collect in twenty-four hours! The box in the attic with all those letters tied up, well, she'd have to go through that tomorrow. All those letters— George's letters and John's letters and her letters to them both— lying around for the children to find afterwards made her uneasy. Yes, that would be tomorrow's business. No use to let them know how silly she had been once.

While she was rummaging around she found death in her mind and it felt clammy and unfamiliar. She had spent so much time preparing for death there was no need for bringing it up again. Let it take care of itself now. When she was sixty she had felt very old, finished, and went around making farewell trips to see her children and grandchildren, with a secret in her mind: This is the very last of your mother, children! Then she made her will and came down with a long fever. That was all just a notion like a lot of other things, but it was lucky too, for she had once for all got over the idea of dying for a long time. Now she couldn't be worried. She hoped she had better sense now. Her father had lived to be one hundred and two years old and had drunk a noggin of strong hot toddy on his last birthday. He told the reporters it was his daily habit, and he owed his long life to that. He had made quite a scandal and was very pleased about it. She believed she'd just plague Cornelia a little.

"Cornelia! Cornelia!" No footsteps, but a sudden hand on her cheek. "Bless you, where have you been?"

"Here, Mother."

"Well, Cornelia, I want a noggin of hot toddy."

"Are you cold, darling?"

"I'm chilly, Cornelia. Lying in bed stops the circulation. I must have told you that a thousand times."

Well, she could just hear Cornelia telling her husband that Mother was getting a little childish and they'd have to humor her. The thing that most annoyed her was that Cornelia thought she was deaf, dumb, and blind. Little hasty glances and tiny gestures tossed around her and over her head saying, "Don't cross her, let her have her way, she's eighty years old," and she sitting there as if she lived in a thin glass cage. Sometimes Granny almost made up her mind to pack up and move back to her own house where nobody could remind her every minute that she was old. Wait, wait, Cornelia, till your own children whisper behind your back!

In her day she had kept a better house and had got more work done. She wasn't too old yet for Lydia to be driving eighty miles for advice when one of the children jumped the track, and Jimmy still dropped in and talked things over: "Now, Mammy, you've a good business head, I want to know what you think of this? . . ." Old. Cornelia couldn't change the furniture around without asking. Little things, little things! They had been so sweet when they were little. Granny wished the old days were back again with the children young and everything to be done over. It had been a hard pull, but not too much for her. When she thought of all the food she had cooked, and all the clothes she had cut and sewed, and all the gardens she had made—well, the children showed it. There they were, made out of her, and they couldn't get away from that. Sometimes she wanted to see John again and point to them and say, Well, I didn't do so badly, did I? But that would have to wait. That was for tomorrow. She used to think of him as a man, but now all the children were older than their father, and he would be a child beside her if she saw him now. It seemed strange and there was something wrong in the idea. Why, he couldn't possibly recognize her. She had fenced in a hundred acres once, digging the post holes herself and clamping the wires with just a negro boy to help. That changed a woman. John would be looking for a young woman with the peaked Spanish comb in her hair and the painted fan. Digging post holes changed a woman. Riding country roads in the winter when women had their babies was another thing: sitting up nights with sick horses and sick negroes and sick children and hardly ever losing one. John, I hardly ever lost one of them! John would see that in a minute, that would be something he could understand, she wouldn't have to explain anything!

It made her feel like rolling up her sleeves and putting the whole place to rights again. No matter if Cornelia was determined to be everywhere at once, there were a great many things left undone on this place. She would start tomorrow and do them. It was good to be strong enough for everything, even if all you made melted and changed and slipped under your hands, so that by the time you finished you almost forgot what you were working for. What was it I set out to do? she asked herself intently, but she could not remember. A fog rose over the valley, she saw it marching across the creek swallowing the trees and moving up the hill like an army of ghosts. Soon it would be at the near edge of the orchard, and then it was time to go in and light the lamps. Come in, children, don't stay out in the night air.

Lighting the lamps had been beautiful. The children huddled up to her and breathed like little calves waiting at the bars in the twilight. Their eyes followed the match and watched the flame rise and settle in a blue curve, then they moved away from her. The lamp was lit, they didn't have to be scared and hang on to Mother any more. Never, never, never more. God, for all my life I thank Thee. Without Thee, my God, I could never have done it. Hail, Mary, full of grace.

I want you to pick all the fruit this year and see that nothing is wasted. There's always someone who can use it. Don't let good things rot for want of using. You waste life when you waste good food. Don't let things get lost. It's bitter to lose things. Now, don't let me get to thinking, not when I am tired and taking a little nap before supper. . . .

The pillow rose about her shoulders and pressed against her heart and the memory was being squeezed out of it: oh, push down the pillow, somebody: it would smother her if she tried to hold it. Such a fresh breeze blowing and such a green day with no threats in it. But he had not come, just the same. What does a woman do when she has put on the white veil and set out the white cake for a man and he doesn't come? She tried to remember. No, I swear he never harmed me but in that. He never harmed me but in that . . . and what if he did? There was the day, the day, but a whirl of dark smoke rose and covered it, crept up and over into the bright field where everything was planted so carefully in orderly rows. That was hell, she knew hell when she saw it. For sixty years she had prayed against remembering him and against losing her soul in the deep pit of hell, and now the two things were mingled in one and the thought of him was a smoky cloud from hell that moved and crept in her head when she had just got rid of Doctor Harry and was trying to rest a minute. Wounded vanity, Ellen, said a sharp voice in the top of her mind. Don't let your wounded vanity get the upper hand of you. Plenty of girls get jilted. You were jilted, weren't you? Then stand up to it. Her eyelids wavered and let in streamers of blue-gray light like tissue paper over her eyes. She must get up and pull the shades down or she'd never sleep. She was in bed again and the shades were not down. How could that happen? Better turn over, hide from the light, sleeping in the light gave you nightmares. "Mother, how do you feel now?" and a stinging wetness on her forehead. But I don't like having my face washed in cold water!

Hapsy? George? Lydia? Jimmy? No, Cornelia, and her features were swollen and full of little puddles. "They're coming, darling, they'll all be here soon." Go wash your face, child, you look funny.

Instead of obeying, Cornelia knelt down and put her head on the pillow. She seemed to be talking but there was no sound. "Well, are you tongue-tied? Whose birthday is it? Are you going to give a party?"

Cornelia's mouth moved urgently in strange shapes. "Don't do that, you bother me, daughter."

"Oh, no, Mother. Oh, no. . . ."

Nonsense. It was strange about children. They disputed your every word. "No what, Cornelia?"

"Here's Doctor Harry."

"I won't see that boy again. He just left five minutes ago."

"That was this morning, Mother. It's night now. Here's the nurse."

"This is Doctor Harry, Mrs. Weatherall. I never saw you look so young and happy!"

"Ah, I'll never be young again—but I'd be happy if they'd let me lie in peace and get rested."

She thought she spoke up loudly, but no one answered. A warm weight on her forehead, a warm bracelet on her wrist, and a breeze went on whispering, trying to tell her something. A shuffle of leaves in the everlasting hand of God, He blew on them and they danced and rattled. "Mother, don't mind, we're going to give you a little hypodermic." "Look here, daughter, how do ants get in this bed? I saw sugar ants yesterday." Did you send for Hapsy too?

It was Hapsy she really wanted. She had to go a long way back through a great many rooms to find Hapsy standing with a baby on her arm. She seemed to herself to be Hapsy also, and the baby on Hapsy's arm was Hapsy and himself and herself, all at once, and there was no surprise in the meeting. Then Hapsy melted from within and turned flimsy as gray gauze and the baby was a gauzy shadow, and Hapsy came up close and said, "I thought you'd never come," and looked at her very searchingly and said, "You haven't changed a bit!" They leaned forward to kiss, when Cornelia began whispering from a long way off, "Oh, is there anything you want to tell me? Is there anything I can do for you?"

Yes, she had changed her mind after sixty years and she would like to see George. I want you to find George. Find him and be sure to tell him I forgot him. I want him to know I had my husband just the same and my children and my house like any other woman. A good house too and a good husband that I loved and fine children out of him. Better than I hoped for even. Tell him I was given back everything he took away and more. Oh, no, oh, God, no, there was something else besides the house and the man and the children. Oh, surely they were not all? What was it? Something not given back. . . . Her breath crowded down under her ribs and grew into a monstrous frightening shape with cutting edges; it bored up into her head, and the agony was unbelievable: Yes, John, get the Doctor now, no more talk, my time has come.

When this one was born it should be the last. The last. It should have been born first, for it was the one she had truly wanted. Everything came in good time. Nothing left out, left over. She was strong, in three days she would be as well as ever. Better. A woman needed milk in her to have her full health.

"Mother, do you hear me?"

"I've been telling you—"

"Mother, Father Connolly's here."

"I went to Holy Communion only last week. Tell him I'm not so sinful as all that."

"Father just wants to speak to you."

He could speak as much as he pleased. It was like him to drop in and inquire about her soul as if it were a teething baby, and then stay on for a cup of tea and a round of cards and gossip. He always had a funny story of some sort, usually about an Irishman

who made his little mistakes and confessed them, and the point lay
in some absurd thing he would blurt out in the confessional showing his struggles between native piety and original sin. Granny felt
easy about her soul. Cornelia, where are your manners? Give
Father Connolly a chair. She had her secret comfortable understanding with a few favorite saints who cleared a straight road to
God for her. All as surely signed and sealed as the papers for the
new Forty Acres. Forever . . . heirs and assigns forever. Since
the day the wedding cake was not cut, but thrown out and wasted.
The whole bottom dropped out of the world, and there she was
blind and sweating with nothing under her feet and the walls
falling away. His hand had caught her under the breast, she had
not fallen, there was the freshly polished floor with the green rug
on it, just as before. He had cursed like a sailor's parrot and said,
"I'll kill him for you." Don't lay a hand on him, for my sake leave
something to God. "Now, Ellen, you must believe what I tell
you. . . ."

So there was nothing, nothing to worry about any more, except sometimes in the night one of the children screamed in a
nightmare, and they both hustled out shaking and hunting for the
matches and calling, "There, wait a minute, here we are!" John,
get the doctor now, Hapsy's time has come. But there was Hapsy
standing by the bed in a white cap. "Cornelia, tell Hapsy to take
off her cap. I can't see her plain."

Her eyes opened very wide and the room stood out like a
picture she had seen somewhere. Dark colors with the shadows
rising towards the ceiling in long angles. The tall black dresser
gleamed with nothing on it but John's picture, enlarged from a
little one, with John's eyes very black when they should have been
blue. You never saw him, so how do you know how he looked?
But the man insisted the copy was perfect, it was very rich and
handsome. For a picture, yes, but it's not my husband. The table
by the bed had a linen cover and a candle and a crucifix. The light
was blue from Cornelia's silk lampshades. No sort of light at all,
just frippery. You had to live forty years with kerosene lamps to
appreciate honest electricity. She felt very strong and she saw
Doctor Harry with a rosy nimbus around him.

"You look like a saint, Doctor Harry, and I vow that's as near
as you'll ever come to it."

"She's saying something."

"I heard you, Cornelia. What's all this carrying-on?"

"Father Connolly's saying—"

Cornelia's voice staggered and bumped like a cart in a bad road. It rounded corners and turned back again and arrived nowhere. Granny stepped up in the cart very lightly and reached for the reins, but a man sat beside her and she knew him by his hands, driving the cart. She did not look in his face, for she knew without seeing, but looked instead down the road where the trees leaned over and bowed to each other and a thousand birds were singing a Mass. She felt like singing too, but she put her hand in the bosom of her dress and pulled out a rosary, and Father Connolly murmured Latin in a very solemn voice and tickled her feet. My God, will you stop that nonsense? I'm a married woman. What if he did run away and leave me to face the priest by myself? I found another a whole world better. I wouldn't have exchanged my husband for anybody except St. Michael himself, and you may tell him that for me with a thank you in the bargain.

Light flashed on her closed eyelids, and a deep roaring shook her. Cornelia, is that lightning? I hear thunder. There's going to be a storm. Close all the windows. Call the children in. . . . "Mother, here we are, all of us." "Is that you, Hapsy?" "Oh, no, I'm Lydia. We drove as fast as we could." Their faces drifted above her, drifted away. The rosary fell out of her hands and Lydia put it back. Jimmy tried to help, their hands fumbled together, and Granny closed two fingers around Jimmy's thumb. Beads wouldn't do, it must be something alive. She was so amazed her thoughts ran round and round. So, my dear Lord, this is my death and I wasn't even thinking about it. My children have come to see me die. But I can't, it's not time. Oh, I always hated surprises. I wanted to give Cornelia the amethyst set—Cornelia, you're to have the amethyst set, but Hapsy's to wear it when she wants, and, Doctor Harry, do shut up. Nobody sent for you. Oh, my dear Lord, do wait a minute. I meant to do something about the Forty Acres, Jimmy doesn't need it and Lydia will later on, with that worthless husband of hers. I meant to finish the altar cloth and send six bottles of wine to Sister Borgia for her dyspepsia. I want to send six bottles of wine to Sister Borgia, Father Connolly, now don't let me forget.

Cornelia's voice made short turns and tilted over and crashed. "Oh, Mother, oh, Mother, oh, Mother. . . ."

"I'm not going, Cornelia. I'm taken by surprise. I can't go."

You'll see Hapsy again. What about her? "I thought you'd never come." Granny made a long journey outward, looking for

Hapsy. What if I don't find her? What then? Her heart sank down and down, there was no bottom to death, she couldn't come to the end of it. The blue light from Cornelia's lampshade drew into a tiny point in the center of her brain, it flickered and winked like an eye, quietly it fluttered and dwindled. Granny lay curled down within herself, amazed and watchful, staring at the point of light that was herself; her body was now only a deeper mass of shadow in an endless darkness and this darkness would curl around the light and swallow it up. God, give a sign!

For the second time there was no sign. Again no bridegroom and the priest in the house. She could not remember any other sorrow because this grief wiped them all away. Oh, no, there's nothing more cruel than this—I'll never forgive it. She stretched herself with a deep breath and blew out the light.

Island

SHIRLEY JACKSON

The isolation of old age is the subject of this story by Shirley Jackson. It would appear that her son and hired companion take excellent care of the elderly, senile Mrs. Montague, but in fact they can provide only for her material comfort. The tragedy of old age is that real comfort does not exist, except in dim memories of the past. Mrs. Montague must endure loneliness and suffer the indignity of being dependent on a person whom she dislikes. As an escape, she creates an imaginary world, an idyllic island where she experiences all the pleasures denied her in old age. Why is her first act to shed her clothes, and why does she bury them in the sand? What determines the appearance and the behavior of the parrot? What is Mrs. Montague's initial reaction to the shrill bird, and why does her attitude toward it mellow? What does this change in mood indicate about Mrs. Montague's personality? Why is it significant that she dreams of an island, and why does the author select this detail as the title of the story?

M rs. Montague's son had been very good to her, with the kind affection and attention to her well-being that is seldom found toward mothers in sons with busy wives and growing families of their own; when Mrs. Montague lost her mind, her son came into his natural role of guardian. There had always been a great deal of warm feeling between Mrs. Montague and her son, and although they lived nearly a thousand miles apart by now, Henry Paul Montague was careful to see that his mother was well taken care of; he ascertained, minutely, that the monthly bills for her apartment, her food, her clothes, and her companion were large enough to ensure that Mrs. Montague was getting the best of everything;

ISLAND From *Come Along With Me* by Shirley Jackson. Copyright 1950 by Stanley Edgar Hyman. Reprinted by permission of The Viking Press, Inc.

he wrote to her weekly, tender letters in longhand inquiring about her health; when he came to New York he visited her promptly, and always left an extra check for the companion, to make sure that any small things Mrs. Montague lacked would be given her. The companion, Miss Oakes, had been with Mrs. Montague for six years, and in that time their invariable quiet routine had been broken only by the regular visits from Mrs. Montague's son, and by Miss Oakes's annual six-weeks' leave, during which Mrs. Montague was cared for no less scrupulously by a carefully chosen substitute.

Between such disturbing occasions, Mrs. Montague lived quietly and expensively in her handsome apartment, following with Miss Oakes a life of placid regularity, which it required all of Miss Oakes's competence to engineer, and duly reported on to Mrs. Montague's son. "I *do* think we're very lucky, dear," was Miss Oakes's frequent comment, "to have a good son like Mr. Montague to take care of us so well."

To which Mrs. Montague's usual answer was, "Henry Paul was a good boy."

Mrs. Montague usually spent the morning in bed, and got up for lunch; after the effort of bathing and dressing and eating she was ready for another rest and then her walk, which occurred regularly at four o'clock, and which was followed by dinner sent up from the restaurant downstairs, and, shortly after, by Mrs. Montague's bedtime. Although Miss Oakes did not leave the apartment except in an emergency, she had a great deal of time to herself and her regular duties were not harsh, although Mrs. Montague was not the best company in the world. Frequently Miss Oakes would look up from her magazine to find Mrs. Montague watching her curiously; sometimes Mrs. Montague, in a spirit of petulant stubbornness, would decline all food under any persuasion until it was necessary for Miss Oakes to call in Mrs. Montague's doctor for Mrs. Montague to hear a firm lecture on her duties as a patient. Once Mrs. Montague had tried to run away, and had been recaptured by Miss Oakes in the street in front of the apartment house, going vaguely through the traffic; and always, constantly, Mrs. Montague was trying to give things to Miss Oakes, many of which, in absolute frankness, it cost Miss Oakes a pang to refuse.

Miss Oakes had not been born to the luxury which Mrs. Montague had known all her life; Miss Oakes had worked hard and never had a fur coat; no matter how much she tried Miss Oakes could not disguise the fact that she relished the food sent up from the restaurant downstairs, delicately cooked and prettily served; Miss Oakes was persuaded that she disdained jewelry, and she chose her clothes hurriedly and inexpensively, under the eye of an impatient, badly dressed salesgirl in a department store. No matter how agonizingly Miss Oakes debated under the insinuating lights of the budget dress department, the clothes she carried home with her turned out to be garish reds and yellows in the daylight, inexactly striped or dotted, badly cut. Miss Oakes sometimes thought longingly of the security of her white uniforms, neatly stacked in her dresser drawer, but Mrs. Montague was apt to go into a tantrum at any outward show of Miss Oakes's professional competence, and Miss Oakes dined nightly on the agreeable food from the restaurant downstairs in her red and yellow dresses, with her colorless hair drawn ungracefully to a bun in back, her ringless hands moving appreciatively among the plates. Mrs. Montague, who ordinarily spilled food all over herself, chose her dresses from a selection sent every three or four months from an exclusive dress shop near by; all information as to size and color was predigested in the shop, and the soft-voiced saleslady brought only dresses absolutely right for Mrs. Montague. Mrs. Montague usually chose two dresses each time, and they went, neatly hung on sacheted hangers, to live softly in Mrs. Montague's closet along with other dresses just like them, all in soft blues and grays and mauves.

"We *must* try to be more careful of our pretty clothes," Miss Oakes would say, looking up from her dinner to find Mrs. Montague, almost deliberately, it seemed sometimes, emptying her spoonful of oatmeal down the front of her dress. "Dear, we really *must* try to be more careful; remember what our nice son has to pay for those dresses."

Mrs. Montague stared vaguely sometimes, holding her spoon; sometimes she said, "I want my pudding now; I'll be careful with my pudding." Now and then, usually when the day had gone badly and Mrs. Montague was overtired, or cross for one reason or another, she might turn the dish of oatmeal over onto the tablecloth, and then, frequently, Miss Oakes was angry, and Mrs. Montague was deprived of her pudding and sat blankly while Miss Oakes moved her own dishes to a coffee table and called the waiter to remove the dinner table with its mess of oatmeal.

It was in the late spring that Mrs. Montague was usually at her worst; then, for some reason, it seemed that the stirring of green life, even under the dirty city traffic, communicated a restlessness and longing to her that she felt only spasmodically the rest of the year; around April or May, Miss Oakes began to prepare for trouble, for runnings-away and supreme oatmeal overturnings. In summer, Mrs. Montague seemed happier, because it was possible to walk in the park and feed the squirrels; in the fall, she quieted, in preparation for the long winter when she was almost dormant, like an animal, rarely speaking, and suffering herself to be dressed and undressed without rebellion; it was the winter that Miss Oakes most appreciated, although as the months moved on into spring Miss Oakes began to think more often of giving up her position, her pleasant salary, the odorous meals from the restaurant downstairs.

It was in the spring that Mrs. Montague so often tried to give things to Miss Oakes; one afternoon when their walk was dubious because of the rain, Mrs. Montague had gone as of habit to the hall closet and taken out her coat, and now sat in her armchair with the rich dark mink heaped in her lap, smoothing the fur as though she held a cat. "Pretty," Mrs. Montague was saying, "pretty, pretty."

"We're very lucky to have such lovely things," Miss Oakes said. Because it was her practice to keep busy always, never to let her knowledgeable fingers rest so long as they might be doing something useful, she was knitting a scarf. It was only half-finished, but already Miss Oakes was beginning to despair of it; the yarn, in the store and in the roll, seemed a soft tender green, but knit up into the scarf it assumed a gaudy chartreuse character that made its original purpose—to embrace the firm fleshy neck of Henry Paul Montague—seem faintly improper; when Miss Oakes looked at the scarf impartially it irritated her, as did almost everything she created.

"Think of the money," Miss Oakes said, "that goes into all those beautiful things, just because your son is so generous and kind."

"I will give you this fur," Mrs. Montague said suddenly. "Because you have no beautiful things of your own."

"Thank you, dear," Miss Oakes said. She worked busily at her scarf for a minute and then said, "It's not being very grateful for nice things like that, dear, to want to give them away."

"It wouldn't look nice on you," Mrs. Montague said, "it would look awful. You're not very pretty."

Miss Oakes was silent again for a minute, and then she said, "Well, dear, shall we see if it's still raining?" With great deliberation she put down the knitting and walked over to the window. When she pulled back the lace curtain and the heavy dark-red drape she did so carefully, because the curtain and the drape were not precisely her own, but were of service to her, and pleasant to her touch, and expensive. "It's almost stopped," she said brightly. She squinted her eyes and looked up at the sky. "I *do* believe it's going to clear up," she went on, as though her brightness might create a sun of reflected brilliance. "In about fifteen minutes . . ." She let her voice trail off, and smiled at Mrs. Montague with vast anticipation.

"I don't want to go for any walk," Mrs. Montague said sullenly. "Once when we were children we used to take off all our clothes and run out in the rain."

Miss Oakes returned to her chair and took up her knitting. "We can start to get ready in a few minutes," she promised.

"I couldn't do that *now*, of course," Mrs. Montague said. "I want to color."

She slid out of her chair, dropping the mink coat into a heap on the floor, and went slowly, with her faltering walk, across the room to the card table where her coloring book and box of crayons lay. Miss Oakes sighed, set her knitting down, and walked over to pick up the mink coat; she draped it tenderly over the back of the chair, and went back and picked up her knitting again.

"Pretty, pretty," Mrs. Montague crooned over her coloring, "Pretty blue, pretty water, pretty, pretty."

Miss Oakes allowed a small smile to touch her face as she regarded the scarf; it was a bright color, perhaps too bright for a man no longer very young, but it was gay and not really *unusually* green. His birthday was three weeks off; the card in the box would say "To remind you of your loyal friend and admirer, Polly Oakes." Miss Oakes sighed quickly.

"I want to go for a *walk*," Mrs. Montague said abruptly.

"Just a minute, dear," Miss Oakes said. She put the knitting down again and smiled at Mrs. Montague. "I'll help you," Miss Oakes said, and went over to assist Mrs. Montague in the slow task that getting out of a straight chair always entailed. "Why, look at you," Miss Oakes said, regarding the coloring book over Mrs. Montague's head. She laughed. "You've gone and made the whole thing blue, you silly child." She turned back a page. "And here," she said, and laughed again. "Why does the man have a blue face? And the little girl in the picture—she mustn't be blue, dear, her face should be pink and her hair should be—oh, yellow, for instance. Not *blue*."

Mrs. Montague put her hands violently over the picture. "Mine," she said. "Get away, this is mine."

"I'm sorry," Miss Oakes said smoothly, "I wasn't laughing at you, dear. It was just funny to see a man with a blue face." She helped Mrs. Montague out of the chair and escorted her across the room to the mink coat. Mrs. Montague stood stiffly while Miss Oakes put the coat over her shoulders and helped her arms into the sleeves, and when Miss Oakes came around in front of her to button the coat at the neck Mrs. Montague turned down the corners of her mouth and said sullenly into Miss Oakes's face, so close to hers, "You don't know what things *are*, really."

"Perhaps I don't," Miss Oakes said absently. She surveyed Mrs. Montague, neatly buttoned into the mink coat, and then took Mrs. Montague's rose-covered hat from the table in the hall and set it on Mrs. Montague's head, with great regard to the correct angle and the neatness of the roses. "Now we look so pretty," Miss Oakes said. Mrs. Montague stood silently while Miss Oakes went to the hall closet and took out her own serviceable blue coat. She shrugged herself into it, settled it with a brisk tug at the collar, and pulled on her hat with a quick gesture from back to front that landed the hatbrim at exactly the usual angle over her eye. It was not until she was escorting Mrs. Montague to the door that Miss Oakes gave one brief, furtive glance at the hall mirror, as one who does so from a nervous compulsion rather than any real desire for information.

Miss Oakes enjoyed walking down the hall; its carpets were so thick that even the stout shoes of Miss Oakes made no sound. The elevator was self-service, and Miss Oakes, with superhuman control, allowed it to sweep soundlessly down to the main floor, carrying with it Miss Oakes herself, and Mrs. Montague, who sat docilely on the velvet-covered bench and stared at the paneling as though she had never seen it before. When the elevator door opened and they moved out into the lobby Miss Oakes knew that the few people who saw them—the girl at the switchboard, the doorman, another tenant coming to the elevator—recognized Mrs. Montague as the rich old lady who lived high upstairs, and Miss Oakes as the infinitely competent companion, without whose unswerving assistance Mrs. Montague could not live for ten minutes. Miss Oakes walked sturdily and well through the lobby, her firm hand guiding soft little Mrs. Montague; the lobby floor was pale carpeting on which their feet made no sound, and the lobby walls were painted an expensive color so neutral as to be almost invisible; as Miss Oakes went with Mrs. Montague through the lobby it was as though they walked upon clouds, through the noncommittal areas of infinite space. The doorway was their aim, and the doorman, dressed in gray, opened the way for them with a flourish and a "Good afternoon" which began by being directed at Mrs. Montague, as the employer, and ended by addressing Miss Oakes, as the person who would be expected to answer.

"Good afternoon, George," Miss Oakes said, with a stately smile, and passed on through the doorway, leading Mrs. Montague. Once outside on the sidewalk, Miss Oakes steered Mrs. Montague quickly to the left, since, allowed her head, Mrs. Montague might as easily have turned unexpectedly to the right, although they always turned to the left, and so upset Miss Oakes's walk for the day. With slow steps they moved into the current of people walking up the street, Miss Oakes watching ahead to avoid Mrs. Montague's walking into strangers, Mrs. Montague with her face turned up to the gray sky.

"It's a *lovely* day," Miss Oakes said. "Pleasantly cool after the rain."

They had gone perhaps half a block when Mrs. Montague, by a gentle pressure against Miss Oakes's arm, began to direct them toward the inside of the sidewalk and the shop windows; Miss Oakes, resisting at first, at last allowed herself to be reluctantly influenced and they crossed the sidewalk to stand in front of the window to a stationery store.

They stopped here every day, and, as she said every day, Mrs. Montague murmured softly, "*Look* at all the lovely things." She watched with amusement a plastic bird, colored bright red and yellow, which methodically dipped its beak into a glass of water and withdrew it; while they stood watching the bird lowered its head and touched the water, hesitated, and then rose.

"Does it stop when we're not here?" Mrs Montague asked, and Miss Oakes laughed, and said, "It never stops. It goes on while we're eating and while we're sleeping and all the time."

Mrs. Montague's attention had wandered to the open pages of a diary, spread nakedly to the pages dated June 14–June 15. Mrs. Montague, looking at the smooth unwritten paper, caught her breath. "I'd like to have *that*," she said, and Miss Oakes, as she answered every day, said, "What would you write in it, dear?"

The thing that always caught Mrs. Montague next was a softly curved blue bowl which stood in the center of the window display; Mrs. Montague pored lovingly and speechlessly over this daily, trying to touch it through the glass of the window.

"Come *on,* dear," Miss Oakes said finally, with an almost-impatient tug at Mrs. Montague's arm. "We'll never get our walk finished if you don't come *on.*"

Docilely Mrs. Montague followed. "Pretty," she whispered, "pretty, pretty."

She opened her eyes suddenly and was aware that she saw. The sky was unbelievably, steadily blue, and the sand beneath her feet was hot; she could see the water, colored more deeply than the sky, but faintly greener. Far off was the line where the sky and water met, and it was infinitely pure.

"Pretty," she said inadequately, and was aware that she spoke. She was walking on the sand, and with a sudden impatient gesture she stopped and slipped off her shoes, standing first on one foot and then on the other. This encouraged her to look down at herself; she was very tall, high above her shoes on the sand, and when she moved it was freely and easily except for the cumbering clothes, the heavy coat and the hat, which sat on her head with a tangible, oppressive weight. She threw the hat onto the hot lovely sand, and it looked so offensive, lying with its patently unreal roses against the smooth clarity of the sand, that she bent quickly and covered the hat with handfuls of sand; the coat was more difficult to cover, and the sand ran delicately between the hairs of the short dark fur; before she had half covered the coat she decided to put the rest of her clothes with it, and did so, slipping easily out of the straps and buttons and catches of many garments, which she remembered as difficult to put on. When all her clothes were buried she looked with satisfaction down at her strong white legs, and thought, aware that she was thinking it: they are almost the same color as the sand. She began to run freely, with the blue ocean and the bluer sky on her right, the trees on her left, and the moving sand underfoot; she ran until she came back to the place where a corner of her coat still showed through the sand. When she saw it she stopped again and said, "Pretty, pretty," and leaned over and took a handful of sand and let it run through her fingers.

Far away, somewhere in the grove of trees that centered the island she could hear the parrot calling. "Eat, eat," it shrieked, and then something indistinguishable, and then, "Eat, eat."

An idea came indirectly and subtly to her mind; it was the idea of food, for a minute unpleasant and as though it meant a disagreeable sensation, and then glowingly happy. She turned and ran—it was impossible to move slowly on the island, with the clear hot air all around her, and the ocean stirring constantly, pushing at the island, and the unbelievable blue sky above—and when she came into the sudden warm shade of the trees she ran from one to another, putting her hand for a minute on each.

"Hello," the parrot gabbled, "Hello, who's there, eat?" She could see it flashing among the trees, no more than a saw-toothed voice and a flash of ugly red and yellow.

The grass was green and rich and soft, and she sat down by the little brook where the food was set out. Today there was a great polished wooden bowl, soft to the touch, full of purple grapes; the sun that came unevenly between the trees struck a high shine from the bowl, and lay flatly against the grapes, which were dusty with warmth, and almost black. There was a shimmering glass just full of dark red wine; there was a flat blue plate filled with little cakes; she touched one and it was full of cream, and heavily iced with soft chocolate. There were pomegranates, and cheese, and small, sharp-flavored candies. She lay down beside the food, and closed her eyes against the heavy scent from the grapes.

"Eat, eat," the parrot screamed from somewhere over her head. She opened her eyes lazily and looked up, to see the flash of red and yellow in the trees. "Be still, you noisy beast," she said, and smiled to herself because it was not important, actually, whether the parrot were quiet or not. Later, after she had slept, she ate some of the grapes and the cheese, and several of the rich little cakes. While she ate the parrot came cautiously closer, begging for food, sidling up near to the dish of cakes and then moving quickly away.

"Beast," she said pleasantly to the parrot, "greedy beast."

When she was sure she was quite through with the food, she put one of the cakes on a green leaf and set it a little bit away from her for the parrot. It came up to the cake slowly and fearfully, watching on either side for some sudden prohibitive movement; when it finally reached the cake it hesitated, and then dipped its head down to bury its beak in the soft frosting; it lifted its head, paused to look around, and then lowered its beak to the cake again. The gesture was familiar, and she laughed, not knowing why.

She was faintly aware that she had slept again, and awakened wanting to run, to go out into the hot sand on the beach and run shouting around the island. The parrot was gone, its cake a mess of crumbs and frosting on the ground. She ran out onto the beach, and the water was there, and the sky. For a few minutes she ran, going down to the water and then swiftly back before it could touch her bare feet, and then she dropped luxuriously onto the sand and lay there. After a while she began to draw a picture in the sand; it was a round face with dots for eyes and nose and a line for a mouth. "Henry Paul," she said, touching the face caressingly with her fingers, and then, laughing, she leaped to her feet and began to run again, around the island. When she passed the face drawn on the sand she put one bare foot on it and ground it away. "Eat, eat," she could hear the parrot calling from the trees; the parrot was afraid of the hot sand and the water and stayed always in the trees near the food. Far off, across the water, she could see the sweet, the always comforting, line of the horizon.

When she was tired with running she lay down again on the sand. For a little while she played idly, writing words on the sand and then rubbing them out with her hand; once she drew a crude picture of a doorway and punched her fist through it.

Finally she lay down and put her face down to the sand. It was hot, hotter than anything else had ever been, and the soft grits of the sand slipped into her mouth, where she could taste them, deliciously hard and grainy against her teeth; they were in her eyes, rich and warm; the sand was covering her face and the blue sky was gone from above her and the sand was cooler, then grayer, covering her face, and cold.

"*Nearly* home," Miss Oakes said brightly, as they turned the last corner of their block. "It's been a *nice* walk, hasn't it?"

She tried, unsuccessfully, to guide Mrs. Montague quickly past the bakery, but Mrs. Montague's feet, moving against Miss Oakes's pressure from habit, brought them up to stand in front of the bakery window.

"I don't know *why* they leave those fly-specked éclairs out here," Miss Oakes said irritably. "There's nothing *less* appetizing. *Look* at that cake; the cream is positively *curdled*."

She moved her arm insinuatingly within Mrs. Montague's. "In a few minutes we'll be home," she said softly, "and then we can have our nice cocktail, and rest for a few minutes, and then dinner."

"Pretty," Mrs. Montague said at the cakes. "I want some."

Miss Oakes shuddered violently. "Don't even *say* it," she implored. "Just *look* at that stuff. You'd be sick for a week."

She moved Mrs. Montague along, and they came, moving quicker than they had when they started, back to their own doorway where the doorman in gray waited for them. He opened the door and said, beginning with Mrs. Montague and finishing with Miss Oakes, "Have a nice walk?"

"Very pleasant, thank you," Miss Oakes said agreeably. They passed through the doorway and into the lobby where the open doors of the elevator waited for them. "Dinner soon," Miss Oakes said as they went across the lobby.

Miss Oakes was careful, on their own floor, to see that Mrs. Montague found the right doorway; while Miss Oakes put the key in the door Mrs. Montague stood waiting without expression.

Mrs. Montague moved forward automatically when the door was opened, and Miss Oakes caught her arm, saying shrilly, "Don't *step* on it!" Mrs. Montague stopped, and waited, while Miss Oakes picked up the dinner menu from the floor just inside the door; it had been slipped under the door while they were out.

Once inside, Miss Oakes removed Mrs. Montague's rosy hat and the mink coat, and Mrs. Montague took the mink coat in her arms and sat down in her chair with it, smoothing the fur. Miss Oakes slid out of her own coat and hung it neatly in the closet, and then came into the living room, carrying the dinner menu.

"Chicken liver omelette," Miss Oakes read as she walked. "The last time it was a trifle underdone; I could *mention* it, of course, but they never seem to pay much attention. Roast turkey. Filet mignon. I *really* do think a nice little piece of . . ." she looked up at Mrs. Montague and smiled. "Hungry?" she suggested.

"No," Mrs. Montague said. "I've had enough."

"Nice oatmeal?" Miss Oakes said. "If you're *very* good you can have ice cream tonight."

"Don't want ice cream," Mrs. Montague said.

Miss Oakes sighed, and then said "Well . . ." placatingly. She returned to the menu. "French-fried potatoes," she said. "They're *very* heavy on the stomach, but I do have my heart set on a nice little piece of steak and some french-fried potatoes. It sounds just *right*, tonight."

"Shall I give you this coat?" Mrs. Montague asked suddenly.

Miss Oakes stopped on her way to the phone and patted Mrs.

Montague lightly on the shoulder. "You're very generous, dear," she said, "but of course you don't really want to give me your beautiful coat. What would your dear son say?"

Mrs. Montague ran her hand over the fur of the coat affectionately. Then she stood up, slowly, and the coat slid to the floor. "I'm going to color," she announced.

Miss Oakes turned back from the phone to pick up the coat and put it over the back of the chair. "All right," she said. She went to the phone, sat so she could keep an eye on Mrs. Montague while she talked, and said into the phone "Room service."

Mrs. Montague moved across the room and sat down at the card table. Reflectively she turned the pages of the coloring book, found a picture that pleased her, and opened the crayon box. Miss Oakes hummed softly into the phone. "Room service?" she said finally. "I want to order dinner sent up to Mrs. Montague's suite, please." She looked over the phone at Mrs. Montague and said, "You all right, dear?"

Without turning, Mrs. Montague moved her shoulders impatiently, and selected a crayon from the box. She examined the point of it with great care while Miss Oakes said, "I want one very sweet martini, please. And Mrs. Montague's prune juice." She picked up the menu and wet her lips, then said, "One crab-meat cocktail. And tonight will you see that Mrs. Montague has milk with her oatmeal; you sent cream last night. Yes, milk, please. You'd think they'd know by *now*," she added to Mrs. Montague over the top of the phone. "Now let me see," she said, into the phone again, her eyes on the menu.

Disregarding Miss Oakes, Mrs. Montague had begun to color. Her shoulders bent low over the book, a vague smile on her old face, she was devoting herself to a picture of a farmyard; a hen and three chickens strutted across the foreground of the picture, a barn surrounded by trees was the background. Mrs. Montague had laboriously colored the hen and the three chickens, the barn and the trees a rich blue, and now, with alternate touches of the crayons, was engaged in putting a red and yellow blot far up in the blue trees.

A Worn Path
EUDORA WELTY

"A Worn Path" presents a portrait of old age that has transcended
all indignity and suffering to assume almost archetypal proportions.
What the old woman says of her sick grandson is equally true of
herself: "He suffer and it don't seem to put him back at all."
Even after the ordeal of her trek, she seems indestructible and
invincible. It is not coincidental that the old woman's name is
Phoenix. What details does the author include to demonstrate
her character's strength in spite of her fragile appearance? What
aspects of her personality are emphasized in her encounter with
the young hunter? With the perfumed lady who ties her shoes?
What is the cumulative effect achieved by the last two paragraphs
of the story—the description of the gift she plans to buy her
grandson, and her exit from the clinic?

It was December—a bright frozen day in the early morning. Far
out in the country there was an old Negro woman with her head
tied in a red rag, coming along a path through the pinewoods. Her
name was Phoenix Jackson. She was very old and small and she
walked slowly in the dark pine shadows, moving a little from side
to side in her steps, with the balanced heaviness and lightness of a
pendulum in a grandfather clock. She carried a thin, small cane
made from an umbrella, and with this she kept tapping the frozen
earth in front of her. This made a grave and persistent noise in the
still air, that seemed meditative like the chirping of a solitary little
bird.

She wore a dark striped dress reaching down to her shoe tops,
and an equally long apron of bleached sugar sacks, with a full

pocket: all neat and tidy, but every time she took a step she might have fallen over her shoelaces, which dragged from her unlaced shoes. She looked straight ahead. Her eyes were blue with age. Her skin had a pattern all its own of numberless branching wrinkles and as though a whole little tree stood in the middle of her forehead, but a golden color ran underneath, and the two knobs of her cheeks were illumined by a yellow burning under the dark. Under the red rag her hair came down on her neck in the frailest of ringlets, still black, and with an odor like copper.

Now and then there was a quivering in the thicket. Old Phoenix said, "Out of my way, all you foxes, owls, beetles, jack rabbits, coons and wild animals! . . . Keep out from under these feet, little bob-whites. . . . Keep the big wild hogs out of my path. Don't let none of those come running my direction. I got a long way." Under her small black-freckled hand her cane, limber as a buggy whip, would switch at the brush as if to rouse up any hiding things.

On she went. The woods were deep and still. The sun made the pine needles almost too bright to look at, up where the wind rocked. The cones dropped as light as feathers. Down in the hollow was the mourning dove—it was not too late for him.

The path ran up a hill. "Seem like there is chains about my feet, time I get this far," she said, in the voice of argument old people keep to use with themselves. "Something always take a hold of me on this hill—pleads I should stay."

After she got to the top she turned and gave a full, severe look behind her where she had come. "Up through pines," she said at length. "Now down through oaks."

Her eyes opened their widest, and she started down gently. But before she got to the bottom of the hill a bush caught her dress.

Her fingers were busy and intent, but her skirts were full and long, so that before she could pull them free in one place they were caught in another. It was not possible to allow the dress to tear. "I in the thorny bush," she said. "Thorns, you doing your appointed work. Never want to let folks pass, no sir. Old eyes thought you was a pretty little *green* bush."

Finally, trembling all over, she stood free, and after a moment dared to stoop for her cane.

"Sun so high!" she cried, leaning back and looking, while the thick tears went over her eyes. "The time getting all gone here."

At the foot of this hill was a place where a log was laid across the creek.

"Now comes the trial," said Phoenix.

Putting her right foot out, she mounted the log and shut her eyes. Lifting her skirt, leveling her cane fiercely before her, like a festival figure in some parade, she began to march across. Then she opened her eyes and she was safe on the other side.

"I wasn't as old as I thought," she said.

But she sat down to rest. She spread her skirts on the bank around her and folded her hands over her knees. Up above her was a tree in a pearly cloud of mistletoe. She did not dare to close her eyes, and when a little boy brought her a plate with a slice of marble-cake on it she spoke to him. "That would be acceptable," she said. But when she went to take it there was just her own hand in the air.

So she left that tree, and had to go through a barbed-wire fence. There she had to creep and crawl, spreading her knees and stretching her fingers like a baby trying to climb the steps. But she talked loudly to herself: she could not let her dress be torn now, so late in the day, and she could not pay for having her arm or her leg sawed off if she got caught fast where she was.

At last she was safe through the fence and risen up out in the clearing. Big dead trees, like black men with one arm, were standing in the purple stalks of the withered cotton field. There sat a buzzard.

"Who you watching?"

In the furrow she made her way along.

"Glad this not the season for bulls," she said, looking sideways, "and the good Lord made his snakes to curl up and sleep in the winter. A pleasure I don't see no two-headed snake coming around that tree, where it come once. It took a while to get by him, back in the summer."

She passed through the old cotton and went into a field of dead corn. It whispered and shook and was taller than her head. "Through the maze now," she said, for there was no path.

Then there was something tall, black, and skinny there, moving before her.

At first she took it for a man. It could have been a man dancing in the field. But she stood still and listened, and it did not make a sound. It was as silent as a ghost.

"Ghost," she said sharply, "who be you the ghost of? For I have heard of nary death close by."

But there was no answer—only the ragged dancing in the wind.

She shut her eyes, reached out her hand, and touched a sleeve. She found a coat and inside that an emptiness, cold as ice.

"You scarecrow," she said. Her face lighted. "I ought to be shut up for good," she said with laughter. "My senses is gone. I too old. I the oldest people I ever know. Dance, old scarecrow," she said, "while I dancing with you."

She kicked her foot over the furrow, and with mouth drawn down, shook her head once or twice in a little strutting way. Some husks blew down and whirled in streamers about her skirts.

Then she went on, parting her way from side to side with the cane, through the whispering field. At last she came to the end, to a wagon track where the silver grass blew between the red ruts. The quail were walking around like pullets, seeming all dainty and unseen.

"Walk pretty," she said. "This the easy place. This the easy going."

She followed the track, swaying through the quiet bare fields, through the little strings of trees silver in their dead leaves, past cabins silver from weather, with the doors and windows boarded shut, all like old women under a spell sitting there. "I walking in their sleep," she said, nodding her head vigorously.

In a ravine she went where a spring was silently flowing through a hollow log. Old Phoenix bent and drank. "Sweet-gum makes the water sweet," she said, and drank more. "Nobody know who made this well, for it was here when I was born."

The track crossed a swampy part where the moss hung as white as lace from every limb. "Sleep on, alligators, and blow your bubbles." Then the track went into the road.

Deep, deep the road went down between the high green-colored banks. Overhead the live-oaks met, and it was as dark as a cave.

A black dog with a lolling tongue came up out of the weeds by the ditch. She was meditating, and not ready, and when he came at her she only hit him a little with her cane. Over she went in the ditch, like a little puff of milkweed.

Down there, her senses drifted away. A dream visited her, and she reached her hand up, but nothing reached down and gave her a pull. So she lay there and presently went to talking. "Old woman,"

she said to herself, "that black dog come up out of the weeds to
stall you off, and now there he sitting on his fine tail, smiling at
you."

A white man finally came along and found her—a hunter, a
young man, with his dog on a chain.

"Well, Granny!" he laughed. "What are you doing there?"

"Lying on my back like a June-bug waiting to be turned over,
mister," she said, reaching up her hand.

He lifted her up, gave her a swing in the air, and set her
down. "Anything broken, Granny?"

"No sir, them old dead weeds is springy enough," said Phoenix,
when she had got her breath. "I thank you for your trouble."

"Where do you live, Granny?" he asked, while the two dogs
were growling at each other.

"Away back yonder, sir, behind the ridge. You can't even see
it from here."

"On your way home?"

"No sir, I going to town."

"Why, that's too far! That's as far as I walk when I come out
myself, and I get something for my trouble." He patted the stuffed
bag he carried, and there hung down a little closed claw. It was
one of the bob-whites, with its beak hooked bitterly to show it was
dead. "Now you go on home, Granny!"

"I bound to go to town, mister," said Phoenix. "The time come
around."

He gave another laugh, filling the whole landscape. "I know
you old colored people! Wouldn't miss going to town to see Santa
Claus!"

But something held old Phoenix very still. The deep lines in
her face went into a fierce and different radiation. Without warning, she had seen with her own eyes a flashing nickel fall out of
the man's pocket onto the ground.

"How old are you, Granny?" he was saying.

"There is no telling, mister," she said, "no telling."

Then she gave a little cry and clapped her hands and said,
"Git on away from here, dog! Look! Look at that dog!" She
laughed as if in admiration. "He ain't scared of nobody. He a big
black dog." She whispered, "Sic him!"

"Watch me get rid of that cur," said the man. "Sic him, Pete!
Sic him!"

Phoenix heard the dogs fighting, and heard the man running

and throwing sticks. She even heard a gunshot. But she was slowly bending forward by that time, further and further forward, the lids stretched down over her eyes, as if she were doing this in her sleep. Her chin was lowered almost to her knees. The yellow palm of her hand came out from the fold of her apron. Her fingers slid down and along the ground under the piece of money with the grace and care they would have in lifting an egg from under a setting hen. Then she slowly straightened up, she stood erect, and the nickel was in her apron pocket. A bird flew by. Her lips moved. "God watching me the whole time. I come to stealing."

The man came back, and his own dog panted about them. "Well, I scared him off that time," he said, and then he laughed and lifted his gun and pointed it at Phoenix.

She stood straight and faced him.

"Doesn't the gun scare you?" he said, still pointing it.

"No, sir, I seen plenty go off closer by, in my day, and for less than what I done," she said, holding utterly still.

He smiled, and shouldered the gun. "Well, Granny," he said, "you must be a hundred years old, and scared of nothing. I'd give you a dime if I had any money with me. But you take my advice and stay home, and nothing will happen to you."

"I bound to go on my way, mister," said Phoenix. She inclined her head in the red rag. Then they went in different directions, but she could hear the gun shooting again and again over the hill.

She walked on. The shadows hung from the oak trees to the road like curtains. Then she smelled wood-smoke, and smelled the river, and she saw a steeple and the cabins on their steep steps. Dozens of little black children whirled around her. There ahead was Natchez shining. Bells were ringing. She walked on.

In the paved city it was Christmas time. There were red and green electric lights strung and crisscrossed everywhere, and all turned on in the daytime. Old Phoenix would have been lost if she had not distrusted her eyesight and depended on her feet to know where to take her.

She paused quietly on the sidewalk where people were passing by. A lady came along in the crowd, carrying an armful of red-, green- and silver-wrapped presents; she gave off perfume like the red roses in hot summer, and Phoenix stopped her.

"Please, missy, will you lace up my shoe?" She held up her foot.

"What do you want, Grandma?"

"See my shoe," said Phoenix. "Do all right for out in the country, but wouldn't look right to go in a big building."

"Stand still then, Grandma," said the lady. She put her packages down on the sidewalk beside her and laced and tied both shoes tightly.

"Can't lace 'em with a cane," said Phoenix. "Thank you, missy. I doesn't mind asking a nice lady to tie up my shoe, when I gets out on the street."

Moving slowly and from side to side, she went into the big building, and into a tower of steps, where she walked up and around and around until her feet knew to stop.

She entered a door, and there she saw nailed up on the wall the document that had been stamped with the gold seal and framed in the gold frame, which matched the dream that was hung up in her head.

"Here I be," she said. There was a fixed and ceremonial stiffness over her body.

"A charity case, I suppose," said an attendant who sat at the desk before her.

But Phoenix only looked above her head. There was sweat on her face, the wrinkles in her skin shone like a bright net.

"Speak up, Grandma," the woman said. "What's your name? We must have your history, you know. Have you been here before? What seems to be the trouble with you?"

Old Phoenix only gave a twitch to her face as if a fly were bothering her.

"Are you deaf?" cried the attendant.

But then the nurse came in.

"Oh, that's just old Aunt Phoenix," she said. "She doesn't come for herself—she has a little grandson. She makes these trips just as regular as clockwork. She lives away back off the Old Natchez Trace." She bent down. "Well, Aunt Phoenix, why don't you just take a seat? We won't keep you standing after your long trip." She pointed.

The old woman sat down, bolt upright in the chair.

"Now, how is the boy?" asked the nurse.

Old Phoenix did not speak.

"I said, how is the boy?"

But Phoenix only waited and stared straight ahead, her face very solemn and withdrawn into rigidity.

"Is his throat any better?" asked the nurse. "Aunt Phoenix,

don't you hear me? Is your grandson's throat any better since the last time you came for the medicine?"

With her hands on her knees, the old woman waited, silent, erect and motionless, just as if she were in armor.

"You mustn't take up our time this way, Aunt Phoenix," the nurse said. "Tell us quickly about your grandson, and get it over. He isn't dead, is he?"

At last there came a flicker and then a flame of comprehension across her face, and she spoke.

"My grandson. It was my memory had left me. There I sat and forgot why I made my long trip."

"Forgot?" The nurse frowned. "After you came so far?"

Then Phoenix was like an old woman begging a dignified forgiveness for waking up frightened in the night. "I never did go to school, I was too old at the Surrender," she said in a soft voice. "I'm an old woman without an education. It was my memory fail me. My little grandson, he is just the same, and I forgot it in the coming."

"Throat never heals, does it?" said the nurse, speaking in a loud, sure voice to old Phoenix. By now she had a card with something written on it, a little list. "Yes. Swallowed lye. When was it?—January—two-three years ago—"

Phoenix spoke unasked now. "No, missy, he not dead, he just the same. Every little while his throat begin to close up again, and he not able to swallow. He not get his breath. He not able to help himself. So the time come around, and I go on another trip for the soothing medicine."

"All right. The doctor said as long as you came to get it, you could have it," said the nurse. "But it's an obstinate case."

"My little grandson, he sit up there in the house all wrapped up, waiting by himself," Phoenix went on. "We is the only two left in the world. He suffer and it don't seem to put him back at all. He got a sweet look. He going to last. He wear a little patch quilt and peep out holding his mouth open like a little bird. I remembers so plain now. I not going to forget him again, no, the whole enduring time. I could tell him from all the others in creation."

"All right." The nurse was trying to hush her now. She brought her a bottle of medicine. "Charity," she said, making a check mark in a book.

Old Phoenix held the bottle close to her eyes, and then carefully put it into her pocket.

"I thank you," she said.

"It's Christmas time, Grandma," said the attendant. "Could I give you a few pennies out of my purse?"

"Five pennies is a nickel," said Phoenix stiffly.

"Here's a nickel," said the attendant.

Phoenix rose carefully and held out her hand. She received the nickel and then fished the other nickel out of her pocket and laid it beside the new one. She stared at her palm closely, with her head on one side.

Then she gave a tap with her cane on the floor.

"This is what come to me to do," she said. "I going to the store and buy my child a little windmill they sells, made out of paper. He going to find it hard to believe there such a thing in the world. I'll march myself back where he waiting, holding it straight up in this hand."

She lifted her free hand, gave a little nod, turned around, and walked out of the doctor's office. Then her slow step began on the stairs, going down.

Notes on the Authors

Elizabeth Bowen

Elizabeth Bowen was born in Ireland in 1899 and lives in County Cork. A prolific writer of short stories, she has published numerous collections of her works: *Joining Charles* (1929), *Look at All Those Roses* (1941), *Ivy Gripped the Steps* (1946), *The Cat Jumps* (1949), *Early Stories* (1951), *A Day in the Dark* (1956), and *Stories* (1959). Among her many novels are *The House in Paris* (1936), *The Death of the Heart* (1939), *The Heat of the Day* (1946), *A World of Love* (1955), and *The Little Girls* (1964).

Gwendolyn Brooks

Gwendolyn Brooks, born in 1917, has lived most of her life in Chicago, where she writes both poetry and fiction. Her second volume of verse, *Annie Allen,* won the Pulitzer Prize in poetry in 1949. She has also published *A Street in Bronzeville* (1945), *Maud Martha* (1953), *Bronzeville Boys and Girls* (1956), *The Bean Eaters* (1960), *Selected Poems* (1962), *In the Mecca* (1968), *Riot* (1970), and *The World of Gwendolyn Brooks* (1971).

Shirley Jackson

Shirley Jackson, born in 1919, was the wife of critic Stanley Edgar Hyman and lived in Bennington, Vermont, until her death in 1965. Known especially for her Gothic tales, she has published *The Road Through the Wall* (1948), which was reissued in 1956 as *The Other Side of the Street, The Lottery* (1949), *Life Among the Savages* (1953), *The Bird's Nest* (1954), *The Witchcraft of Salem Village* (1956), *Raising*

Demons (1957), *The Sun Dial* (1958), *The Haunting of Hill House* (1959), and *We Have Always Lived in the Castle* (1962). A posthumous collection of three novels and eleven short stories entitled *The Magic of Shirley Jackson* was published in 1966.

Mary Lavin

Mary Lavin was born in Massachusetts in 1912 but has lived most of her life in Ireland, where she is a member of the Irish Academy of Letters. She has published both short stories and novels. Her works include *Tales from Bective Bridge* (1942), *The Long Ago* (1944), *The House in Clewe Street* (1946), *The Becker Wives* (1946), *Mary O'Grady* (1950), *A Single Lady* (1951), *The Patriot Son* (1956), *A Likely Story* (1957), *Selected Stories* (1959), *The Great Wave* (1961), *In the Middle of the Field* (1969), and *Happiness* (1970).

Doris Lessing

Doris Lessing was born in Persia of British parents in 1919. She grew up in Southern Rhodesia and later moved to England. Her five-volume work, *The Children of Violence*, was written between 1950 and 1969 and contains *Martha Quest, A Proper Marriage, A Ripple from the Storm, Landlocked,* and *The Four-Gated City*. She has also written *Five Short Novels* (1953), *Retreat to Innocence* (1955), *Going Home* (1957), *The Habit of Loving* (1957), *In Pursuit of the English* (1959), and *The Golden Notebook* (1960). Her most recent collection of short stories is entitled *A Man and Two Women* (1965).

Katherine Mansfield

Katherine Mansfield, born in New Zealand in 1888, lived in England for many years until tuberculosis forced her to travel to warmer climates. She married critic John Middleton Murry, who introduced her to the artistic circles of London, but her life was plagued by unhappiness and ill health. She was a prolific writer of short stories and produced a number of collections, including *In a German Pension* (1911), *Bliss* (1921), *The Garden Party* (1922), and *The Dove's Nest* (1922). Since her death in 1923, *The Short Stories of Katherine Mansfield* (1929) has been published along with *The Journal of Katherine Mansfield* (1927) and *The Letters of Katherine Mansfield* (1928).

Mary McCarthy

Mary McCarthy, born in Seattle in 1912, now resides in Paris. Equally skilled at writing critical essays and fiction, she has published a number of political studies, including *Vietnam* (1967), *Hanoi* (1968), and *Medina* (1972). Among her essays on contemporary culture are *Venice Observed* (1956), *The Stones of Florence* (1959), and *On the Contrary* (1961). Her fiction includes *The Company She Keeps* (1942), *The Groves of Academe* (1952), *The Group* (1963), and *Birds of America* (1971).

Carson McCullers

Carson McCullers was born in Georgia in 1917. During the depression she went to New York to study music, but financial difficulties led her to turn to writing instead. Chronic ill health hampered her career, especially after she suffered a series of partially crippling strokes. Her works include *The Heart Is a Lonely Hunter* (1940), *Reflections in a Golden Eye* (1941), *The Member of the Wedding* (1946), *The Ballad of the Sad Café* (1951), and *Clock Without Hands* (1961). *The Mortgaged Heart* (1971) was published after Miss McCullers' death in 1967.

Anaïs Nin

Anaïs Nin was born in France in 1903 and lived in Europe until World War II. Her association with a number of famous writers and artists such as Henry Miller, Antonin Artaud, Lawrence Durrell, and Djuna Barnes is described in her *Diary*, four volumes of which have been published. In addition to writing, she practiced psychoanalysis under the direction of Otto Rank, and this interest in psychology has influenced her works. Her novels include *The House of Incest* (1936), *The Winter of Artifice* (1939), *Under a Glass Bell* (1944), *Ladders to Fire* (1946), *Children of the Albatross* (1947), *The Four-Chambered Heart* (1950), *A Spy in the House of Love* (1954), *Cities of the Interior* (1961), *Seduction of the Minotaur* (1961), and *Collages* (1964).

Joyce Carol Oates

Joyce Carol Oates, born in New York in 1938, lives near Detroit and teaches at the University of Windsor in Ontario, Canada. In addition to two volumes of poems, she has published three collections of short stories: *By the North Gate* (1963), *Upon the Sweeping Flood* (1965), and *The Wheel of Love* (1970). Her novels include *With Shuddering Fall* (1964), *A Garden of Earthly Delights* (1967), *Expensive People* (1968), *Them* (awarded the National Book Award in 1970), and *Wonderland* (1971).

Flannery O'Connor

Flannery O'Connor was born in 1925 in Georgia and was educated there and at the University of Iowa. She moved to New York, but when she developed an incurable skin disease she was forced to return to her family's farm, where she lived until her death in 1964. Although able to write only when her health permitted, she produced an impressive body of work, including two novels, *Wise Blood* (1952) and *The Violent Bear It Away* (1960), and a collection of short stories, *A Good Man Is Hard to Find* (1955). Two posthumous works have been published: *Everything That Rises Must Converge*, which received a special tribute by the National Book Awards Committee in 1966, and *Flannery O'Connor: The Complete Stories* (1971), which contains twelve previously unpublished pieces.

Dorothy Parker

Dorothy Parker was born in 1893 and died in 1967. Noted for her sharp wit, she wrote biting satires both in prose and in verse. During the 1930s she was a member of New York's Algonquin Round Table, which included many prominent writers and intellectuals. Later she moved to Hollywood, where she wrote movie scripts and was politically active in liberal causes. Her poetry includes *Enough Rope* (1926), *Sunset Gun* (1928), *Death and Taxes* (1931), and *Collected Poems: Not So Deep a Well* (1936). Her volumes of short fiction are *Lament for the Living* (1930), *After Such Pleasures* (1932), and *Here Lies* (1939).

Katherine Anne Porter

Katherine Anne Porter was born in Texas in 1894 and has lived in Mexico, Europe, and the United States. A well-known short story writer and journalist, she has published *Flowering Judas and Other Stories* (1930), *Pale Horse, Pale Rider* (1939), and *The Leaning Tower* (1944). Her volume *Collected Stories* won the National Book Award in 1965. Her one novel is *Ship of Fools* (1962).

Elizabeth Taylor

Elizabeth Taylor was born in Berkshire, England, in 1912 and is a prolific writer both of novels and of short fiction. She is a frequent contributor to *The New Yorker* magazine. Her works include *At Mrs. Lippincote's* (1945), *A View of the Harbour* (1949), *A Wreath of Roses* (1950), *A Game of Hide-and-Seek* (1951), *The Sleeping Beauty* (1953), *Angel* (1957), *The Blush* (1959), *In a Summer Season* (1961), *A Dedicated Man* (1965), *The Soul of Kindness* (1964), *Mossy Trotter* (1967), and *The Wedding Group* (1968).

Constance Urdang

Constance Urdang was born in New York City and attended Smith College and Iowa State University. A poet as well as a fiction writer, she has published a collection of poems entitled *Charades and Celebrations* (1965). "Natural History" won first prize in *The Carleton Miscellany* fiction contest for 1967 and was later published as part of a novel by the same name. Wife of the poet Donald Finkel, Miss Urdang lives in St. Louis, Missouri.

Mary Elizabeth Vroman

Mary Elizabeth Vroman was born in the British West Indies and attended Alabama State University. Several of her short stories have appeared in *The Ladies Home Journal*. The first Negro woman to become a member of the Screenwriters Guild, she has written a number of movie scripts, including one for her short story "See How They Run." The movie was released in 1953 as *Bright Road.* Her novel, *Esther,* was published in 1963 and her history of Delta Sigma Theta sorority, *Shaped to Its Purpose,* appeared in 1964.

Eudora Welty

Eudora Welty was born in 1909 in Jackson, Mississippi, where she has lived for most of her life as a writer and photographer. Her fiction depicting rural life in the South includes three volumes of short stories: *A Curtain of Green* (1941), *The Wide Net* (1943), and *The Bride of the Innisfallen* (1955). Her novels are *Delta Wedding* (1946), *Golden Apples* (1949), *The Ponder Heart* (1954), and *The Optimist's Daughter* (1971). In 1971 she released *One Time, One Place,* a collection of her photographs of black Mississippi taken for the Work Projects Administration during the depression.

Jessamyn West

Jessamyn West was born in 1907 in Indiana and now lives in California. She is best known for her novel *The Friendly Persuasion* (1954), which she later adapted for the screen. Her other works include *A Mirror for the Sky* (1948), *The Witch Diggers* (1951), *Cress Delahanty* (1953), *Love, Death, and the Ladies' Drill Team* (1955), *To See the Dream* (1957), *Love Is Not What You Think* (1959), and *South of the Angels* (1960). She has written movie scripts for several films, including *The Big Country,* and has edited an anthology, *A Quaker Reader.*

Virginia Woolf

Virginia Woolf, born in London in 1882, was the daughter of Sir Leslie Stephen, a British biographer and literary critic. A brilliant novelist, essayist, and critic, she was a member of the Bloomsbury Group, a circle of literary and artistic intellectuals who met in the Bloomsbury section of London. In 1917 she and her husband, Leonard Woolf, founded the Hogarth Press, known for its limited editions of the works of twentieth-century British writers. Her critical works and essays include *The Common Reader* (1925), *A Room of One's Own* (1929), *The Second*

Common Reader (1932), *Three Guineas* (1938), and *The Death of the Moth* (1942), published posthumously. Among her novels are *The Voyage Out* (1915), *Night and Day* (1919), *Jacob's Room* (1922), *Mrs. Dalloway* (1925), *To the Lighthouse* (1927), *Orlando* (1928), *The Waves* (1931), and *The Years* (1937). Mrs. Woolf committed suicide in 1941.

Bibliography

1 Promise and Disappointment

Eliasberg, Ann. "Are You Hurting Your Daughter Without Knowing It?" In *The American Sisterhood,* edited by Wendy Martin. New York: Harper & Row, 1972.

Howe, Florence. "The Education of Women." In *The American Sisterhood,* edited by Wendy Martin. New York: Harper & Row, 1972.

Mannes, Marya. "The Problems of Creative Women." In *The Potential of Women,* edited by Seymour M. Farber and Roger H. L. Wilson. New York: McGraw-Hill, 1963.

McCarthy, Mary. *Memories of a Catholic Girlhood.* New York: Harcourt Brace Jovanovich, 1959.

McClelland, David C. "Wanted: A New Self-Image for Women." In *The Woman in America,* edited by Robert Jay Lifton. Boston: Beacon Press, 1964.

Mead, Margaret. *Male and Female.* New York: William Morrow, 1949.

Putney, Gail Jackson. "Children: In Dreams Come Unexpected Responsibilities." In *The Challenge to Women,* edited by Seymour M. Farber and Roger H. L. Wilson. New York: Basic Books, 1966.

Rossi, Alice S. "Equality Between the Sexes: An Immodest Proposal." In *The Woman in America,* edited by Robert Jay Lifton. Boston: Beacon Press, 1964.

Weisstein, Naomi. "Psychology Constructs the Female, or The Fantasy Life of the Male Psychologist." In *Women's Liberation and Literature,* edited by Elaine Showalter. New York: Harcourt Brace Jovanovich, 1971.

2 Expectation and Defeat

Bird, Caroline. "The Androgynous Life." In *Voices of the New Feminism,* edited by Mary Lou Thompson. Boston: Beacon Press, 1970.

Cyrus, Della. "Why Mothers Fail." In *The American Sisterhood,* edited by Wendy Martin. New York: Harper & Row, 1972.

de Beauvoir, Simone. *The Second Sex.* New York: Bantam Books, 1968.

Friedan, Betty. *The Feminine Mystique.* New York: Dell, 1963.

Fromm, Erich. *The Art of Loving.* New York: Bantam Books, 1967.

Goldman, Emma. "Marriage and Love." In *The American Sisterhood,* edited by Wendy Martin. New York: Harper & Row, 1972.

Janeway, Elizabeth. *Man's World, Woman's Place: A Study in Social Mythology.* New York: William Morrow, 1971.

Merriam, Eve. "Woman's Expectation: Mirage or Reality?" In *The Challenge to Women,* edited by Seymour M. Farber and Roger H. L. Wilson. New York: Basic Books, 1966.

Rostow, Edna G. "Conflict and Accommodation." In *The Woman in America,* edited by Robert Jay Lifton. Boston: Beacon Press, 1964.

3   Success and Failure

Albert, Ethel M. "The Unmothered Woman." In *The Challenge to Women,* edited by Seymour M. Farber and Roger H. L. Wilson. New York: Basic Books, 1966.

Amundsen, Kirsten. *The Silenced Majority: Women and American Democracy.* Englewood Cliffs, N.J.: Prentice-Hall, 1971.

Bird, Caroline. *Born Female: The High Cost of Keeping Women Down.* New York: David McKay, 1968.

Epstein, Cynthia Fuchs. *Woman's Place: Options and Limits in Professional Careers.* Berkeley: University of California Press, 1971.

Greer, Germaine. *The Female Eunuch.* New York: Bantam Books, 1970.

Gunderson, Barbara Bates. "The Implication of Rivalry." In *The Potential of Women,* edited by Seymour M. Farber and Roger H. L. Wilson. New York: McGraw-Hill, 1963.

Koestenbaum, Peter. "The Interpretation of Roles." In *The Potential of Women,* edited by Seymour M. Farber and Roger H. L. Wilson. New York: McGraw-Hill, 1963.

Woolf, Virginia. *A Room of One's Own.* New York: Harcourt Brace Jovanovich, 1929.

4 Triumph and Death

de Beauvoir, Simone. *The Coming of Age.* New York: G. P. Putnam's Sons, 1972.

Henry, Jules. "Forty-Year-Old Jitters in Married Urban Women." In *The Challenge to Women,* edited by Seymour M. Farber and Roger II. L. Wilson. New York: Basic Books, 1966.

Moss, Zoe. "It Hurts to Be Alive and Obsolete: The Aging Woman." In *Sisterhood is Powerful: An Anthology of Writings from the Women's Liberation Movement,* edited by Robin Morgan. New York: Random House, 1970.